BOOK OF KNUT

a novel by Knut Knudson

by Halvor Aakhus

“Halvor Aakhus is the smartest and most wildly inventive young writer to come around since David Foster Wallace. Knut rules!”

– David Leavitt, author of *The Lost Language of Cranes* and *The Indian Clerk*

“Behold, the bastard child—thrice removed—of Padgett Powell, Barry Hannah, and Samuel Beckett. There’s something very wrong and very right about the wires crossed in his head.”

– Benjamin Percy, author of *The Wilding* and *Refresh, Refresh*

“This wonderful novel is excessive—beautifully and humanely and ecstatically excessive. I urge you to give yourself up to it.”

– Chris Bachelder, author of *U.S.!* and *Bear V. Shark*

“Halvor Aakhus should be paralyzed from depression and knowing too much. He has two or three doctoral dissertations, never consummated, in his head.... The reader should gird his or her loins if loins can be in one’s head.”

– Padgett Powell, author of *You & I, Edisto,* and *The Interrogative Mood*

BOOK OF KNUT

a novel by Knut Knudson

by Halvor Aakhus

Jaded Ibis Press
sustainable literature by digital means™
an imprint of Jaded Ibis Productions

ISBN: 978-1-937543-08-2

Library of Congress Control Number: 2012936198

Published by Jaded Ibis Press, sustainable literature by digital means™ An imprint of Jaded Ibis Productions, LLC, Seattle, WA USA jadedibisproductions.com

Book design and art by Halvor Aakhus

This book is also available in full color, digital and fine art limited editions. Visit our website for more information.

TABLE OF CONTENTS

LIST OF TABLES

LIST OF FIGURES

BOOK OF KNUT

SECTION ZERO

SECTION 0
THE FIRST PARAGRAPH OF BOOK

I've just read the first paragraph of *Book*.

Now, I am having an emotion. It is unpleasant, disturbing. And also undefined. Call it 𝕏.

A sample of emotion 𝕏: *I hate Knut Knudson.* Yes, clearly, 𝕏 is irrational. But 𝕏 is not irrelevant: My mother was artsy (she's dead), much like this Mr. Knudson, an unpublished wannabe writer, who was my lover and left me for my mother. (He died this morning.)

So let 𝕏 hate writers like Knut if it wants to. I'm not a writer—I am a mathematician—and before I met Knut, life was simple: Waking up meant my students learned d/dx (sin x) = cos x and I hadn't spoken to my mother in a decade. But now he's dead and, suddenly, halfway through my life, like Dante in a dark wood, I am lost and broke and unemployed: And 𝕏 is angry because the simple life is gone, because getting out of bed won't mean students learn d/dx (cos x) = –sin x, because my mother was a slut, because I've begun reading *Book*, because I'm wet and I can't sleep, because I've been possessed by an unpublished dead writer and have nothing to say… (That sounds a tad crazy, doesn't it? Well, I'm not crazy.) Let's start over:

Proposition 0.1. *Writers are crazy.*

Example 0.2. Knut Knudson. He lived with me, so I got to see crazy firsthand. At first, when things got serious, when Knut started proposing marriage at night and taking it back when he woke up with a hangover, I wasn't worried: This is your standard dynamic for the two-dimensional flow of "insecure" love—the writer is attracted by your love and terrified of his own—easily modeled by a 2D linear system.[1] However, when this direct relationship between the frequency of rescinded marriage proposals and blood-alcohol concentration began

---

[1] Let HIM = his love at time t, and let YOU = your love at time t. Then the dynamical system

dHIM/dt = aHIM + bYOU

dYOU/dt = bHIM + aYOU

is a two-dimensional system of simultaneous first-order homogenous linear ordinary differential equations with constant coefficients a and b, so that $a < 0$ and $b > 0$ (where a is a measure of the fear of one's own love and b is a measure of one's attraction to the other's overt expression of love) models flow of love between "insecure" lovers.

Case 1: if $a^2 > b^2$ then you have a stable node and your love extinguishes.

Case 2: if $a^2 < b^2$ then you have a saddle point and love explodes.

Cf. Romeo and Juliet in S. Strogatz, *Nonlinear Dynamics and Chaos* (Cambridge: Perseus Books, 1994), 138.

to seem irregular, when I realized that our dynamic might be nonlinear, that the principle of superposition no longer applied, that I might be dealing with a crazy person, with chaos on a strange attractor, that's when I did the research: What is the writer and how do you fix it? Creativity seems to be the primary problem. Cognitive psychologist Hans J. Eysenck is particularly lucid on the subject: Of all creative people, who by definition are "not really psychotic" but merely score "high on psychoticism," writers are at the top of their class—in every subject. Indeed, Eysenck cites Barron, who found that even "the *average* creative writer, in fact, is in the upper 15 percent on *all* measures of psychopathology."[2] In short, these findings reinforced what I already knew: My writer was crazy, extremely sensitive to initial conditions, and had a drinking problem.[3]

Remark 0.3. It follows from Example 0.2 that Knut was nuts and drank a lot of bourbon, which is why I drove to the river bottoms last night, where even the homes on stilts had been abandoned because of the spring rains, where he'd be. When the levee broke at dawn, the river took my writer.

So now I'm reading *Book*, that novel-in-progress he never let me touch, this unpublished manuscript of *Book* he never let me see, and it is—

(Interpolation 0.4. Concession: I don't read much. At least, not what most people call reading. People like Knut who could never grasp my passion for Szabo and Ostlund's *Modern Quantum Chemistry* or Webern's *Symphony* or Lang's *Algebra*. People who'd rather read poems about gyres or the Pope's penis, and will never know what it's like to lose yourself in a diagrammatic representation of Rayleigh-Schrodinger perturbation theory, or the D_{24} symmetry of Webern's serialism, or Abel's mostly correct proof of the unsolvability of the general quintic in 1829 (just before, at the age of 26, impoverished and unemployed, he died of malnutrition and tuberculosis) and its subsequent perfection by Galois in 1832 (just before, at the age 20, he was killed in a pistol duel over a love affair). People like Knut who'll never know

[2] This, Eysenck subsequently explains: Compared to a score of 50 for the general population, "creative writers average MMPI [Minnesota Multiphasic Personality Inventory] scores of 63 (for Hypochondriasis), 65 (for Depression), 68 (for Hysteria), 65 (for Psychopathic Deviate), 61 (for Paranoia), 64 (for Psychasthenia), 67 (for Schizophrenia), and 61 (for Hypomania)" (see p. 156 of H. J. Eysenck, "Creativity and Personality: Suggestions for a Theory," *Psychological Inquiry* 4.3 (1993): 147-78).

[3] On the other hand, the existence of a third unknown, the mother variable, would come as a bit of a surprise.

how the genres of quantum chemistry, atonal music, or abstract algebra can cleanse, conciliate, purify to the core, far more than a poetic pondering of papal penetration. *End interpolation 0.4.*)

—yes, Knut's *Book* is crap, but I keep on reading it (now well beyond the first paragraph) because I've been possessed by 𝕏, I'm wet, and I have nothing to say. And what is 𝕏? 𝕏 is crap. By sitting here, reading it, all damn day since dawn reading it, sitting at my dead mother's desk, my clothes still damp from the flood, his keys still clutched in my hand, always clutched, by reading it, I've been possessed by all his crap. The transmigration of crap. The river got a writer and I got a book: lies, warped, things he had no right to say. Granted: I'd always suspected *Book*'d be full of math and music and chemistry. A writer is a species that turns every conversation into an inquisition, not because he cares about your interests, but because you're a source of information, and he thinks he's being sly, but it's so obvious—he's nice...—and you pretend he cares and teach him how 5-limit just intonation forms a free abelian group <3, 5>, teach him because it's the only time he smiles and his looks have a look, and you smile back at his (nauseous) response, as he explains how 5-limit just intonation hinges on the music of the spheres and the harmonics of regular polygons in Kepler's *Harmonices Mundi*. You do this because it hurts, because this is your origin, your impulse function, what love ought to be, a real line which is zero everywhere, except at the origin, where it is infinite.[4] You have to have a wound to heal... That said, I'd never suspected the first paragraph of *Book* (the opening of its "Prologue") would be this shitty:

> **Book Excerpt 0.5. (Prologue: Paragraph 1.)** Concerning Knut's hurtful first paragraph which is shitty, soaking wet, and splattered with paint.
>
> Our story has three heroes. Unfortunately, they can be boring as hell. As disciples of algebraic number theory, quantum chemistry, and classical music, their lonely pursuit of truth has led to neither the meaning of life, nor a sense of humor, nor suicide. Only murder. So let's begin with setting.

[4] That is, a function δ on $\mathbb{R}(-\infty,\infty)$, with identity $\int \delta(x)\, dx = 1$, such that $\delta(x) = \infty$ at $x = 0$ and $\delta(x) = 0$ for $x \neq 0$.

Bullshit. Nobody murdered anybody. (Not really.) So perhaps I do have something to say (Knut's full of shit), and I could be objective because I'm not a writer: I do math, I do simple. Erdos defines a mathematician to be "a device for turning coffee into theorems." This implies that a writer is a device for turning bourbon into obfuscated bullshit. For Knut, simplicity is wrong: If you whittle down a writer with Ockham's razor, all that's left is narcissism, denial, and a smile. Art nails you to yourself.

Yes, I'll be simple, objective, and tell you why it's crap. We'll keep his book *Book*, but I'll add to it, annotate it, tell you the rest of the story, his story, our story, my mother's story, and—I never told him everything. (And he never told me where he hid her money.) Let's start over...

SECTION ONE

SECTION 1
A FEW PRELIMINARIES: SETTING & HERO TRIANGLE

In section one, we review some background material: In particular, after an introduction to *Book*'s setting in its "Prologue" (Excerpt 1.1) and its three characters in "Chapter One" (1.2, 1.3, 1.4), students of *Book* shall be better prepared to tackle the homework problems at section's end.

Book Excerpt 1.1. (Prologue: Paragraphs 2 & 3.) *Concerning Knut's setting, a college town in southern Indiana where I taught mathematics and Knut flunked out of school.*

Twenty-four hours from now, there's this thing with a shotgun, but our story begins pleasantly enough the night before, in the small college town of Napoleon, Indiana, on the Ohio River, where you smell the river before you see it, college town does not mean an oasis of culture, and, as far as Napoleon locals—that is, not students, nor anyone born outside Napoleon—are concerned, any association of their hometown with a French emperor is a false one. Not even the word: Just as Louisville locals reduce their city name's syllabic count to two (something like "Lou'v'lle"), Napoleon might be approximated best by "Nap'lung," accent on "Nap." Essentially, this French association has been repressed because of the unfortunate arrival of Madame "Dupper" (Dupré) shortly after "the war" (World War II) and her creation of the "Institution" (Napoleon Institute of Music). But that's another story.

Our story begins in Napoleon, Indiana, in the year 2007, a year of iPod phones and Facebook friends, a year when, in Berlin, after 55 years, Margaret Wegner finally decides to have a pencil surgically removed from her head and, in California, Jennifer Strange dies from water intoxication in a drinking-water-without-pissing contest; a year when Barry Bonds breaks Hank Aaron's homerun record, but is indicted for perjury, and World Wrestler Chris Benoit hangs himself with a weight-machine cord, after sedating his wife and son and strangling them to death; a year when Pluto's not a planet anymore, vajayjay's the word for vagina, happiness means antidepressants, and the Yangtze River Dolphin becomes extinct; a year when the oldest living animal is a 405-year-old clam living off the coast of northern Iceland;[5] a year when the US hunts down foreign terrorists, zealous evildoers, while its own students shoot their classmates at Virginia Tech for no reason; and more precisely, in Napoleon, our story begins just after midnight on Wednesday, May 2, 2007—2059 days before the Mayan Apocalypse of 2012—the night when, quite accidentally, our three heroes all come together, for the very first time, on the grassy piazza of St. Gengulphus Community College and, quite uncharacteristically, they decide to act like heroes: The first digs, the second climbs a tree, and the third calls the police.

Book Excerpt 1.2. (Hero #1 Digs.) *Concerning Knut's fictionalization of my dead mother (a tree-hugger with a penchant for political protests) as a man (an ex-professor of mathematics named Slob, whose management of "The Christmas Tree Protest," a late-night tree-planting on the lawn of the college that fired him, is not going well).*

He digs. He doesn't want to dig anymore. He is ashamed.

After all the planning he's done, the training of his workforce, all of them ignorant of mathematical tests for primality and aliquot iterations, after "finding" an eclectic cause to unite these eleven gentlemen, each with his own distinct domain of inquiry, be it Medieval French literature (esp., Guerin's *The Chevalier Who Made Cunts Talk*), toilet cleaners (esp., the Clorox® ToiletWand™ System), "generalized" hieroglyphics (i.e., originally Mayan glyphs, but more recently, the message transmitted by any shape or image), counting techniques (i.e., the stocking of liquor stores), the revival of Latin (i.e., as a spoken language [i.e., marked by a stubborn refusal to speak in any language other than Latin]), flipping burgers (esp., 5oz and 8oz patties), applied organic chemistry (i.e., marijuana), or "universal" ESP (i.e., not restricted to communication between humans), after channeling all these sundry passions into a collective concern for deforestation, the War on Terror, a dislike for Christmas, and the Mayan Apocalypse, after ringing bells like girl scouts outside Wal-Marts (alt., Walmex in Mexico, Seiyu in Japan) from March to May to collect donations for the "charitable" purchase of 75 Christmas trees (only 40 of which, given 13 last-minute civilian casualties in Kandahar and the fact that 2^{20} =

[5] Knut neglects to inform us that, in order to determine its age (405 years), scientists had to kill the clam.

1,048,576, they will use in tonight's on-campus tree-planting), after the "borrowing" of eight shovels from unwatched on-campus landscaping and construction sites, after three months of planning and crippling parsimony, all the 99-cent double cheeseburgers, un-chilled cases of Keystone, 25-cent Sam's Choice Colas, black-market Valium, and now, all this digging, at his age, a senior citizen, after all this (despite a personal pleasure in vandalizing college property [and a private hope that the Dean of Science and Engineering, Dr. Steven Mendenhall, the man who fired him, will inadvertently walk by {and a secret desire to make his daughter,[6] to whom he hasn't spoken in a decade, proud}]), everything's going wrong. The Christmas Tree Protest is turning out to be a disaster.

The "disaster," it's not the weather. On this night, May 2, 2007—2059 days since the 9/11 attacks, precisely 2059 days before the Mayan Apocalypse of 2012—the climate conditions (at least those forecasted on www.weather.com at 22:57, three minutes before the college library closed) are optimal: visibility at 16.1 km, UV index of 0 Low, wind from the WNW at 8 km/h, pressure at 1022.0 mb., 93% humidity, dew point of 1°C, temp. at 21°C—yes, humid for digging, but they still have three 30-can cases of Keystone to go. And to supplement the campus lampposts and nearby streetlights, a full moon, or rather, given that the full moon actually occurred at 10:10 a.m., a waning 0.96297905203204942562023361328314 moon.[7] So no problem with man versus nature.

And it's not that the on-campus tree-planting operation has been sabotaged. It's clear the protest has remained a well-kept secret and—beyond belief—has attracted little or no attention: Claim: Despite protest's small size (12 total members), location of dig site and scope of tree-planting operation should still attract attention. Grounds: 8 diggers digging the first 4 of 20 pairs of holes, to be evenly spaced in a circle around the flagpole of the grassy College Piazza on the highly trafficked corner of College and 3rd. Rebuttal: (1) "Mop," appointed lookout man, crouches behind the hedge that lines College Ave., (2) "Scriber," scribing the protest's commemorative poster at a picnic bench by said hedge, hides the Keystone under said bench, and (3) it's the first week of summer classes, this is Napoleon, etc. Defense: (1) empty beer cans

[6] Me.

[7] This calculation has been left as a homework exercise. (See Problem 1.3 at the end of §1.)

strewn across the lawn, (2) the smell of pot, and (3) Johnny, unconscious on the mound of forty Christmas trees piled at the flagpole's base. Anomaly: It hasn't. No attention attracted.

And no, it's not the condition of his laborers, none of them gardeners (unless you count Johnny, AKA Johnny Potseed, who's been tossing pot seeds all over town for 10-plus years to no avail…thus far), and not even the fact that Mop's drunk as hell, Wolfer's high as Everest, and Johnny, whose delicate constitution cannot handle pot followed by beer, has already passed out, sleeping soundly on the hill of trees.

No. All that's inconsequential. Slobodon, "retired" professor of mathematics, is ashamed of his egregious miscalculation, a simple math error he must soon confess to his eight diggers, who—beyond belief—seem so focused, so engrossed in substantive dialogic inquiry with their partners at neighboring hole vertices as they merrily mutilate the Piazza's well-mown lawn, and about whom Slob feels so proud, proud of how far they've come in just three months:

Vertices 1 & 2: Silence. This is the exception. The digger at hole 2 is not talking to Slob at hole 1, because Digger 2 never talks, except in Latin, which none of them can understand.

Vertices 3 & 4: "No cop's gonna tell me I can't plant a tree." "Usufruct, man, usufruct." "You said it, chief. We're digging holes. Land's ours." "Fucking libertarian, socialism, proletariat." "That's right. No cop's gonna give us social contract up the ass. I ain't no tree hugger, but I'm planting trees." "Property is theft!" "The hell with property. Not like university dirt's getting scarce. No, man, we're planting trees. This here's a protest. This here's an idea." "Usufructing an idea, man. Usu-fuckin-fructing." "You said it, chief. Planting trees isn't your intellectual property type. No owners. I looked that shit up. The things that don't have owners gonna include: non-intellectual ideas, seawater, *parts* of the seafloor (UN thing), gasses in the atmosphere, wild animals (except for New York), planets and stars and shit in outer space, and Antarctica." "And we're planting trees." "And it's an idea." "And we're doing it." "Usufruct."

Vertices 5 & 6: "All I'm saying is we dig for coal, man, and oil, you know?" "Yeah, that's a wolf, for sure." "Yeah it is. Fill the planet with holes, so we can build shit that has right angles." "Yeah, that and straight-looking wolfs: buildings and a flagwolf." "Straight doesn't exist, man; we just want it straight. Being straight's being honest." "Wolf up tall and straight." "Straight ain't gay. Straight's a buncha bullshit." "Buncha bullwolf." "Bullwolf is right. No straight line from men to women." "Can't wolf a guy with a gun, if the bullet doesn't travel in a straight wolf." "Now, we're getting somewhere."

Vertices 7 & 8: "So we sure about the date and all? I mean, I been hearing shit, like how the Gregorian calendar's got problems." "No, no, Boss got it straight. You know how particular he is with his numberings. Julian puts the zero in there where it belongs." "Yeah, OK, but that's the whole deal. It's Cervantes-Shakespeare all over again. Got Spain going Gregorian, Brits doing Julian, and you get Cervantes dying the same date as Shakespeare and ten days before him at the same time." "Yeah, that doesn't make any sense." "I know." "Kinda like the power of 2 thing." "Yeah, Boss seems upset. Doesn't like the number 2." "No, he sure as hell doesn't."

This is true about Slobodon and 2, for what can Slob do with a number modulo 2, a reductive number distending with horrid dualism—good and evil, God and Devil, mind and body, interactionism versus epiphenomenalism and parallelism, and hence, the existence of zombies—so utterly antithetical to his profound devotion to prime, perfect, pentagonal, and amicable numbers. And although this has nothing to do with Slob's shame, it has everything to do with arranging Christmas trees around a flagpole: How was Slob supposed to know that, at the very last minute, *Vertex 8* would discover an American MQ-1 Predator airstrike in Kandahar's Maroof district had resulted in thirteen civilian casualties, raising the War on Terror body count to 1,048,576—how unfortunate! Slob had spent the entire evening at the college library staring over *Vertex 8*'s shoulder at CNN.com, praying that this thirteen was an erroneous, premature toll, praying that just one more of the wounded would die. What are the chances that *Vertex 8*'s grand death toll, on the night of the Christmas Tree Protest, would land precisely on a power of 2 ($1{,}048{,}576 = 2^{20}$), the next power of 2 over a million numbers away, the previous over half a million behind, powers of 2 being, by definition, what mathematicians call "almost perfect numbers"...in short, they are evil.[8] And to think that just yesterday, before *Vertex 8*'s latest tally—before the loss of *two* American lives (Pfc. Zachary R. Gullett and Lance Cpl. Johnathan E. Kirk) in Iraq, the beheading of *one* eighteen-year-old

[8] To elevate Knut's use of the term above a mere...neurotic idiosyncrasy of Mamma Slob's character, a *perfect number* is one being the sum of its positive divisors excluding itself, whereas this sinister *almost perfect number* is one being "almost" or "one off" such a sum. In other words, let σ be the number-theoretic function $\sigma\colon \mathbb{N} \to \mathbb{N}$, $\mathbb{N}$ the set of natural numbers, s.t. $\forall n \in \mathbb{N}$, $\sigma(n)$ is the sum of the positive divisors of n. Then a perfect number is any $n \in \mathbb{N}$ s.t. $n = \sigma(n) - n$, whereas an $m \in \mathbb{N}$ with $m = \sigma(m) - (m - 1)$ would be almost perfect. In the above case, then, Mamma Slob is absolutely correct that powers of 2 are almost perfect, since, for the geometric series $\{2^k\}$, we have the sum $2^0 + 2^1 + \ldots + 2^{k-1} = 2^k - 1$, and hence, $\forall k \in \mathbb{N}$: $2^k = \sigma(2^k) - (2^k - 1)$.

police officer in Kandahar's Panjwayi district, the successful kill of *one* Senior Minister of Information of al-Qaeda-in-Iraq (Muharib Abdul Latif) during Operation Rat Trap, and, to top it off, this last-minute *thirteen* civilians—just *seventeen* deaths ago, the grand toll had been 1,048,559, a prime number, the spirit of which so perfectly (i.e., perfect in a prime-al sense) encapsulated the essence of the protest: the indivisibility, a unity no factor can divide, a symbol for a global community, a *whole* new world where, starting tomorrow, every day at work, perhaps even through her office window, his daughter, now a tenured professor of music theory, could admire his protest's arboreous monument, a Christmas tree configuration signifying the War on Terror's grand death toll. But now, they're stuck with 2^{20}. And no, they can't wait for another airstrike (nor review *Vertex 8*'s potentially dubious research methods) because the trees, especially the Douglass firs, are browning and losing needles—so Slob has no choice:

$$1{,}048{,}576 = 2^{20} = 2\times2\times2\times2\times2\times2\times2\times2\times2\times2\times2\times2\times2\times2\times2\times2\times2\times2\times2\times2$$

And yes, all he can come up with is a circle of 20 radial pairs of trees, 20 pairs of vertices evenly spaced around the circle's circumference, with the American flag as the circle's center—

but all of that's irrelevant, Slob's aversion to 2 having nothing to do with his shame, with his miscalculation: so simple, so elementary, so common sense, so humiliating, so—

"Stop!" Slob shouts. Then louder into the ear of his digging neighbor, *Vertex 2*: "Hey, Digger, get them all to stop."

A moment on names: Why Digger? Why's this six-foot-two middle-aged Michelin Man of a man with a Marxian beard, about whom nobody knows much, except he's a Latin-speaking "mime" who only wears a far too small wrestler's uniform, called Digger? Well, first of all, Digger's out of work. The majority of Slob's workforce is out of work (as is Slob), and secondly, Slob is terrible with names. Never could remember his *real* students' names, either. He remembers what people do. So employment helps. Take Wolfer: He's head cook at Gator's Hut, but what he really does is say "wolf" compulsively. Nobody really knows why. We've already met Johnny Potseed, failed chemist; Mop's a janitor on campus; and Shell's a clerk at a Shell station. On the other hand, the names of the unemployed change continuously, names dependent on the action of the moment. Slob had toyed with the idea of assigning numbers to them, but numbers of interest aren't practical. For example, though the first two perfect numbers are $P_1 = 6$ and $P_2 = 28$, the twelfth smallest perfect number is $P_{12} = 1447401115466$

4524427946373126085988481573677491474835889066354349131199152128.[9] No, it's far less

[9] And that's nothing—what if Knut had doubled their number? What if Mamma Slob's protest had two-dozen members? Just imagine, the twenty-fourth smallest perfect number is P_{24} = 931144559095633232126208229355
238422113850001463928526808806653402284611978749773848642502745750235886919222407060185428
231306967732769619297281980013350268777824022423404756395906567785248155561826937944274833
923740390738824148161290823737958049820530398382439492832706492858419464598676976671688576
142502366891340675317316068681637697880248732846321904750966833997786001310309120200658282
221257336135929549036550061744409632977209462990688392010483186577025080300505439154842173
051698566164323597521225148982722159154848051890417225579119019977474646952420072055433453
392979599830638030975858156817574776780857341603739955310186275693823208522361746650294135
982762631493630260440296242118468111690424024695941774984622208982218618787780694924886218
778595539018846269180783840820529157483442192326809757233038818278544351098716756104360371
402697649699164323488272794689303493004189224068600900181118538604424551652725042304722435
816376266218433390388603467644466976804547146425331054951217184378808424332594083925155182
832982159472615515341902108058720683125578959246931848261495828997178013596845354199917231
980482567869955990167995854554369523190165573912977297180517149433490823604959047106378112
471005314643822269585007087011538145234339976728853532157602057543904854629411274605932452
870579488991136609732783784240829791448744610083328129267239508122032214799670476779843822
277970343325829695026816171414545909246304506930111866504135926405519019485655865133813526
497856795284293716128205000594291097962910935411393815561583572518472526153732001163761279
287251157701495751404054444689143593271181671602022147407445873060064270454341879102067171
675018670710714987235637425866272941497627166081868801157360822250810027481889585013016212
899852611785157751883076569980821005079969072926332554680153173203338895070032638658125840
653573916883039399935205543633951745787466690148089826117117657243257831657490663938781351
381116227572241303232981886250802697969239959292657608118217229209868159447930961381937884
588700550406298008045498293126305784409533501560556090108578930955711133879336299254332440
191128196520251089959813244850562833458669019574381336018553192547527343317574562714945709
282767542782834028937942861974148687366349450158945232645655529909220798953989715911622989
782045344361002309344806739336182244938807418669931703683027377130379084982853098491659259
855158405090971105251458954586624908411643177901332132814809468112362687318141930579642820
018914283045529654443063613539101426483305748985917507581455754515369023026743836247852886
535453326728082133293522658642331299935796928130018030818480422677538838956965601212138419
154504967380526838935143775254906586599197415240575166801220910819705656742197761039950106
686690504779097552831986565102429725804173266014453685290093114526437292440433960407175657
685239915448099815850006730551255316627302862473641786008563606524605856693636013521258486
299931348131511348406427540000225321607508389698318653719703860084453081285512996165699980
676629804843537956663791253691330505074156414151320627989060040000179137136101782284956220
042393073773213059204000566325536754294942468703966475952502877230496251160230446734493623
723583120643305322843080431596659694553074795834727587261348452761015593999698133378994147
496753076572214545249782028809681236010544352042918173982949324045843213997500927747289206
255344505998813223363642439670241693488614984891331249010095994349944716123699267807724265
007800163927104447490846345745949793759867901511944664572141882770787332308892319710394555
706353736788900616352398568174198209109851841035446175481815157168443566194952287646095582
408991213117937155107996775981980408528970628895197912029371688886349466383341466845939920
071587708899546725111932158136397260332482343898814170739226439579850193142206959785448094
168749960987350969632746340539747621176639385390914364875988478383944443359214440140902774
834231916430993589280322176500958811116810247681936245520297425538031923074282967992614836
681385929972546222335925060234676206978067676890857594910151246926089454427102994337686657
605459558034155226706786813285016447366735703175320197499956300746056046025223803945221000
309623868131688157661431915379851843326247774988476781849670899247695476647289863894085661
155646760184301642424778879265758120778052963325596750282735202259067839282546552122284318
569321373166030338881595799900424527448286933683599831931697521936312912186779550013236563

233357017656167902265204723932072407915437555841001651929656271896225468035432161624208383
013288008176043752445489964561523824301518519589295060026337804737645546962822214476355386
509435728553369449179154910838189392696799279828498200356495478656067045604231857599722587
667905660006500704018219509458973117938900141103236945291639167579196843196491081624912480
118833206573562435500796465801433325491148403338625389895171161620423239959958028576907979
260625288510598304246063276100557664043037019646077655342110517465058058795315235754472729
840224279105469929954865835973189577796001999607794313526433694462036570650431188191095943
686626899813538516152201255109484858519776280255840315096974446197470078870139104310156576
796085569535530444764892922528705542824326882343868748685737882562018708983899422574630100
067754165868793580710053909215444365946463095569689379848510581543040740385238615369362912
814417863410613343685695921514222546585751447873232477185120031331124425336600155149234468
119499588081480046942630182154398154100290513491341501279670005704427624997845301255410888
008631271778703291991671676072348900511543898473421512234883777985447514247030459817249264
809321336777566203485140278429462979723457867098434006175387723749320607209331551423558236
391128098154843251759636346798267183062146430491937244685381750958728334948222216825688745
617529096278658251271936077514062764766396784323111987521932860198805005593967248711774812
535999967653213860730899151881047096921500545532706600825273588899006473066729110197662897
119865915989570612538923014109557129410747734118494982081343812268567653146808857906672946
006002047955736893123822251642500374931860091336637778294429299964598430473348422309965502
604481402629942056019613146053399027000684239514840525205181325118182106162763966758912791
816742521921672780852147090642256925388789393744308634543261238689762110771389722167845575
748732590629180364896316949155971181662724428860305506839049769694051474503692860332811132
673250835067159115434172543541550179457364857476422333499876547261156046952577604650762452
910572665984710654777112390243286525513430539790948088946878283900276715395882464342636874
485581596029563902413241866827648084857821540942490539559960754896869324211084713518100137
037746424318025500509727748178870478328058303473643692954421197226299278408882009554014193
872269524265646083629260691324693030276253363801051047696248540081844639379543524625752165
198099483302601974027253958017067691799039549414194757517547200170457875303358509036719640
018006002882274214700409756219860351866595160517010152297965751373553512459142590184813989
792767713317335692994611825002730112262836830960036679665676980152636930481081790714009078
235715276501439365863373061932594679503332457414460860816859522814089000110794296203262297
437466957020110058161359038633951548053525522128505696419748930295629946033753061381308922
833974781646054765703108598344622439265279334313666419202564908209099426821516744797183226
491888898283758180245531699540890747352798058165118264772970753358612331049981847676238430
745896174595759416037463684266670488554617360079433927593145407300154913845131713644045496
907904546558342023012518908166333573154503183198780499993463478011954436879279858220657031
419507256566228389546946647506901312402374220779318214233395890450617215253186546048075354
077095767527130545470868316702154561131280878917303331290092362287932195995086762813942988
338872619529634931584985374953173523111299932681633042076306818564338219024926945217147837
886148189607497231993645666468756197920434375977508094402017263819578398097544923345282134
032726672459240329724622873155001654584109366897100258573981354226915312707211637029583435
523073887719388235822521973991211888125074628735012342305044429597332597213200409974705846
370720637183286264731281965906825541778108552940108296728437448234144747146139338620028480
233484930048861823085542463506338441437575643009897463416330649339568818663783446319496653
729042595238658137960756432228513320218091001004745891335102561240390413324427084452455423
397218879456675399221636077770282548422090980856831062969004310617009873788662440643487294
339934475841761423064584833841167196530745088098089036504100975671332805186035802031768297
142581474100864708292760282499057279066135166344088523700033335380763004143297714490622599
1404356029295301971964057730175663542733279916696675695381955784866686068341676311315038362
764996385179103397970959991857011531983127760228694099660060696987967294331330736706919888
636678963672397074058124865622392128920906432406771139134645845977728916839813106511057294
966584582879030626854572141015492101340264210380297788949266366763908409732717702137484038

cumbersome to just be what you do. So that's why "Digger."

Digger hasn't said anything, but Slob's workforce—Lookout Guy, Scriber, and eight diggers—gathers around Slob by the flagpole and Johnny, still unconscious on the hill of trees.

The moment of shame: Slob adopts a lecture tone, but looks nobody in the eye, his gaze wandering from his feet to the moon, to whatever. Nerves. He needs a chalkboard. "All wrong," he says. "If we quarter a ring of 20, we can't dig holes at the 1, 5, 10, and 15 positions. That'll only give us 19 hole-pairs total. The four cardinal vertices must be 1, 6, 11, and 16."

"Wolf," Wolfer says in his stoned, John-Wayne-like drawl. It should be noted that Wolfer, chef premier, with his polished cowboy boots and weathered cowboy hat, could be John Wayne's twin, if he weren't anemic and didn't have a silky, dirty-blond, foot-long beard.

"What you talking about?" Shell asks. "We divided up the pie in quarters, just like you

---

0562867395281119081263528753474177111881607593678760604150949402905158954151985879125136013652366676872214959178039586930293855168643619813589497701632078754772586823721838253025543305617225073517800578087778403229931645833028221433518111856524748832439568318834582926640907172513105422830232026136387371665450431213084477843169628403559438547443017189272409599049580339283613649369932465498219335506378270808498759945952623169148884953272679160142022314354925539315048757060658158597332649881239404039427101476862935386969148503024648159833698041724137174619166726502977907645957729346267538718764007398605209459501258906975897889318751207326710735278845720006184589786125019045148018784639676870188750681462098366391823698090897525258493023226406965747260059380686776044927232538515874113894145391944897398582267207297387371225880081374254936822704006710872791229047059539898084692490013664550193685657215266565150284975129052470692409612674914677095159665478264296823980804637335442468731284152733719305116524859660571668659604468834720954512546564832496943352185906054978300143277160937894791585649072290966093085274052722436185026332487009788014651761775101262813501593214342425600168374915215022143292096834408109682555624314335786678764958351451331690560030714589134198116751064722153779034808187969232891252807422941932467373834309308159018704719044946589559428402308181632310848448016059547351345652080284741735211148140589809474629590660819110670249181025551156847761893409833368312030550859525537308283294727058492276596193533647485076951272742138845020929178355095761584488761326966940669718413724462410806152359547453754940191343682906322088951888866474285681345898012318671961368230331843649007849122722898867243016458134187704589865827187499011526814771015284339350255272385800383201557462741733084320745899041148745633094746495914305550395042271240146872227394301072274347017382921048936570619293657501329188800243434151310648142808441021806777630246458392617385085970067794242626495999201170742121338803418145666354692170351607276579224054324711955457801832666705171173586853193899419423525448425210199759456403280276160906385391055606330051713589888977830300480104038349925560203571167671240912307065130796821637926351767958073116220111694326695139148940590546612644091838019144959558333813216202601205256486774423346465377265338386139263475358574168880152530220751471652150113210338983356687861144756678709204848247127103049373788823812705451533237260824314038334425512602792123046214020003487636298708946526943105153300358507412405861321759301866491488343950259289372093166265194635072798357319110171025407642205407866059219326471414894875294451715486164207403383486022857039666550157020508372487281239879620109438677367061490117686464623335698746904185778929576765384858187046351529502472895440525571551556804439354704656737335369812127771059435824443479027194265 6.

said, and 20 divided by 4 is 5. So it's gotta be 1, 5, 10, and 15." Shell's not a cowboy. He's the disheveled kind of guy who incorrectly quotes anarchists he's heard about secondhand. He'll always want a leader to follow and a government to blame.

"Yeah," Slob says, "well, what's 10 minus 5?"

"Five," Shell says, like he's having flashbacks of first grade, when his identity was founded upon answering the teacher's questions before anybody else.

"Uh huh, and what's 5 minus 1?"

"Oh." Shell sucks the last of his beer dry. Digger passes him another.

"So," Slob says, "we need to fill these four pairs of holes back up and start over."

Shell raises his hand, but doesn't wait to be called on. "But, sir, 20 minus 16 is 4."

"Never you mind that," Slob says, but he crosses his arms and looks the problem-student straight in the eye. He's tempted to review cyclic groups, but there isn't time. "Look, we're dividing the rings"—he sighs—"we're dividing the *pies* into quarters, so 4 divides 20, so we'll have trees at the—OK. Look. If the ring's a clock, we'll have trees at the 3, 6, 9, and 12 o'clock positions. So if you're counting 1, then shift the clock digits counterclockwise one position and you'll have 4, 7, 10, and 1. So this is the same thing, except there's 20 hours in a day instead of 12—or, I guess, 40 hours in a day instead of 24. You get the—"

"But," Wolfer shouts, "that still ain't gonna make 20 wolf 16 equal 5."

"Listen. The difference between the 1 and the 16 is 5. The 1 is really a 21."

"So you're saying we got 21 pairs of trees to plant?"

"No, darnit, there's either a 1 or a 21. Not both. 21 mod 20 is 1."

"Oh, the mod wolf." Wolfer pulls a pre-rolled joint out of his breast pocket. He fires up.

"Put that out," Slob barks.

Wolfer exhales happily, but flicks the cherry off the end of the joint and pinches the smoking tip—"wolf"—then twists the tip shut, like it's brain surgery. He drops it back in his pocket and clears his throat. "Right," he says, "I got it, Boss. We're doing a 20-mod wolf."

"Yes, mod 20. Just divide by 20." Slob sighs, accepting, as expected, how making just one little error can ruin your credibility (cf., the "incident" and a daughter who shuns you for ten years). "And 20 mod 20 is 0. Simple division. OK, so—"

"But wolf, Boss, 20 divided 20 is 1. You sure that—"

"Wolf it, Wolfer," Shell says. "Why don't you go join Johnny. No way you're—"

"No, wait!" Wolfer shouts. "I'm starting to get it. 21 minus 1 is 20, so it's got to work out, somehow, even though it doesn't make any sense. I need a smoke. Who's got my lighter?"

Digger, the big one in the tiny wrestler's uniform, hands him a lighter, then speed-walks back to his hole. There, at Vertex 2, he digs urgently: Chunks of dirt soar over his shoulder, and his uniform's tight shoulder strap burrows like wire into the wrestler's flabby trapezius.

"OK, gentleman, the lesson's over," Slob says. "Big Digger's right, except he's digging—darnit, Digger, I said refill. We're doing new holes, now…" (Digger digs.) "Hopeless. All right, the rest of you gentleman, it's 1 a.m. right now—or 12:58, to be exact—so that gives us 5 hours and less than 2 minutes until the janitors unlock the doors. So get the holes filled, and I'll come around and show you where you're supposed to dig."

They obey (except for Digger) and Slob thinks how 5 hours is perfect. How that's 4 pairs or 8 total trees per hour, and they have 8 shovels—but—but refilling the holes will eat into the 5, will mess up everything. No. No, it's wrong.

"Wait!" Slob shouts. "Never mind about refilling the holes. Need to start digging right away. It's 12:59. Less than a minute to assign new digging vertices. Stop, I said." They do, except for the big one: "Digger, I said stop digging there. You listen—"

"Boss," says Mop the Lookout Guy, "Boss, don't know how. Came out of nowhere. Someone's coming. Out of nowhere."

Chaos ensues: "Quick! The beer, hide the beer."

Disaster, Slob thinks. One catastrophe after another. It never ends. Never.

This scrawny, pale kid—student, no doubt—has the gall to walk right up to Slobodon and ask, "What you doing?"

Book Excerpt 1.3. (Hero #3 Calls the Police.) *Concerning Knut's fictionalization of me as the villain, a professor of music theory and "closet" computational chemist named Claire.*

As Claire, peering around the corner of the Music Annex at a dozen drunken dolts digging up the piazza lawn, calls the police, she thinks: Slobodon is not my father. Not anymore.

No, she's not worried about her job—Claire has tenure—but it's not been easy teaching at the college that fired her father. Her path to tenure has been a lonely one: Changing her name from Bisera to Claire has not stemmed gossip among the faculty; nor has the new course title of her freshman-level theory course "Melody, Meter, and Me" increased her popularity among students. Her creation of the Napoleon Asexual Society has been regarded as curious, at best. To cope, Claire has her hobbies: oil painting and, more recently, computational chemistry.

Waiting for the cops to arrive, Claire peruses the pages of Szabo and Ostlund's *Modern Quantum Chemistry.* She'd like to chemically model her most recent painting. She knows that the pigment of her oil paint Phthalo Blue is copper (II) phthalocyanine, which looks like this:

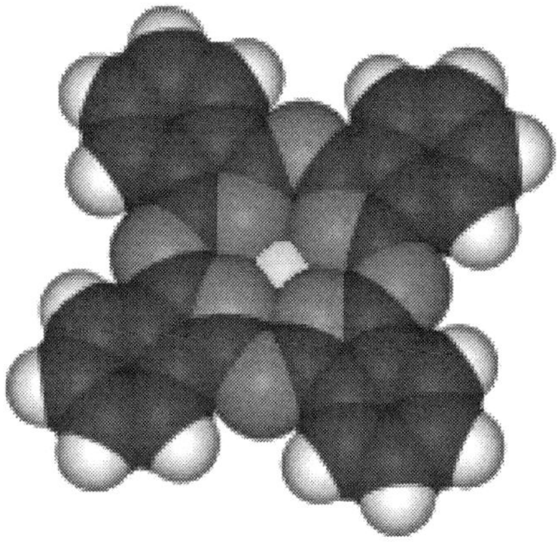

Figure 1.1. Claire's pigment. ($C_{32}H_{16}N_8Cu$, 1.468×0.498×1.960 nm.)

But what about the rest of her painting, which looks like this:

Figure 1.2. Claire's painting. (Oil on wood, 13"×19"×3/16".)

But Claire is distracted from her reading:[10] Suddenly, across the lawn near the corner of 3rd and College, some guy falls out of a tree.

Book Excerpt 1.4. (Hero #2, in a Tree.) *Concerning Knut's fictionalization of himself.*

Weird.

Torbjorn has no idea why he's sitting in this maple tree, twenty or so feet above the ground, drinking a two-liter bottle of Diet Mountain Dew and gin, spilling it all over himself each time he stubbornly raises the shaking bottle to his lips with only his right index finger around the bottle's neck, and thinking how this branch is a real pain in the ass (literally), even though it's cool how, as he leans back against the trunk, the leaves and branches emanate from him, how the moon spears back, the wind churns the leaves—jagged bits of glass, superimposed—and leaf layers *kaleidoscope* the moonlight.

The gin's shit and he hates the moon. Moonlight's got to be Debussy's "Claire de Lune" or something Ravel, got to have the same wholetone sound, same cloud-like hover, gotta be all that love and werewolf you haven't got. Moon's a stop sign that reminds you how alive's alone. He doesn't have time for that shit. So that's why he's doing the Diet Mountain Gin: It slaughters werewolf love with a silver bullet, and tomorrow, he is going to be a composer, even though he doesn't want to be, but it's hard to be a concert pianist when you only have nine fingers.

How to get into the Napoleon Institute of Music's composition program: Start playing piano at the age of three, practice piano for thirteen years, lose your right-hand thumb, drop out of high school, work graveyard shifts at gas stations for ten years, survive on beef, beer, and Everclear, find women with beds and air-conditioning (jazz and de-thumbed Chopin works well on most women), let Steve the Homeless Guy bathe in the station's unisex restroom because he'll give you a journal article called "The Effect of Country Music on Suicide," write a symphony by operating on a concatenation of crap like Billy Hill's "There's Too Much Month at the End of the Money" and Alfred Reed's "How Can a Man Stand Such Things and Live?",

[10] That's OK. She should probably abandon this project, anyway: At this scale of magnification (as in Figure 1.1), a chemical model of her painting would be too large to fit on the planet earth. See homework Problem 1.5.

call the symphony "Go Ahead and Kill Yourself," apply (as a joke) to some prestigious music school in the middle of nowhere, get accepted, let the woman know it's been fun, find Napoleon on a map, move there, avoid women, do the dorm thing, get permission to take summer classes before the fall semester because there's nothing to do in Napoleon and you don't know how to write music, apply for gas-station jobs, don't get one, remember not to drink so much before your interview, get a kitchen job, climb a tree.

He unscrews the cap of his Diet Mountain Gin with his left and spills it down his shirt with his right index finger. He's gonna take this opportunity to let this opportunity change his life. Already, things are turning around, already. *Already Number One*: He's got a tree—he'll write in it—a perfectly located tree at the corner of Third and College, on the front lawn of the Music Annex, this colossal stone cube housing the opera theater, six stories of windowless rock across Third Street from *Already Number Two*: this kitchen job at a restaurant-bar that's got shit going on: jazz nights, a foreign-film series, stands of free anarchist newsletters by the toilets. And after the alreadys, we got *The Tomorrow*, his first day of college, when he is a composer, when he is coffee and 8AM Music Theory and write and kitchen and coffee, and don't forget *The Also Tomorrow*, when he is still coffee but also won't forget his private composition lesson at noon with some guy named Long—Google said Chinese-Frenchman, Rome Prize, Kronos commissions, operas in Mexico City—should be OK. And finally, *The Someday*, when he has that shack on the edge of a cliff overlooking the Atlantic, where he grows tomatoes, beans, and jalapenos, maybe even some fruit trees, pears or olives—need one big enough to sit in—and grapevines for his own little vineyard, and a cow or goat, maybe, whichever's cheaper, and corn or something, whatever cows and goats eat—but absolutely, under no condition can there be a woman. Done with women. Done with beef, beer, and Everclear. On to school, Ramen, and no women. Then someday, on to cliffs, beans, and goats, and no women.

More Dew, no spillage. Bottle seems empty, so it falls to the ground.

Alcohol: Alcohol's almost as bad as women. Actually, they're pretty much the same: Hot chicks are a can of beer, good Norwegian farm girls (those big-ass Valkyries that mothers introduce you to) are bottles of Everclear, and on beyond bottles…getting slapped doesn't hurt much on beyond bottles. Yeah, done with alcohol. Like women, the shit interferes with work and has been known to induce *Sleep*: Sleep's the downfall of the human race, a biological one, making it difficult to ignore. Sleep falls in line right behind alcohol and hairy-boobed Valkyrie-like farm girls, and it can contribute to their cause.[11] Done with sleep.

So yeah, what we got here is a moment of clarity: Women, alcohol, and sleep are the same thing and, at all costs, must be *eschewed*; but even with all his alreadys, tomorrows, also tomorrows, and somedays, that doesn't change the fact that Torbjorn's fucked. In his head, being fucked sounds something like this:

Figure 1.3. The sound of being fucked in your head.[12]

Outside his head, we got *Fucked Number One* (The Digging Dozen's Alcohol): To his right, somewhere between ten to twenty yards away, this guy, squatting behind the hedge of bushes that ends at Torbjorn's tree, is drinking beer, and maybe a certain number of yards away from Bush Squatter, there's another guy sitting at a picnic bench, drinking a beer, and writing on something biggish, a landscaping plan, Torbjorn thinks, because in the center of the Annex's front lawn, somewhere between ten to a hundred yards from his tree, there is a flagpole rising out of a hill of trees—you know, not planted in the ground—upon which one guy's passed out and around which eight or so guys were digging, but now, they're getting yelled at by their manager, probably, and they're all drinking beer. *Fucked Number Two* (The Two-Can Babe): To his left, many, many, but not *that* many yards away, this young dark-haired woman, a two-cans-of-beer species in a dark red summer dress, talking on her cell phone, peers around the corner of the Music Annex at the dig site. *Fucked Number Three*: Said fuckeds must be avoided.

Starting tomorrow. He starts climbing down his tree—difficult—humming the melody of his new "Being Fucked" theme (*BF*). He hugs the trunk, tightly. *BF* isn't helping the descent. He looks over his right shoulder: Two Can's still around the corner, waiting. No longer on her

[11] Valkyries, the so-called "choosers of the slain" and daughters of Odin, are not indigenous to southern Indiana.

[12] Figure 1.3 illustrates that being fucked in Torbjorn's head is not like the moon's Debussy/Ravel-ish wholetones, but something more dissonant, with melodic major sevenths, minor seconds, and tritones.

phone. Flipping through the pages of some book, a text for class, most likely. And waiting—but. But. Not yet. Not ready. Order must be preserved: beer, then woman. Then never again.

He's on the wrong branch. Definitely didn't come up this way. Fuck it: He jumps the eight feet to the hard ground. He lands on his ass—pain—but gets up and feels his *BF* theme gather steam. He laughs at the moon and kicks a clump of mowed grass into the air in celebration of his last chance to get fucked-up before Ramen and, ultimately, grapes and goats.

The kick is an alarm. Bush Squatter—forgot about him—just four bushes down, springs to his feet and runs straight to—no, runs back and gets his beer out of a bush—runs straight to the old guy. Whatever Bush Squatter says is an alarm. The Digging Dozen scurries with yelps of "The beer, hide the beer." It's clear this old guy's the boss. He'll be in charge of the beer.

Torbjorn looks left: Yes, Two Can's still there, standing around her corner, reading some book. Waiting. Yeah, two beers should do it.[13] He hides his *weird* thumb-less right hand in his pocket, then walks across the lawn, *BF* in his step, right up to the boss, standing tall in front of the American flag's cloud-like hover above the hill of trees.

"What you doing?"

Facing Torbjorn, the Dozen lines up behind Boss, who (almost) has that *debonair* old-man look, shirt (wrinkled) tucked into his high-riding slacks (inches above the ankles), and the professor sport coat (no leather elbow patches); and his band of troops, armed with shovels in one hand and beers in the other, trench dirt caking knees and palms, some in the uniforms of second jobs—janitor, Shell clerk, cowboy—are stone-still, except for the cowboy, who walks, feline-quiet, to the end of the line and lights a partially smoked, hand-rolled cigarette.

Boss stares. A cloud crosses the moon in that look, suddenly, like the look just drove its truck across the median and crashed into your eyes in a head-on collision. "Digging," Boss says.

"Landscape work, huh?" Torbjorn asks. Now up-close, he surveys the arc of a dozen-plus holes and haphazardly tossed chunks of dirt, mostly clay, clumped together like boulders with roots and grass. Bomb site. No bags of fertilizer or mulch to be seen, just disturbed earth, beer cans everywhere, and a pile of pine trees, roots intact, but trees browning, some nearly needle-less.

---

[13] I.e., two *cans* of beer?

A cloud of smoke from the cowboy's exhale drifts to Torbjorn: pot.

Back to head-on collision with Eyes: "Planting trees," says Boss.

"Yeah, I'm new in town. Just got a kitchen job, but this kinda work looks like mo—"

Hiccup. Bush Squatter, embarrassed, like this is church, gulps down his beer. Hiccup.

"Doesn't look too bad, though," Torbjorn continues. "Hell, way it is, right? Shoot work full of holes, and you got the definition of life."

"We're planting trees," says Bush Squatter.

"Drop it, Mop," Boss says. "Look, son, these trees need to be up before dawn. So, unless you're going to grab a shovel, why don't you let us do our jobs? Hit the books, maybe."

"Yeah, I don't have the textbooks, yet. But anyway, you know, if it's cool with you, sir, I'd like to join you guys."

"Wolf, Boss, this kid just wants a beer. No Christmas in years to come, not with the a-wolf-alypse." The cowboy takes another drag, his beard stained nicotine-yellow about the lips.

"Well, I say no, Boss," says the Shell clerk. "Kid's a liability. Just look at him."

"Wolf, you're right. Pale, wearing black. Wolf looks like a school-shooter."

Torbjorn asks: "School-shooter?"

"You know, your school-shooting wolfs got a certain look to them."

"I agree," Shell says.

A big guy with a bushy, Brahms-like beard offers Torbjorn a beer. His wrestler's uniform is *way* too small.

"Hey, Digger, don't give the kid a beer."

Kid: Torbjorn gets that a lot—thirty years old and still gets it—so with can of Keystone in his left, he pops the seal with his right, then chugs. Afterthought: *like a kid.*

"Holy wolf! School-shooter's missing a thumb."

"Hey, that's cool," Shell says. "You born like that?"

"Wolf's like some kinda terrorist on top of the whole school—"

"All right—fine," Boss says, handing his shovel to Torbjorn, "you're wise to the beer. You're hired, but the wage is one beer per erect tree. Same goes for all of you. So, come on, everyone. Back to work. Scriber, get that sign done. Mop, watch diligently, and stop drinking. Rest of you, we need to assign your digging vertices. Now listen, kid, we only have eight—"

Sirens. Two city cop cars with flashing lights fly down College, slow as they pass along the bushes, then stop at the intersection by Torbjorn's tree. Two cops, bulky, black and two-dimensional behind their flashlights, jog around the maple—straight for them.

"Quick," Boss shouts, "toss the beers and line up. Need to hide Unconscious Guy."

Torbjorn'd forgotten about Unconscious Guy: He'd be dead, if it weren't for the beads of sweat. "Is he OK?" Torbjorn asks, taking a spot in line, next to Boss, on his left.

"Yeah, Johnny's fine—Wolfer!"

"Yeah, Boss?" he asks, hopping in line, on Boss's right.

"Get rid of your—your smoke."

"Wolf, you're right." He tosses the joint behind them, over his shoulder into the hill of trees. "Wolf," he mutters, "should've saved her for later."

"Hey, what you doing?" asks a pair of flashlights, blasting them with brilliant white light. Not moonlight. "We had a call. What's going on here?"

More sirens. Two more cop cars, flashing blue and red, pull up behind the first two, and two more flashlights jump between the bushes and jog across the lawn.

A walkie-talkie spits with static, the sound coming from the nearest flashlight, its brightness still shrouding the largest silhouette:[14] "Yeah, there's a bunch of them….Yeah, the backup just got here….Copy that, but we might need more."

The walkie-talkie's flashlight lowers, and a walrus of a woman steps forward into the light of the other flashlights, her hand resting on a holstered gun that's too tiny for her hip, which is also her ass and her thigh. "All right, gentlemen, let's drop the shovels."

Shovels drop.

"Had a call come in," says the Walrus, slowly, vowels as round as herself. "Y'all got permission to be digging?"

"Yes, officer," Torbjorn says, "we gotta get these trees planted by—"

"Silence, son," Boss says. "Not another word."

"Yeah, don't listen to that wolf. Might be a school-shooter."

"What's that?" Walrus says.

[14] The physics of this silhouette is suspect: These cops are "fore-lit," not backlit.

"Possibly a terrorist." Cowboy holds up nine fingers, right thumb behind his palm.

"Shush, Wolfer!" Boss shouts. "Sorry for the interruptions, officer. To answer your question, we are planting trees to honor the dead."

"What's that?" she asks.

"Christmas Tree Protest," Cowboy says, "and it's a wolfie, too. Gotta quarter the pie like it's a clock with twenty hours."

"Excuse me." No, that wasn't Walrus' voice.

Flashlights swing right and spotlight the two-can babe. Two Can's summer dress is different, no longer dark and earthy in the moonlight. Her flashlight dress is bright and scarlet.

"Bisera!" Boss shouts, beside Torbjorn. The Boss' flashlight face has also changed: older, oddly translucent, lines gouged into a wax face. Not fear, not fatigue. Sadness. Shame.

"What's that?" Walrus asks him.

"Nothing, officer," says Two Can, "my apologies for intruding, but these men have no right to be here. They've been drinking heavily for hours now, disturbing the peace, and vandalizing college property. Just a bunch of hobos. And dangerous, by the looks of them."

"And who are you?" Walrus asks.

"I made the call. Frankly, I don't know how students are supposed to feel safe walking home at night, with men like this on campus."

Bitch, Torbjorn thinks. "Look here, girl. These men work for the college and—"

Someone punches Torbjorn's left shoulder. It's the Shell station guy.

Torbjorn whispers to Boss, "Well, you do, don't you?" But Boss is silent, head hanging.

"Just look over there," says the Two Can Bitch, pointing behind the cops to the picnic bench, "three open cases of beer. Public intoxication. And this young man," she says, nodding at Torbjorn, "looks to be underage. Serving alcohol to a minor, and I'll—is something burning?"

"No, officer," Boss says, chin up, "we don't work for the college. We're just honest, hardworking citizens, exercising our right of free speech. Our tree-planting is a creative nonviolent act in protest of the War on Terror. Scriber, why don't you show this lady the sign?"

"Nobody move," Walrus says.

"OK. OK, officer, you'll see," Boss says, "it's over there behind you on the picnic bench by the—by our beverages. Please, just take a look."

"Mike," Walrus says, "take a look."

The officer to her left heads off.

The Scriber (or that landscape architect, thinks Torbjorn) whispers: "Boss, we weren't quite done with—" "Shush," Boss interrupts. "And, Boss, girl's right, we got a—" "Shush up!"

Four more cop cars pull up and half a dozen more flashlights run to join the frontlines.

Officer Mike returns with a four-foot-ish poster. Walrus points her flashlight at it. In thick black magic marker, the text, reducing in size and increasingly cramped from left to right to fit on the board, reads: "On this day, May 2, 2007, because $2^{20} = 1{,}048{,}576$."

"Clearly," Two Can Bitch says, "they're all intoxicated. And one gentleman, somewhere, is unconscious. Don't know where—all right, something's definitely—"

"OK, gentleman," says the Walrus, going for handcuffs, and the rest of the cops follow suit, "gentleman, you have—"

"Officer," Two Can interrupts, "where's all this—"

"Mam,"[15] Torbjorn says, "honestly, I didn't—"

"Son, you have the right to remain silent, and I suggest—Jesus, what's burning?"

"Told you, Boss," says the Scriber/Architect.

Scream. An absurd, silly sort of scream.

The Dozen all spin around, then part and scatter, as Johnny, absurd-silly screaming, crawls away from his bed of trees, his smoking bed of trees, smoke growing fast and thick.

"Wolf," Cowboy says, "definitely should've saved her for later. Darn shame of a wolf."

And with that "darn shame of a wolf," yellow flames leap high from the mound of trees, and clouds of black smoke rise and dim the moon.

PROBLEMS

1.1. *Fiction.* Pretend you're a critic (if you are a critic, pretend you're not a critic pretending to be a critic) and write a review of my writer's three-paragraph Prologue (Excerpts 0.5 and 1.1) that considers the following:

(a) Is my writer the narrator and not the writer pretending not to be my writer inviting you to pretend to be three dull bookish characters who just happen to share my passion for math, music, chemistry, etc., or not?

[15] I can only assume that Knut means "ma'am;" Mam is the language and name for a Native American people in Guatemala who are considered to be pre-Columbian members of the Maya civilization. Yes, I think it is safe to presume that Walrus is not a Mam.

(b) If so, if the narrator is simply a figment of your imagination, is (s)he reliable?

(c) As Burke-ian critic, argue whether or not such excerpts could "be treated as equipments for living, that size up situations in various ways and in keeping with various attitudes" or, as he elsewhere designates them, "strategies" for dealing with "typical, recurrent situations."[16]

(d) Assuming that authorial intention is problematic, adopt the stance of Rabinowitz to characterize the following: **(i)** my writer's authorial audience, **(ii)** my authorial audience, **(iii)** your authorial audience.[17]

(e) Include a response to Roland Barthes' "The Death of the Author" (1967).[18]

1.2. *Hyperhydration.* Suppose you are Jennifer Strange during a drinking-water-without-urinating contest and you're about to die because you want to win a Nintendo Wii game console. Furthermore, suppose you weigh 115½ lbs, your body's interior is composed of one type of cell having a single sodium ion channel and no organelles (i.e., simply a plasma cell membrane filled with water and sodium ions), and your body's exterior (your "skin" that holds water and interior cells together) is simply one giant impermeable membrane having a single orifice for drinking water so that, as the contest begins with your first sip of H_2O (all water drunk being pure, having no ions of any kind), the voltage potential across all internal membranes is balanced. Finally, at sea level with a temperature of 273.15 degrees Kelvin and air pressure of 1 atm, calculate, to 4 significant digits, the number of liters of water you, as Jennifer, will have drunk at the moment of your death.

1.3. *Mamma Slob's Moon Fractions.* Given that the full moon occurred at 10:10 on May 2, 2007, and the subsequent new moon will occur at 19:28 on May 16, 2007, compute the fraction of moon ("a waning 0. 96297905203204942562023361328314 moon") corresponding to the moment of Slobodon's calculation in the college library at 22:57 on May 1, 2007. (*Mamma Slob's Hint*: Convert times to Julian Days, i.e., to 32 decimal places, the number of 24-hour days that have elapsed since noon on Monday, January 1, 4713 BC.)

1.4. *Vertex Eight's Dubious Research Methods.* Suppose the Christmas Tree Protest had been postponed a day, or even held the night before, rather than stubbornly starting at midnight between the first and second of May (2007) to celebrate the midpoint day between the 9/11 attacks (2001) and the Mayan Apocalypse (2012). Using *Vertex 8*'s spreadsheet of casualties in the War on Terror (see Table 1.1 below) and his latest tally of 1,048,576 deaths (just before the library closed at 23:00 on the eve of May 1), find new death toll tallies for

(a) the eve of May 2 (24 hours later)

[16] Kenneth Burke, "Literature as Equipment for Living," *The Philosophy of Literary Form* 3rd ed., University of California Press, 1973.

[17] Recommended reading: Peter J. Rabinowitz, "Who Is Reading?" and "Rules of Reading" from *Before Reading: Narrative Conventions and the Politics of Interpretation* (1986): 20-46.

[18] For text you might consult the American journal *Aspen* or Barthes' collection *Image, Music, Text* (1977).

(b) the eve of April 30 (24 hours earlier)

Then calculate the prime factorizations of each new tally and propose alternative Christmas tree configurations that would appeal to Mamma Slob's number-theoretic aesthetic.

Table 1.1. Vertex 8's "Grand Death Toll"

DATE	iraq	Afg	Dead People Description
4/30	20		20 CIVILIANS (*in Khalis, Shi'ite enclave north of Baghdad*): Suicide bomber kills *at least* 20 at funeral; 25 others wounded.
4/30	4		4 CIVILIANS (*western Baghdad*): Suicide car bomber kills 4 at police checkpoint.
4/30	2		1 CIVILIAN, 1 IRAQI GENERAL (*headline*): "In other parts of the capital, a bomb killed one person and gunmen killed a former general in Saddam Hussein's army."
4/30	5		4 INSURGENTS, 1 POLICEMAN (*Mosul*): 4 insurgents killed attacking police station; car bomb kills policeman.
4/30	9		8 MILITANTS, 1 IRAQI SOLDIER (*Shi'ite district of Baghdad*): US/Iraqi raid kills 8 militants, 1 soldier.
4/30		56	"NEARLY 60 KILLED" (*Helmand Province, opium-producing Sangin Valley = drug world stronghold*): 56 killed, Afghan general said (5/3), in Operation Achilles' Operation Silicon.
4/30		5	5 INSURGENTS (*near Gereshk*): "Air Force MQ-1 Predator fired a Hellfire missile at 5 insurgents observed to be carrying weapons...missile successfully hit targets."
4/30		4	4 INSURGENTS (*near Shindand*): "Air Force F-15E Strike Eagle dropped a GBU-38 on four insurgents with weapons...achieve the desired effects."
4/30	2		2 INSURGENTS (*Kamiz al-Hajj*): Airstrike kills 2 insurgents trying "to set an improvised explosive device on a local street."
4/30		1	1 AFGHAN GUARD OF US SECURITY FIRM (*Kandahar*): Taliban suicide bomber killed guard, wounded 3.
5/1	1		PFC. ZACHARY R. GULLET: Died at approximately 10:30 a.m. of non-battle causes
5/1	1		LANCE CPL. JOHNATHAN E KIRK (*Al Anbar*): Died May 1 from wounds received while conducting combat operations on Apr 23.
5/1	1		MUHARIB ABDUL LATIF (*the Senior Minister of Information of al-Qaeda-in-Iraq*): died in Adhamiiya, part of Operation Rat Trap.
5/1	15		15 ENEMIES (*in Operation Rat Trap*): over 72 hours, 95 enemy personnel retained, 15 enemy killed . . . Maj. Gen. William Caldwell IV confesses no evidence (DNA) of Abu Ayyub al-Masri's death exists; Omar al-Baghdadi's entire existence is uncertain.
5/1	5		5 "ARMED MEN" (*west of Taji*): Al-Masri originally reported killed during battle in town of Taji (but = false: see above).
5/1	14		14 CIVILIANS ON HIGHWAY: Near Al-Iskandariyah gunmen ambush bus and kill 11 (women + children); but near Al-Latifiyah, gunmen fire on civilian cars and only kill 3 (plus 5 wounded).

5/1		5	5 MEN FIRING GUNS (*at checkpoint in Sara Kalay village*): 8 men exit speeding vehicles & open fire -- 5 killed, 3 escape.
5/1		4	4 MILITANTS (*Spera district of Khost province*): 4 killed after 12 attack administration office.
5/1		1	1 POLICE OFFICER BEHEADED (*Kandahar*): Captured in village of Mushan in Panjwayi district, 18-yr-old police office is beheaded -- head left in a school in the village
5/1		13	13 CIVILIANS IN US-LED BOMBING (*Maroof district*): 13 killed in US-led bombing raid near Pakistan border.
5/2	2		1ST LT. RYAN P. JOHNES, SPC. ASTOR A SUNSIN-PINEADA: Killed when vehicle was struck by an IED in a S. Baghdad.
5/2	1		PFC. KATIE M SOENKSEN (*Baghdad*): died from wounds from IED detonated near vehicle.
5/2	11		11 CIVILIANS (*on bus heading to Hilla, south of Baghdad*): Bomb on bus explodes, kills 11.
5/2	3		3 CIVILIANS (*Mahmudiya*): Mortar shells kills 3, wound 15.
5/2	4		4 CIVILIANS (*in Green Zone*): US embassy reports rocket attack killed 4 contractors working for US gov't (1 Philippine national, 2 Indians, 1 Nepalese national).
5/2		1	1 SENATOR (*Kabul*): Senator Abdul Saboor Farid (prime minister, 1992) shot outside home.
5/2		12	5 SOLDIERS, 7 MILITANTS (*Zurmat*): 5 soldiers & 7 militants killed when Czech diplomat from Kabul was fired on by gunmen

1.5. *Claire's Awkward Model.* Show that, given the scale of Claire's pigment $C_{32}H_{16}N_8Cu$ (here magnified to 2.5"×2.5" Figure 1.4), a two-dimensional model of Claire's entire 13"×19" painting (Figure 1.2) would have a height greater than the diameter of the planet earth.

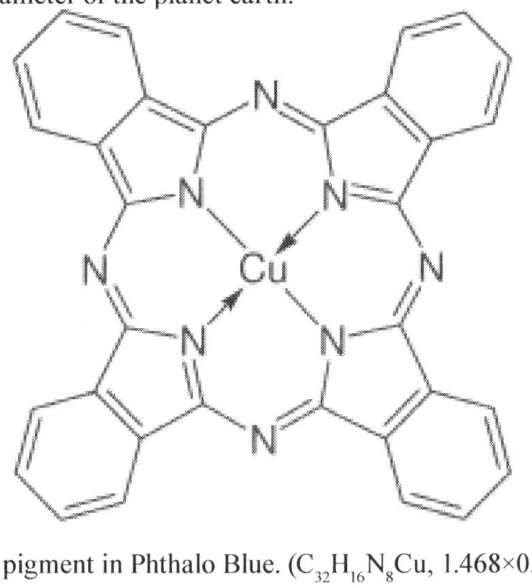

Figure 1.4. The pigment in Phthalo Blue. ($C_{32}H_{16}N_8Cu$, 1.468×0.498×1.960 nm.)

1.6. *Being Fucked.* Compose a set of variations on Torbjorn's being fucked cell (Figure 1.3) for

(a) piano solo

(b) string quartet

(c) brass quintet

(d) quintet for harmonica, sleigh bells, musical saw, almglocken, and slide whistle

1.7. *The Fluid Dynamics Surrounding the Death of the Author (Part 1 of 3).*

Dear Dead Knut, did I kill you, did you kill yourself? Can I blame a river? (Your keys clutched in my hand, always clutched.) What about chaos, nonlinearity? What about fluids…

(a) FLUID 1: *Rain.* Last night. Long after midnight. I remember the rain, weeks of rain. The cold and the dark. I remember how, last night, just hours before dawn, the dawn the river takes you, I sit here in the dark, my laptop on the desk in front of me, my dead mother's desk. I am alone, waiting for you. For weeks, I've been waiting here, alone in the dark, without electricity, in my dead mother's house. Her house is empty, cold and dark, because of you. Because of you, I lost it all—job, house, life—and we'd sold everything (*her* everything), everything except the walls, my mother's white walls, this desk, my laptop on her desk, and the beer cans—your beer cans—these empty Keystone cans on her desk. They've been here for a while. You have not. After she died, you disappeared…because of me. But you'll come back. You must: You've got her money—*our* money…It's my fault you disappeared: It was me that called the cops.[19]

Now, where are you? You and the money. Last I saw you, you had your box: your novel, your research, your whatever, all of it in your box, box you never let me touch. This was weeks ago, before the rain came and never stopped. And you were sitting on it, your box, in the middle of the street, in front of the hospital where she finally died. And me, standing on the sidewalk, I needed the money, but all I could do was stand there and look at you from the sidewalk, look at all the dirt—dirt on your face, jeans, black Subcomandante Marcos T-shirt—and you not looking, not at anything, just sitting on your box, staring at the street between your feet, and causing a traffic jam, as cars honked and people yelled…things. Then, suddenly, I laughed—Why?—I don't know. Perhaps I felt bad about the money thing. Perhaps you reminded me of Diogenes, who was said to have eaten (and masturbated) in the marketplace, urinated on people who insulted him, and defecated in the amphitheater.[20] But I'm sorry I laughed. It was inappropriate, untimely. It was the precise moment the authorities appeared and took you away. Box, too. You and your box, they took you. (Yes, Knut, it was I who'd called the police…I

---

[19] Cf. Claire in Book Excerpt 1.3.

[20] Apparently, eating in public was considered rude: See Diogenes Laërtius, *Lives of Eminent Philosophers*, trans. RD Hicks (Cambridge: Harvard University Press, 1972), vi, 46, 58, 69. For shitting in an amphitheater, see Dio Chrysostom, *Discourses* (Loeb Classical Library, 1932), 8.36.

was worried.)

So that's why your beer cans are still on the desk. That's why I'm squatting in my dead mother's house. With no electricity, no heat. And nothing to eat. Just the cold and the dark, and me staring at my laptop's screen. And there's nothing to stare at, the screen is black, battery's dead—no electricity, no money—how long ago did it die? And they took you, because of me.

The front door opens behind me.

(b) FLUID 2: *The Linear Two-Dimensional Flow of Insecure Love (with a, b < 0).*[21] Last night, behind me: You open the front door. You and your box, you enter. You do not shut the door behind you. You are clean, the dirt is gone. But I smell the bourbon.

The rain. Knut, you enter, the door left open, and I think of rain. For weeks I'd heard it, listening—blinds shut, no lights—listening, as I watched my black computer screen and remembered how it was before the rain, how, sitting here at sunset, beams of light would skewer through the slits of the Venetian blinds and gold dust would fall in the beams, around them, over them, dust and light like rain, those beams stretching across the room from west window to me, to my reflection on the unlit laptop screen, my face shining in the slanted stripes of golden light, and I liked how I looked. But now, the door opens, Knut enters, and door left open, the rain has a different sound.

And Knut, you are different, standing there, some ten feet away, in front of the open door, your weight shifted to one side, whole body strained under the weight of the 13"×19"×11" box balanced on one shoulder, whole body soaked, water dripping down your face like dust in light, and you are different: bones, cheek flesh carved out, hollow, head shaved. Yes, Knut, you needed a haircut, but I do not like this: Beads of water drip from your clean bald head to my dead mother's hardwood floor, and the sound of droplets slapping floor is loud and different. I do not like it. I have been staring at black screens in the dark. I am carved out.

But box crashing to the floor beside your feet, I know that sound: panic in my chest.

You kick the box towards me. It moves an inch, and you suck in air, sharply, at the pain.

I want to say things, say how I'd gone looking, had looked for you everywhere, had called every facility, but couldn't find you, so I'd sat at this desk, the laptop battery beeped itself dead, and the days passed, but rain did not. I want you to know I didn't care anymore—the job, the foreclosure, her money—I do not care: Toss me in the street, I will stand in the rain. (Beside you.) I want you to know the truth about her death, the guilt. But my writer is bald, now. I cannot speak.

You do: "It's done," you say. Your voice is different, too—cracked and confused—vowels too large, like you hadn't spoken for a long time and tongue had gone to sleep.

---

[21] See footnote 1.

It is different. Too much. I shut my eyes, I wait for you.

Waiting, eyes shut, I listen: Footsteps, yours. Creaks, her floor. Slam, her door. Door shut, rain has the right sound. But you are gone.

I say, "Come back."

(c) *Her money isn't in your box of crap*: I leave my dead mother's house and follow you into the storm.

(d) *To be continued…*

SECTION TWO

SECTION 2
CONCERNING §2'S BEING OPTIONAL[22]

This second section is optional because Knut's second chapter (titled "The Twins: Sex") is a waste of time. In short, the chapter is over 200 pages long and nothing happens: Claire is asleep, Torbjorn and Slob sit in a crowded drunk tank, and chapter three begins the following morning.

Ergo, students of *Book*, having committed to memory the following plot necessities, may skip to Section 3 without experiencing significant disorientation:

Plot Necessities 2.1. *Before skipping to §3, commit the following to memory:*
(i) *Slob has a brain tumor.*[23]
(ii) *With her father incarcerated, Claire goes home and falls fast asleep.*
(iii) *Torbjorn observes a salamander tattoo on the ass of a fellow drunk tank inhabitant.*

We are now ready for §3.

[22] As its title suggests, this section is optional, provided Plot Necessities 2.1 be committed to memory.

[23] As did my mother.

SECTION THREE

SECTION 3
CONCERNING T&A: TRITONES AND ASS

The moral of §3: Sleeping with your students is bad—lose your job, lose your home, lose your life—but falling in love with them is worse. Asexuality is preferable.

Book Excerpt 3.1. (B&F.) *Concerning Knut's reduction of my "mother issues" to Claire's exploding head syndrome, her symptoms marked by musical tritones, satanic incest, etc.*

7:00 A.M.: Claire does not believe in the devil, she believes in B and F.

She should get out of bed: Today is Wednesday, the beep of her alarm clock is nearly A (A is good), and she is happy with last night's success, with how quickly the cops arrived and arrested her father and how—problem solved—she went home and fell fast asleep. Unfortunately, she dreamt of B and F again: the tritone, that is, as a harmonic interval, the diabolus in musica, diabolus per somnia loqui. When her head explodes, she wakes up.

But it's OK now: Her alarm is almost A (slightly sharp of 440 Hz), her bedroom is white (white is good), and she does not believe in the devil. And she never has, not really. At least, not religiously: She was raised on Big Bang Theory, rather than the Bible, so her childhood concepts of Lucifer, to the horror of her babysitters, were scientifically skewed. For example, there was the giant bioluminescent praying mantis that bites off the heads of mischievous children. As her mother had taught her, bioluminescent creatures, such as Photinus pyralis (the firefly) or the Jack-o-lantern mushroom (Omphalotus olearius), emit light via the oxidation of the pigment luciferin, a reaction catalyzed by the enzyme luciferase, which, as her father had taught her, is far more efficient than incandescent light bulbs.[24] These days, though, Daddy's the devil.

Claire feels scattered. She gets out of bed and shuts off the alarm. She makes her

[24] A bit oversimplified? Though Mamma Slob the Father may have meant well—if, by "efficiency," he meant nearly all the energy in luciferin's reduction is converted to light, whereas light bulbs dissipate about 90% of their energy as heat—the reaction, however, is more complex, having multiple steps involving ATP; i.e., to simplify:

$$\text{luciferin} + \text{ATP} \rightarrow \text{luciferyl adenylate} + \text{PP}_i$$
$$\text{luciferyl adenylate} + \text{O}_2 \rightarrow \text{oxyluciferin} + \text{AMP} + \text{light}$$

bed, smoothes the wrinkles out of her sheets. She thinks how her hands are irons (she likes ironing) and decides to eat a Reduced Sugar Chocolate Peanut Butter Protein Plus PowerBar with a glass of soymilk for breakfast. Her bed is made—wrinkleless—but first she has to use the bathroom.

And scattered is not good. Today is Wednesday, May 2, the first day of Summer Session I, when she teaches 8 A.M. Music Theory II, a survey of Renaissance and Baroque music from Palestrina to Bach, which is good, she thinks, has some thought behind it, much like 20th century (the serialism of Schoenberg and Webern, the soundscapes of Birtwistle and Adès) and unlike the "dark ages" in between. The history of music is a canyon with a pair of dark ages, Classical and Romantic, at the bottom: *Dark Age One*: always the same chord progression (iii → vi → IV → ii → V → I) but people like Classical because Beethoven's deaf and Mozart laughs funny in the movies, followed by *Dark Age Two*: the endless whining of Chopin and Rachmaninoff (for what? A sequence of doubly diminished seventh chord simultaneities? A secondary dominant or two? Perhaps some rootless ninths, elevenths, or thirteenths?), all their whiny wandering crap, spinning 360-degrees at the bottom of a canyon without aim or purpose: Claire flushes the toilet.

Hands washed, she looks in the mirror above the sink and sees this:

Figure 3.1. Claire's bathroom mirror. (Mixed media on glass, $23\frac{3}{4}$" × $23\frac{3}{4}$".)

The face in her painted mirror makes her happy: As staunch asexual, Claire has no use for mirrors, for any reminder that she has a body. However, as closet computational chemist, her bathroom mirror will be harder to model in ChemBioDraw: In addition to oil-based pigments, her mirror's self-portrait also contains cosmetic media: various brands of nail polish, lipstick, etc.

She opens her face, this painted mirror that's also the door of the cabinet above the sink. Inside the cabinet, there are seven shelves of tiny travel-sized bottles—35 bottles, to be exact—each shelf containing five bottles of a different color (the top shelf has five yellow bottles, the second shelf has gray, third has red, then blue, purple, green, and bottom shelf has black). But today is Wednesday. So she selects shampoo and conditioner in the blue bottles (fourth shelf).

Claire takes a shower.

Claire's Shower-time Reflections: The goal of today's lecture: Begin with Medieval modes and make it to Palestrina, whose counterpoint coheres, has rules: minor sixths ascend, eighth notes proceed in pairs, stepwise, on unaccented beats, and leaps return in contrary direction—yes, she must get to Palestrina. So there will be no time to discuss her silly syllabus. And no student introductions, either—no "Let's go around the room and say your name, your major, and what you did over the summer"—because, frankly, what's the point? (1) Claire won't remember their names, (2) There's no need reinforce instrument/major stereotypes (composers as arrogant, pianists as anal, and voice majors as airheads—in one vocal cord and out the other), and (3) How do all music majors spend their summers? They practice—*duh!* And no, Claire won't even introduce herself. Instead, she'll plunge into a lecture on modes—except for Hypophrygian whose dominant (F) forms a tritone with its tonic (B):[25]

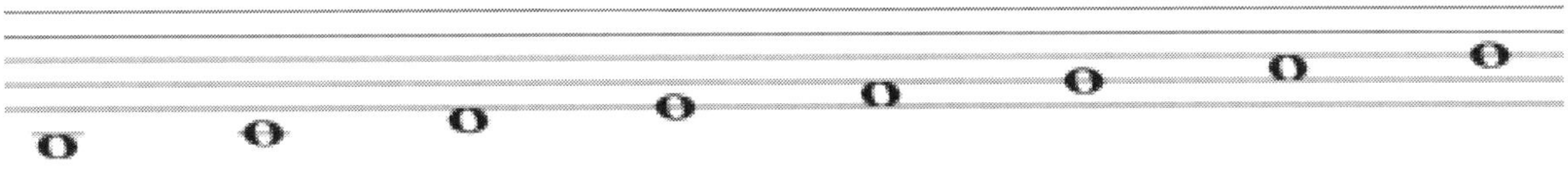

Figure 3.2. Hypophrygian mode.

No, there will be no Hypophrygian mode in Music Theory II.

Today is Wednesday: blue towel...

Claire's *Problem of the Day*: B and F are the devil, but which is the culprit, B or F?

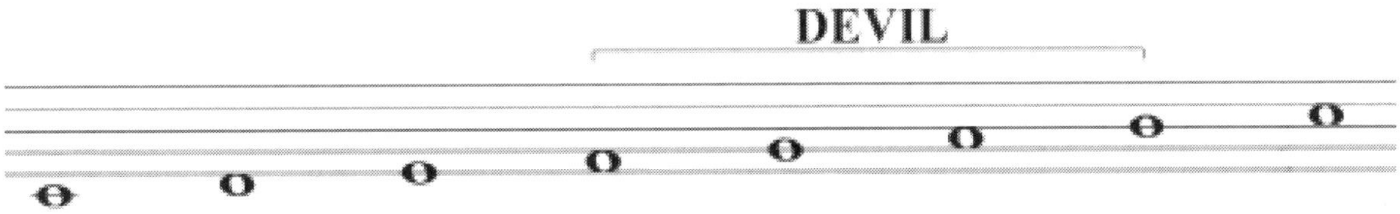

Figure 3.3. Problem: *B* + *F* = *Devil*.

Solution: There will be no B in Music Theory II, only B-flat. Even in Gregorian chant, they knew that B (not F) was the troublemaker: They excised B and invented B-flat: *musica ficta* ("false music")...a term invented to confuse voice majors and interrupt class with questions.

Claire is dry, her hair wrapped up in a blue-towel turban. But she must wear clothes.

Except for its structural design (size, shape, and function) and its contents, her bedroom closet is the same as her bathroom cabinet. It is Wednesday, so from a row of fourteen identical

[25] What about transpositions? Are we really limited to the conventional listing of modes (the convention attempting, of course, to minimize accidentals) so that Hypophrygian *must* begin on B (as tonic) and have F as dominant.

(barring color) summer dresses on hangers, she chooses the eighth dress from the left or second of two blue dresses (like toiletry items, dresses one and two are yellow, the next two are gray, then two red, two blue, two purple, two green, and finally two black).

She puts on the blue dress. She is happy—blue is good—but it's only now, as she adjusts her dress, smoothing out the wrinkles at her hips, that she realizes she has a new problem—*Sub-problem*: Now, with B excised, B-flat and E form a tritone.

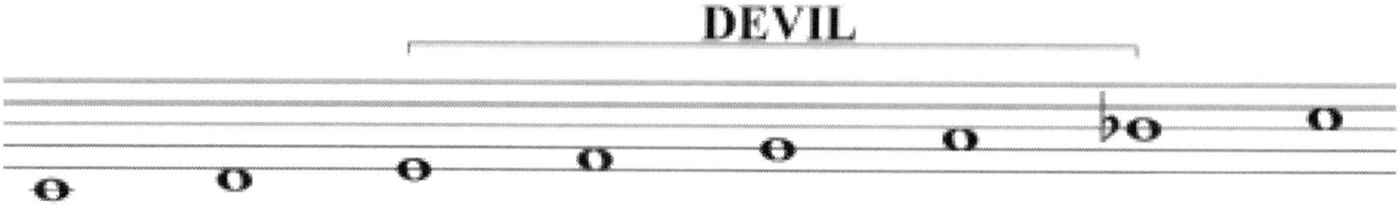

Figure 3.4. Sub-Problem: Now, *B-flat + E = Devil.*

Clearly, Claire is tired. She hasn't been sleeping well, due to B-and-F's Exploding Head.

7:43 a.m.: Sitting in her white-walled dining room furnished with white china cabinet, a dead plant in a white ceramic pot, and a ring of six small tables arranged in a circle around a video camera on a tripod, Claire takes a sip from her glass of soy milk, followed by a nibble of her Chocolate Peanut Butter PowerBar® ProteinPlus™ Reduced Sugar, also made with soy, and wonders if her B-and-F's Exploding Head is governed by the second law of thermodynamics...[26]

How it always starts: It is hot. But there can be no air-conditioning because her AC unit hums the tritone, B and F. And there is no ice—soymilk, warm—because the refrigerator's been unplugged, its tritone must be stopped. And no water, B and F between the leaky faucet's drips. But it's no use—wherever she goes, whatever she does—the tritone, B and F, just spreads and increases, from AC to fridge to faucet and onward: no lights, light bulbs buzzing B and F; and no laptop, the hum of the monitor; and no PowerBars, the grind of her chewing; and no walking, tritones in her tiptoes; and no moving, tritones in her tendons cracking, in the movement of her dress' cloth, in the bits of dryer lint she can't pick off her dress, the removal of lint like the rip of Velcro, like Bartók's snap pizzicati; and no earplugs, the blood pumping in

[26] See Problem 3.1.

ears, like timpani tuned to B and F; and no breathing through the nose, only through the mouth, which dries out mouth like bad tequila; until finally, it's the thinking, the thoughts you cannot stop, the tritones in the leaps between the thoughts, between the words and images, emotions and memories, B and F, and you try to blank your mind, but the thoughts, full of tritone, just burst into the blankness on their own, and you can't stop thinking—the more you blank, the more they burst—until finally, you scream: "Stop!"[27]

And then the dream: Everything's gone. What's left: the same drone of B and F inside her, like eardrums are timpani, like tremolo-ing timpani, but outside, all is black—except for him.

Him: six feet away. He is naked and lit by no source. He is the source of his own light: If alive, he'd be bioluminescent. But he's not fleshy—if she amputated his arm, Claire has the feeling there'd be no bleeding and, also, arm'd grow back like a starfish's—he's more like a plastic manikin, his pose fixed, arms at his sides, rigid, and one foot forward like an Early Egyptian statue of Amun-Re, and glowing, especially the eyes, same as his scaly skin, glowing red.[28] But he is not the devil, the devil has horns. No, he is her father. *Scaly Slob*: He will not bite off her head. Her father is not a praying mantis with scales. He is like a fish, a red lantern-eyed flashlight fish,[29] a nude Amun-Re-standing/bioluminescent-fish version of her father.[30]

But here's the crazy thing: Claire can't see herself. Her hands, she can feel them, feel them move, but when she holds them in front of her face, they do not block him from sight: He is still there, six feet away, standing still, arms at his sides, naked.

---

[27] I have serious worries about this "metaphor," or whatever it is. I fear Knut is making the thermodynamical substitution *heat* = *tritone* so that the intensity of the tritone Claire hears (and its subsequent tendency to infect all her possessions, actions, and ultimately her thoughts) is somehow a measure of entropy which...which is bullshit.

[28] This is consistent with bioluminescence. Even fireflies. The light, generated by bacteria that live in special pouches, is often red in color.

[29] Some confusion in terminology here? The term flashlight fish applies either (1) to the family Anomalopidae (also dubbed lanterneye fish) in the Beryciformes order (the sawbellies) or (2) to various species, not in Anomalopidae (e.g., the 200-plus species of deep-sea lanternfish in the family Myctophidae, order Myctophiformes), but mostly to *Photoblepharon steinitzi* (which might be a subspecies of *P. palpebratusis*) found in the Red Sea or Indian Ocean.

[30] And here, this allusion to Amun-Re seems forced, an unnecessary distraction from the fabric of Knut's narrative: Yes, Amun-Re has been associated with the devilish symbol of the horned ram (though earlier with the goose); and yes, Amun-Re, as (self-created) creator, was known to regenerate (like a starfish) by becoming a snake (not a fish) and shedding His scaled skin; and yes, as divided divinity, though Amun remained "hidden," revealed Re is associated with a *light source*, namely, the sun—but frankly, what's the point?

"Do you have hands?" says Scaly Slob.[31] She hears him speak over the tritone drone, but his lips did not move. He stares. His opal eyes. The tritone's hum coming from his eyes.

Claire shuts her eyes. She feels her eyelids slide down and clench tightly shut: He is still there. His luminescence, undimmed. She turns her head away: He is there, same place, hasn't moved. She turns her back to him, feels her steps turn her around: still there.

"Stop it," she says.

"Stop what?" he says, his lips firmly shut. "It's your doing, dear. If only you'd studied harder in chemistry and learned your Gibbs free energy."[32]

"Go away," she yells. And she feels her throat yell. But the sound of her voice is soft, calm, gentle, a purred tritone. Though inside, she feels the panic and the heart pound.

"You don't want me to go," he says, lips shut. "You like it."

"No, I don't," she screams. Or tries to scream, feels the scream rip her throat. But, instead, she hears herself speak happily, yearningly, flirtatiously—like a voice major—hears herself say: "Yes, thank you, Daddy. I do."

He is closer. But he hasn't stepped: He is just closer now, a yard away.

She steps back. She feels the stepping, feels her soles finding firm ground behind her, but she hasn't moved: He remains the same distance from her. "Let me go," she tries to say. She doesn't hear herself speak, and feels herself wanting the opposite, wishing he'd come closer.

She runs: He is there, same place, without moving. She turns, runs faster in the opposite direction. Nothing: still there. She is out of breath and stops running. Sides hurting, she gasps and gasps. But she can't hear herself breathe.

She leaps towards her naked father and punches him in the jaw, and she can't see her arm when she punches him, but her hand hurts—pain—the pain of punching a marble statue, but he doesn't budge. And instead of anger, she feels herself becoming overwhelmed with happiness: They are inches apart, stuck inches apart.

"What are you afraid of?" he asks.

---

[31] The following quote from Descartes' *Meditations* seems relevant: "Suppose then that I am dreaming, and that these particulars—that my eyes are open, that I am moving my head and stretching out my hands—are not true. Perhaps, indeed, I do not have such hands or such a body at all." See Descartes, *Meditations on First Philosophy: with Selection from the Objections and Replies*, trans. John Cottingham (Cambridge University Press, 1996), 13.

[32] What the fuck? (See Problem 3.1.)

"Nothing!" she screams. But hears herself say, "You, Daddy," and say it seductively.

"I would never hurt you." He hugs her, embraces tightly: He hasn't moved. She sees him standing several inches away, arms at sides, but she feels his arms wrapped tightly around her, trapped in a tight marble cocoon, squeezed, suffocated, as if she's submerged in wet concrete and waiting for it to harden, waiting to drown in concrete—and held there in his arms, she feels herself fill with false desire, wanting him.

She struggles, feels herself pushing him away, feels her fists pound his chest, feels her muscles doing it, brain ordering muscles to contract and smash his face to hell—but nothing: just his warm embrace, his bare chest tight against her breasts, and her arms hang at her sides, relaxed, gentle like the tritone drone.

"Tell me you love me," he says. The tritone is louder.

"No," she shouts—*louder, the tritone*—"Fuck you. Fuck you. Fuck you. Fuck you."—*and louder*—but she hears herself softly say, "Yes. I love you. I love you. I love you. I love you." And the tritone drowns her out.

And he, inches away, arms at sides, lips shut, he kisses her. His tongue jackhammers past her teeth. So loud, the tritone.

She strikes him and screams, but the tritone screams louder. She feels herself kissing him back. And she feels herself like it.

She suffocates in him.

The tritone explodes her head.

The dream ends: She always wakes up when B and F explode her head, and the alarm is always beeping nearly A, and A is good.

Ridiculous, Claire thinks. She washes down a delicious, long-ago-melted-in-her-mouth nibble from her Reduced Sugar Chocolate Peanut Butter ProteinPlus™ PowerBar® with the last of the soymilk and saves the second half of her PowerBar for lunch. Ridiculous, she thinks, it was just a dream. Her father's kiss had tasted like the barbequed potato chips she'd had before bed. They're good, the best—Tim's Reduced Fat Hawaiian Luau BBQ Potato Chips—and Claire is disgusted: How could she have forgotten to brush her teeth?

Claire brushes her teeth. Today is Wednesday, she thinks. Wednesday is a big day: 8:00 A.M.: Teach Music Theory II. (No syllabus, no intros, no Hypophrygian.)

11:00 A.M.: Meet with colleague Dr. P.S. Long. (Update status of their joint research grant.)
NOON – 5:00 P.M.: Office hours. (Shut office door at 1 P.M. and work.)
5:00 P.M.: Attend rehearsal of Long's new string quartet. (His "contribution" to their grant.)
7:00 P.M.: Host dinner party for Napoleon Asexual Society. (Record "dinner" for YouTube.)
7:51 A.M.: Claire locks her back door and then, laptop bag over her shoulder, quickly descends the back alley stairs of her second-floor flat. She has less than 10 minutes to get to work, and can't be late. She should probably move, she thinks: Her flat, the second floor of a Second Empire three-story building, is so noisy—yes, above her, the third floor is vacant (the old cat lady who lived there finally died last year), but below her, on the ground floor, is Gator's Hut, a restaurant/bar frequented by students for its late-night entertainments (the jazz on Saturdays is nice, but today is Wednesday…Karaoke Night)—but, she thinks, it's also so convenient.

She walks across Third Street from her building to the small parking lot behind the Music Annex, the faculty lot. She spots her blue Chevy Malibu Hybrid[33] in the lot—*so convenient*: Now that she has tenure, she parks at work, in *her* spot in the faculty lot, rather than at home, across the street, where spots get stolen by Gator's customers. She walks past the lot and heads for the Annex front door—*7:52 A.M.*: Claire is early. The mound of burnt Christmas trees is still there. The Piazza lawn, still dug full of holes. Is her father still in jail? Her father…

It is warm and sunny outside, the sky is clear and blue: After class, she will drive her Malibu to Starbucks. Starbucks is her asylum. She will take her laptop to Starbucks, order a sugar-free soymilk mocha with a double shot of amaretto, eat the other half of her Peanut Butter Chocolate PowerBar; and once she's changed her blank desktop's color scheme from "Brick" to "Twilight" and checked her horoscope at www.astrology-online.com, after that, she'll then figure out how, regardless of transposition, to exorcise the devil from musical scales, starting with B and F—she'll discover a scale where tritones are impossible…and then drive back to campus in time for her 11 A.M. meeting with Dr. Long.

Her father: It was just a dream, she thinks. As Freud said, "A dream then is a psychosis."[34] But Freud also had a cocaine problem, Claire does not. Claire is awake. Claire is in control:

---

[33] My car…

[34] Probably in Freud, *An Outline of Psychoanalysis* (London: Hogarth Press, 1940), but I can't find the page number.

Today is Wednesday, the day of Mercury, the day of change. Blue is a Mercury color. Her Malibu is blue, like her dress, like the sky. Being awake—consciousness—is the management of dreams. Her eyes are open. She enters the Annex.

Book Excerpt 3.2. (Clocks as Scales.) *Concerning Knut's fictionalization of my ass.*

"Shit, you're a teacher?"

The Two-Can Bitch is his teacher. And everyone is silent—waiting. And Torbjorn stands there in the doorway of the classroom—paralyzed. And Two Can, standing there with a look that paralyzes—a Medusa look—her mouth hanging open, ready to devour, standing there in a light blue dress professors don't wear, standing there at the chalkboard—waiting.

Just moments earlier, twenty minutes late to his first-ever college class, clutching his sides, gasping for breath, and dripping with sweat after a two-mile sprint from the county jail to the Music Annex—no sleep, no food, no shower, no coffee, no books, no pens, no paper, no beer, nothing but a public-intoxication ticket stuffed in his back pocket—just moments ago, Torbjorn burst into the classroom, panting hard, and shouted: "Shit, you're a teacher?"

It came out wrong. He'd meant to enter the classroom quietly, meant to be invisible, and try, discreetly as possible, to find an empty seat without a word, with averted eyes. But instead, his exhausted body, ready to collapse, crashed through the classroom door, and he heard himself shout: "Shit, you're a teacher?" And now, the classroom is silent. And Two Can, in her blue dress, with her Medusa look, her mouth is hanging open. And Torbjorn, in his sweat-drenched track-and-field attire (blacks jeans, black T-shirt, black jungle boots), is preparing for the worst, for her to shout, Welcome to Music Theory II—now get the fuck out of my classroom! But instead, all he hears is a monotone Medusa: "As I was saying, with respect to Gregorian chant, the eight modes were divided into four pairs or maneriæ." And all she does is: Two Can turns to the chalkboard behind her and writes "maneriæ" on the board.

And what Torbjorn does is: He takes the open—and only open—seat in the front row. And there he sits and sweats, squeezed between two young ladies, two big-boned curly-haired

Bottle-of-Bourbon blondes, glossy-lipped, glittery-cheeked, and both wearing enough perfume to asphyxiate, enough jewelry to sink a ship. How sad, he thinks. He's heard about it, the sad fate of six-foot voice majors who, doomed to roles as Wagnerian Valkyries, have got to eat that pre-performance "Pavaratti turkey" to hop around stage, to shriek and wave swords like good stalwart Valkyries do, but who then, offstage, overdo their makeup and perfume to look thin.

The Left Valkyrie bumps his arm. She smiles at him...You'd have to break out the carpet cleaner to remove all that makeup. Also, she looks hungry. He imagines her grabbing his arm and eating it, and his interrupting class again by screaming he's not a turkey. He exerts a little self-control, however, and smiles, trying to blank his mind as he shifts his attention to Two Can, who's still writing on the chalkboard, her back to class, as she lectures: "Protus, deuterus, tritus, and tetradus, each maneria consisting of an authentic form and a plagal form..."

By "tetradus" Torbjorn is done for: He just sits there in the front row—hypnotized—and admires how her ass is a well-lighted place, how slender beams of slanted morning light connect her ass to the window, how these beams first skewer through the slits of the windows' Venetian blinds, then spear across the room in a parallel series of horizontal golden beams streaked with gentle falling dust, and finally end in scintillating slashes across her curvy rear, slashes shining bright upon the thin fabric of her tight blue dress.[35]

This course kicks ass, he thinks. And he can't stop, can't take his eyes off that ass, the V on her ass, the ridges, the crests of dark underwear, beneath the thin blue fabric. It's wrong. This Two Can, all wrong: Her calling the cops last night and getting him thrown in a drunk tank so he'd be late to class and, now, her reserving this open seat in the front row between two Valkyries with rose-scented perfume designed to aggravate hangovers and Two Can wearing dark underwear just to torture him. Unlike that one guy, he thinks, in the drunk tank last night, the short middle-aged Asian dude who couldn't keep his gray-and-white-striped pants on—he

[35] This is my ass, Knut was my student, and now we know why Knut flunked my class, despite his good attendance record: Students of mathematics, especially in upper-level courses, get a lot of ass. In fact, orientation of ass, the student soon discovers, is profound, emerges from mathematicians' *Three-stage Pedagogical Strategy*: (1) Adopt a Springer textbook with a yellow cover, (2) By standing in front of what you're writing, with your ass facing the student body, read and copy verbatim your yellow-covered textbook onto the chalkboard, and (3) The students, who can't hear what you're saying to the chalkboard, shall wait patiently for you to finish and move out of the way so they can copy from the board what you've copied from your yellow-covered textbook into their notebooks, their own yellow-bound books lying open on their desks to double-check the accuracy of their notes, which they'll then recopy after class. For more on ass in the classroom, see Problem 3.2.

wasn't wearing underwear. He had tattoo of a lizard on his right ass cheek.[36]

And now, having written "authentic" and "plagal" on the board, Two Can turns to face the class: "Any questions?" she asks.

Silence, no questions from students. Only her long dark hair, her large dark eyes, slashes of sunlight in the dark of her eyes—looking at him. This is too much for Torbjorn—*Is class over yet?*—he stares at the clock above the chalkboard behind Two Can.

"No questions? OK, good," she continues, "then let's list the modes: Dorian, Hypodorian, Phrygian, Hypolydian, Mixolydian, and Hypomixolydian…"

As she writes the modes' scales on the board, he continues staring at the clock, like it's a Magic Eye thing,[37] just stares at the secondhand tick: Dorian (the mode starting on D), and tick: Hypodorian (on A), and tick: Phrygian (E), and tick: Hypolydian (C), and tick: Mixolydian (G), and tick: Hypomixolydian (also on D)—*But wait a second*, he thinks, *only six modes?*

"However, Glareanus," she continues, "in his *Dodecachordon* (1547), introduced two…"

Yeah, sure, he thinks, *but what about the modes starting on F and B, like Lydian and that one other one?* Suddenly, Torbjorn shouts: "Hey, you missed two!"

Two Can stops, chalk in hand, her "Glareanus" half-written on the board.

"Sorry, professor," says Torbjorn. "But I was just wondering…it seems like, you know—shouldn't there be a B and F, too?"

Two Can, paralyzed. Chalk, still hovering by the "Glare-" of her half-written Glareanus.

Torbjorn, now embarrassed, tries again: "I mean, you know, like Lydian or whatever?"

Silent, she writes the scale of the Lydian mode on the board…

But not that one other one. And Torbjorn, embarrassed for interrupting class like a jackass, does what he always does when he's embarrassed for being an ass: He keeps acting like a jackass. "Yeah, sorry, professor," he says, "but that's still only seven. Weren't there eight?"

Two Can, nothing. Ass-to-class, she writes the "-anus" of Glareanus on the board and then, ignoring him, continues: "So it was Heinrich Glareanus in his *Dodecachordon* (1547)…"

Blah, blah, blah—Torbjorn can't believe it: Ignoring me, he thinks. Ignore-ance is bliss.

---

[36] Actually, it was a salamander. (See Plot Necessities 2.1.)

[37] An autostereogram?

Her ignorance, my night in a drunk tank. Her ignorance, my getting no coffee and no sleep, and cramped between two Valkyries and no Aspirin. Her ignorance, her forgetting that one mode starting on B. Fuck this, he decides, and as she continues in the same mode—"…Aeolian and Hypoaeolian, Ionian and…"—he focuses on the board: *Which mode*, he thinks, *is missing?*

Figure 3.5. Torbjorn trying to think.

Torbjorn remembers—he doesn't worry about shouting: "Hey! You forgot Hypophyrygian!"

Still, she ignores him: "And—and Ionian," she continues, shouting, "Hypoionian—"

"Which," Torbjorn shouts, trying to interrupt, "no matter the *transposition*, are the same scales as Hypolydian and Mixolydian."[38]

But the teacher keeps on ignoring him: "And you'll notice how, whether Ionian and Hypolydian have the same scalar notes or not, the dominants are different…"

Suddenly, Torbjorn's left-hand Valkyrie whispers to him, "What's a transposition?"

"I don't know," Torbjorn whispers back. "You should probably ask the teacher."

Left Valkyrie's hand is up. But Two Can doesn't notice this, still going on about dominants: "…the Ionian having a G-dominant and the Hypolydian having an A-dominant…"

But Right-hand Valykyrie doesn't need to raise her hand: "Uh, professor?" she calls out.

Ass-to-class, Two Can continues circling the modes' dominants, but responds: "Yes?"

"I'm confused," says Right Valkyrie. "I thought dominants were like the Five chords."

Apparently, Two Can *can* answer questions: "It's how you use them," she replies. "This isn't like the major/minor tonal system. Ionian is the authentic form…"

But, as Two Can explains whatever, Torbjorn feels sorry for Left Valkyrie, whose hand

[38] Good for Torbjorn. (Cf. footnote 25.)

is still up, ignored. "Ask about Hypophrygian," he whispers in her large, thrice-pierced ear.

"The phry-whatsit?" she asks him, as Two Can goes on talking about dominants.

"The Hypophrygian mode," he whispers again.

"But professor," says Left Valkyrie, waving her hand in the air, arm fully extended.

Damn, that's a lot of armpit, and hairy, Torbjorn observes, but arm's a good fan, nice and cool. As her waving arm fans his sweaty brow, he stops staring at her hairy pit and, returning to the wall clock above the board, makes a remarkable discovery: A musical scale's got 12 notes, and so does the clock.

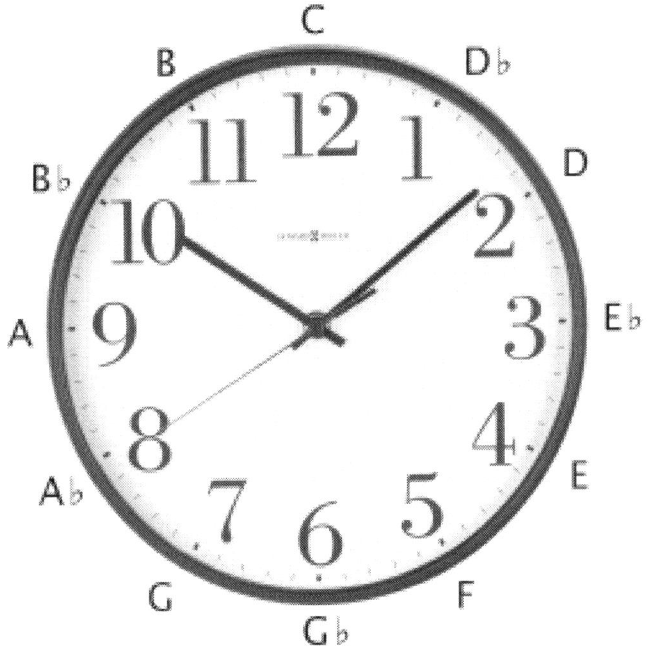

Figure 3.6. Torbjorn's remarkable discovery.[39]

For example, labeling the half-steps of an octave 1 through 12, Hypophrygian starts on B. On his clock, B is 11. Then up a half-step, C is 12. And up a whole-step, D is 14—no wait, on his clock, 14 is a 2—yeah, E is 4, F is 5...So, on his clock, Hypophrygian is 11, 12, 2, 4, 5, 7, 9, 11.

[39] See Problem 3.3.

Torbjorn's discovery is awesome. But below his clock, Two Can's still answering Right Valkyrie's question—"and, whereas the authentic modes' dominants are the fifth notes of…"—still ignoring his left-hand fan, which is waving faster: "Professor?!" And faster: "Professor?!"

"Yes, OK, fine," says Two Can—finally: "Yes, what is it? What do you want?"

"Yes, thank you, professor," says Left Valkyrie, "but what about Hippo-fridge-in mode?"

"Hypophrygian," Torbjorn whispers, noting her mispronunciation—a Freudian slip?

But Two Can is not amused, not à la mode: "That's it," she says, her voice *crescendo*-ing to a shout: "No more interruptions!"

Left Valkyrie tries to apologize: "Sorry, professor, but I was just—"

But Professor Two Can interrupts: "Yes, I know, that's nice, thank you, but there are no tritones in…"—the teacher trails off, *diminuendos* into silence. She sighs. Then, composed, she returns to her lecture drone, *mezzo-piano e legato*: "So where were we? Yes, dominants, the fifth notes, for authentic modes. Yes. But for plagal modes, typically the sixth or seventh—"

"Like Hypophrygian," Torbjorn interrupts, "which is the coolest mode because its One and Five are B and F which form a tritone."

"No tritones—no!" she screams, *subito fortissimo*. "There are no tritones in Palestrina."

"Who's Palestrina?" asks Left Valkyrie.

Professor Two Can, her mouth's hanging open again…

Happy with where class is going, Torbjorn plays the clock again, which is sort of like math, he thinks: Tritones split your clock in half, are always opposite, always 6 apart, like B and F: $B - F = 11 - 5 = 6$. And the four quadrants—12, 3, 6, 9—split clocks into minor thirds…

But suddenly, Two Can's open mouth has bad news: "Unfortunately, we're going to end class early, today." She starts erasing the board. "But for homework, I'd like you to—"

"What about the syllabus?" asks Right Valkyrie, without raising her hand.

"It's online," Two Can says, softly, *pianissimo*, but erasing the board violently—*feroce, con fuoco*. Yeah, her eraser is a weapon. "I'll put the syllabus online," she adds, "but for homework, I want you to construct a mode that—"

"What's a mode?" asks Left Valkyrie, arm up and waving—her fan back in action.

And Two Can, back to *forte*: "Fine! No modes." Her eraser attacks the board, a blank region of the board with nothing to erase. "Fine, we won't call them modes. Just construct a seven-note scale that has no tritones between any pair of notes and then compose two—"

"That's impossible," Torbjorn shouts, checking his clock.

Two Can drops the eraser on the floor. She leaves it there, board half-erased. "So, the homework assignment, no tritones in the scale and compose two eight-measure phrases with it."

"Yep, impossible," he repeats, double-checking clock. "Can't have more than six notes."

Big Surprise, the teacher ignores him: "So, does everybody understand the assignment?"

"Look, professor," he says, "if you got seven notes, it's impossible to not have a tritone. Look, it's like the clock. Just look at the clock," he says, pointing above her head.

Right Valkyrie slugs him, in his pointing arm. She doesn't eat it, just whispers, "Will you shut up? I'm sure she knows what she's doing. She's the teacher." Then she smiles.

Torbjorn stands up quickly—or tries to…getting out of a chair between two Valkyries is like driving bumper cars—but on his feet, free at last, Torbjorn then speed-walks to the door. There, by the door, he stops to wait for Professor Two Can, who's packing up her bag to leave.

But with Torbjorn out of the way, Left Valkyrie has a question: "So, professor—uh, yeah—Miss Professor, how do you get syllabuses online?"

"Never mind," says Two Can, swinging her laptop bag over her shoulder. "I'll bring copies next time."

But Left Valkyrie is persistent: "But what textbooks are we supposed to get?"

"They're on the sylla—we'll go over it next time." Two Can heads for the door, as her students, yet seated at their desks, stuff away notebooks, but still have questions, their hands still raised—except for Torbjorn who's holding the door open for the teacher. And except for Right Valkyrie, who doesn't do the raised-hand thing: "But I like totally don't get all this mode stuff."

"Don't worry about it," says Two Can. She walks through Torbjorn's open door, and he bows to her as she—

She is already gone. He catches up and walks down the hall beside her. "Look, professor, seriously," he says, "it's like a clock—12 notes, 12 numbers—you know what I'm saying?" He opens the door to the stairwell for her: She steps through it, but says nothing. So, stepping down the stairs beside her, he tries again: "Now, tritones, they bisect the 12-note scale, which is like a difference of 6. So that means, on clocks, tritones are opposite each other, like 6 and 12, or 1 and 7. See what I mean?" He opens the door for her at the bottom of the stairs, but she still says nothing. And same with the Annex front door—same nothing. So, outside, he tries facing her, walking backwards on the sidewalk in front of her, as students behind him hop onto the grass: "So, professor, what I'm saying is there's only six pairs—you know, on a clock—only six can be opposite. So, for any seven-note scale, you always got two notes being opposite, and that shit's a tritone, so your homework can't be done—you get it?" But she's still got nothing, and his back slams into some guy—"Hey, man, watch where the fuck you're going, why don't you?"—and more nothing, as she crashes into his chest and he says, "Oh shit, professor, sorry—you all right?" But eyes averted, she just walks around him into the parking lot behind the Annex: "Hey, professor, what's your name? At least tell me that."

Nothing: He doesn't follow her, just watches her ass depart, as she walks to the far end of the faculty parking lot, to a blue car in the last row by the Dumpsters. She never glances back, not once...What the fuck is he doing? he thinks. He's a composer, now—remember? He's done with women, alcohol, sleep—done with all that shit. And he's got his first composition lesson at noon and hasn't written anything. He should go find a piano. And something to write with.

Torbjorn changes his mind: Across the lot, Two Can is trying to unlock her door, when out of nowhere, or rather, out from behind the Dumpster nearest her blue car, the Boss—that Slobodon dude—suddenly appears.

There is shouting: Slob shouts the word "Bisera!" "That's not my name," Two Can shouts back, still trying to unlock her car door. "Stay away from me."

There is something in Slob's hand. He is aiming it at Professor Two Can's back.

Torbjorn charges to the rescue, to the far end of the lot, where the old man, still aiming, shouts again: "I'm sorry. I didn't mean to. Please, Bisera."

And Torbjorn, running, still half across the lot, hears his teacher scream: "I mean it! I said stay away. That's not my name." Her door is unlocked. She opens it and—

But the old pervert is too quick: The object in Slob's hand is small, but he points it straight at her, at her back, as he charges her from behind: "Please," Slob shouts, "at least, tell me what it means. The code, what's the—"

But as he attacks from behind, Two Can's laptop bag swings through the air and smashes into the old man's head: Slob falls back, hitting the Dumpster, and collapses to the ground.

Torbjorn has finally arrived: And Slob, prostrate beside the Dumpster by her car, does not move. But kneeling down beside him, Torbjorn can see the old man breathe—breathing hard—can hear his wheezing. The object in his hand, the weapon: It appears to be a 3×5 note card. But what about Two Can? The car door slams: Torbjorn looks up.

Two Can is in her car. Torbjorn stands, then hops over Slob's body to stand beside her driver's-side door. "Professor," he shouts, knocking on her window, "are you OK?"

She rolls down her window: "Help him," she says. She starts the engine and adds: "And tell him it's easy. Tell him it's as easy as your ABCs and 123s."

"What?" Torbjorn asks.

"Wait! You, stop!" she shouts. Torbjorn is not going anywhere, standing outside her window. With her engine running, Professor Two Can retrieves a scrap of paper from her glove compartment. A receipt perhaps. On the back, she scribbles a brief message with a black pen. Finished, she folds the scrap of paper—folds it four times—then hands it to Torbjorn through the window. "You give it to him," she says. "I'm going to Starbucks."

"OK," he says, putting the tiny folded square of paper in his pocket, "but I was just—"

"I don't care." Her stick jams into reverse—"And you," she says, backing out of her spot, "you stay away from me"—reverse shifts to drive, her tires squeal, she's gone.

Torbjorn kneels back down to Slob. The old man is not moving, but he is wheezing, and the weapon, this old 3×5 note card, stained and taped around the edges, trembles in his right hand. Torbjorn shakes the old man's shoulder gently. "Can you move, man?"

Slob doesn't move, but says—or wheezes, rather—wheezes more than says: "I'm sorry."

"For what?"

"I didn't mean to kill Barney," Slob says. And he chokes and drops the card.

Torbjorn picks up the dilapidated 3×5 note card and reads its handwritten message:
10001100

1011100011101011101011000111011011110001011100001100011101000 11.

PROBLEMS

3.1. (a) *Nonsense*. Is Claire's "Exploding Head" governed by the second law of thermodynamics? Or—for some isolated system (e.g., her home with AC unit, fridge, leaky faucet, etc.) in which the total entropy (of the tritone B and F) tends to increase through time (in her dream) and approach a maximum value (until her head explodes and she wakes up)—is this just bullshit? An asinine misusage of sound scientific concepts? Is it nonsense? Is it fashionable?[40] Is it rape?

(b) Does this really warrant Scaly Slob's non sequitur apropos Gibbs free energy?

3.2. *Ass in Class.* As my student, Knut had to buy a yellow-covered textbook. It was repulsive—literally. Its cover illustrated a "butterfly" Lorenz attractor with a large Rayleigh number, with $\rho = 28 > 24.74$-ish. (See Figure 3.7.) "Butterflies" emerge from the Lorenz equations—$dx/dt = \sigma(y - x)$, $dy/dt = x(\rho - z) - y$, $dz/dt = xy - \beta z$—in xz-plots, when $\sigma = 10$, $\beta = 8/3$, and ρ is varied. For small ρ, the system is stable and yields one of two fixed-point attractors; but for $\rho > 24.74$-ish, the fixed points become repulsors, eternally evolving without ever crossing:

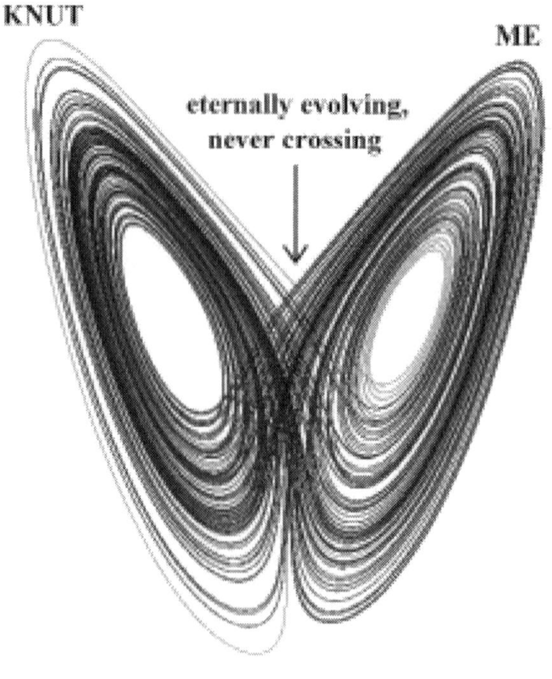

Figure 3.7. Student-teacher relationship. (Strange attraction with $\rho = 28$.)

~~"Butterflies" emerge from the Lorenz equations—$dx/dt = \sigma(y - x)$, $dy/dt = x(\rho - z) - y$, $dz/dt = xy - \beta z$—in~~

[40] First, cf. Alan Sokal's "Transgressing the Boundaries: Toward a Transformative Hermeneutics of Quantum Gravity," *Social Text* 46/47 (1996): pp. 217-52. Then, cf. Sokal and Bricmont's *Fashionable Nonsense: Postmodern Intellectuals' Abuse of Science* (1998). Finally, cf. Problem 3.2.

~~xz-plots, when $\sigma = 10$, $\beta = 8/3$, and ρ is varied. For small ρ, the system is stable and yields one of two fixed-point attractors, but for $\rho > 24.74$-ish, the fixed points become repulsors, eternally evolving without ever crossing.~~

(a) Is my textbook cover's $\rho = 28$ an apt model for student-teacher etiquette, for a strange attractor distinguished by repulsion?

(b) Does $\rho = 28$ really look like a butterfly?

(c) Or is it an ass?

(d) Is it a good reason to screw students in your office and get fired because you don't have tenure?

(e) Why would my ass be connected to lasers, dynamos, waterwheels, and convection rolls in the atmosphere?

3.3. *Clocks in Class.* Use Torbjorn's wall clock (Figure 3.6) to prove the following:

(a) For musical scales having seven or more pitch classes, tritones are unavoidable. (*Hint*: Apply the Pigeonhole Principle.)

(b) Construct a six-note scale in which tritones are impossible. How many such scales exist?

(c) How does the quartering of a clock as a musical scale (Torbjorn's stack of minor thirds in §3) differ from the quartering of a clock as ring of Christmas trees (Slobodon's error in §1)?

3.4. What am I doing? (Sitting here, writing homework problems—why?)

3.5. *The Fluid Dynamics Surrounding the Death of the Author (Part 2 of 3).*[41]

(a) Fluid 3: *The Ghost of Nonlinear Two-Dimensional Saddle-Node Bifurcations ($-\infty < \mu < \infty$).* Last night, I drive and cannot see. But I keep on looking for my writer, in the dark and the storm.

It's near dawn—*the* dawn, the dawn Knut dies—my dashboard says 4:37, which means (1) it's a little after five and (2) I don't know how to fix the damn clock. The rain has lightened—that's what I keep telling myself—and I keep driving south, out of Napoleon, south to where there are no streetlights, just my Chevy's headlights' brights, south to where the river overflows.

At first, I'd been able to follow him, heading for the bottomlands, but—with Knut driving his Jeep fast and drunk and forgetting to turn on his headlights like a crazy person—I soon lost him. So now he's gone, again. Guzzling bourbon, again. Again, I hunt his drunk ass driving in the river bottoms, somewhere along the levee. "It's done," he said. *What?* I think. *What is done?*

Yes, it's done. Damn that old dead bitch: It's her fault Knut's...the way he is. Not mine. Not my fault he had to go and love her—or whatever the hell it was—and wannabe a writer. But my mother's money wasn't in the box. I looked. It was just paper, notebooks, drafts, musical scores, graphs, paintings,

[41] You may wish to review Problem 1.7 before diving into its sequel, 3.5.

the manuscript of his "novel" on top: *Book*. That's the title. Ridiculous.[42]

[42] Recall: In Problem 1.7, Knut showed up at my dead mother's house with a shaved head: He dropped his box on the floor, then left—but, before I followed, I did rip open his giant box of crap and dump the following on the floor:

- A manuscript of a "novel" called *Book* by Knut Knudson (ca. 1000 pages, not paginated, but water-damaged and splattered with paint)
- A bunch of oil paintings on wood: Aside from "Claire's painting" (Figure 1.2) and her self-portrait in the bathroom mirror (Figure 3.1), I found several works not appearing in *Book*:

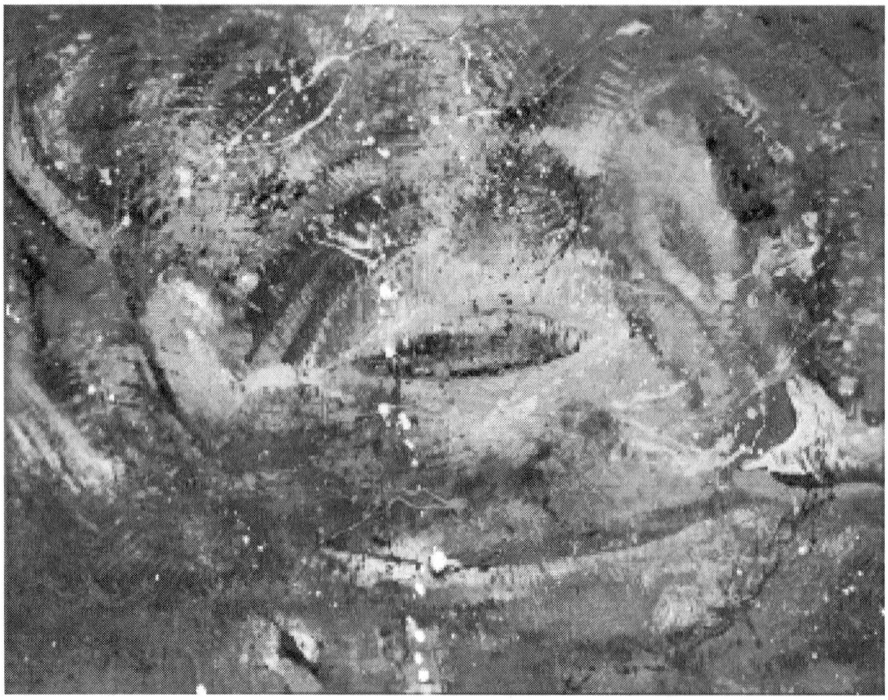

Figure 3.8. Example of painting not appearing in Book. (Oil on wood.)

- A bunch of musical scores, such as Torbjorn's "Being Fucked" theme (Figure 1.3), but also a string quartet—my mother's "Requiem"—and the following handwritten excerpt for cello solo that appears to be unplayable:

And now, I can't see shit. My headlights don't reach too far, my brights' beams like a pair of tunnels ending too soon in cloudy orbs of rain-streaked light. Ghosts, I think: orb = *ghost*, tunnel = *bottleneck*. It's math. What happens when you're near saddle-node bifurcations: Fixed points collide and leave behind a "ghost," a saddle-node remnant. And then, the ghost takes you, slowly; slowly it pushes you down the tunnel, slow passage through the "bottleneck" that sucks in trajectories and delays them, holds them back, before permitting passage out the other end.

And then I see it: headlights, incoming. A semi-truck. (Not Knut.) But I can't see shit, so I roll down the window: The cold rain burns my cheeks like crystal bullets, and this semi, incoming, its brights blind my eyes. The truck's horn blares, like speech: "Weave right," it screams, "you're in the wrong damn lane." Head out the window, I shout back: "Fucking ghosts!"

Indeed, I think, fuck it all. I shut my eyes: no truck, no storm, just the slick sliding traction, four wheels on flooded road, just the semi's blaring horn. And eyelids clenched, I see the two-dimensional system—$dx/dt = \mu - x^2$, $dy/dt = -y$—its sequence of phase portraits, its ghost rising from the collision of fixed points:

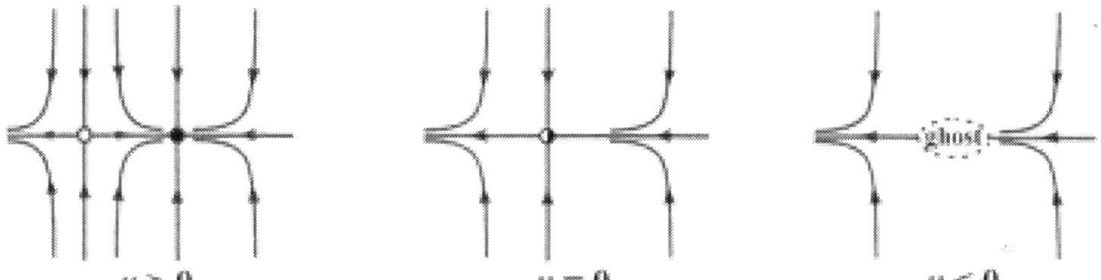

Head-on Collision: Chevy vs. Semi

Figure 3.10. Saddle-node bifurcations. (The emergence of ghosts as μ varies.)[43]

Figure 3.9. Impossible-to-play cello solo. (Pencil on paper.)

- A bunch of other crap:
  - A dead leaf from a maple tree (brown, crumbling)
  - Xeroxes of "research" which have been copiously scribbled on (ca. 4000 pages)
  - More art crap: papers, brushes, inks, paints (including Phthalo Blue), etc.
  - A rewritable CD labeled "Music Shit" in a black marker (Knut's handwriting)
  - Six cartons of cigarettes (Clipper Lil' Cigars, filtered Full Flavor 100's)

But no money fell out of his giant box of crap onto my dead mother's hardwood floor, so I ran out the door and followed Knut into the storm in my Chevy Malibu Hybrid.

[43] This phase portrait, as μ varies, provides a more accurate "visualization" of ghosts emerging from the fixed

Suddenly, I feel it: The semi thunders past, my Chevy shoved right in the truck-wind, like a leaf. Open, I think. Open your eyes…

Never mind: It wasn't a semi. Too small. Just a pickup truck. But biggish, possibly an F-250.

(b) FLUID 4: *Phase Portrait of a Reversible System with Nonlinear Center as Origin and with Saddle Points Joined by Heteroclinic Trajectories.* I drive. And drive. And have been driving. Have driven. Drove. I drive. Driven. Drive.

Driving, I steer into the southernmost bend of Riverside Road. From left to right, an inch of river flows across the road: On my left, the Ohio River streams slowly over the stacks of sandbags that line the road, then runs across the road beneath me, and finally cascades into the ditch on my right. It's here I see you parked on Oil Creek Bridge, your Jeep's driver's side facing me, your lights and engine off, but my brights *bottleneck* through the pouring rain and light your profile, your forehead resting on the steering wheel, your hands gripping it, and the brightness of your bald skull glares back, though blurred by the storm between us.

I roll to a stop in the middle of the road, just off the edge of the bridge you've blocked, your Jeep's length cutting diagonally across both lanes of the narrow bridge, as if you'd turned sharply left from the right lane and parked to face the flood, to watch the river coming straight at you through the windshield. It's here I find you, in the worst parking spot in Perry County, parked just feet north of the nonlinear center of a reversible system—$dx/dt = y - y^3$, $dy/dt = -x - y^2$—I know it's silly. But it's how I remember you: near the origin in the phase portrait in Figure 3.11.

---

point annihilations of saddle-node bifurcations. Figure 3.10 depicts a prototypical example—$dx/dt = \mu - x^2$, $dy/dt = -y$—where for $\mu > 0$, we have two fixed points, a stable node at $(\sqrt{\mu}, 0)$ and a saddle at $(-\sqrt{\mu}, 0)$. Thus, as μ decreases, the saddle and node approach each other until they collide at $\mu = 0$, and disappear when $\mu < 0$. But from this "head-on collision" there rises a ghost and a "tunnel" that sucks in all trajectories and delays passage out the other end.

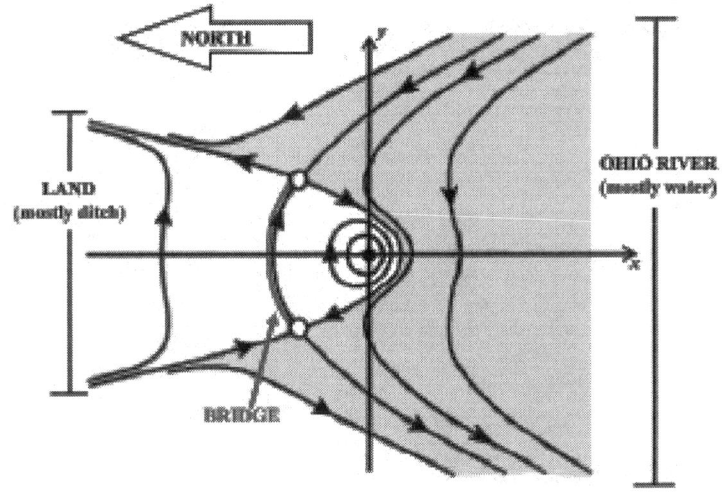

Figure 3.11. Phase portrait of where I find Knut. (Microsoft Paint.)

I kill the engine, I kill the lights, and your head disappears in the darkness. I open my door: The wind punches and the cold rain stabs, but I am not afraid. For once, I must help you. As I step out of the warmth of my car, I see what I missed behind me—a happy cliché: along the eastern horizon, a frayed ribbon of blue-green light clenched between black and black, nascent sunrise clasped from above by the faraway rim of black cloud and from below by the nearby crest of black backlit sandbags, the river sliding over their solid shapes, like dust in beams of sunset light. I have my cliché: Dawn is hope. And now, this once, I know I can help.

I turn and run, away from the beginning of day and into the end of night, and know it.

(c) More on that later.

(I'm tired.)

Let's get back to Knut's fourth chapter, to Mamma Slob lying prostrate in a parking lot.

SECTION FOUR

SECTION 4
100011001011100011101011101011000111011011110001011100000110001110100011

Like Chapter Two, Knut's fourth chapter (titled "10001100101…") is waste of paper (Georgia-Pacific, 8½"×11") and fraught with flashbacks. I have cut Slob's entire life story down to three brief flashbacks, which concern the origin of his 3×5 note card and Barney's murder, and labeled them Evisceration 4.3, 4.4, and 4.5. The remaining Book Excerpts stick to the present…mostly.

Book Excerpt 4.1. *Concerning Mamma Slob's reasons for hiding behind a Dumpster.*

He's fine. In the shade of three large oak trees, hidden between a garbage Dumpster and a concrete wall, the perimeter wall of the faculty parking lot behind the Music Annex, Slob waits for his daughter to finish teaching, waits for the right moment to casually bump into Bisera and say something. Even a "Hi" or an "Excuse me" would change everything. Yes, "Hi" is a place to start: You can't have love without a "Hi," can't have a "Hi" without staking-out a parking lot, hidden behind a Dumpster, where old colleagues in the math department won't see you. And her car, her blue Malibu, is just feet away, parked beside this Dumpster. When she exits the Annex and heads to her car, that's when Slob will casually bump into her and tell her about the tumor.

But how? Slob hasn't spoken to his daughter in over a decade, not since "the incident."

So he can't just say: "Hi, I got this tumor, so I'm saying hi before I die, I love you too."

Nor should he bring up "the incident." Nor pre-incident incidents: (*x*) the DUI or (*y*) he "quit" his job. Nor post-incident repercussions: (*z*) the wife is gone, all because of this 22-year-old named Barney, and his daughter shuns him for ten years, even though he quits drinking.

Nor should he say: "Ah well, could be worse. For example, your daddy could live here, behind this Dumpster. And Daddy could be a hungry homeless beggar with a drinking problem, who'd sit on the sidewalk in front of XYZ Liquors and accost pedestrians with his sad tale of unemployment and his wife leaving him, all because of Barney, that Prometheus A. Barney: 'Hey, you! My wife left me for a twenty-two-year-old!' Daddy'd shout at passing pedestrians. 'Why?' they'd ask. 'Well,' he'd explain, 'it's all due to three reasons:

'*Reason X*: attempted murder,
'*Reason Y*: Barney,
'*Reason Z*: her divorcing me.'

And then Daddy'd hold out his cup and say something about Jesus: 'Think you could spare a buck? I need to eat. Like Jesus, even Jesus eats. Me and Jesus.' But then they'd notice how Daddy's sitting on the doorstep of XYZ Liquors and say, 'Sorry, sir, no cash on me, just debit.' And Daddy'd start saying he had no problem taking debit cards, but then he'd notice he's alone."

Nor can he simply claim that Daddy's changed—that now, hiding behind a Dumpster, things are different (e.g., sober for ten years)—nor argue that it wasn't his fault, that his whole life has been nothing but bad luck, an iteration of failures that weren't his fault, like a malevolent fractal, the Cantor set (C_∞), with its repeated disembowelment of your open middle third:[44]

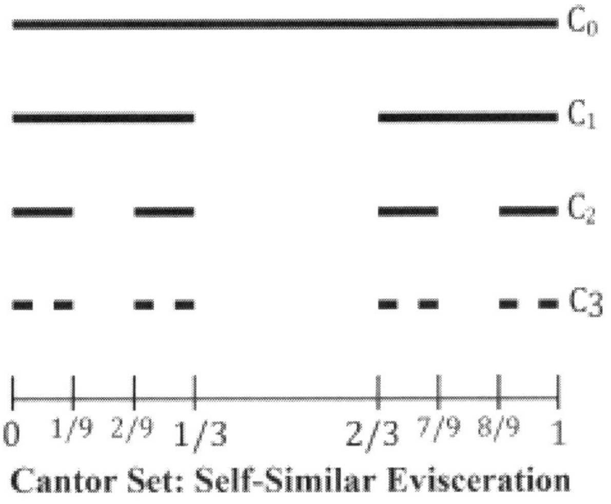

Figure 4.1. Repeated disembowelment of your middle third. (C_i: $0 < i < 3$.)

Nor is she likely to care how this process of disembowelment has remarkable properties. For

[44] **Definition 4.2.** The CANTOR SET C_∞ is a self-similar fractal created by repeatedly deleting the open middle thirds of a set of line segments. Let C_0 be the unit interval [0, 1]. Delete the open middle third (⅓, ⅔) from C_0 to yield:

$$C_1 = [0, \tfrac{1}{3}] \cup [\tfrac{2}{3}, 1].$$

Next, delete the open middle third of each of the segments in C_1, leaving four line segments:

$$C_2 = [0, \tfrac{1}{9}] \cup [\tfrac{2}{9}, \tfrac{1}{3}] \cup [\tfrac{2}{3}, \tfrac{7}{9}] \cup [\tfrac{8}{9}, 1].$$

Continue *ad infinitum*, with the *n*th set given by

$$C_n = (\tfrac{1}{3} \cdot C_{n-1}) \cup [\tfrac{2}{3} + (\tfrac{1}{3} \cdot C_{n-1})].$$

Thus, C_∞ is the set of all points in [0, 1] that are not deleted at any step in this infinite process.

example: *The Cantor set C_∞ has infinitely many points, but has zero length.*[45]

No, she is more likely to mention that Daddy spent last night in jail because she called the cops. Because she'd want to remind Daddy that: Ah well, things have been worse. For example, digging through Daddy's extensive criminal record, we have his first arrest, over ten years ago, for the DUI, when (much like last night) Daddy'd gone to jail, where he'd been ordered to strip and spread apart his ass cheeks as some cop hosed him down. And then, outfitted in gray-and-white stripes, Daddy'd been given a private cell (unlike last night), where he sat Indian style on his bench because the toilet had overflowed who knows when, a lake of sewage already on the floor when they'd locked him in, and waited for the wife to show up and to bail him out. And Daddy waited. And waited. And Daddy was dehydrated, but the water fountain built into the top of the toilet was broken. So Daddy memorized the graffiti on the walls, all cursing white racist motherfuckers, and waited, until lapping up the floor's water seemed like a good idea, and poor thirsty Daddy just wanted to sleep, but they'd tossed Daddy's complimentary blanket and inch-thick mattress into the floor's sewage and never shut off the lights, so Daddy waited.

And when the wife finally arrived to pay the bond, she brought Daddy's little girl, his teenage daughter, Bisera, dressed in funeral black. But the wife was dressed like a Christmas tree, sporting a chest full of necklaces like they were medals of honor. And Daddy, seeing his wife sparkle, so out of place in the jail lobby, all he could say was, "Darnit, I need a drink."

And off went the wife: "A DUI. Divorce, Slob. I'm so damn sick of it. All your bullshit. And Barney, thank God he's OK. Jesus, if this weren't a prison, Slob, I'd—"

"Mom—"

"That's right, Bizzy. No need. Barney'll take care of him."

"Mom—"

"Quiet, Bizzy, this is between me and your father."

Bisera obeyed, and Daddy saw the *please* in her eyes, the "Please try, Daddy. For once."

[45] *Naïve Proof of Mamma Slob's Remarkable Property*. By definition, C_∞ is the set of points not deleted from the unit interval [0, 1] of length 1. But the total length deleted is given by the geometric series:

$$\sum_{n=0}^{\infty} \frac{2^n}{3^{n+1}} = \frac{1}{3} + \frac{2}{9} + \frac{4}{27} + \frac{8}{81} + \ldots = \frac{1}{3}\left(\frac{1}{1-2/3}\right) = 1$$

So the undeleted proportion has length $1 - 1 = 0$. Hence, the set C_∞ has measure zero. *QED*

But Daddy was a loser and said, "Your mother's right, Bisera." But what was Daddy supposed to say? Daddy had his reasons for being a loser—and always has: *X*, *Y*, and *Z*…

Evisceration 4.3. (Slob's pre-incident Reason X: Attempted Murder.) *Concerning Mamma Slob's DUI arrest.*

Firstly, as Barney is strangling him to death, Daddy attempts to remain calm, objective, and forgive Barney, because it's not his fault. Indeed, consider the following: It's Sunday, they live in Indiana, and Daddy's marriage is going to hell. During the week, Daddy asks his undergraduate students to call him "Slob," as he drinks his coffee half-and-half—half Sumatra, half bourbon—and teaches post-graduate algebraic number theory in their remedial pre-algebra course. But this morning, when Daddy'd sucked the last drop of bourbon from his bottle, he recalled the following: It's Sunday and he lives in Indiana—no liquor sales in Indiana on Sundays. So Daddy had to drive to Illinois to get another bottle. And yes, naturally, Daddy brought his "best friend," Barney, to keep him company during the 4.5-hour roundtrip. Anyway, it was just plain rotten luck that Daddy and Barney got pulled over on the bridge—the *middle* of the bridge—crossing the border. It's also unfortunate that, surrounded on all sides by the flashing lights of a dozen cop cars from Indiana and Illinois (the cops trying to decide just where on the bridge, exactly, the state line really was—a measuring stick was called for), Barney lost it and began to strangle Daddy. No, dear, it isn't Barney's fault.

Nor does Daddy blame the cops, who made no attempt to rescue him, as they stood outside the driver's-side window of Daddy's unlocked vehicle and, pointing their flashlights in his eyes, made comments like: "What the fuck?" "No way I'm getting between the two of them." "Why? Who's in there? Who are you—holy shit!"

However, Daddy did find this particular cop's question annoying: It should have been obvious that Daddy, mid-strangulation, couldn't explain who Barney is. Then again, considering Daddy's audience, it would have been futile to answer the question: "Who are you, Prometheus

A. Barney?" Much less explicate the following permutation,[46] of which Daddy is so proud:

Let S *be the set* $\{P, R_1, O, M \ldots N, E_3, Y\}$ *of the letters of the string*

$$\Psi = P\,R_1\,O\,M\,E_1\,T\,H\,E_2\,U\,S\,A_1\,B\,A_2\,R_2\,N\,E_3\,Y$$

where, in ascending order, the repetition of the letters R, E, *and* A *are made distinct via subscripts; and let* F: S → S *be the bijective function such that*

$$F(P) = 1,\ F(R_1) = 2,\ F(O) = 3 \ldots F(E_3) = 16,\ F(Y) = 17.$$

Now, let Φ *be the permutation*

$$\begin{pmatrix} 1 & 2 & 3 & 4 & 5 & 6 & 7 & 8 & 9 & 10 & 11 & 12 & 13 & 14 & 15 & 16 & 17 \\ 11 & 2 & 5 & 13 & 12 & 9 & 14 & 4 & 8 & 10 & 16 & 1 & 17 & 6 & 7 & 3 & 15 \end{pmatrix}$$

where $1 \to 11,\ 2 \to 2 \ldots 17 \to 15$. *Then* Φ[F(S)] *is a product of disjoint cycles* α *and* β

$$\alpha = (1 \ \ 11 \ \ 16 \ \ 3 \ \ 5 \ \ 12)$$

$$\beta = (4 \ \ 13 \ \ 17 \ \ 15 \ \ 7 \ \ 14 \ \ 6 \ \ 9 \ \ 8)$$

and, hence, it follows that Φ[F(Ψ)]

$$= \Phi[F(P\,R_1\,O\,M\,E_1\,T\,H\,E_2\,U\,S\,A_1\,B\,A_2\,R_2\,N\,E_3\,Y)]$$
$$= \alpha(\Psi)\beta(\Psi) = \alpha(\Psi)[P\,R_1\,O\,A_2\,E_1\,U\,R_2\,M\,E_2\,S]$$
$$= A_1\,R_1\,E_1\,A_2\,B\,U\,R_2\,M\,E_2\,S\,E_3\,P\,Y\,T\,H\,O\,N$$

And indeed, Barney, you ARE A BURMESE PYTHON, and Daddy loves you, but Daddy doesn't blame the stupid cops for being frightened of a 22-year-old, 22-foot-long, 235-pound snake with a mouth full of teeth in a head the size of a cantaloupe.

Evisceration 4.4. (Slob's pre-incident Reason Y: Barney.) *Concerning a "Student Transcript of Slobodon's Final Lecture as Associate Professor of Mathematics."*[47]

---

[46] I.e., anagram.

[47] "Amendments" are not mathematical…Nor do corollaries often follow from axioms. But whatever. (I'm tired.)

THE TEN PYTHON MOLURUS BIVITTATUS AXIOMS

Axiom 1: It shits like a horse.

Axiom 2: At 3 yrs, 10 ft, 40+ lbs: done with rats → on to chickens.

Amendment 1 to Axiom 2: Outbreak of Salmonella → free-range chickens.

Amendment 2 to Axiom 2: At 15 yrs of age, it graduates to goats and pigs.

Axiom 3: It is an escape artist, and the wife won't let you eat dinner until you find it.

Corollary 3.1: 3 ft newborns need 55 gal tanks.

Corollary 3.2: At 2 yrs, a large partition of your study must be converted into a hardwood, Plexiglas aviary you have to build yourself.

Corollary 3.3: Must use unprinted newsprint to remove mite-infested mounds of shit.

Amendment to Corollary 3.3: Frequent diarrhea → use mulch.

Amendment to the Amendment to Corollary 3.3: Pine, cedar, and redwood shavings get stuck in its throat, and the wife will force you to dislodge such bodies → snakebite.

Axiom 4: It needs a hiding place. Cardboard boxes are sufficient and inexpensive.

Amendment to Axiom 4: It will piss and shit in its box.

Corollary of the Amendment to Axiom 4: Modified garbage cans are suitable substitutes.

Amendment to the Corollary of the Amendment to Axiom 4: At 3 yrs and 10 ft, w.r.t. its hiding place, you must build a solid wooden enclosure, within the aviary, within your old study, and it must have a door w/ latch s.t. you may shovel shit with ease.

Axiom 5: Proper temperature range is essential to keeping it healthy.

Corollary 5.1: The ambient air temperature must be kept at 85-88°F with a basking area of 90°F and 20°F lower at night. Any deviation will prohibit digestion → no dinner.

Corollary 5.2: Lights must be turned off 12-14 hrs/day to mimic the photoperiod; since, otherwise, it will experience severe stress and may become ill → no dinner.

Axiom 6: It is always hungry.

Corollary 6.1: It will voraciously consume prey that is far too large and regurgitate it.

Axiom 7: Monitor its tub of water at all times, since it will drink, bathe, and shit in it.

Axiom 8: When grabbed by a mouth full of inward-facing teeth, relax, since, if you struggle, it will bite harder and initiate the coil-and-constriction process, whereby it asphyxiates, then swallows you.

Corollary 8.1: Refrain from smelling like food.

Axiom 9: When your wife is present, do not mention any of the following: (1) the blood and gall of young, 3-5 ft Burmese are used in folk medicine; (2) they are a Chinese delicacy; (3) last year, the number of deaths caused by such pets tripled; and (4) in Everglades National Park, a 13 ft Burmese swallowed a 6 ft alligator and exploded.

Corollary 9.1: Do not mention "whales," "toads," or "ants," given (1) internet footage of whale explosions; (2) in Germany, a significant population of toads exploded by over-puffing while under attack of crows; and (3) the ant species *Camponotus saundersi* explodes as a defense mechanism.

Corollary 9.2: Do not discuss medieval history, since William the Conqueror exploded when his attendants forced his corpulent corpse into his stone sarcophagus.

Amendment 1 to Corollary 9.2: Use neither the word "history" nor "fat."

Amendment 2 to Corollary 9.2: No Monty Python, given penchant for exploding animals.

Axiom 10: Under no circumstance, given any level of eagerness, sexual frustration, and/or inebriation, should one accept it as a gift from in-laws on your wedding night.

Corollary 10.1: Divorce is an arduous process, esp. given existence of daughter.[48]

Evisceration 4.5. (Slob's post-incident Reason Z: Her Divorcing Me.) *Concerning the last time Mamma Slob spoke to his daughter.*

Although the decapitation of a snake couldn't constitute a literal violation of his DUI probation, the honorable Judge Julie Simmons was not impressed with Daddy's clear neglect to "sober up," and, aided by the wife's statement, corroborated by Officer Stein's report, it was determined that Daddy's spearing of Prometheus A. Barney through the right eye with a 19th century African artifact and subsequent sawing off of the victim's cantaloupe-sized head with a French Sabatier chef knife, could qualify as "possession of a firearm or other dangerous weapon." In short, fifteen days of jail time, and, although the wife never visited, on the eleventh

[48] Yes, my mother had a snake, but she didn't name it Barney.

day, Bisera made an appearance.

"Mom's too busy," she said, sliding the divorce papers through the slot beneath the window of the visitation cubicle.

"That's fine." Daddy raised his knees to his chest, the chain from wrists to ankles too short for him to otherwise reach the opening.

"Well, you were drunk."

A guard provided a pen, and Daddy signed beside the many X's. The guard promptly took back the weapon and departed. Daddy wondered if this was the right moment to bond with Bisera, to finally tell her about the war, the fall of the KKE, the child-refugee camps. But Daddy needed a drink.

"Bisera, I want to tell—"

"I don't want to hear about it," she said.

"But, you deserve to—"

"No, Dad, I really don't care. I just came for the signatures." She stood up. "And don't try to contact me, either. Not ever. Also, I'm changing my name."

"Bisera, it—"

"That's not my name. Not anymore."

"OK, honey, but it doesn't have to be this way."

"No, and it never did." She turned and walked away.

"Bisera?"

She came back. "I forgot." She slid an index card through the slot without looking at him. "Bye," she said and left.

Daddy flipped over the card and read her goodbye note: 1000110010111000111010111010110001110110111100010111000011000111010001.

Book Excerpt 4.6. (Decapitation.) *Concerning Torbjorn's helping the elderly, by not clobbering their cancerous skulls with decapitated Buddha heads.*

This Slob dude's not dead. Torbjorn's propped him up against the Dumpster: He's fine.

Last night, Officer Mike had said "pervert." Torbjorn doesn't remember much from last night—too much to drink—but he does recall Officer Mike's warning: "You stay out of trouble, son," he'd said, removing Torbjorn's handcuffs. "That gang of protestors, I'm saying stay away from them. Nothing but trouble. And I probably shouldn't be saying it, but that old professor, Professor Slobo-something, we've had trouble with him stalking a nice young lady. Pervert's what he is." Officer Mike shook his head and yawned. "Okey-dokey, then." And with that okey-dokey, Mike had locked Torbjorn in a drunk tank, where he was greeted by a lizard tattooed on an ass.

This morning, Professor Two Can, having knocked the pervert to the ground with her laptop bag, where he'd lain prostrate on the asphalt, asked Torbjorn to "help." *Help*: Torbjorn's propped the pervert against the Dumpster where, sitting up, the old guy's still mumbling incoherently about killing some guy named Barney. *Now what?*—Torbjorn's Jeep[49] is nearby, just across the street in the student lot, the gravel parking lot across Second, but he's not sure whether to take the old man to the hospital or the cops. Data. Torbjorn needs more data.

So now, waiting for answers, Torbjorn sits on the ground beside the murderous Mumbler, their backs against the Dumpster, and examines the evidence. He stares at Slob's note card: 10 0011001011100011101011101011000111011011110001011100001100011101 00011, but Torbjorn hasn't slept—no sleeping in a drunk tank—and the 1s and 0s just mix, blend, multiply, as his tired eyes struggle to focus. And so does his brain, from too much data: So, this card here, he thinks, it's old, stained, taped-up around the edges, and…it's got 0s and 1s on it. This Slob dude had asked Professor Two Can what it meant, called her "Bisera," and confessed to killing some guy named Barney. But her name's not Bisera, so she clobbered him with a laptop, then asked her student for help, and drove off to Starbucks. She also mentioned something being easy, something ABCs and 123s. And, oh yeah, she also scribbled a note and folded it up, a note for Slob. He should read that note. Where'd he put that—

"Gosh darnit!"

Torbjorn jumps. *Pervert alert*: Slob's not mumbling, he's sitting up straight now, alert, looking about wildly. His hands clasp his face, then scrape down his unshaven cheeks, like he's

[49] Knut's Jeep…?

trying to rip away the wrinkles, his face as old and creased as his sport coat. Then he notices Torbjorn sitting beside him: "Darnit," he says, "am I a prisoner?"

"No, dude." But Torbjorn needs to be cautious: The old guy's confessed to murder. And Torbjorn has no weapon, much less a laptop. So he adds, "You're sitting against a Dumpster."

"Oh." Slob turns to see the Dumpster behind them and slaps its metal belly with his palm: It makes a hollow *gong* sound, and Slob seems happier: "Where are my glasses?" he asks.

"Oh," says Torbjorn. Then, for the first time, he notices a pair of eyeglasses lying in Two Can's old parking spot, a couple yards beyond their feet. "Broken," he says. He gets up to retrieve the glasses from the empty spot: the frame is all bent and the right lens seems badly scratched, but the left lens is shattered, bits of glass scattered and *ground* into pavement. He returns to his seat and restores the broken spectacles to their owner, who accepts them silently.

But not gratefully: "You," he says, pointing at Torbjorn, "you attacked me."

"No, that was Two Can."

"What's that?" Slob is still pointing his broken glasses in Torbjorn's face.

"My music-theory professor. She must've knocked 'em off your head and run 'em over."

"Oh." Slob stops pointing. He collapses, physically and emotionally (perhaps mentally), back into the Dumpster—*gong*. "I think I hit my head," he says, and puts the glasses on his face.

"Yeah," Torbjorn says. But he's got more important questions: "So, who's Barney?"

"What's that?"

"You know, this Barney. This Barney guy you killed?"

The old guy is silent, remote, like he's not listening, just looking silly as shit in broken glasses, aloof but silly. Suddenly Slob bursts into laughter.

As the laughing fit continues, Torbjorn recalls that, in his Jeep across the street, he *does* own something: not a laptop, but a twenty-five-ish pound, solid stone, decapitated Buddha head, a Christmas gift which, by gripping its large dangly earlobes, he's used primarily as a dumbbell for *left* bicep curls (no right thumb), but which now could be used as a weapon, if necessary.[50]

Eventually, laughter subsides: "Oh, hell," Slob says, "don't know why I'm laughing. So

[50] Knut's use of my Christmas gift, a fourth-century Buddha of Sarnath with his princely elongated earlobes and sagacious protrusion from the top of his head, is appalling. But not unexpected.

you know about old Barney, do you? Yeah, lost the job over that. And the wife. House, money, daughter. And a *darn* good library of yellow books."

"Yellow?"

"Yep, had to sell them all."

OK, Torbjorn thinks, perhaps the guy's just crazy. But he asks, "You sold phonebooks?"

"No, Springer-Verlag, of course," Slob says, but there must be a funny look on Torbjorn's face because Slob elaborates: "the *publisher* of math textbooks, the yellow ones."

Slob's laughing again. His laugh is villainous, but mirthful and *ho-ho*-ish…like Santa Claus. "But I sure don't remember chopping off Barney's head," says Homicidal Santa, scratching the top of his balding head. "They all said I blacked out. And it's true I passed out, was out cold when the police arrived—don't remember *that* at all. But the weird thing was—*do* remember this—how Barney kept twitching so long after the decapitation."

"Yeah," Torbjorn says, "that's impossible."

Santa gets all serious. "No," he says, "actually, it's quite common, all the muscles contort, contract. And if you're not careful, a chopped-off head's liable to bite you. But Barney's head didn't bite anyone"—*ho! ho! ho!*—"and that darn head, bigger than a grapefruit."

"That seems small," Torbjorn says. The stone Buddha head in his Jeep, for example, is much larger than a grapefruit.

"What?" Santa seems sincerely concerned. "Come on, son, don't talk crazy. Grapefruit was plenty big for his size."

"He was small?" Torbjorn says. Then angrily: "Barney was a child?"

"No, son, he was in his early 20s, more than 200 pounds. Clearly you've never seen a—"

Santa's lost his jolly spirit: His arm's up, and incoming, his fist flying at Torbjorn's face. But it stops, as if Santa's crashed into an invisible wall: His fist just hangs, clenched and aimed, as if to stab Torbjorn's neck with an invisible knife. Silent, stuck, and still, they stay this way: invisible wall versus invisible knife. Finally, the fist begins to shake, preparing to "decapitate" its next victim. But Torbjorn has options: He could probably outrun this senior citizen, whom a skinny music-theory professor just conked out with a laptop. Also, if he hopped across the street to his Jeep and back again, he could smash Santa's skull with his 25-pound stone Buddha head.[51]

"Give it to me!" shouts Homicidal Santa.

"What?" Torbjorn shouts back. (And thinks: Buddha head in Jeep.)

Slob lowers his fist and, once again, collapses back—*gong*—into the Dumpster. "Please, son. Please give me the card." He holds out his hand, palm up, like he's scolding a schoolboy.

The card. Torbjorn is still holding the card, clamped between the index and middle finger of his thumb-less right hand. And suddenly he feels sorry for old Santa: If you threw this card off a cliff, Slob would jump after it. No, he decides, Slob dude is not Santa. Nor should Santa be sent back to jail. Perhaps a mental hospital. But then, just as suddenly, Torbjorn feels sorry for himself: Today, he is a composer, his first-ever composition lesson is at noon, and he still hasn't written anything. So he decides to torture Slob for no reason. "No," says Torbjorn.

"No?" Slob asks. "What do you mean, No?"

"I mean, No, I won't give you the card. But I will give you a lift home, if you need it. Or take you to a mental hospital, whichever you prefer."

Slob is faster than expected: Suddenly, both Slob and Torbjorn have hold of the card, Slob with the advantage, with two thumbs. His surplus thumb is stronger than expected. And so is the card, as old and stained and creased as Slob's face/jacket—the paper fibers would rip if it weren't for the tape. But Torbjorn isn't thinking about the durability of Scotch packing tape. He's thinking how he's got "issues" with old people—he dislikes them—and, whether this dislike emerges from a fear of death or not, it gives him strength: Torbjorn rips the card free with his four-fingered right and shoves the old man back with his left. Slob hasn't fallen supine on the pavement, but Torbjorn is the clear winner. He has the card.

Slob doesn't take his loss in thumb(-vs.-no-thumb)-war like a loser. More like an addict: "Please, son," he says, voice shaking, "you must give it to me. Please. I *need* it. It's important."

"Why?" Torbjorn asks.

---

[51] I probably should have mentioned this earlier, but Knut's loathing for Santa Claus (and Christmas, in general) is commonplace in Napoleon. It arises from the existence of Holiday World, a theme park in Santa Claus, Indiana, a small nearby town in Spencer County (38°7′8″N × 86°55′17″W). The park now features Christmas, Halloween, Thanksgiving, the 4th of July, and has the brown canine "Holidog" as mascot, but originally, when it first opened in 1946, nine years before Disneyland, its founder Louis J. Koch had dubbed it Santa Claus Land and the hegemony of Christmas persists to this today, physically in its rides/attractions, and mentally in the minds of Napoleon natives.

Slob doesn't respond. He's just staring at the card in Torbjorn's hand like an addict, like Slob's a smoker and, all the sudden, this decrepit 3×5 note card is the last cigarette in the galaxy.

"Fine, whatever, man," Torbjorn says. "Look, I got shit to do. But tell you what: I'm parked just across the street there. You need a ride home? I'll give you a ride home."

Slob's gaze jerks from side to side, then all around, like a hunted animal, an addict looking for quick fix…and looking pathetic as hell in broken glasses.

Torbjorn sighs. "And if you tell me why it's so important," he adds, "I'll give it back."

"You'll give it to me?" Slob asks.

"If you talk," Torbjorn says.

Slob stands. He adjusts his collar, then flicks the cuffs of his wrinkled coat, like a concert pianist preparing to perform. Thus composed, he stands there, still and waiting, full of potential energy, like the silence before the pianist's first note, the suspense before you jump off a cliff.

Torbjorn, sitting on the ground against the Dumpster, breaks the silence: "So you need—"

But Slob spins 180 and takes off, speed-walking away from Torbjorn and his Dumpster.

Where's he going? Torbjorn wonders. "Hey, wait up!" he says and stands up. Slob's left the faculty lot and appears to be crossing Second Street. But Torbjorn has not slept, is not in the mood to chase down speed-walking senior citizens, not in the mood to "help." And anyway, Torbjorn's no good at help, helping, being helped, asking for help, nothing to do with help. Done with help. Every time he tries to help people, they just disappear. And now, so has Slob. And Torbjorn has the card. And, oh yeah, that note. That folded-up note from Two Can to Santa. Where'd he put that note? Here it is, in his pocket. He should read—

Car alarms. More than one. A shitload of car alarms, in the student lot across the street. Perhaps Slob is not gone for good/bad. Torbjorn chases after Santa.

In the students' gravel parking lot, the car alarms of dozens of Lexus-Mercedes-something-or-others (one goddamn Jaguar), they're all going off—deafening—except for one shit Jeep. Slob is sitting in the passenger's seat of this shit Jeep, the only vehicle, apparently, without an alarm. Torbjorn gets into his shit Jeep, behind the wheel, and asks Slob, "How the fuck'd you know this is my car?"

Slob is leaning forward, seatbelt buckled, hands in lap, his posture the *paragon* of excitement, like a little kid sitting on Santa's lap. "Isn't it obvious, son?" he says.

"No," Torbjorn shouts over the earsplitting alarms.

"Was the only car that wasn't locked." In Santa's lap, the stone Buddha head.

"Oh right, *obviously*." Then louder, over alarms, Torbjorn shouts: "Gimme Buddha!"

"What's that?"

"Give me back my Buddha head."

"Gimme card," Slob shouts, fingering the decapitated Buddha head's long earlobes.

"Fine." Torbjorn won't return the card, not yet, not until he gets some answers, so he starts the engine. Nope. He tries a second time. On the fourth attempt, the engine starts, just as, in his rearview mirror, he spots a security guard, driving one of those parking-ticket/golf-cart things, pull into the gravel lot through the EXIT ONLY entrance—"Damn it, Slob, you some kinda fuckin' cop magnet."

"Not my fault, son," Slob shouts over the car alarms.

"Right." Torbjorn jams the stick in reverse and backs up, stirring up a cloud of grayish gravel dust, then shifts—nope—he now shifts into first successfully and drives, heading for the ENTER ONLY exit. Torbjorn can no longer see Golf Cart Security through the fog of gravel dust behind him, and Slob *helps* with a "Go, son, go!" as Torbjorn exits the lot then tears down Second Street, shifting from first to third, because second gear doesn't work too well.[52]

They soon lose the golf cart. And following Slob's directions, Torbjorn drives south, out of Napoleon, to the river, and thinks about Two Can's blue dress and how to help out Santa…

How to help Santa: Finally, turning onto Riverside Road, with neither stoplights nor signs in sight, only cornfields, with nothing but the wind through his rolled-down window to sting his tired eyes, Torbjorn thinks of a way to help: Steering with his right, he holds his left arm out the window. And holding Slob's note card out his driver's-side window, Torbjorn threatens Slob: "Tell me, or I drop it!" And Torbjorn knows he can keep his word, because he's done having old people issues with death and he has five fingers on his left hand. With nothing but a straight stretch of road ahead, he floors the gas.

[52] Yep, definitely Knut's Jeep.

Book Excerpt 4.7. (Devil's Staircase.) *Concerning Slob's helping the youth, by not dying and applying the Cantor function.*

Not only is the crazy youth holding Slob's card (Bisera's card) out the window and making threats—"Tell me, or I drop it!" (just what, exactly, Slob's supposed to tell him has remained obscure)—he is also driving between 10 and 12.5 mph over the speed limit.

"Well?" says Crazy Youth. "Look, man, I'm just trying to help you. Seriously, you got issues. I can help, man."

But Slob can't see how driving over the speed limit and holding his daughter's card out the window is supposed to help. Nor to what the "issues" of his Well?-Look,-man,-I'm-just-etc. statement refer. Slob does know Crazy Youth has a name—Tubular? Trafalgar? Trigonometry? Tabernacle?—and T-something's missing thumb suggests instability, a dark past. In summary,

<over-the-speed-limit> + *<I-can-help,-man>* + *<*$3^2 = 9$ *fingers>* + *<etc.>* = *<catastrophe>*

So Slob must take control of the conversation, must divert discourse away from nonsensical notions of "help" and toward something concrete, to firmer ground: Slob must appeal to Crazy Youth's rational side, must rationalize in baby steps, by starting small, simple, with something he can handle, and, ultimately, must convince Crazy Youth that, even if, for several kilometers, this stretch of Riverside Road be straight and unhindered by stop signs, speeding is dangerous.

"You're driving over 55 mph," Slob says.

"So what?" Crazy Youth says.

This is good, Slob thinks. The first baby step toward balancing the equation between crazy and conservative, between him (youth) and me (prime of life), between over and under the speed limit, is always the hardest: With his "So what?" Crazy Youth proves he is conscious of his environment and, hence, his speedometer. Now, all that remains is to prod the rest of the baby steps, to manipulate, one at a time, a sequence of irreducible baby steps such that sequence converges monotonically toward a limit L = *<sanity>* = *<speed-limit>*.

Baby Step #2: "Well, son, the speed limit is 45."

"And?"

Excellent, Slob thinks, acknowledgement of speed limit. All Slob has to do is persist, i.e., proceed with manipulative sequence of iterations which demand convergence toward a limit of rational thought (L) and, hence, rational behavior. All rational thought has its limits. *Baby Step #3*: "So," Slob says, "can you tell me what 45 mph is in mps, meters per second?"

Silence. Crazy Youth is thinking, Slob thinks. And speeding: Through his passenger's-side window, Slob sees the cornfields blur, the Jeep's speed blurring the young stalks into a homogenous block of green. (No, it's not his broken glasses.) And through the windshield: The segmented strips of the straight road's passing zone *blur* into a continuous, no-passing line.

Still thinking, thinks Slob. Crazy Youth is taking too long—Slob'd been hoping to get to derivatives, soon: position, velocity, acceleration—and speeding: Through the driver's-side window, through a break in the trees, the Ohio River appears, as it bends closer (nearly tangent) to the straight road, and the river's breakers blur into a flat surface, like smooth blue-gray stone.

Yes, Slob decides, much too long. Clearly, Crazy Youth is struggling with *Baby Step #3*: "An estimate is sufficient," Slob says. "The crucial conversion factor is roughly 1.609 km/mile."

No answer. It seems baby steps aren't working, are going nowhere, like baby steps on the Devil's Staircase,[53] which is Slob's definition of life: At any particular moment you're going nowhere, but somehow, in the long run, via repeated disembowelments of open middle third, things happen and you get from 0 to 1 without ever noticing it and then you're dead.[54]

---

[53] **Definition 4.8.** The CANTOR FUNCTION (or Devil's staircase) is a function $D(x)$ on [0,1] defined as follows:
1. Express x in base 3. If possible, use no 1s (e.g., let the decimal 0.1 = 0.022222...).
2. Replace the first 1 with 2 and everything after it with 0.
3. Replace all 2s with 1s.
4. Interpret result as a binary number. The result is $D(x)$.

[54] Mamma Slob's "definition of life" seems overly reductive: The Cantor function (or Devil's staircase) is an example of a function that is uniformly continuous, but not absolutely continuous, and has zero derivative almost everywhere. That is, locally, for any given value of x, its derivative is either zero or nonexistent—i.e., $D(x)$ is not rising, but horizontally level—however, globally, as x proceeds from 0 to 1 (along the horizontal axis), the staircase $D(x)$ still rises "continuously," taking on all values, from 0 to 1 (vertical axis).

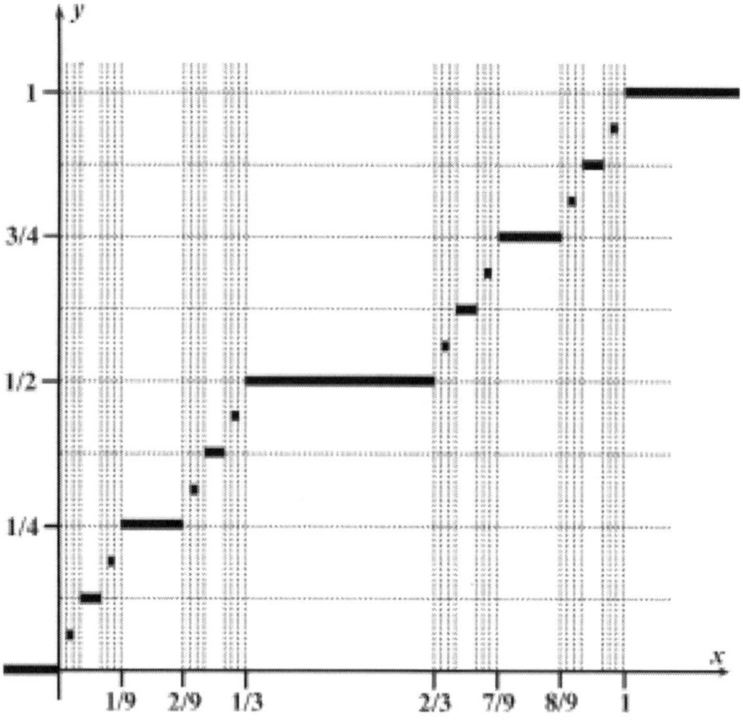

Figure 4.2. Slob's definition of life. (The Devil's Staircase.)

Or, Slob thinks, perhaps Crazy Youth has simply forgotten the question. "Do you need help?" he asks. "It's all right, son, if you do. Never be afraid to ask for help if—"

"Shut," says Crazy Youth, "up."

Slob is worried. Crazy Youth didn't yell this, his "shut up" was muttered, croaked, an isolated expression with nothing before or after, a hole of utterance, apathetically bottomless, bottomless-ly apathetic, a last dying word, a staircase to Hell. But Slob is more worried about Crazy Youth's plumbum foot:[55] The Jeep is traveling over 62.5 mph…perhaps: Barring Slob's bad angle from the passenger's seat (and his broken glasses), the reliability of the speedometer must be called into question, the instrument's needle—defective—continuously quivering, quivers punctuated by more violent oscillations (esp., over potholes) which may or may not—*not*, Slob thinks—be attributed to the plumbum foot. And these thoughts on lead lead Slob to the

[55] Here Mamma Slob means "lead foot:" In Latin lead is *plumbum*, from which we get its chemical symbol, Pb.

question: Does Crazy Youth want to die? Slob can't die yet, Slob has obligations: Slob must talk to Bisera one last time, must crack the card's code—the card now bending sharply in the out-the-window wind—must do many things he can't remember right now, given plumbum foots.

"OK," says Crazy Youth, in his plumbum voice, "we'll do this in baby steps, start small and simple with like, you know, something you can handle. Ready?" (For what? Slob thinks.) "OK," Crazy Youth begins, "first off, what do these numbers mean?"

Slob assumes Crazy Youth means the card's sequence of 0s and 1s, even though he's still holding the card out the window. "I don't know," Slob answers, honestly.

"Wrong answer!" Crazy Youth shouts and accelerates (at least from Slob's angle) to 65 mph: youth's plumbum shout bound to plumbum foot. "Who was Barney?" he says.

Slob is confused: He thought Crazy Youth knew about Barney. But who Barney is—was—is irrelevant. What is relevant: They're going 20 mph over the speed limit, and baby steps didn't work. So Slob yields to Crazy Youth's Q&A: "He was—Barney was my wife's pet."

"What? You mean lover? She cheated on you, so you killed him?"

"No, you don't understand: Barney wasn't human."

"You mean what, exactly? You didn't get along?"

"No, Barney was a snake." Again, Slob thinks, Barney = snake = irrelevant. What is relevant: Straight ahead, a kilometer or less ahead, Slob sees the grove of tall oaks where, finally, this straight stretch of Riverside Road bends—*snakes*—sharply, before it arrives at his driveway leading to his trailer = home. And he can't help think how, speeding, Jeep will blur road's bend.

"Right, a snake," Crazy Youth mutters apathetically (not plumbum-ly). "Slob, dude, just tell the truth. It'll help—trust me—I know it'll help."

"No, it's the truth. A python, a Burmese. But ahead, the trees ahead—"

"Wrong answer!" he yells, back to plumbum, accelerating to 70 mph.

"No, honestly, Barney = python = pet. But the oaks ahead, please slow—"

75 mph: "I said, Wrong answer!" The shaky speedometer oscillates violently (no pothole) between 70 and 80, much like the rest of the vehicle, shaking and jerking: "shit Jeep" pushed to the limit. And card bends back in the wind. And the oaks, its hidden bend, less than half a kilometer off, grow. And more plumbum from the youth: "What you got on Two Can?"

“Who?”

“Wrong answer!” Now breaking 80, perhaps—speedometer impossible to read—but faster, as Shit Jeep rattles, jumps, croaks, and the road is smooth, and the oaks are closer, the bend in the road closer, too close, so close—“Last Chance,” he says, “why are you stalking my music-theory professor? Why’s she afraid of you?”

The oaks, perhaps 200 meters off: “You mean Bisera?” Slob asks.

“Her name’s not Bisera. She said so. Just say it, man. Admit you’re in love with her.”

The oaks, 166⅔ meters: “Slow down!” Slob shouts. “The road. It’s about to bend—”

Oaks, 133⅓ meters: “Jesus, dude, just admit you’re in love with her, admit you’re obsessed, stalking her—I’m doing this for you, man—you need my help.”

100 meters: Help? With what does Slob need help? He is being blackmailed, his fragile card bending in the wind. What Slob needs is to not smash into an oak tree and die, and, to facilitate his not dying, Crazy Youth, the blackmailer, stipulates Slob, the father, admit he loves his own daughter. Well, he does. And yes, obsessively. But Crazy Youth wants something sexual, a false confession of incest, perhaps. And if Slob doesn’t confess, they’ll both die—how cunning! And Slob must hurry, for Jeep rattles and oaks grow ever closer, bigger, deadlier…in seconds, they’ll be dead. So analyze—now, Slob—analyze now. *Analysis*: Suppose Slob says he wants to have sex with his daughter. Will this really help? Will the card be returned? Won’t they just be dead, when Jeep collides with tree? Suppose they don’t die and Crazy Youth really is trying to help, to lend a helping four-fingered hand, the other holding card out the window—what does Crazy Youth want to hear? Should Slob get vulnerable, tell him secrets nobody knows, not even Bisera? Tell him, say, about Communist refugee camps for kids? Or perhaps the brain tumor? Would that really help? Plus, supposing they don’t die, Crazy Youth knows Bisera, and won’t he, first chance he gets, just blab his secrets to her because, knowing him, he’ll think that’s help? Help: Slob could smash Crazy Youth’s skull with this giant stone Buddha head in his lap—would that help? (No, they’re going too fast.) The hell with help: There’s no time, not now, trees closer, Jeep shaking itself to pieces, to death in a grove, at road’s bend. And no, Slob won’t tell him secrets because, no, he won’t have his Bisera hear them, not from someone else, and no, she won’t hear Daddy wants to have sex with her, either, not from anyone. *Conclusion*: Slob must think of a good excuse not to have sex with his daughter—and fast…

50 meters: Slob thinks of a good excuse: "That's impossible," he says.

The oaks don't blur up-close: "Why?" says Crazy Youth.

Slob's excuse: "I'm gay."

"What?"

But it's too late. They are in the woods. Slob prepares himself for death—"Bisera," he whispers, "I'm sorry"—for, say, crashing into a tree, his seatbelt decapitating him, and his head, like a stone Buddha's, smashing through the windshield, then soaring through the air...and flying perhaps far enough to plop into the river with a gentle splash, followed by an aesthetically pleasing burst of concentric rings emanating from his head's point of entry.

But, as Slob prepares for decapitation and Crazy Youth slams on the brakes and the Jeep swerves and Slob's body slams against his door then forward then back then door then etc., as the brakes screech and the seatbelt tightens at his neck, Slob notices none of these things: Rather, Slob, distracted, beholds shafts of sunlight spearing through the gold-green leaves of the oak tree canopy, leaves glowing like shards of glass, like stars, like a stained-glass window vaulting above and over them in a dome, this oak grove's domed ceiling framed with a lattice of branches, glassy leaves burning green between the branch lattice; and as Shit Jeep swerves violently back and forth between the slanted shafts of light, Slob observes how the blurring of this complex network of glassy leaf bits, poorly partitioned by a chaotic crisscrossing of branches, into a simple whole, an ideal, a single gold-green dome, is terrible to behold, but he'll be dead soon enough.

Slob's home: Crazy Youth pulls up beside Slob's trailer and parks his car in front—inches in front—of the Wrestler, who hadn't moved during the Jeeps' wild ride down Slob's gravel drive, nor at its near collision into him, and who, now, still hasn't moved (and won't), but remains standing in the same stooped pose, hunched over with legs spread and palms on knees, elbows locked, as he stares back at them (or between them, rather) through the windshield.[56] Past the stationary Wrestler through the windshield is *Slob's home*: his isolated four-acre strip

[56] This odd behavior of "the Wrestler" (alt., "Big Digger" in §1: the obese, bearded gentleman who never speaks, except in Latin, and always wears a far too small wrestler's uniform) was explored at length in Chapter Two. If necessary, we shall return to it later.

of land along the Ohio River, just off Riverside Road near Oil Creek Bridge,[57] where he's lived happily since the divorce in his secluded trailer on stilts, four-foot stacks of concrete blocks that keep his bed above the rising river. But now—stilts or no stilts—Slob, not dead, is upset.

Crazy Youth kills the engine, but leaves the keys—i.e., lone key, along with bottle opener—dangling in the ignition. Crazy Youth had not killed them at road's bend, even the card survived, though yet held out the window, and once again, nothing is blurred. "So," Crazy Youth says, addressing Slob, but staring "back" at the immobile Wrestler, "so you're gay?"

But Slob is still upset: "We almost died." Then adds, "Are you crazy?"

Crazy Youth relapses to his bottomless-ly apathetic mutter: "Yep."

"But we almost died."

Crazy Youth stops staring at the Wrestler to look at Slob. "What do you mean?" he asks.

"I mean we could have been killed."

Like the giant's through the windshield, the youth's posture suggests an inquisitive nature. "How's that?" he asks.

To be more upset would be impossible: "How's that? *How's that?* You were driving like a madman, doubling the speed limit—at least."

"No, I wasn't."

Revision: Slob's upset has no upper bound: "Of course you were. You think I can't read the darn speedometer? You were going 90 mph in a 45 mph zone."

"No, I wasn't."

Revision corroborated: "Darnit, son, you really are crazy."

"Not this time," he says. Then worse: He laughs. The laugh continues longer than laughter's lasting ought. "Look at the speedometer," he says.

Slob doesn't want to look, doesn't want anything to do with Crazy Youth, but he does:

1. The Jeep—engine, radio, lights, battery, everything—is off.
2. The speedometer needle is still shaking, oscillating widely.
3. Oscillations fluctuate randomly on an interval of approximately 60 to 90 mph.

Slob is no longer upset. He is something else, and it's much worse. Doubt's involved.

[57] Where Knut died last night. See Problem 4.1.

Crazy Youth does not share Slob's something else. "Seriously, man, the shit's broken—wanders around 75 no matter what—it takes a while to get used to. But seriously, man, I could tell we were going around 45. Definitely not more than 50."

The card is inside the Jeep. Crazy Youth offers the card to Slobodon.

Discarding Buddha head, Slob takes the note card. He is ashamed. Shame is appropriate when you're traveling 50 mph and think you're going 100, when the world blurs into something simple, when you think you're going to die and death simplifies light-speared trees into stained-glass domes. And now, the card: the string of 0s and 1s he doesn't understand, the worn paper fibers, the yellowed strips of tape. Slob's thumbs burrow into the 0s and 1s. He feels better: He wants it, the card, and wants not to want it. And he is ashamed because now, card in hand, he is happy—yes, he thinks, happy. Thinking is a good tool for warping how you feel: Feelings warp.

"So," Crazy Youth says, "you're gay?"

Slob parries this question by adopting a look-through-the-windshield tactic. No good: The Wrestler—his giant size, his too small wrestling uniform, his mysterious Latin aphorisms nobody can understand—is still there. Slob shuts his eyes and, world blurred into black, thumbs burrow. "No, I'm not," he says. "I just didn't want to die."

"What're you—oh right, because you thought we were speeding?"

Better topic, Slob thinks. "Well, we probably were," he says, "the speedometer doesn't work." He opens his eyes, then parses, once again, the meaning of the message he finds through his side window: OBJECTS IN MIRROR ARE CLOSER THAN THEY APPEAR.

"So, not gay. So you *are* stalking Two Can—or…or this Bisera—or whatever?"

Slob is bored of the message in his convex side-view mirror. He should go. He opens his door—heavy—and exits Shit Jeep. Outside, he notes how his back, damp with sweat, is cool in the gentle riverside breeze. Too cool to shed his heavy houndstooth sport coat. But instead of slamming the Jeep door shut and heading for the sanctuary of his trailer, he bends down—*ouch, lower back*—to glare at Crazy Youth through the open door and say things: "You there," he says, his lower back still spasm-ing, "you have no darn—ouch—know nothing." Slob slams the door.

Crazy Youth gets out of the Jeep, slams his own door shut, and then…joins the Wrestler. Crazy Youth looks the giant up and down (no response from Wrestler), then mimics him, palms on knees, but the youth, being shorter (not a giant), has to stand stooped on his tiptoes and stretch his neck up, straining to see over the Jeep's hood and through the windshield. Holding the Wrestler pose, Crazy Youth asks, "Does he do this a lot? You know, he was standing like this, exactly like this, before we parked in front of him. So I don't think he's looking in the Jeep. I bet he's probably still looking past or…you know, *through* the Jeep."

Slob is embarrassed for/by the Wrestler. "Of course he's looking through it. But he's better now." That's not what Slob'd meant to say. His back hurts and he's thinking of last night, how active the Wrestler had been as digger during the protest. Last night, it had been suggested (or hoped) that it was a passing phase, that Big Digger was making up for lost time, that his newfound mobility was simply an equal and opposite reaction to years of standing still on street corners and staring into intersections and, hence, somehow satisfied Newton's Third Law of Motion. But now, seeing the Wrestler back to "normal" and staring down a Jeep, Slob is sad. Slob stands up straight, his back feels better.

But Crazy Youth is still bending over, holding the Wrestler position. "Yeah, think he's trying to see through it, but, man, I don't know. Kinda fucked-up, if you—"

Slob's wrath: "Darnit, you don't know what it's like. Wrestler here, you don't know the first thing about him. You, thinking you can help people, see through them, overlooking who they are." Slob stops. That's not what he meant to say, either.

Crazy Youth is not being a short wrestler: He's standing tall, facing Slob.

So Slob says something else he doesn't mean to say: "I'm not gay, she's my daughter."

"Oh," Crazy Youth says. "Really?"

"Yes, really, but we've been out of touch, and I'm sick," Slob says, meaning some—

Someone is shouting (in trailer): "Hey, Don Slob, guess what? The shotgun's missing."

Then another someone (also inside Slob's trailer): "Looky there, it's Boss-wolf."

Out of Slob's trailer emerge two trespassers:[58] Cowboy Wolfer, doing what he does (smoking dope), and Camouflage Pants, doing something worse (carrying a bifurcated stick [willow] for his new water-witching "vocation"…thus far, his search for work as a dowser in Napoleon, a river town, has been unsuccessful), these two trespassers join the trio by the Jeep.

[58] Probably *Vertices 5 & 6* in last night's protest (*BE* 1.2). But Mamma Slob's naming system can get pretty hairy…

"And looky there, he's got his wolf with him." Wolfer drags deep then, holding drag, addresses Crazy Youth in a raspy, high-pitched voice: "What's wolfin', School Shooter?"

"He is trying to help," Slob says, which is pretty much what he meant to say. But he recapitulates for Wolfer and Camouflage Pants, who couldn't have known what he meant: "Trying to rescue us all. Crazy Youth here thinks he's our savior, no doubt."

Wolfer exhales, then adopts a docile tone, like John Wayne gone Catholic schoolgirl: "Yep, that's School Shooter, always doing your good manner of wolfs—wanna grab a beer?"

"Actually," Crazy Youth says, "I got to get going. Got my first composition lesson at—"

"Holy wolf!" The joint falls out of Wolfer's mouth. "Will you look at that: Roman Wolf's checking out the Jeep." Wolfer does not retrieve the smoking joint from the ground. He is staring at the Wrestler, who is staring "through" the Jeep.

Camouflage Pants swats the ground with his stick. "Of course he's checking out the Jeep," he says, and sparks fly. He is swatting the joint. "Checks out whatever, whether it's there or not."

Wolfer whistles—whistles badly (essentially, un-pitched blown air)—then adds: "Checking the *wolf* out of that Jeep." He blows air again, with better results. Then addresses Boss-Wolf: "Oh, Boss, almost forgot: The shotgun's missing."

"What's that?" Slob asks.

"Yep, shotgun's not by the oven-wolf, we checked. Also, running low on beer—only got your un-alcoholic and no regular, so us wolfs was thinking—"

But in butts the youth: "Like I said, I got to go, but I'm supposed to give you something," he says to Slob. From his pants pocket, Crazy Youth removes a small square of folded paper. He hands this square, no bigger than a postage stamp, to Slob and says: "Yeah, it's from your daughter. Or whatever she is. Look, I got to get going, but Two Can said some funny shit after she knocked—I mean, before she had to go. You know, like something about your card, maybe: ABCs, 123s—whatever, we'll talk later. Sorry you been sick. But I got a lesson. Gotta go."

With that *gotta go,* he gets back in his Shit Jeep, waves bye to the Wrestler, starts the engine on his third try, and, just like that, Crazy Youth's *gotta gone.*

But Slob's not watching the departure—he is reading Bisera's note, scribbled on the back of a Wal-mart receipt: It seems he's been invited to dinner.

PROBLEMS

4.1. *The Fluid Dynamics Surrounding the Death of the Author (Part 3 of 3).*[59]

Problem 4.1 is complex. In general, with respect to Jeep's interior and exterior, the problem can be broken down as follows: (1) Inside the Jeep, we have (1*a*) the screeching of Black Angels, a string quartet, whose electric insects blare full-blast from Jeep's speakers, and (1*b*) a comatose writer, Knut, who's drunk himself unconscious; and (2) outside the Jeep, the river is coming. In particular, however, it wasn't that simple:

(a) FLUID 5: *Relaxation Oscillations: Limit Cycles for the van der Pol Equation for* $\mu >> 1$*...*[60]

Having abandoned my Chevy Malibu Hybrid and run to his Jeep on Oil Creek Bridge, away from the dawn and into the wind and cold rain, and not giving a damn because I knew I could help, and having made it to the passenger's side, my feet soaked, water rushing over my shoes, like ocean waves above the ankles, when I opened the door to the inside lights, blinding like a flashbulb, and to *Black Angels*, blaring so loud, when I climbed into his passenger's seat, floorboards covered with beer and bourbon bottles, and when I grasped the inside door handle to jerk shut the car door, but wind slammed it for me—and when and when and when—when I did all these things, all the while, Knut hadn't moved, and he hasn't.

And he isn't: his forehead lying 12 o'clock on the steering wheel, hands hanging from 4 and 8, his torso bent unnaturally forward, strained but "relaxed," like the cruel poses of Rodin's women, like the flexibility of broken bones, and no jacket to hide his ribs through soaked white T-shirt, countable ribs I'd never seen like that—he always wore black T-shirts—and, still, he doesn't move. No, hopelessly drunk, he is relaxing to the screaming of insects—"Threnody I: Night of the Electric Insects," the first movement of Crumb's string quartet *Black Angels*—that blares full-blast from his Jeep's CD player. Their screeching, like ambulance sirens in your ears. Knut hadn't been allowed to play it at home—it's all war and death and devil, all numbers 7 and 13 (see Problem 4.2)[61]—I'd forbidden it, not because it's not music, but because the CD was a gift from *her*, from my mother, because he'd become obsessed with "modern" music, passionate about something because of her, and now she's dead and speakers blast this

[59] That is, the third and final installment in the saga of homework Problems 1.7 and 3.5.

[60] In a phase plane analysis of the van der Pol equation—$d^2x/dt^2 + \mu\,(x^2 - 1)\,dx/dt + x = 0$—for $\mu >> 1$, limit cycles tend to be *strongly nonlinear*, characterized by an alternating sequence of a slow buildups and sudden discharges, or "relaxation oscillations," which arise in various contexts, such as the bowing of violin strings (their so-called "stick-slip" oscillations), the firing of current-driven nerve cells, and the helping of Knut in part (a) of Problem 4.1.

[61] George Crumb's string quartet *Black Angels*, inspired by the Vietnam War, exploits an arsenal of sounds, including shouting, chanting, whistling, whispering, gongs, maracas, and crystal glasses, but its score bears two inscriptions, *in tempore belli* and "Finished on Friday the Thirteenth, March, 1970," which could explain its numerological dependence on 7 and 13, and allusions to the Devil, whether overtly with "black angel" (fallen angel) or musically with ubiquitous Diabolus in Musica (tritone) and Trillo Di Diavolo ("Devil's Trill," after Tartini).

"Threnody," the song of mourning you compose in remembrance of the dead.[62]

And Knut, motionless in the driver's seat, he'd be dead, too, if it weren't for the vein: In a battle of blue lights—the CD player's screen, cold and constant and electric, versus the blue-green behind him, through the driver's-side window, beyond the river and the rain, the horizon's nascent dawn—in this battle of blue, I can see the vein in his neck (or artery, maybe—whichever).[63] Its pulse is slow, but large and violent, like the vessel isn't big enough, like a ghost driven down a cramped tunnel after fixed point's annihilation. I'm here to help.

But me, I don't know what to do. Don't know how to *fix* him. He is comatose, and there isn't time: The river is coming, and the Jeep shakes and rocks in the wind—wind, battering ram—and he cannot be carried. Knut will fight against me, like blood against a vein. I am small.

I turn off *Black Angels*. The screen's electric light goes out.

Discharge: Knut turns on, like a catapult: His torso snaps back into his seat, his head ejected from the steering wheel his hands yet grip, pushing. He is not relaxed: Hands strangling the wheel, arms shaking, he keeps pushing against the wheel, pushing himself into the back of his seat—an isometric exercise, like a jet pushing against the earth, like the river against the levee's rock wall—and the "vein" is large. The violence of the vein. The violence of the river and the rain. And he pushes and shakes. And me, I am like a steering wheel. He does not touch me, but I am strangled. He strangles me from a distance. Is this love?

"Stop it," I say.

Relax: He obeys: Arms crash to his sides, his right hand first banging into the knobbed handle of the stick shift, then collapsing, deadweight, into the well of the parking brake—no—*onto* the well filled with empty Miller Light bottles. His bottles are always empty. And his bald head also falls, slowly, like nodding to sleep. And fallen, chin to chest, head just hangs. But I see a further "fall" in this hanging, see the post-shake pain flowing down his face, slowly, like dust in light, like a river overflows then falls, sinking down into the wet earth, and earth drinks. I preferred the shaking: With this "fall," he is leaving me. And I want to fall with him, to follow him, to be the ghost that slows him down. He is leaving behind a body, and what can I do with a body, with ribs, bones—what? Shaking can be stopped, but this, this nothing, this bald head hanging, how can I help cheeks carved out, help a hollow, hold a hollow—how? Flowing things are hard to hold in cupped hands: perhaps dust, but not water; perhaps dust, but not light. When bodies get left behind, they turn to dust.

---

[62] Aside from *Black Angels*, notable examples of the threnody would include Krzysztof Penderecki's *Threnody to the Victims of Hiroshima* or Charles Mingus' "Goodbye Pork Pie Hat" written in memory of Lester Young.

[63] I've never studied the biological sciences…only the physical sciences, the abstract, theoretical ones. The science of living things is messy, and doesn't concern me.

And then my writer speaks: "You." His head is up. Knut is looking at me…perhaps—his eyes have the glazed unfocused drunk-as-fuck look. "You," he says, "what you doing here?"

I don't know what to say. I have to get him out of here, out of his Jeep and into my Chevy—but how? I can't just say, I'm here to help. Nor appeal to his rational side by shouting: Get out, or die. Nor can I simply drag him out by his hair: He is large, I am small, and he is bald now.

"River's coming," he says. But his speech, slurred, sounds like: *Rover's comin'.*

"No shit," I say. But I don't add, It was coming when I got here. And has been coming.

And it is: With Jeep parked diagonally across this southernmost bridge of Riverside Road, we face the flooding levee wall so that, just beyond the rusted rail of Oil Creek Bridge, the river comes, straight at us, then falls beneath us, filling the riverside ditch our bridge overpasses and wall keeps dry—*Straight Ahead*: Through the windshield, just past bridge's rail and just above our eye-line, the river flows over the top of the levee wall, and then, waterfall-ing down the heap of sandbags that rise, stacked, from the bottom of Oil Creek Ditch to the summit of the levee's dam-like wall of rock, the river slowly fills the ditch under our bridge, slowly swallows from beneath. *Beneath*: I feel it swallow, feel how the ditch fills from all sides, how here, on this southernmost tip of peninsular land, all water flows towards us, then down the ditch's steep sides, and fills beneath us. I can not see it fill. Can't see how fast the water level rises, but know it does, know how it will rise to the underside of the bridge, then over it, rushing past the Jeep's wheels, then rising up the tires, up my passenger's-side door, how it will rise up my window, then flow through us, then over us, far over us, how I won't be able to stretch my neck above the water—*Above*: The rain batters the roof above our heads, just as it batters the world—underwater, can you hear the rain smack the river's surface?—there is no time. I turn away from the world outside, back to my—

"You wanna beer?" he says. My writer, bent forward, is reaching down, fumbling through the trash around his feet. He produces an unopened Miller Light.

"No, I don't want a beer." I grab the bottle out of his hand. Opening my door quickly, I toss the bottle into the storm, behind us, off the bridge and into the fast-filling ditch, and wind slams door back shut.

"What the fuck you take my beer?" His bald head is looking at me, and his eyes, those blue-gray eyes, eyes that, depending on the light, change—sometimes blue, sometimes gray—they are like the river: blue beneath clear skies, gray under clouded, but now, colorless in the dark. And both are coming, eyes and river, looking/coming at me: to, through, and into me. This is not Knut sitting on a box in the street and staring between his feet, it is *look* and *into*, it is pierce, it is overflow, submerge, drown, and *into*. There is no levee between me and his eyes: Is this love? Staring, he does not speak.

I do: "Come back," I say.

His lips: Lips part. They tremble, parted, just wide enough to kiss, but do not speak.

"Please," I say. "Please, let's go, get out of here. The river's coming."

"Rover's comin'," he says.

Flash of white—lightning. Lightning is not love, lightning rips apart the air. I am not afraid of lightning (the chance of getting struck is small[64]), but lightning loves water: The river is large, I am small. Then comes thunder: At first, not loud, it is far away. I listen to it grow: the rumbling, deep and long, like the moan of a giant thing, moan dry and cracking in a wet world, but evolving, growing—living—in itself, an echo of itself. I listen to it fade.

Knut has found another beer, bottle already in hand. I try to take it, but he flings away my groping arms, brutally: His bottle nearly strikes my face. It's no use. He twists off the cap, then chugs.

"No," I say. I did not shout. I'd meant to, the shout was in my head, the distant object of a shouted thought, hushed, at the edge of thunder, an echo of myself. I am muzzled. I don't know what to do. How can I help? There is no echo between us.

I ask, "Where have you been?"[65]

He snorts, then sips his Miller Light. But does not speak.

I ask, "Where's the money?"

Still nothing, not even a snort.

So I ask, "Why'd you shave your head?"

"Why'd you call the cops?" he asks back.

"I'm sorry!" I shout. And didn't mean to.

"Yeah," he says. "You and the fucking money." His bald head turns away. I see the back of his head. But then I look with him, to the *east*: Through his driver's-side window, past the beads of water dripping down the glass, and through the rain, and past my Chevy, and over the wall of sandbags behind it, and across the river to the Kentucky side, to the faraway horizon, and into the dawn we look: a feather of orange and yellow fanning from a sinuous thread of red light, clamped below by Kentucky's black

---

[64] Granted: Nearly 2000 people are injured yearly by lightning strikes and, in the US, between 9-10% of those die. (Indeed, according to OSAA Safety Facts, lightning is the "#2 weather killer" in the US—second only to *floods*—killing 100 yearly and injuring ten times more.) That said, the odds of being struck by lightning are only 1:700,000, and park ranger Roy Sullivan, who was struck seven times in his 35-year career, survived his seventh strike, despite the loss of his big toe nail. For further reading, see J. Cherington et al., "Closing the Gap on the Actual Numbers of Lightning Casualties and Deaths," *Preprints: The 11th Conference on Applied Climatology* (1999): 379-80.

[65] Recall: As outlined in Problem 1.7*a*, after my mother died, Knut sat on his box in the middle of the street, so I called the cops: They took him—but where? For weeks and weeks, I called and looked—everywhere—but couldn't find him, so I sat in my dead mother's house, in the cold and the dark, and waited, until, last night, he suddenly appeared, with box, but bald (1.7*b*). So, yes, this would seem a natural question to ask.

backlit treetops and above by the outer edge of black storm cloud, its outer rim highlighted with purple, this single cloud, just one, that stretches back, from the beginning of day, over and past us, to the *west*: Through my passenger's side, I see the end of night, where all is black and dark and rain, and cloud never ends.

But it's facing east my writer speaks: His voice, slow and soft and distant, full of gentle thunder, underwater, facing hope, he says, "A sunrise is a striptease between day and night."

Not really, I think: Sunrise is between night and day, not day and night. But I keep this to myself.

He reaches over the steering wheel, to the ledge of the dashboard, and takes something I had not seen, an envelope. He holds it, above the wheel, close to his face and looks at it. He flips it over, and in the dim light of sunrise, I can see the envelope is unaddressed, but sealed. Then, without looking at me, he hands me the envelope, hands it gently, reverently—proposal, wedding ring—I take it. It is blank and sealed. There is no time, but I poke my index finger beneath the edge of the sealed flap to open—

Discharge: He grabs my wrist, his hand slamming fast, like a guillotine blade. He looks at me: no anger, no fear, just a look. "Sorry," he says. He lets go of my wrist. "Go ahead."

I open the envelope. Inside, I find an 8½×11 sheet of paper with the following handwritten message:

10110001111000101100010110001111101100011000101100000111010001110000111100000011000111000
1110010110000111110101110000011010001100010111111001011000011000000111001011111000011101 1
1000111001110100011010001100000011001100010111100110010110001110110101011000011100011100 1
0110011010001110110001101000111000011101000110100011000000110001011010001101000011100001
1010101100001100011100001110100011010001100000011001011100011001100101111001011100101101
1000000110101011000000111000011100110100011000101101010110000001110000111101010110001110
1011101000111000110000111110000011000111000011010001100111010110000001100011010000110000
1110100011001011100001100000011010101110001110010110000111110000111011100011100001101011 0
1000110000001100010110000011110101011000011000110000011110101011100011001110001111100001
1010101100001110001110010110001110000110011000101110100011001001101010110001110111000011 0
1000110101011000111000011010001100010110100001100001111010101110001101010111001011000011 0
1000110000001110101110110001011000111110110110000001101010110100001100011001111100001110 0
1110001101011000000110001011000110101011000011110101011010001100000011010101110101111010 1
0110001100010111101010110101011000011000110001110000111011010001110011011010001101000110 0
1011…

I don't say, "What the fuck?" There's no time. The river overflows, and there is a sunrise, but it is far away, black cloud covering the rest of the sky, just as it covers the world with rain. I say, "All right, it's time to go now." I stuff his letter in my jacket pocket. "Come on," I say. "Please, let's go. We'll take my car. I'll take you home." I am afraid, but I reach out to him. "Please come," I say. I touch his wrist.

He flings away my hand, violently. Once again, his fist nearly hits me in the face.

It's not his fault. That's what I tell myself—it is narcissistic rage and he's drunk—but we don't have time for that. The river rages. "We're going now," I say. "I'll drive."

He sips his beer, nearly empty. Then, in the underwater voice, the confused one that thinks dawn's a stripper, he says: "I met someone."

This sentence I can grasp. "What?" I ask. "You mean besides my mother?"

"In *rehab*," he adds.

"Rehab? What do you mean, rehab?"

He downs the rest of his beer. "I'm leaving," he says. He reaches to his keys. I had not seen them. They are in the ignition. But I am faster. I grab the keys and pull them out of the ignition. I hold the keys, grip them tightly in both hands, hold them to my chest. Him, driving—no—it is death drive.[66] I hold them.

He drops his empty bottle, but doesn't take back his keys. He does something worse. It is awful: He turns, turns his bald head to me, and its lips, they smile, smile falsely, like he's posing in a TV commercial, advertising for toothpaste. "River's coming," he says.

"Please don't! Just come with me." For the first time, I've shouted and mean to. I reach for his arm, but he raises his—I stop, remembering the rage. And finally, I get it, know it, know there's nothing I can do. Me, I cannot help. Can't. And never will. Never could, never did. I must find help: *phone*. My writer has no phone. But I do, my cell phone, in my car. We will call for help. Must. While there's still time. The phone, in my car, in the well between the seats.

With his keys clutched to my chest in my left, I open the door with my right. It is hard. The wind. I push, like it's a steering wheel. It opens. And keys to my chest, I jump into the rain and wind and run. Around his Jeep, water splashing my knees, I run to my Chevy and the sun, to a sliver of the red sun's upper arc, singeing the black Kentucky treetops. But once again, I hear it. Behind me, from his Jeep, I hear the screeching of *Black Angels*, blasting into the dawn.

(b) Fluid 6: *Basin of Attraction, or The Lotka-Volterra Model of Competition, or Rabbits vs. Sheep.*

It's not in my car.

My phone. My cell phone is not in my car.

And river rushing across the road under me, the river is quickening: Slowly it flows over the sandbags lining Riverside Road, but faster now. Definitely faster. And when I ran across Oil Creek Bridge to my Chevy, I saw how the ditch is deep, but more than half full, filling faster. How did people

[66] I suppose this isn't really a pun: Freud primarily associates death drive—defined in *Jenseits des Lustprinzips* (1920 [*Beyond the Pleasure Principle*, trans., 1922]) as "an urge inherent in all organic life to restore an earlier state of things" (SE 18:36)—with soldiers returning from World War I, with their observed tendency to revisit wartime experiences in violation with the pleasure principle. My writer tended to seek pain, as his attention-getter.

cry for help before cell phones?

I start my car. It starts on the second try. On the first, my brights flash on: I see him, Knut, see his bald skull glaring back in my headlights like before, but now, even in the storm, in my car, with engine running and windows up, I can hear the screeching of Black Angels, hear Crumb's death and devil—Knut's window is rolled down. And the river is quickening, water rushing past my wheels, from behind. And the sunrise, burning from behind. And Napoleon, two miles north, two miles behind…two miles to that gas station at town's outer edge. Gas stations have phones. And it's half past five, so the station might be open—probably—but maybe not: This is fucking Napoleon. Napoleon, so goddamn backwards and behind. Behind, I think, it's always behind: You fear what comes from behind, it's tough putting things behind you, but once behind you, it's water under the bridge. The water under Oil Creek Bridge isn't going anywhere. Yes, I decide, go to station, find phone, call for help.

First, I have to turn around. I crank the steering wheel left and back up a few feet, back into the sandbags, then pull forward a few feet, cranking right, forward towards the ditch. And again, I back up with left, forward with right. Going forward, backing up: dancing to Black Angels.

I am turned around. I drive against the river's overflow, water splashing high on either side of me, in a V-shape, geysers spouting from my sides, river halfway up my tires, perhaps—don't know, can't see—driving into the thin red line, a scratch of sunrise, a paper-cut bleeding along the horizon, and driving under ten damn miles per hour, I am getting nowhere, and I can't—

A bright white light passes through me. (Not lightning.) From behind, it passes through my car from left to right. Passing, like a shiver down my spine, but horizontal: hand, arm, chest, arm, hand.

The light is gone. I roll my car to a stop. It could be help, the light.

The light is back. Again, it swings through me, from left to right. The rain pours, but in the rearview mirror, a long column of bright light sweeps across the rear windshield. It is gone.

It is back: a tunnel, a column, a beam of bright light swinging around, in a circle, I think, from a center. From the river. Like a revolving lighthouse light. Hope is brightness across Hell's river. There are no lighthouses in Napoleon.

So what? What do I do? Caught here, river quickening and bottleneck of light revolving—what? I am stuck: a basin of attraction. (See Figure 4.3.[67]) Two ways. One or the other. Two, I think, it's always

[67] Incidentally, 4.3's portrait of a basin of attraction, the 2-dimensional nonlinear system given by

$$dx/dt = x\,(3 - x - 2y)$$
$$dy/dt = y\,(2 - x - y)$$

with x and $y > 0$, is also a particularly apt model of competition between, say, sheep and rabbits over grass or comparable food source; i.e., an example of the Lotka-Volterra model of competition between said species, with

$x(t)$ = population of rabbits
$y(t)$ = population of sheep

both fighting over grass at time t.

two, always opposite—backwards forwards, north south, yes no, help can't, can can't, nothing infinite, cause effect, rise set, beginning end—two sides to any river, to any mind, conscious and unconscious: A psychopomp ferries souls between riversides, from the living to the dead.[68] And two ways is never two-dimensional—no space, no surface—because two ways is a line, two directions, a tunnel, and your decision is the ghost that pushes you down the bottleneck. And between two choices, between option and decision, question and answer, stuck in that betweeness, you hesitate, empty, waiting for the answer that comes from nowhere, out of nothing. The complement of nothing, the empty set, is infinity, the universe.

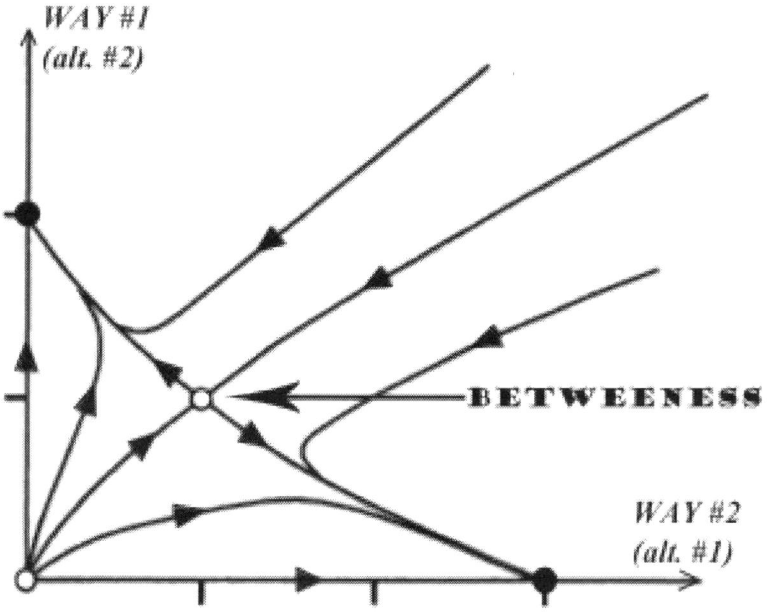

Figure 4.3. Basin of attraction.

Decision: Why the fuck did I leave him? Sitting here, his keys clutched in my hand. I must turn around. Back to my writer.

But once again, from left to right, the column of light sweeps across me, through me.

I get out of my car and look: I see light's source, a barge.

[68] From the Greek ψυχοπομπός, "psychopompos" (literally the "guide of souls"). But Jung also used the term of psychopomp for a sort of mediator between the unconscious and conscious realms.

(c) FLUID 7: *The River λήθη.*[69] At dawn, standing beside my car, I watch the river take my writer: I was over a hundred yards off, far enough away that the river couldn't get me, so I didn't tumble into the ditch, along with bridge and bags and rock, and wasn't crushed like my writer, when the barge's revolving light was upon him and the levee crumbled:

Yes, Knut, it's there, at Oil Creek Bridge, where I'd left you sitting in your Jeep, window down, with Black Angels blasting into the dawn, but without your keys, your keys some 100 yards away, clutched in my hands, clutched hard like I was holding your hand, in fear; it's there, at Oil Creek Bridge, where the Ohio River bends sharply in a U-shape around the southernmost tip of peninsular land, that the driver of the barge, backing up to swing the barge's long nose around the river's U-shaped bend, couldn't see any edge of land, couldn't see the levee's rock wall and sandbags over which the river slowly flowed; so it's there, backing up at Oil Creek Ditch, at the point, and only point, where the levee is not a solid bank of ground, but a wall of rock, that the driver in his tugboat's tower, even with its revolving column of bright white light, backed over the submerged wall of rock and sandbags, and his barge slid and scraped backwards, always backwards, and tipped; and it's there I saw the barge scrape over the wall, saw how the wall crumbled, how it crushed beneath the barge and blasted like a grenade into shrapnel, blasted in one direction, as the river poured like Niagara and the sandbags and crushed rock all crashed into the bridge, how that grenade-like explosion only had one direction, one choice, one of two ways, only two, how the bridge collapsed and tumbled in one direction, as the river blasted nothing into infinity, into the fast-filling ditch, and your Jeep followed as it did, and the shriek of Black Angels went out.

4.2. *Problem 4.1.* Compose a rhetorical analysis that compares/contrasts homework Problem 4.1 with the thirteen movements of George Crumb's string quartet *Black Angels*:

Table 4.1. Numerology in Crumb's *Black Angels*

Part	Title	Numerology
I. Departure	1. THRENODY I: Night of the Electric Insects	13 × 7 and 7 × 13
	2. Sounds of Bones and Flutes	7 in 13
	3. Lost Bells	13 over 7
	4. Devil-music	7 and 13

[69] The river is really the Ohio, but I've written *Lethe* because it's obscure and artsy: Lethe or λήθη ("forgetfulness" or "concealment") is one of Hades' rivers, and those who drank from it, often in a "transmigration" between lives, experienced complete forgetfulness; e.g., in the "Myth of Er" at the end of Plato's *Republic*. However, there have been more recent usages, such as Martin Heidegger's use of "lēthē" to symbolize the "concealment" or "forgetting of Being" in his analysis of, for example, Nietzsche (Vol 1, p. 194); and more "concretely," in Alaska, a River Lethe runs through the Valley of Ten Thousand Smokes: latitude 58.40, longitude 155.4.

	5. Danse Macabre	13 × 7
II. Absence	6. Pavana Lachrymae	13 under 13
	7. THRENODY II: BLACK ANGELS!	7 × 7 and 13 × 13
	8. Sarabanda de la Muerte Oscura	13 over 13
	9. Lost Bells (Echo)	7 × 13
III. Return	10. God-music	13 and 7
	11. Ancient Voices	7 over 13
	12. Ancient Voices (echo)	13 in 7
	13. THRENODY III: Night of the Electric Insects	7 × 13 and 13 × 7

SECTION FIVE

SECTION 5
CONCERNING KEPLER AND FIBONACCI

Here, in section five, we cover more music crap.[70] To this end, we begin with a seventeenth-century discussion (Kepler's) of thirteenth-century mathematics (Fibonacci's) in Excerpt 5.1, and conclude with sleep-deprivation in Excerpt 5.2. (For more ambitious students of *Book*, supplementary excerpts are available in footnote 85 and homework Problem 5.1*e*.) The guilt surrounding the death of my mother is introduced in footnotes 92-140.

Book Excerpt 5.1. (The Harmony of the Spheres.) *Concerning Claire's joint research grant on Kepler with Dr. Long, a fictionalization of Knut's collaborative composition of a requiem (i.e., string quartet) for/with my mother.*

10:59.25: Claire must knock. It is time for her weekly meeting with her colleague and collaborator, Dr. Long, to review the progress of their joint research grant on Kepler. And Claire is ready to knock: Facing his office door, with her blue binder held in her left, her right fist is ready, suspended at eyelevel, its knuckles inches from the door. But the door is orange. Last week, his door had not been orange—here, on the second floor of the Music Annex, all the doors of this long corridor of offices are an insipid beige—but now, Long's door has been painted orange, and painted brusquely, its brush strokes random, its bristled thicket of paintbrush marks left well-defined, as if, she thinks, his door had been branded with bawdy graffiti and swiftly censored. This is quite possible. The Chinese-Frenchman's full name is Peng S. Long, and despite the esteemed composer's mandate that he be called "Long"—and Long alone—numerous uncouth nicknames have continued to circulate the student body: Nobody knows what the "S" stands for, but with the recent discovery that *Long* means *dragon* in Chinese, coupled with *Peng S*'s homophone, variations on the title "Long Dragon Penis" have become particularly popular.

10:59.50: Claire's right fist yet hovers, inert, a floating doorknocker. She recalls that today is Wednesday, that both her dress and binder are blue, the complementary color of door's

[70] That is, a condensation (cf. §4) of Knut's fifth chapter, a stack of un-paginated Georgia-Pacific ca. ⅞" tall.

orange, but still she wavers, still her knuckled knocker will not rap. *Nerves*: Dr. Long is special, and his résumé—Rome Prize, Paris Conservatory, Kronos commissions—is impressive, but it's not his creative genius that intimidates Claire, it's his Armani silk suits and the bleached cones of his black spiked hair, it's his photo-/phono-graphic memory for not only avant-garde concert music but also the works of Tool and Nine Inch Nails, it's his frequent quotation of favorite lines by Beavis and Butthead, and more recent insertion of midget sex into any conversational context, and finally, it's the fact that his office, where his private lessons with students are also held, has a queen-sized bed in it—and frankly, all this "specialness" has made their collaboration, *her* research on Kepler and *his* composition of a string quartet, rather ineffectual. Even so, her contribution to this grant-funded project, which played a pivotal role in her being awarded tenure, has changed her life, and she looks forward eagerly to tonight's first rehearsal (5 P.M.) of Dr. Long's contribution, his newest composition, *Dissociative Fugue: Seven Planets for String Quartet*, the quartet's seven movements corresponding to the musical interval "sung" by the seven planets in Kepler's *Harmonices Mundi*.[71] It is genius. And beyond genius, Claire considers Long a friend, who tonight, as the first registered member of the Napoleon Asexual Society, will play the role of cameraman in her post-rehearsal "dinner" party (7 P.M.), the performance of which she plans to post on YouTube, and to which, this morning (via Wal-mart receipt), she's now invited her father, whom (via laptop) she knocked unconscious in a parking lot. (On seeing him, she'd had a bad attack of exploding head: B and

[71] There is also a direct correspondence between the seven movements of Long's string quartet, *Dissociative Fugue*, and Claire's "life-changing" obsession with colors, planets, metals, and days of the week.

Table 5.1. The influence of Dissociative Fugue on Claire's life

LONG'S STRING QUARTET	DAYS	COLORS	PLANETS	METALS
Movement Zero: Sun	Sunday	Yellow	Sun	gold
Movement One: Earth	Monday	White	Moon*	silver
Movement Two: Mars	Tuesday	Red	Mars	iron
Movement Three: Mercury	Wednesday	Blue	Mercury	mercury
Movement Four: Jupiter	Thursday	Purple	Jupiter	tin
Movement Five: Venus	Friday	Green	Venus	copper
Movement Six: Saturn	Saturday	Black	Saturn	lead

* Knut substitutes earth for moon in celestial music. (In Kepler's time, the sun and moon were planets.)

F, unbearable. Her incestuous dream last night did not help.)

11:00.00: Claire knocks. Punctual, she is brave.

11:00.01: Late, she fears.

11:00.02: She hears Dr. Long's voice, shouted through the door, but muffled. He might have said "Come in." Or possibly "Go away—ET no home." Both likely.

She turns the doorknob silently. Then pushes, slowly, open the door…

Through the slowly widening crack between frame and door, she beholds Dr. Long, typing: Sitting at his desk, he types on a keyboard with two fingers, the left middle finger and right index, each key jabbed, pounded, stabbed. (Each month, Long purchases a new keyboard. He is proud of this: "Keep losing my keys!" he often shouts, then always adds: "It my time of the month!") And now, between stabs of key, he jerks his neck forward—far forward—the edge of his desk digging into his chest, his neck straining to reach his Dell UltraSharp 32-inch flat screen computer monitor, which is not a desktop, but hangs, across the yard-long depth of his desk, on the wall in front of him, far above his eyelevel. And now, Dr. Long, having deciphered something on the distant screen, collapses back, violently, into the back of his office chair, his neck arching downward, chin to his chest, so he can see the keyboard (also against his chest), and—pow! pow! pow!—he stabs three keys, each stab accompanied by a sharp grunt and verbal "Pow!" Then, the acrobatic process repeats itself: He pops back forward, torso and neck straining to check the aftermath of his "Pow!" on the wall monitor, and then slamming back into chair for another "Pow!" session, and so on, this cycle of thrusting back (to keyboard) and forth (to monitor) continues. His frequent complaints of neck-/head-aches, however, have not prompted him to request a desktop monitor, nor to increase the zoom-level of his far-off flat screen, nor the font size of its texts. Nor will he take off his large mirrored sunglasses—absurdly large, like a chemist's protective lab glasses—which he wears indoors and out, night or day, perhaps even asleep. As Long himself puts it, proudly: "They blind man glasses!"

11:00.11: Crash!—the door slams into the bookcase (doorstopper) behind it, and Claire, having been leaning into the slowly opening door in her hazardous high heels, stumbles forward and almost falls onto the queen-sized bed before her. She does not like that bed, it has not been made, its comforter is wrinkled—it is bad. The "big bad bed," Dr. Long dubs it. Claire composes herself in the open doorway. Long, typing at his desk, has yet to acknowledge her entrance. "Good morning, Dr. Long," she says.

Dr. Long, whose blue Armani suit *complements* the golden bleached-then-dyed conical spikes of his otherwise black egg-yolk-spiked hair, does not respond.

"Dr. Long?" she repeats.

"Pow!" he replies. "Puh-pow! Pow! Puh-puh, puh-pow!" Ignoring her, he continues to compose what appears to be an email, one stab at a time, one of two fingers at a time.

11:01.00: Claire enters, shutting the door behind her, and then, blue binder in hand, walks between the back of his office chair and the bed, a tight squeeze, to the far wall of his office and takes a seat on the piano bench of the furthest of two Steinway concert grands (as far from bed as possible). Claire is used to being ignored by Dr. Long: She stubbornly arrives on time to their meetings, which often begin 15 to 20 minutes late.

11:14.40: Each week, Claire endures by tallying the odd objects in Long's sparsely decorated office—odd, literally (or numerically, rather)—the number of objects being an odd square, $25 = 5^2$ (or, to include Long and herself, the odd cube $27 = 3^3$):[72]

A. *The Desk Region*: (1) desk, (2) computer, (3) office chair, (4) wastebasket, (5) Dr. Long.

B. *The "Doorstopper" Region*: (6) the "doorstopper" itself, a floor-to-ceiling metal bookcase, its shelves empty, except for the bottom shelf containing (7-9) three worn books, two coverless, with Chinese titles, (10) *Larousse's French-English English-French Dictionary*, in pristine condition, still wrapped in plastic, (11) a mound of ledger-sized sheet music, and the top shelf containing (12-18) seven computer games.

C. *The Piano Region*: (19-20) two Steinway grand pianos, with (21) Claire seated at one and (22) a well-sharpened BAZIC # 2 Premium Yellow Pencil on the music stand of the other.

D. *The Indeterminate Region*: (23) a mobile Styrofoam coffee cup (on desk, at present) purchased for Dr. Long by some "suck-up student" at Main Street Coffee Shop.

(*11:29.19*: "Pow!"—a notably loud pow!, drawn-out and high-pitched, like a battle cry...but only intermediary [not signifying meeting commencement], since pow!s continue...)

E. *The Wall Region*: (24) clock and (25-26) two framed prints, hanging side-by-side above the tail-ends of the two Steinways to face the seated keyboardists, each print depicting the profile of an identical male nude, but their profiles *reflected* and hung so that the nudes, as mirror images, have their backs turned to each other. If prints' positions were

[72] I like this chick!

reversed, they'd face one another.

F. *The Unmentionable Region*: (27) Big bad bed.

11:33.07: Yep, it's all there. Office objects, perfect attendance. So far, Wednesday has been notable for its attendance. In particular, the attendance of her disruptive criminally inclined problem student, who seems to be a "slobber," as she calls her father's groupies, one of his so-called protestors: Torbjorn, that's his name, according to the registrar's records. And a composer, no less, with a knowledge of B and F.

11:42.11: "I thought you dead!"

Clearly, Claire's been zoning-out.[73] The Long Dragon Penis is sitting beside her, on the other piano bench, next to hers. This is acceptable, he is far enough away. But the coffee cup is not. It is far too full for the feral gestures, sudden and spasmodic, that accompany Long's vocalic outbursts, shouted, crass in kind. At present, the cup has been placed above his piano's keyboard, beside its raised music stand. It is safe there, for now. Unlike Claire.

Concerning her alleged death: Claire has survived many meetings with Dr. Long, so she knows his stock phrases, his little perturbative maxims, but this belief that Claire is dead—his "I thought you dead!"—this is uncharted territory. She is intimidated by this renowned composer's childish behavior. She must proceed with caution, but feign infantile. Must mimic jive, but feign jejune. Must impress him with crass, though witty, acumen à la Long Dragon Penis. She's on the spot. Entire seconds of silence pass. Several more seconds pass. Finally, she panics: "Nothing beats midget sex!" she squeals.

How tactless. Granted: Lately, this has been one of Long's more popular aphorisms, first manifesting during the Dragon's end-of-semester party—for students only (mostly female), no faculty allowed (except for Claire)—at his large suburban house (mostly empty). The party was interesting…and not just because of the stripper, who was definitely not a local, and for whom Long paid, or so he said, a fortune. This peerless stripper: a 125-pound, curvy, blond, middle-aged, 3-foot-7-inch, male midget with the stage name "Lawnmower," who sang, in the style of Edith Piaf, a song (only one), an original work titled "Love Is a Field, But Sex Is a Lawnmower" (or maybe it was sex is field, love is lawnmower—also, confusion with "Long-more"), the

[73] The statement bugs me. Is it because "Clearly Claire" is a sort of cross-lingual redundancy? Or is it that the adverb *clearly* modifies a state of being (zoning-out) in contradiction to clarity of vision?

lyrics of which had nothing to do with mowing a lawn. However, that's not why Claire's squeal is inappropriate. No, her lack of tact concerns subsequent party events. After Lawnmower left early (in a limousine), as did most students (on bicycles), Dr. Long had an(other) unexpected outburst: Out of nowhere, he mentioned how, for two years, before his escape to Paris, he'd lived in a Communist concentration camp. The Dragon broke down. The remaining students stayed until he recovered. This did not take Long long, his quick recovery marked by exclamations of "Hey, Mommy, nothing beats midget sex at commie camp!" The party was over.

So yes, tactless, Claire-ly.[74] The result, Claire-ly catastrophic: Long picks up his coffee cup and sips, but doesn't put it back by his stand. It remains in hand…

11:43.29: *The Notorious Jumping Cup of Dragon Penis Office*: Their meeting finally begins with a large coffee cup, nearly full (ca. 16 fl oz). In reply to Claire's midget sex squeal, Long shouts, "I think you go crazy before you makes it to graduate schools!"

Claire is a tenured faculty member, not a student. "Long, you know I have a PhD just—"

"Oh yes, I forget this not a lesson." Long pauses, then shouts: "But I thought you dead!" (Here, a dangerous swaying of cup…for a loss of ca. 1 fl oz, leaving the cup with 15 good fluid ounces to go. The missing fluid ounce is on his silk Armani slacks.)

"Why?" Claire asks.

15 fl oz: "You always late to meeting!" (A meager loss between his legs, ca. 0.5 fl oz.)

"But I'm never—"

14.5 fl oz: "We meet at 11. Almost noon." This reply, though less shouted, accompanies a magnificent feral gesture at his wall clock, as well as far less coffee in his cup (ca. 11 fl oz remaining): 3.5 fluid ounces of coffee drip from his Steinway's keyboard to the puddle between his feet. Long wipes the keyboard with the jacket cuff of his blue Armani suit. Then continues: "Noon soon. Meeting almost over."

"But you…" Claire stops: Defending her prompt arrivals may increase the rate of coffee loss. "Yes, you're right," she says. "I'm sorry. But I can stay later. Nothing else scheduled for today. Until our *five o'clock* rehearsal," she adds. Long needs reminders.

---

[74] Apparently, Knut anticipated footnote 73.

But not this time (11 fl oz): "And then Asex-you-well party—I the cameraman!"

"*Asexual*," Claire corrects, "and yes, you are, but—"

10.5 fl oz: "A-sucks-you-well."

"Yes, Long, but I mean now. I have time now. Nothing scheduled until rehearsal."

10 fl oz: "Ah, poor Claire. Lonely Claire is have the: No life!"—giggle (feral cup in flux: ca. 10 fl oz, but changing rapidly)—"I think I too tough on my students. I say, Suck big time! I fear they may sue me!" (7.5 fl oz remaining.)

"Well, I'm not a student, I'm a—"

7.5 fl oz: "Yes, yes, I know. You is *tenured.* But I have new suck-big-time student come at noon. So hardly gives not much time for meeting. Not my fault you is always—how you say?—tardy the meeting."

"But, Long, you were…your email, and—oh yes, I see, it's my fault."

7 fl oz: "Yes, I notice it. But just a little of kidding." Long sips half an ounce of coffee, then continues—6.5 fl oz: "But no time argue! Student come now soon. Show me!"

"What?"

6 fl oz: "No time for nonsenses. Show me!" He is pointing at her blue binder.

"Show you what?" she asks. "You want to look at Kepler's—"

5 fl oz: "Yes, it Keebler time!"

Claire hesitates. In the past few weeks, "Keebler time" has not been highly productive. In particular, Long tends to be distracted by biographical facts such as:

1. Kepler's Mommy is a witch.
2. Kepler is concerned with the volumes of wine barrels, because Mommy is a witch.[75]
3. Kepler is fond of hens: 3*a. Astrology.* Although he compares the methods of astrology to "evil-smelling dung," Kepler worked as an astrologer his entire life, a profession in which, as an "industrious hen," one may find "a good little grain." 3*b. Music Theory.* In musical scales, the leading tones, Kepler notes, are "like a hen ready to be mounted by cock."[76]

---

[75] Knut is probably referring to Kepler's *Nova stereometria doliorum vinariorum* (composed in Latin in 1613, but published in Latin in 1615), a quite practical mathematical treatise on the volume measurements of containers. For further discussion (in English), see James A. Connor, *Kepler's Witch: An Astronomer's Discovery of Cosmic Order Amid Religious War, Political Intrigue, and the Heresy Trial of His Mother* (San Francisco: Harper, 2004).

[76] This is a direct quote from Kepler's Harmonices Mundi:

4. Given Mommy issues, Kepler's math and music is sexually confusing: In music, major thirds are masculine, minor thirds are feminine. In mathematics, the gender of geometrical solids (dodecahedron, masculine; icosahedron, feminine; tetrahedron, androgynous) is more complex, but the sex of Fibonacci numbers[77] (2 and 10, masculine; 3 and 24, feminine) is easy to visualize, when denoted geometrically by squares:

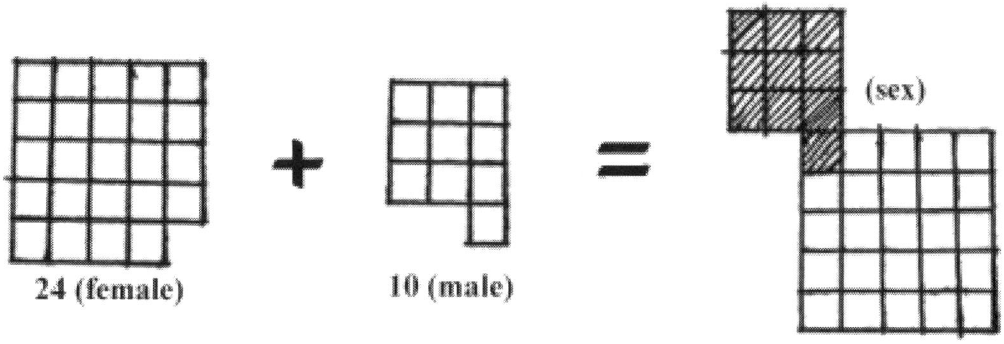

Figure 5.1. Sexual penetration of female by male. (24 + 10 = 34.)

5. The hexagonal symmetry of snowflakes…[78]

But that's not why Claire is hesitating. She is thinking about the five ounces of coffee left in Long's cup, and the full-color facsimile of Kepler's *Harmonices Mundi* that she brought in her blue binder. The facsimile was expensive—*not* in grant budget—and she'd paid top dollar for it, out of her own pocket. But then she observes the following:

1. *Inverse Relationship*: Given heavy coffee loss and fixed cup size, the intensity of feral gesture must now be greater for coffee to surmount the steep sides of his half-empty cup.
2. *Day of the Week*: Today is Wednesday.

So, she decides, it would be apt to discuss the musical scale of the planet Mercury in Book V:

---

semper se, veluti gallina, sternit
humi, promptam insessori gallo.

(See Kepler's *Gessamelte Werke*, vi, ed. Max Casper [Munich 1940], 176.)

[77] See Problem 5.1.

[78] See Kepler's New Year's gift to his longstanding patron Baron Wackher von Wackhenfels: a pamphlet entitled *Strena Seu de Nive Sexangula* (i.e., *A New Year's Gift of Hexagonal Snow*).

Figure 5.2. The musical range of planet Mercury.[79]

Claire opens her binder's facsimile to Book V. The coffee cup is still in Long's hand: She will not let Long hold her precious facsimile. Reaching across him, she places her open binder on his Steinway's music stand.

5 fl oz: "What this?" he asks. Long places his coffee cup above the keyboard, beside her Kepler on his raised stand. (It is safe there, she decides, for the moment.) He jerks forward, like he's typing at his desk, to see the pages. He does not remove his large sunglasses. "What? Is it planet scales, we do them already. Didn't you research *anything* this week?"

"Well," Claire begins, eyeing his cup, yet at rest, by her Kepler, "well, I thought—"

"I do!"

"You do what?"

"I do research. On ant book."

"What?"

"Superstring! Ant book, I show you," he says, standing up, with a hop. He lifts his

[79] Though Mercury's scale (which Kepler derives from the planet's extreme speeds at the aphelion and perihelion) is often notated melodically,* Kepler's planetary music is not restricted to such melodic steps, to the tones and semitones we associate with the earthbound scales of Western tonal music (e.g., the black and white keys of a piano). Rather, Kepler's planetary scales describe the continuous acceleration and deceleration of heavenly bodies, and thus, when some planet emits sound, it does so on a continuous interval—not discrete—so that Mercury's range would correspond to the frequencies obtained from, say, the glissandi of unfretted string instruments, like the violin:

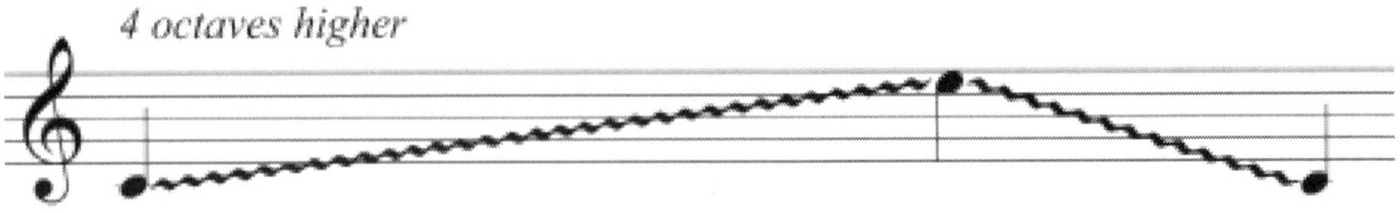

Figure 5.3. The actual range of planet Mercury.

* See Kepler, *Gesammelte Werke*, vi, ed. Max Caspar (Munich 1940), 321-22.

bench's lid and removes a book: *The Elegant Universe* by Brian Greene. "Ant Book," he says, yet standing, paging through his book, "my string quartet is an ant! I find ant page to explain—"

There is a loud knock on the door behind Long's back, just one knock, but loud, like a gunshot: Before Long, startled, has a chance to say anything, not even "ET no home," the slobber Torbjorn bursts into the office, the door smashes into bookcase (second shot), and Dr. Long, more startled, has a characteristic spasm—in hand, Greene's *Eleg-Ant Universe*, feral, flies, colliding, in flux, with cup then stand, then narrowly missing Claire's head—as stand collapses, facsimile falls, as does cup, and five ounces of coffee spill on fallen Kepler.

12:04.48: 0 fl oz.

Book Excerpt 5.2. (Lesson.) *Concerning Knut's Norwegian name and his familiarity with sleep-deprivation as fictional fodder for Torbjorn's first composition lesson.*

Torbjorn's thought of the day: The door is orange.

There was a Tuesday once when he woke up at 8AM. On this Tuesday, he had more than one thought and it's even possible that he was happy: He'd scored a kitchen job, he was going to be a composer, and someday there were gonna be goats. That 8AM was 28 hours ago.[80] Since then he has not slept, has been arrested by Walrus, helped out Santa, and eaten lunch.

His lunch made him feel sick. After giving Santa a lift home, he'd gone to a Village Pantry convenience store next to Gator's Hut. He'd then taken his lunch to his tree, just a jaywalk across Third, and there, sitting under his tree—not in it (too tired to climb)—he ate lunch: a four-pack of Red Bull and six ephedra-licious Yellow Swarm Energy Pills. Yep, he's an ephedra fan: The livid bumblebee logo is cool, plus it means a horse's ass.[81] But now he's sick. And he should probably drop out of school, as soon as he knocks on this door and goes to his lesson.

He returns to *Thought #1* (door's orange) and acts: He knocks with his right, turns

[80] Which is a perfect number of sleepless hours: $28 = (1 + 2 + 4 + 7 + 14 + 28) - 28$. (See footnote 8.)

[81] Not really. The Latin *ephedra*, meaning "horsetail," comes from the Greek *ephedrā*, the feminine of *ephedros*, meaning "sitting upon," composed of the word parts *ep(i)-* and *hedrā*, with *hedrā* meaning "seat."

doorknob with left, and opens door with body. His multitasking works well, until the door smashes into a bookcase—

Thought #2: Why has Professor Two Can come to my lesson and what the *hell* is he—?

But his second thought is interrupted by a miracle: There's a big-ass bed in front of him, queen-sized. Without further thought(s), he falls face-first onto this gift of bed. Bliss: His face slamming onto the mattress is bliss, like a gentle mist of cool water on his sunburned head after an unseasonably hot day on the planet Mercury, or Venus, whichever's closer to the sun.[82] Behind an orange door, Torbjorn has found all he needs: He's done with school, done with thoughts, done with being awake—he's done being done. Life has been good to him, and now, he's just looking forward to dying here, having half-landed on this bed—torso on bed, legs hanging off—*Thought #3*: If he be alive, his grave is like to be his professor's bed.[83]

"Who are you doing?!" shouts some guy. It's not the voice of God. Nor is it just some guy. He recognizes the voice, he'd know that tenor voice anywhere—*Joy to the World!*[84]—but he cannot answer, much less move. He is powerless, recalling salamanders, in the arms of this supermagnetic bed...which means he must be magnetic. And hence, a conductor. You know, of electricity, not orchestras. Animal magnetism. And blah, blah, bed. Blah, blah. Blah.

Despite all that is good and animally magnetic in this crazy world, people are talking: "Hey, who you?!" "Dr. Long, you've ruined—" "Hey, you the new student suck big time?!" "But look, your coffee's just ruined—" "Answer teacher who talk at you!" "Look, your ant-book has ruined Kepler—" "Police! If you not talk at teacher, I say: police!, police!, police!..."

The repetition of the word "police!" has a rousing effect on Torbjorn: He flips over, drags his ass up onto the bed, and sits. He looks at his roommates (flashback to his second thought: Two Can's here) and even talks out loud: "I am not the police," he says. But he's not sure why he said this. He wants to vomit. But he probably shouldn't, because people are talking.

[82] Planetary distance from the Sun is irrelevant: The mean surface temperature of Mercury is 100°C, but ranges from –220°C to 420°C, due to the absence of an atmosphere. On the other hand, though nearly twice Mercury's distance from the Sun, Venus' extremely thick CO_2-rich atmosphere, having an atmospheric mass 93 times that of Earth's and thus the strongest greenhouse effect in the solar system, generates constant isothermal surface temperatures of over 460°C, making Venus hotter than both Mercury's minimum and maximum surface temperatures.

[83] Cf. "If he be married / My grave is like to be my wedding bed" (Shakespeare, *Romeo and Juliet*, I, v, 134-35).

[84] See subsequent footnote.

People Talking: Sitting behind a Steinway grand piano, *People #1* is saying, "But, Dr. Long, you've spilled coffee on Kepler with your ant-book!" *People #1* is Professor Two Can, who snatches a big blue binder from the top of the other Steinway, where *People #2* is sitting beside her. *People #2* is wearing giant mirrored sunglasses and, as Torbjorn recalls from last night in a drunk tank, *People #2* has a tattoo of a salamander on his ass, and also a thing for Christmas carols.[85] He is wearing pants now. He is talking, too:

---

[85] Recall that §2 was optional because Knut's second chapter was a waste of time. And it is. For most of the chapter Torbjorn's hippocampus has been compromised; that is, he is the victim of a full-blown en bloc blackout. However, the following brief excerpt, regarding Dr. Long's bare ass in a drunk tank, may now be of interest. Three "slobbers"—Shell, Mop, and Wolfer—are also featured:

Waste of Time 5.3. (Facially proximate lizard.) *Concerning Torbjorn's emergence from a blackout.*

Suddenly, in Torbjorn's face: a lizard.

"Joy to the world!" sings an ass, small and flabby, but shaved to flaunt its lizard tattoo which, hanging limp from the right cheek, swings from side to side on a pendulum of loose blubber suspended from thrusting hips, from which beneath extends the jiggling adipose tissue of quite hairy legs, hairy down to the ankles, with feet hidden by the gray-and-white-striped trousers of a prison uniform, which had fallen so suddenly to share a lizard with Torbjorn's face.

Torbjorn is perplexed: What do you say to flabby, shaved, facially proximate asses?

The ass proceeds to sing the Christmas carol "Joy to the World"—however, it has modified the lyrics:

Figure 5.4. Salamander's song. ("Joy to the World," modified.)

Yet singing, Lizard Ass rips off his shirt, flings it high into the air, then flips around to face Torbjorn. Lizard Ass, a short middle-aged Asian dude, is tiny and circumcised, the rest of his tattoo-less body now flexed, mimicking some kind of Mr. Universe pose as he sings, his black head of hair spiked, with conical spikes' tips bleached and dyed gold. His flung shirt lands far behind him, into the middle of the debating protestors.

"Looky there," says Shell, "guy's got a lizard on his ass."

Bending at the waist, towards Torbjorn, Lizard Ass shakes his ass for his new audience and sings.

"Don't be a stupid big time!" Salamander shouts at Two Can. He is holding a book and shaking it at her. She is holding a big blue binder, which is dripping…

Torbjorn deduces her big blue binder must be wet. And *his* book, not dripping, ergo dry. But why Prof. Two Can would call it "ant book" is a mystery. *What's not a mystery*: the connection between Salamander's ass and SoBe beverages. SoBe drinks have lizards on them, taurine in them, on top of caffeine, and lizards resemble salamanders. Also, he's heard too much taurine will give you bull testicles.[86] So far, no bull testicles…*Thought #4*: Wouldn't it be funny, if drinking milk gave you udders? If it did, though, he would not let other people milk him.

"What you doing here?!" Salamander shouts.

"Yes!" Torbjorn shouts backs, because this seems to be how Salamander talks, in shouts.

"Yes, what you mean by the yes?!"

"I'm your student!"

"Wolf."

Wolfer, Shell, and Mop approach the singing ass from behind. They stop a safe distance away (at least a yard or so) to further examine the lizard.

"Not a lizard," says Mop, "that's a salamander."

"How you know?"

"Looks like a salamander."

"And it's got foreign wolf on it."

"Yep, that's Latin." Shell reads with a mispronunciation beyond description: "*Nutrisco et extinguo.** Damnit, where's the Wrestler when you need him?"

"Good tattooing for a wolf."

"Yep, that's professional."

"Joy to the world! I wanna fuckin' die…"

* *This quotation reveals that the tattoo is the personal emblem of François 1er, i.e., a stylized salamander, which did indeed have the inscription: "Nutrisco et extinguo"—Francois' motto: "I nourish and extinguish."*

[86] Taurine is a sulfonic acid ($C_2H_7NO_3S$): Sulfonic acids do not turn people into bulls. However, blindness is risk of taurine deficiency in cats. *Attn all cat lovers*: Your cat can't synthesize taurine. Too little taurine causes a cat's retina to slowly degenerate (CRD), leading to irreversible blindness, as well as hair loss and tooth decay. Fortunately, taurine is now a requirement of the Association of American Feed Control Officials (AAFCO), so make sure your dry/wet food product is AAFCO-approved and contains a minimum of 0.1% (dry) / 0.2% (wet) taurine.

"Stop shouting, everyone—*please!*" says Prof. Two Can, who is also shouting.

Torbjorn makes a personal note to himself in his head without shouting it out loud: If I had udders, he thinks, Two Can could milk me. He decides not to think this a second time.

"What your name?" Salamander is whispering, now.

Torbjorn catches on—that is, on to the fact that they're whispering, now—and he also knows the answer: Torbjorn. But then, suddenly, he's frustrated because saying his name is always a pain in the ass (you say "Torbjorn" and people go "What?", so you say it again and people go "How you spell that?", and you spell it and people go "You foreign?", and you say "Nope" but they don't believe you, so you say "Indiana, born and raised" and they go blah, blah, blah, and so on), so Torbjorn decides to give Salamander the English translation of his Norwegian name and, simultaneously, attempt a John Wayne impression he's heard locals use: "They call me Strong Bear," he says.[87] But he's never tried a John Wayne impression before, so it sucked. He also forgot to whisper. So he tries, again: "They call me Strong Bear," he whispers. Still nothing like John Wayne. His third attempt is interrupted by Salamander:

"Forget the graduate school, he too crazy for the undergraduate schools!"

"His name is Torbjorn," Prof. Two Can says.

Torbjorn hears the word "Torbjorn." But, once again, Prof. Two Can has the blank look, the nothing face—null face, black-hole face—he's seen this face before. She is a sucker. A nice face, but it sucks. Sucks you like a black hole, sucks in the universe, so nobody knows who she is. And suckers stuff: The sucker takes and takes, never gives, but then complains: "Nobody knows who I really am." Torbjorn: been there, done that. Suckers can only suck/stuff so much, before they explode. Abandonment is kind. Done with suck-hole-face.

Salamander's back to shouting: "I like the Bear better—Strong Bear! I am Dr. Long."

"Hi," says Torbjorn, looking at Two Can, who's looking at her lap, which is interesting. Big blue binder in her lap, wet.

"But—they calls me Long!"

"Hi, Long."

"Care Bear! I call you Care Bear for the now on. Care Bear, you interrupt our meeting!"

[87] Just as Torbjorn means "Strong Bear" (alt., "Thunder Bear") in Norwegian, Knut means "Knot." Enough said.

"Sorry, Long."

"Care Bear always interrupt the meeting all the times!" Long shakes his head and then, laying his dry book gently on his Steinway, adopts a histrionic inside-voice: "O Ant Book, just look what you done." Still shaking head, he seizes the big blue binder from Two Can's lap: "O Kepler," he begins, opening her binder and regarding its pages, "you all wet and falling apart." He stops shaking his head (*Dizzy?*) and addresses Two Can, who's still engaged by her lap, now empty: "O Tenured, see what Ant Book done to Kepler?"

She nods at lap, her nod jerked, gawky, like the motion is a new experience for her neck.

Long is no longer dizzy: "Good! You fall apart is good. Kepler, you too pretty and make us work hard all the times and waste our time." And then, binder to breast…he sings: "I feel pretty, oh so pretty, I am Kepler and pretty and gay!" He stops singing (*Thank God!*) to regard the binder more closely: "O Kepler," he says to binder, his gargantuan-for-his-head sunglasses nearly touching its wet pages, "you pretty from a distance, but closer look and you sloppy inside all over. Beauty and Beast, you both!" He tosses "Kepler" on the piano, where it lands on Ant Book, and proceeds to conduct (*in four-four time?*) the song he sings: "I feel soggy, oh so soggy, oh so soggy and sloppy and gay!" This refrain is repeated. Twice repeated. Finally he stops: "Care Bear," he says, out of breath, "what you think my singing-bird voice?!"

It sucks, Torbjorn thinks. But then thinks, Wow! This guy's incredible: I'm glad I found his bed, instead of dropping out of school. However, he decides not to voice these thoughts.

"It suck big time!" Long shouts, rhetorically, at his student. Then addresses his colleague, Two Can: "O Tenured, meeting over. Now, time for Care-Bear lesson. He share music with the teacher." Long slides off his bench. He continues sliding on an imaginary bench, as he heads to his desk across from bedridden Torbjorn. Arriving at desk chair, Long stops sliding: "It share time, now. My student is the Care Bear." He sits: "I teach, Care Bear share."

Two Can stands up and sidesteps over to Long's piano. There, cramped between bench and piano, she lifts her soggy binder from the Steinway, then tenderly (*too tenderly?*) hugs it across her chest. She doesn't leave, just stands there, and Torbjorn sucks in a long look at that blue dress…and suddenly, in pops Santa: He helped Santa.

"Those pictures," she says, like she's in a trance, "the drawings, I mean. It's such fine work. Who's the artist?" She nods at the wall opposite her, across the pianos. In bed, Torbjorn leans forward to get a better view of two framed pictures on the wall behind him, a view of two male nudes. Nothing special, just sketches of two Hellenic statues, discus throwers. And they're prints, not drawings. And Torbjorn needs to tell her about Santa, but people are talking:

"Who knows," Long says, "they was in here when I moved in—just two nude dudes!—but hey, you, Asexual Girl, with the tenure! Meeting over. It is only the Care Bears, now."

Two Can heads for the door, not looking at Torbjorn as she passes between the two men, between bed and desk, but walking with a poise that says: Hey, look at me. And Torbjorn thinks: Yeah, just tell her how you helped out Santa and delivered her note, then maybe she'll stop ignoring you—and tell her now, before she leaves: Opening the door, with the same dramatic bearing, aware of her audience, and without banging door into bookcase, she stops in the doorway to adjust her hair. This is Torbjorn's chance: "So, professor, I gave—"

But she interrupts him: "So, Dr. Long, shall I come back later, before the rehearsal?"

"Yes, it OK, after lesson. Come back in hour—I explain, my string quartet is an ant."

"Of course," she says, "and don't forget the party tonight?"

"Yes, yes, A-sucks-you-well Girl. I say I be there, I be there. Or I no Care Bear."

Prof. Two Can smiles and walks out. The smile is not pretty.

"Bye," Torbjorn says. "But hey, I gave that Slob dude your—"

Ah shit, it's too late: The door softly shuts. She is gone.

And suddenly, everything is wrong. With door shut and Two Can gone, Dr. Long acts strangely: He spins his chair around to face Torbjorn and transforms…

The undressing of his disguise: First, he removes the giant sunglasses, folds them shut, and slides them into the inner breast pocket of his blue silk suit. Then the pruning sequence continues: a tug at each (coffee-stained) cuff, followed by that adjustment of the suit jacket, a lift at the collar and shrug of the shoulders for that perfect relaxed fit. Then downward: a tug at the knees, a brush of the thighs, and then a crossing of the legs (crotch, also coffee-stained). And finally, his fingers interlock and, hands in lap, thumbs begin to tap— the signal that Dr. Peng S. Long is now ready, and waiting, his thumbprints tapping each other, slow and steady, like a batter stepping up to the plate, getting those last few practice strokes in before the pitcher winds up, waiting for Torbjorn to unleash a fastball. And Torbjorn hopes this is all a bad dream, that any second now, the crass buffoon will erupt from this pretentious pose, shout some profanity, and charge the mound. The Two Can Bitch, it's her fault: She shuts the door like the black hole she is, sucking up their life force and turning Salamander Ass into Professor Peng S. Long.

Torbjorn gets out of bed and walks over to the pianos. With back to Dr. Long, he regards the composer's framed pair of male nudes. Yep, they're prints, not drawings. They suck, too. "So, these pictures, they're intaglio prints, aren't they?"

"Yes," Long says, and his yes is formal, somber. "Yes, I am rather fond of them."

Torbjorn glances behind him, over his shoulder at Dr. Long, expecting to see someone else: What happened to the shouts, the giggles, the Chinese-French accent? Turning back to the prints, Torbjorn notices the two nudes have tattoos of salamanders on their shoulders.

Dr. Long continues, soberly: "Mere trifles, of course. Reproductions I bought from a bookseller on the Seine—Place du Châtelet, I believe…yes. Anyway, Torbjorn, shall we—"

"They call me Strong Bear," Torbjorn interrupts. No attempt at a John Wayne. Just one last attempt to reverse Two Can's spell, her door softly shutting.

"Yeah, sorry about calling you that, but—"

Last-last attempt: "So did you get your Grand Theft Auto in Paris, too?" Still facing prints, Torbjorn points a blind thumb over his shoulder, indicating the computer games on the bookshelf. He points with his right hand, like a hitchhiker, on purpose. No right-hand thumb.

"Oh, yes," Long says, "those silly things, they actually *were* in here when I moved in. I keep forgetting to toss them." His tone, now, too embarrassed—Long's lying.

Torbjorn goes back to bed. But he doesn't lie down. Sitting up, cross-legged, with boots on the bed and hands in lap, he mimics Long's tapping thumbs and waits.

"Anyway," Long says, "we were pleased with your application portfolio—mature work. The influence of Adès, for example, is obvious. Especially his newer work, *Tevot*, for—"[88]

"So," Torbjorn interrupts, still thumb-tapping, "did you get that tattoo in Paris, too?"

"Excuse me?" The thumbs of Dr. Long freeze up.

Torbjorn's tapping quickens: "You know, the salamander on your ass. French, isn't it?"

Long, not tapping, looks pale: "Last night?" he asks.

[88] Very new, given that today is May 2, 2007, and *Tevot*, for orchestra, premiered in Berlin on February 21, 2007.

"Yep. Don't you remember? 'Joy to the World' and shit. In a drunk tank."

Long's folded hands strangle each other: "I'd appreciate it if we kept this between—"

"Come now, you weren't so bashful last night."

"What did...what happened?" Dr. Long is eyeing Torbjorn's *prestissimo* thumb-tapping.

Torbjorn should stop, but can't: "Come on, man, it was hardly forgettable."

Long is paler, especially his self-strangled hands: "You mean...Did I—"

"Yes," Torbjorn interrupts.

"So we...We were—"

"Yes." *Thought #5*: Long's got more than stripping on his mind?

Long asks: "What do you want?"

Torbjorn wonders: What is this, *blackmail*? Then asks: "How well do you know this Little Miss Asexual?"

"Well, she—she's hosting a party tonight."

Torbjorn's thumb(s) stops: "Where?" he asks. He only has one thumb.

PROBLEMS

5.1. *Kepler's Fibonacci Sex*. Let $\{f_n\}$ be the sequence of Fibonacci numbers {1, 1, 2, 3, 5, 8, 13, 21...}, defined by the recurrence relation $f_n = f_{n-1} + f_{n-2}$ with $f_1 = 1$ and $f_2 = 1$. In his *Harmonices Mundi*, Kepler notes that, though f_{n-1} is equivalent to the difference of f_n and f_{n-2}, its square does not equal their product (i.e., $f_{n-1}^2 \neq f_{n-2} \times f_n$); however, it *almost* does, the product $f_{n-2} \times f_n$ alternately exceeding or falling short of f_{n-1}^2 by unity—in brief, when the product exceeds the square, this number is masculine; when it falls short, feminine:[89]

Table 5.2. The sex of Fibonacci numbers

gender	*m*	*f*	*m*	*f*	*m*	*f*	*m*	*f*	*m*	*f*	*m*	*f*	*m*	...
$f_{n-2} \times f_n$	2	3	10	24	65	168	442	1155	3026	7920	20737	54288	142130	...
f_{n-1}^2	1	4	9	25	64	169	441	1156	3025	7921	20736	54289	142129	...

Kepler is particularly interested in how this gender is linked to the golden ratio in ancient Greek mathematics, i.e., to the "divine" division of a rectangle (having length φ and width 1) into a unit square (1×1) and a

[89] Kepler, *Gesammelte Werke*, vi, ed. Max Caspar (Munich 1940), 175.

smaller rectangle (having length 1 and width φ – 1), where φ satisfies the equation $\varphi^2 = \varphi + 1$, equals ½(1 + √5), and also emerges in the intersection of the pentagon's diagonals. Use these facts to complete the following:

(a) Derive the closed-form formula for the *n*th element of the Fibonacci series:

$$f_n = \frac{1}{\sqrt{5}} \cdot \left(\frac{1+\sqrt{5}}{2}\right)^{n+1} - \frac{1}{\sqrt{5}} \cdot \left(\frac{1-\sqrt{5}}{2}\right)^{n+1}$$

(b) Verify the following continued fraction for φ:

$$\varphi = \cfrac{1}{1+\cfrac{1}{1+\cfrac{1}{1+\cfrac{1}{1+\cfrac{1}{\ddots}}}}}$$

(c) Calculate the binary and hexadecimal expansions of φ to show that

1.618033988749894842 = 1.10011110001101011 = 1.9E3779B97F4A7C15F39

(d) Evaluate the following excerpt from Kepler concerning the gender of Fibonacci numbers, the God-like golden section, and the progeny of the pentagon:[90]

> Haec cùm sit natura hujus sectionis, quae ad quinquanguli demonstrationem concurrit; cùmque Creator Deus ad illam conformaverit leges generationis; ad genuinam quidem et seipsâ solâ perfectam proportionem ineffabilium terminorum, rationes plantarum seminarias, quae semen suum in semetipsis habere jussae sunt singulae: adjunctas verò binas Numerorum proportiones (quarum unius deficiens unitas alterius excedente compensetur) conjunctionem maris et foeminae: quid mirum igitur, si etiam soboles quinquanguli Tertia dura seu 4•5 et mollis 5•6 moveat animos, Dei imagines, ad affectus, generationis negocio comparandos?

(e) Evaluate the following excerpt from *Book*'s Chapter Two (cf. fn. 85), a superfluous flashback included here because it reveals Slob's ardor for φ, the golden ratio, and reminds me of Thanksgiving dinner.

Waste of Time 5.4. ("Prolegomenon to the Christmas Tree Protest" [*Book*, Ch. 2].) Concerning Knut's fictionalization of Thanksgiving dinner as Mamma Slob's flashback, the fruit of Slobodon's just punishment, as he sits in a drunk tank and ponders (1) why he's here and (2) the true nature of justice.[91]

It all started a couple months ago in early March, on the day Slobodon decided not

[90] Ibid., 175-76.

[91] **Footnotes 92-140. (Thanksgiving.)** ***The guilt surrounding the death of my mother (part 1 of 3).***

to shoot four "homeless" people and, instead, told them $1 + 1 = 10$.[92]

Whether they were homeless or not is beside the point, they *were* trespassing on Slob's land, his unmarketable riverfront property (springtime floodplain), an isolated four-acre strip of land on the Ohio, where, since the divorce, he's lived happily alone in his secluded trailer on stilts, four-foot stacks of concrete blocks that keep his bed above the rising river. This particular March, however, had been unseasonably dry, so these four trespassers, squatting in his vast front yard, were not underwater, as Slob hid in his trailer—watching them—with both his cat, Ramanujan, and a shotgun on his lap.

Slob's generalized loathing for homeless people had begun long ago, when St. Gengulphus banned smoking and Professor Slob was forced to quit cold turkey.[93] Slob got fat.[94] Solution: He walked to work for exercise. The problem: He was consistently accosted by homeless guys begging for change (especially near liquor stores) and could never say no. Word got around. Soon every walk to work became an ambush, and Slob became well-acquainted with Napoleon's homeless community.[95]

So, this March, when the first "squatter" arrived, Slob recognized him: the Wrestler. And Slob was worried. Although the Wrestler had been, for decades, a regular fixture of Napoleon's street corners, nobody knew much about this obese, bearded gentleman, who always wore the same too small wrestler's uniform, and who neither spoke nor moved. All he ever did: He simply stood on street corners, always remaining perfectly still, never distracted by passing cars or pedestrians stepping around him, and always adopting the same stooped pose, hunched over with legs spread and palms on his knees, like a base runner preparing to steal, and, thus postured, he stared into the intersection.[96] So one fine March morning, when Slob, peering through his trailer window as the sun rose and fog

---

92 It all started last Thanksgiving, on the night we decided to concoct a plan to get my dying mother's money…

93 When Gengulphus banned smoking, Knut didn't quit.

94 So Knut didn't get fat. Instead, he flunked out of school and became "politically active."

95 In short, Knut's political activism involved less bathing and more smoking/drinking across the street from campus where he, along with a bunch of other homeless-looking guys, made "Smokers United" posters, beat bongo drums, and chanted nonsense in protest of whatever—the War on Terror, deforestation, the hegemony of Wal-mart, etc.—but primarily the Gengulphus smoking ban.

96 And these Smokers United guys were crazy: There actually was this big fat guy who, rather than a wrestler's uniform, wore one of those hunting hats with ear flaps (I called him the Hunter) and stared into intersections…Knut became the Hunter at the dinner table: Each night, after a hard day's smoking/drinking/drumming on their street corner, Knut's activist zeal would vanish at dinner, as I chattered desperately and he, silent, stared.

cleared, noticed the Wrestler staring at the intersection of Riverside Road and his own private gravel driveway, Slob realized he was trapped, could not leave his trailer, and resolved to sit on his rocking chair and stroke his shotgun until the Wrestler left.

Slob should not have had a shotgun. But the weapon was an antique, a valuable pre-'64 Winchester, and a memento of marriage—of the *obsessive* ex-wife (e.g., her strict maintenance of temperature control for her pet snake's health, her large collection of antique rifles, her reorganization of their library according to the call numbers of the Library of Congress, making it impossible for Slob to find his books)—and, hence, of the daughter, who's shunned him this past decade. He'd like to speak to her before he dies.

Anyway, what Slob should have had: more food. Waiting for the Wrestler to find a new intersection, Slob, who tended to buy food in small quantities because he stored his books in his refrigerator (the height of its shelves nearly coinciding—just a hair higher for that perfect fit—with the height of his Dover edition math texts),[97] soon became hungry. But the days passed, and the Wrestler never left, never even moved. And Slob, trapped in trailer, began to wonder if this giant man could sleep standing up like a horse.

Two mornings after the Wrestler's arrival, three more gentlemen appeared (their trespassing ignored by the unflinching Wrestler) and set up camp about twenty yards from Slob's front door. At about noon, they built a campfire and, sitting around it, drank a case of beer. Though smaller than the Wrestler, one of the new arrivals seemed to be a cowboy (boots, hat, giant belt buckle), the second sported a blue jumpsuit, like a janitor's, and the third wore camouflage pants. They appeared to be unarmed…

Darnit, thought Slob, yet stroking the cat and gun barrel in his lap, as he rocked in his chair, stared at his wall, and, listening to this new trio's increasingly drunken laughter outside, thought how here, inside the sanctuary of his trailer, life is simple (e.g., on his wall, below a poster of Pascal's triangle [11¼" × 11¼"], he's taped a hard-to-find photo of a young

97 This reminds me of the first time I saw Knut's apartment: After we'd been dating for several months, before he moved in with me, he finally allowed me to see his apartment, and, indeed, Knut kept both books (Penguin and Dover editions, primarily) and DVDs in his refrigerator (fridge always unplugged, of course, with door left wide open) because of their precise fit in its shelves. Knut seemed particularly proud of this, and we spent my first evening in his apartment sitting on the floor in front of his refrigerator, as we drank wine and then did other things. In short, I bought Knut a bookcase. He did not put his books and DVDs in the bookcase: The shelves were too tall and space was wasted—he had a profound concern for not "wasting" things, like time and space—ergo, my gift remained empty, and his fridge, full. However, later, when he moved in with me, he was not permitted to put books in my refrigerator. This did not discourage Knut: My gift of bookcase still not an option, he spent several days measuring cardboard boxes, then cut each box apart into its six sides, removed strips from these sides, and finally taped the sides back together to form boxes having the desired dimensions. It was into these boxes that he put his books and DVDs, which fit perfectly in the boxes, all boxes completely filled, so that no box-space was wasted.

Irene Papas [7" × 11¼"], her photo positioned horizontally and precisely beneath Pascal's triangle so that their combined edge lengths satisfy the golden ratio…granted, Irene's photo [originally 8½" × 12"] has been doctored with scissors, a ¾" strip of sky cut off the top and another 1½" strip off the right side that, though severing a large portion of her left breast, salvaged the nipple);[98] but outside his trailer, the world is confusing (e.g., the last time he left his trailer, a doctor told him he had a brain tumor).[99] Still, Slob did have a gut feeling: *Darnit*, he thought, *I can't just shoot a bunch of homeless people*.[100] No, but he'd teach them a lesson they'd never forget.

First, however, Slob needed to get dressed. He wasn't naked, but boxers and undershirt could give the wrong impression.[101] He retrieved a trash bag full of old clothes from the cabinet under the kitchen sink. The right impression: his old houndstooth sport

---

98 And this reminds me that we need homework problems: For salvaged nipple, see Problem 5.2*d*.

99 And this reminds me that, when I lost my job (because of Knut) and Knut (out of school) just had a kitchen job at St. Gengulphus Hospital, we sold all my furniture, but still couldn't pay the bills, so we devised a plan to get my mother's money: A plan was both necessary, because I'd been formally disinherited, and easy to initiate, because she had a brain tumor and was, eventually, an inpatient at the hospital, where Knut "cooked" her food.

100 And no, we couldn't just shoot her; so yes, this flashback reminds me of Thanksgiving dinner, of the night we decided to concoct a better plan to get her dirty oil money: It was about five months ago, last Thanksgiving, the end of the good times (Knut's sober period), when I thought I'd partially fixed my writer, when it wasn't all about sex, when I'd been teaching Knut math for fun, and he was staying away from the Smokers United street corner, and his writing, without liquor, he confessed, had been going well—he could actually think—and so had the math.

But Knut was late for Thanksgiving dinner, a marinara meat pasta with lots of red pepper and meatballs—Knut liked beef, as well as red pepper—and I promised myself not to get angry when he didn't eat the noodles and dumped extra red pepper on everything, which was always a waste because he'd pick through it all for the meat. But it was more than meatballs: By removing the shelves from Knut's empty bookcase and placing it facedown on his largest box of books, I'd made a table (dining-room table having been pawned to buy Halloween candy for the brats who'd egged my Malibu the year before) and set this "table" with real plates (not paper), napkins, and candles.

101 And I'd even dressed up for the occasion (not naked) and purchased lipstick, and dinner was ready, but no Knut. He hadn't been late from work, not once, during this sober period, but I should have known better, shouldn't have started boiling the pasta until he got home. I'd filled the large pot to the brim with water and turned down the heat, but little bubbles kept rising. (I don't cook much.)

And then, the unthinkable: Three members of the Smokers United gang showed up on my lawn. They'd never done this before, but I guessed they were looking for Knut, who'd been shunning them. And these three trespassers—the Hunter and two others, one with a shaved head and wearing camouflage, and the second wearing a trench coat and a cowboy hat—did not leave, just stood there on my front lawn, smoking and drinking from two-liter bottles of Diet Mountain Dew. And I was alone, with no weapon to protect myself, wearing heels and lipstick, and the candles were dripping wax onto the back of the bookcase. And three large men on the lawn. And no weapon.

coat and black slacks, and no belt needed, both professor-days habiliments seeming, though unwashed, to have shrunk. But the pen, he couldn't teach them a lesson without his pen—pen missing: not in pants pocket, not in fridge, not under rocking chair. He did find a black Sanford King Size Permanent Marker in a shoebox in the oven, and, having no breast pocket (nor holster), he stuck it down his tight slacks at his hip, marker half-showing like a pistol.[102]

Slob exited his trailer. The Wrestler hadn't moved, still hunched and staring into the intersection of Slob's driveway and Riverside Road, a safe distance away. But sitting around their campfire and working on a second case of beer, the new squatters—COWBOY, JANITOR, and CAMOUFLAGE PANTS—were dangerously close. Even so, it wasn't until Slob stood over them and cast his early afternoon shadow across their campfire that the seated trespassers noticed Slob.[103] It was three against one: *I must observe them vigilantly*, thought Slob. *The bearded trespasser, smoking a hand-rolled cigarette and sporting polished boots, weathered hat, and giant belt buckle with turquoise cabochon the size of a fist, speaks first*:

COWBOY: Wolf.

JANITOR: (*to Slob*) Hey there, old man.[104]

COWBOY: You an old wolf.

SLOB: What's that?

CAMOUFLAGE PANTS: Guy says wolf a lot.[105]

---

[102] Fortunately, I found one of Knut's Japanese Uni-ball Vision Micro black pens—the only pen he used, other brands resulting in writer's block—and, crouching with my back to the front door, I removed the pen cap, baring the micro-sharp point, and held the pen ready like a knife.

Suddenly, a loud knock, pounding the door at my back.

[103] I hadn't heard the three trespassers approach the front doorstep. I stayed still on the opposite side of the door. They knocked again. It was locked, but I held pen high and ready.

[104] A shout: "Hey there, honey, open up!" It was Knut's voice. "It's fine, just open up," he shouted in slow, drunkenly slurred syllables. "Can't find my key. Come on, it's fine."

[105] Knut said "fine" a lot, and I hated it. But I had a pen, so I opened the door. They stood outside, I stood inside, we faced each other—everyone, silent and waiting. I would not permit them to enter: The Army Guy in camouflage wore boots caked with mud (my floors were spotless), the Hunter's shirt bore the logo of the Napoleon Taxidermy Society (he hurt deer), and the Detective Cowboy in trench coat and cowboy hat stared at my breasts (not naked). I held my pen in stabbing position. No one moved.

Finally, the giant Hunter pointed to the doorknob and said, "Bonk."

"What?" I said.

"Bonk, knob."

SLOB: Why?[106]

CAMOUFLAGE PANTS: Couldn't say, chief.[107] We call him Wolfer.

Cowboy blows a smoke ring, then holds his joint up to Slob, offering the old man a hit. Slob declines, smelling marijuana.

SLOB: I'm afraid you gentlemen are going to have to leave.[108]

JANITOR: (*to Slob, but spilling beer at Cowboy*) Why's that, man? (*then to self*) Shit.[109]

"Guy says words backwards," said the shaved-head one in camouflage. "That is, if backwards words make words: sometimes sound-wise, sometimes letter-wise."

"Knob, bonk."

"That's letter-wise backwards."

106 "Why does he do that?" I asked.

107 "Who knows?" said Knut.

The Hunter spoke lightning fast: "Bonbon, knob-knob. Doorknob, bonk-road."

"And that there's sound-wise backwards."

Knut introduced them, but I wasn't listening: They were all smoking, drinking what I knew to be 80-proof Diet Mt. Dew (the Knut/Torbjorn method), and wearing dirty clothes, and their smelly smoke was entering the home I could no longer afford, staining its bare walls and ceiling.

"Watch it there, *Nut*, your girl's got a pen."

Nut, I thought, is a stupid nickname. But I lowered the pen.

108 "I'm afraid you gentlemen are going to have to leave," I said.

"Come on, woman," Knut said. "It's Thanksgiving."

Woman, I thought. Knut was clearly wasted. Once, quite drunk, he'd called me "woman," and I gave him a lecture on feminism and the Bible. He'd said it a second time, so I threw a lamp at him.

But (K)*nut* was a slow learner: "Come on, wo—"

"Don't say it," I said, raising the pen.

"Sorry. But it's Thanksgiving," Knut said, nodding at his "homeless" cronies. "Come on, it's fine."

"If you say 'fine' one more—"

109 Fizzing. I heard fizzing. In the kitchen. "Shit," I said, "the pot's boiling over."

"Pot, top."

"Stop doing that," I said.

"Stop, pots. Spots, stops."

"Just leave," I shouted and ran to the kitchen. But I should have slammed the door in their dirty unwashed faces: I heard them enter behind me, then shut the door. With no doors between us, just archways, the living room opening to dining room opening to kitchen, I could hear them whisper (loudly): "Man, put out your

SLOB: You're trespassing. This is my property, and it's time for you to go.

Janitor poses surprise rebuttal:

JANITOR: What about you, old man? How we know you're not trespassing?

CAMOUFLAGE PANTS: (*to Janitor*) Yeah, chief, who's to say the old guy ain't lying?

COWBOY: (*to joint*) Lying wolf.[110]

SLOB: (*dropping "the bomb"*) If you don't leave, I'll call the cops.[111]

CAMOUFLAGE PANTS: Whoa there, chief. Why you got to be so like—you know—all argumentative and shit?

SLOB: (*fingering his Sanford King Size Permanent marker*) Cops.[112]

JANITOR: Injustice, man, we're not doing nothing.[113]

---

smoke." "Fine. Sorry." "No smoking—injustice, chief."

"What's for dinner?" Knut shouted—at me, I assumed.

"Probably pot-food, chief," said one of the trespassers. "Pots can overflow."

110 "Flow, wolf. Wolfer, re-flow. Flower, re-wolf."

"Goddamn, chief, cut it out with the backwards—Nut's girl don't like it."

"Goddamn, mad dog. God mad, damn dog."

"Just ignore it," Knut said. "It's OK. She'll be fine."

"She'll, leash."

I could hear them in the next room now, the dining room. "There's no drinking and *no smoking*," I shouted from the kitchen, "and, Knut, they have to leave—not enough food."

"No smoking, knee-combs own."

111 "I mean it," I shouted: "If they don't leave, I'll call the cops."

"Call, lock."

I peeked around the corner into the dining room. Detective Cowboy and Army Guy were seated at the romantic candlelit bookcase for two, Knut sitting on the back of the case, and the Hunter stooped across the room, palms on his knees, and staring at the kitchen entrance, right at me.

112 "Cops," I said, showing him the pen.

"Cops, Spock. Scope, pokes. Scopes, spokes."

"And Knut, no drinking." I returned to the stove. The pasta was far overcooked, sludge-like, but they'd just have to wait for the marinara meat sauce, which I'd forgotten I'd turned off and, now, wasn't even warm yet.

113 "We're not drinking," Knut said. "It's just Mountain Dew."

"Dew, wed."

"Bullcrap," I shouted.

"Crap, park. Craps, spark. Sparks, scraps."

CAMOUFLAGE PANTS: (*to Janitor*) You said it, chief. What we been saying all day—injustice and shit.

COWBOY: Un-wolf-like manner of all your types of… (*fading off, returns to joint*)

JANITOR: (*agreeing with Camouflage Pants*) Yeah, conspiracies and shit—New World Order, Google Maps, fuckin' Federal Reserve—all to like cause inflation.

CAMOUFLAGE PANTS: Yep, it's 9/11 up the ass, just to get some oil.

COWBOY: Oil-wolf up your ass. That and cops outlawing your weed-wolf.[114]

SLOB: (*louder, crossing arms*) Cops.

Arm-crossing ignored by Trespassers.

JANITOR: (*to Camouflage Pants*) Yeah, man, Peak Oil's what it is. Bet old guy's got oil peaking up something or other. (*to Slob*) Hey, old man, you got oil?

SLOB: (*adopting a new "lure them in" strategy*[115]) No.

JANITOR: Well, it's conspiracy.

CAMOUFLAGE PANTS: (*to Slob*) You know any conspiracies, chief?

The Trespassers are talking to Slob, Slob proceeds with Luring Method:

SLOB: Watergate.

JANITOR: Shit, man, that's a scandal, not a conspiracy.

CAMOUFLAGE PANTS: (*to Slob, about Janitor*) Yeah, chief knows his scandals. He's

---

"Shit, no drinking. Unjust, man. Like the smoking ban. Same thing."

"Same, mace."

114 "Yeah, not like smoking's against the law."

"Law, wall. Walls, slaw."

115 I walked back to the kitchen entrance and adopted a new strategy: "Fine. You can all stay, as long as you give me those bottles."

They held out their bottles. I hadn't expected this. I took them two at a time (Knut'd taken the Hunter's, Hunter still stooped and staring). Back in the kitchen, I poured the bottles' alcoholic contents into the sink, then checked the stove: "OK, gentlemen," I said, stirring the soup-like pasta, "but no dinner. Not enough food."

"Funny, enough."

"And you, shush up!" I shouted from the stove.

"Pushup, pushup."

The sauce was sort of warm. I drained the pasta in the strainer, then dumped it into the sauce pan and stirred.

"So, honey, what's for dinner?" said Knut.

"It's a surprise," I said, which inspired the following dialogue:

been memorizing "-gates," right down to those chess guys and—what was it?—right, and their Toiletgate. (*to Janitor*) Hey, chief, do the food ones, again.

JANITOR: (*to audience*) Man, there's a shitload: You got your Corngate, got Obama's burgers for your Dijongate, San Francisco cops doing Fajitagate, Cadbury chocolate bar for your Flakegate, and then your Pizzagate,[116] your Tunagate,[117] your Wheatgate, your—

SLOB: (*shouted*) I said *cops*!

JANITOR: Shit. (*Janitor stands up—keeping balance, difficult—then points to the stone-still Wrestler.*) And what about the big man? You gonna call cops on his ass, too?

SLOB: Yes.

Janitor appears forlorn: He sits back down—by falling—and splashes beer on crotch.

JANITOR: Fuck.[118]

COWBOY: Wolf-fuckin'—unjust.

CAMOUFLAGE PANTS: You said it, chief. Wolfed his crotch up.

Setback: Janitor exhibits a startling second wind, with introduction of (irrelevant) counterargument:

JANITOR: (*scrubbing crotch*) Old people, thinking they all powerful and shit.

CAMOUFLAGE PANTS: (*to heavens*) Got the power!

COWBOY: Wolfin' all the property and saying it's theirs.

---

116 "Pizza?"

"Pizza, a zip."

"Spam?"

"Spam, maps."

117 "Tuna?"

"Tuna, a nut. Tongue, nut. Stun, nuts."

Etcetera.

I heard the sound of Knut's other well-filled boxes (living room chairs), being dragged into the dining room. The bookcase was four-shelved, but not big enough to seat five.

I poured the mixed pasta and sauce into the serving bowl and—

118 And I spilled half of it on the floor—"Fuck." I scooped up the spilled pasta and dumped it back in the bowl. I'd decided I wasn't going to eat, anyway.

"Hey, man, what's with the boxes?"

"No chairs, chief."

JANITOR: Yeah, man, whoever's got the power, they tell you what's what—justice is whatever they say when they go all *what's-what-ing* on your ass.

CAMOUFLAGE PANTS: (*to Janitor, but regarding Slob*) Right on, chief, calling it justice, all because they got the power, and they got the money, and they're old.

SLOB: (*exposing irrelevance*) I don't have any money.[119]

Camouflage Pants detects argumentative strategy:

CAMOUFLAGE PANTS: (*to Slob*) Chief, why you being all argumentative? Hell, we know what's up.

COWBOY: What's wolf.

JANITOR: What's *what's-what-ing.*

CAMOUFLAGE PANTS: Chief, all we want's a little justice.

SLOB: (*countering with interrogative blitz*) What's justice?

JANITOR: Letting us sit here and drink our fuckin' beer.[120]

SLOB: (*blitz continued*) How's that justice?[121]

COWBOY: (*shaking head*) Argu-wolf-ative.

CAMOUFLAGE PANTS: (*to Cowboy*) That's right, chief—asking questions all argumentatively. (*to Slob*) Listen here, old man, justice ain't your define-able type of word: Justice just is.

COWBOY: Just-is-wolf, that be justice.

---

119 Knut whispered: "Yeah, we don't have any money."

"And whose fault is that?" I said, entering with the pasta and four forks, no serving spoon. All four idiots were seated around the bookcase, even the Hunter. I dropped the bowl on the center of the bookcase. A candle fell over. Nobody picked it up. So I had to. I tossed the four forks into the pasta, then took away the two plates. "I'm not eating. But you guys are welcome to it."

"What about plates?"

"You have forks," I said

"Injustice, lady. You holding the plates right there. We'll share."

I didn't move, hugging my plates. They hadn't washed their hands.

They all grabbed forks and ate anyway, spilling pasta on the way from communal bowl to respective mouths.

120 "You said it, chief," said Army Guy, with mouth full and two unwashed elbows on the bookcase/table, "unjust to let us sit here and eat without fuckin' plates."

121 "How's that injustice?" I asked.

"How's it not, chief?"

"Not, ton."

CAMOUFLAGE PANTS: Damn, chief, you're right: Justice is just-is.

SLOB: Would you please get off my lawn?[122]

Ignorance of blitz is bliss, but trespassers appear disoriented and subsequent conversation spirals downward:[123]

CAMOUFLAGE PANTS: Just just-is.

JANITOR: (*to Camouflage Pants*) Man, would you stop saying just-is?

COWBOY: What's up your wolf?

JANITOR: The word just-is, man, it sounds like jizz.

CAMOUFLAGE PANTS: No, it don't, chief.

JANITOR: Whatever—reminds me of jizz.

COWBOY: Justice ain't jizz-wolf.

CAMOUFLAGE PANTS: That's right, chief. That's like saying jizz sounds like Jeez, so jizz reminds you of Jesus Christ.

JANITOR: Whatever, man, there's no need to tell us how, when you masturbate, you're thinking about Jesus.

COWBOY: Wolf, jizzing to Jesus.

SLOB: (*shouted*) Shush up![124] I'll give you five minutes to get you and your beer off

---

122 Eight unwashed elbows on the back of a bookcase. "Would you get your elbows off my table?"

123 They ignored me, so I just stood there, hands at my hips, and listened to their infantile conversation—I couldn't believe it:

"Not, ton. Tons, snot."

"Man, would you stop it with the tons of snot thing."

"Yeah, chief, making food taste all—you know—snot-ly."

"Snot-ly, eel tongues."

"Noodles are sort of runny, man. Wish we still had some Dew. Hey, Nut, you got anything else to sip on?"

"Sip, piss. Spit, tips."

I couldn't take it. "Enough!" I shouted.

"Enough, funny."

"And you, Hunter, that's not funny."

"Funny, enough."

124 "Shush up!" I shouted.

"Pushup, pushup."

I could feel myself losing my temper. And I never lost my temper. Or rarely, at least. Rarely/Never.

my lawn. Then I'm calling the police.

CAMOUFLAGE PANTS: (*to Janitor*) There he goes, chief—argumentative.

SLOB: (*shouted*) No, I'm not!

JANITOR: You *are not*? Shit, old man, justice is all about *is*. You got justice when you *is-ing*.

CAMOUFLAGE PANTS: (*to Janitor*) Hey there, chief, *is-ing* still sounds like—

JANITOR: I don't give a damn. When you *is-ing*, you are who you are,[125] doing what you should be doing—flipping burgers, building rockets, transplanting organs, drinking beer—doing what you're good at,[126] when the elderly power bitches (*nodding at Slob*) don't go all *what's-what-ing*—that's justice.

SLOB: (*back to blitz*) What about murderers? It's just, if they're good at killing?[127]

JANITOR: Argumentative. Old guy don't know what's what.

COWBOY: (*excitedly, to someone*) Old wolf thinking he got the power because wolf's got money and saying property's his[128] and calling cop-wolfs like we're all murdering

---

125 "Jesus, girl, why not just let big man do his thing? Nothing he can do about that kind of thing—the way it is: You are who you are."

"Era, are."

126 "See? He's good at that shit. So let big man do what the big man does good. Way it should be: Do what you're good at."

127 "Oh yeah," I said, "what about bad people, homicidal maniacs and rapists? What if you're good at killing?"

"Kill, lick. Slick, kills. Licks, skill."

I couldn't lose my temper in front of them. I ran into the kitchen.

"What's up with her, Nut?"

"Don't worry, guys. It's fine. She's just worried about money and shit. Foreclosure and all. She's fine."

I decided that, as soon as I calmed down, if Knut said "fine" one more time, I'd throw the large pot at him.

128 "Yeah, man, I know what you mean. Money and property: Got the money, got the power."

"You bet, chief, makes it easy."

"No worries, guys, she's fine."

Fine. I hadn't calmed down yet, but the pot was in reach. I considered heating it back up on the stove first.

"Rich kids, man, they got it easy."

"I don't know," Knut said. Then he started whispering, too quietly for me to hear—for once—but I have exceptional ears and could make out the words: "shit," "cancer," and "fuckin-A."

Suddenly, the Hunter, who does not whisper, shouted: "Mom, mom!"

manner of wolfs.

CAMOUFLAGE PANTS: (*agreeing*) Yeah, murdering: That's just a circumstantial situation.

JANITOR: (*also in agreement*) Yeah, taking *is-ing* and particularizing *just-is* with *murder-is-ing*. Old man here can't say what's what. All he's got is *what's not*—being all argumentative for argument's sake.

SLOB: No, I'm not![129]

JANITOR: Old guy just contradicting whatever you say.

SLOB: No, I'm not![130]

JANITOR: (*to Slob*) OK, old man, here's the deal: You stop contradicting us, and we'll

---

"Hey, quiet down there, bud. Nut's girl gonna hear."

"Nut, tongue."

"It's OK," Knut continued, no longer whispering, "like I was saying, cancer and shit, but she's actually pretty cool. We talk all the time now."

I hadn't calmed down, but couldn't help it. "You talked to her?" I said, reentering the dining room.

"Oh good, chief, look at that. She's chilled out."

129 "No, I have—"

"No! Don't—OK? Thought you were being cool now."

130 "No, I am—"

"No, don't!" shouted Detective Cowboy. Then, gaze fixed on my breasts, he whispered: "Don't you remember? Don't get the big man going on the N-O-T word."

I calmed down. My hair was in my eyes. I fixed my hair.

"There," Knut said, "see guys? She's fine, now."

I'd left the pot in the kitchen. "No, I'm—"

"No!" they all shouted, all of their mouths full.

"Fine…" I started.

"Fine, knife."

"…just leave!" I finished.

"Leave, veal."

There followed an uncomfortable silence. I found it quite comfortable.

Knut interrupted the tranquil discomfort: "But there's still pasta left."

There was. But most of it was on the bookcase. I didn't say "leave." Disquieting silence was more effective.

take off.[131]

COWBOY: Gallop off like a wolf.

JANITOR: Man, Wolfer, pretty sure wolfs don't gallop.

COWBOY: You got all different kinds of wolfs out there.

JANITOR: Whatever, man, we're making a deal with the old guy. (*to Slob*) So, old man, want us to hit the road? Then stop it with all your counter-argue-diction.

CAMOUFLAGE PANTS: (*to Slob*) Yeah, chief, stop negating us. Say some positive shit.

JANITOR: Give us some *is-ing.*

SLOB: (*defeated*) What do you mean?[132]

Victors clarify:[133]

JANITOR: Tell us something that *just is*, man. Don't go contradicting and argumentative-ing and questioning and all that shit.

COWBOY: (*for further clarification*) All that jizz-wolf.

CAMOUFLAGE PANTS: Shut up, chief.

And that's when Slob made a life-changing decision: *Must teach victors a different type of lesson*, he thought: "Fine," he said, "follow me." Slob took the marker from his pants and walked to his white (except for the rust) trailer. He preferred chalkboards, but if you can write with a marker, you can write on a trailer.

Alternative lesson: When the three presumptively homeless trespassers (along with their case of beer) finally made it to the trailer where they focused on standing up, Slob reverted to the old reliable, what he'd always asked on the first day of class. With the black marker, Slob wrote the following on his trailer:

A. 1 + 1 = 10
B. 1 + 1 = 2
C. 1 + 1 = 11
D. 1 + 1 = 0

Then turned to his trespassers: "Multiple choice question. Which is correct: *A*, *B*, *C*, or *D*?"

---

131 "OK, chief," Army Guy said to me, "tell you what. You say something nice to us, and we'll take off."

132 "What do you mean?"

133 "What do *you* mean? Chief, you been like bitch—I mean—first you took our Mountain Dew, and then you took our plates. So how about you say something nice?"

"Yeah, man, just one nice thing about us."

Who, I thought, says something nice about somebody to make them go away? "Well, you're—you're just—"

Victors appear somewhat piqued: "Listen here, old man," said Janitor, "this is bullshit." Cowboy agreed, "Bunch of bull-wolf."

"Which one?" Slob asked again.

Suddenly, a voice from behind the trespassers: "Unus et unus est duos."[134]

Barbarian invasion: The trespassers swung around (Janitor fell to the ground) and beheld the Wrestler. Even Slob, who'd been facing the trio, hadn't noticed the approach.

"The wolf can talk," said the Cowboy.

The Wrestler repeated himself: "Unus et unus est duos."

Camouflage Pants (dis)agreed: "Yeah, Wolfer, but that ain't talking too well."

The Wrestler stepped around the trio (Janitor remained on the ground) to the multiple choice question, then smiled at Slob and said, "Latin."[135]

Slob backed away from the large barbarian.

Then, pointing successively to each symbol in answer *C*, the Wrestler repeated his statement, one word per symbol: "Unus" (pointing to 1), "et" (to +), "unus" (1), "est" (=), "duos" (11). Still beaming wide, the Wrestler then turned back to Slob and said, "Latin."[136]

"The Wrestler is correct," Slob said, as if this giant were a model student.[137]

The Trespassing Trio regarded Slob. Their facial expressions were blank, much like the uniform expression of 99.9% of all the students (who were awake) that Slob had ever had.

---

134 But I stopped: The Hunter had removed the last meatball from the bowl and set it gingerly on the back of the bookcase in front of him. Then, suspending the fork above the meatball by pinching the handle's tip between thumb and index finger, the pronged end swaying between him and meatball like a pendulum, as if he were dangling a mouse by the tail above a cat's reach to tease it, fork thus swaying back and forth (between his direction and mine) and the pronged end, with each rock of fork, almost tapping the meatball—suddenly—with one mighty swing of fork, he knocked the meatball onto the floor. It rolled between my high heels and into the kitchen.

Silence.

135 The Hunter smiled and said, "Flog."

"What's that, chief?"

136 Still with the smiles: "Flog, golf."

137 "Shit, man, that's right: playing golf with a meatball. Nice shot there, big man."

"Whatever, chief, back to more important matters—so, Miss, how about saying something nice about us?"

"You're—you're just all so…"

"*So* what? What do you think of us?"

"You're fine," I said. "Each and every one of you, you're all fine."

"Roman numerals, gentleman," Slob explained.

Blank faces pay attention: "Hey, chief, I seen those before," said Camouflage Pants. And Cowboy nodded: "Speaking Roman-wolf."

"Good," Slob said, "and in fact, all the choices—*A*, *B*, *C*, and *D*—are correct."

Students frustrated: "Bullwolf," Cowboy said. And Janitor challenged the teacher from the ground: "OK, old man, how's *one + one = ten*?"

"*One-zero* is *two* in *binary*," Slob said.

Long silence…finally, Cowboy asked, "And the zero-wolf?"

"*Zero* is *two* in *mod two*."

I taught them a lesson, indeed: The Trio nodded. The Wrestler said, "Latin."[138]

Retrospective complication: None of them left.[139]

In fact, they never did leave:[140] Over the next two months, Slob befriended more beer-drinking trespassers (some of whom, living in tents and trucks, now call Slob's lawn "home"), and soon there was no more space on Slob's trailer, for it had become completely covered with mathematical expressions of *1 + 1 = something equivalent to 2*, such as $1 + 1 = -2e^{i\pi}$, and Slob became "the boss" (having rejected the nickname Slŏb), Camouflage Pants (in search of true justice) became fascinated with the philosophy of property law, Wolfer improved his John Wayne impersonation, and ultimately, together, Slob and a dozen or so "disciples" organized the Christmas Tree Protest, a tree-planting on the grassy Gengulphus Piazza.

---

[138] "Flog, golf."

[139] They all stood up to leave.

"Thanks a lot, ma'am."

"Yeah, chief, we think you're fine, too."

"Hey, Nut, let's get some beer."

"No, I'm fine."

"OK, chief, but we'll be seeing you. In the meantime, I say get some money out of that old cancer lady."

"Sure, guys," Knut said. He feigned a laugh. "No prob. I'll get every penny."

"Is that a promise?" I said.

Knut looked me in the eyes. He never did that. (Rarely/Never.) He didn't look fine. "Sure," he said.

[140] But they actually did leave. And I held Knut to his promise.

(*To be continued…*)

5.2. (a) Compare/contrast the above excerpt (5.4) from Knut's *Book* with the opening of Plato's *Republic*. How do the Slobodic and Socratic methods differ? In particular, your analysis should include:

- **(i)** Slob as Socrates versus Slob as Cephalus.
- **(ii)** Writers (alt. poets) as evil and, hence, justly banished from the state.
- **(iii)** Would you make a good philosopher king? Why or why not?

(b) Find ten more solutions to the equation *1 + 1 = something equivalent.*

- **(i)** How many such solutions exist?
- **(ii)** How does the equation *1 + 1 = 3* make you feel?
  - Relaxed?
  - Hysterical?
  - Sexual?

(c) Cf. Tubeofknut's "Class of Knut 1: Do you desire to smash the teacher's laptop with a hammer?"

(d) Show that Slob's juxtaposition of a "doctored" photo of Irene Papas (originally 8½" × 12", now 7" × 11¼") beneath a poster of Pascal's triangle (11¼" × 11¼") to satisfy the golden ratio is slightly erroneous. (See Figure 5.5 below.) That is, show that the width of Irene's photo should be [$\sqrt{(9949)}/8 - 47/8$]" ≈ 6.9529", not 7", and the width of strip removed from Irene's left breast should have been [$115/8 - \sqrt{(9949)}/8$]" ≈ 1.5471", rather than 1½".

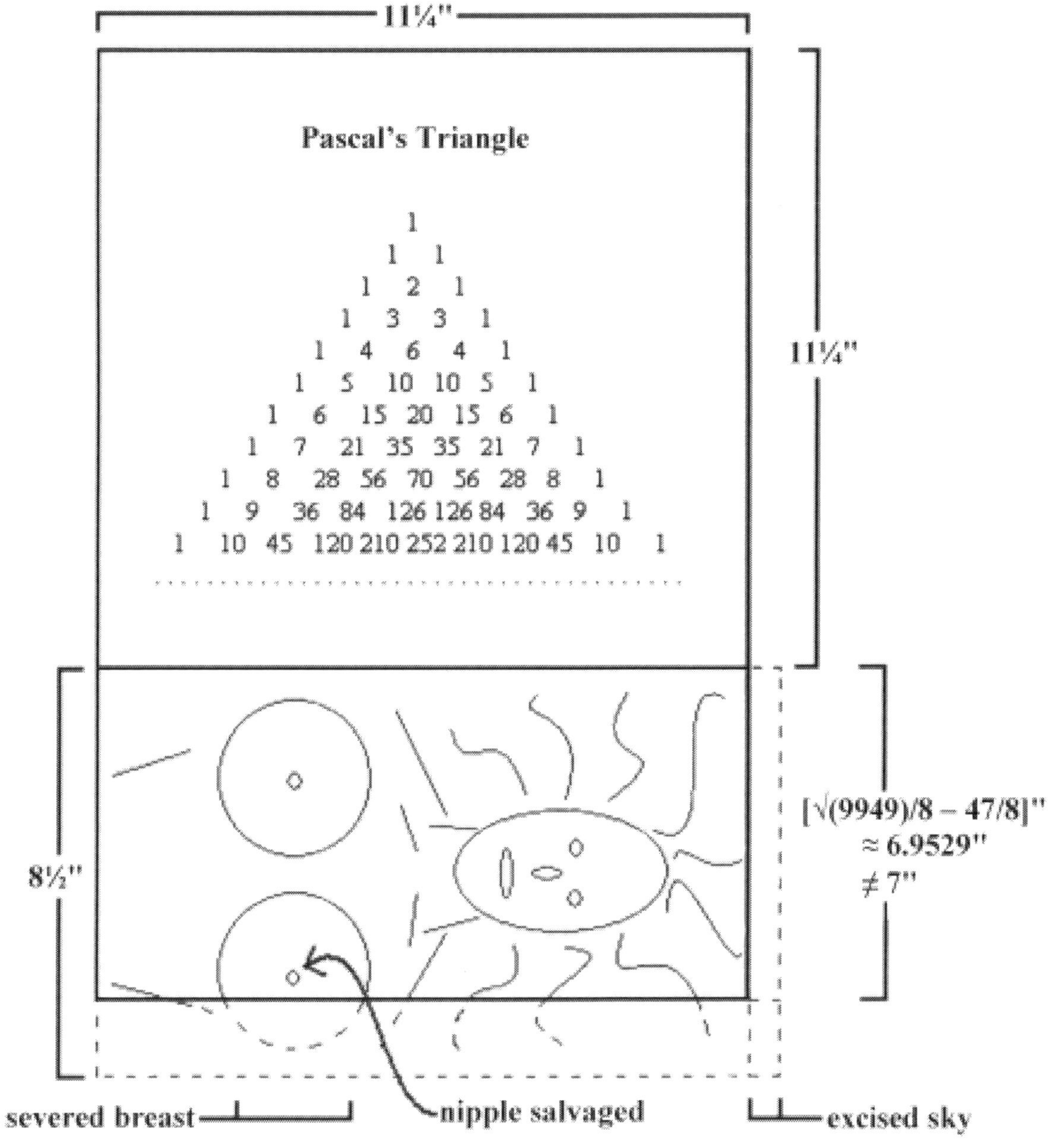

Figure 5.5. Inside Slob's trailer. (*Simple Life* ≡ φ + *Nipple Salvaged.*)

SECTION SIX

SECTION 6
CONCERNING GOD AND A PAIR OF KEYBOARDS

And here, in this penultimate section, we cover the rest of the music crap.[141] Its two excerpts have been subtitled Keyboard #1 and #2; God is featured heavily in footnotes 147 and 148.

Book Excerpt 6.1. (Keyboard #1.) *Concerning God and nudity as a distraction from the fact that Knut doesn't know shit about music.*

At 4:30 p.m., looking for a piano, Torbjorn stops by his tree. His empty two-liter Diet Mountain Gin bottle is still there. Last night, it had been: I'm gonna write in this tree. But he can't, not now, because he doesn't have anything to write with. He looks at the corner of the Music Annex, where he first *espied* Professor Two Can, but she's not there anymore. Across the street, though, the restaurant-bar Gator's Hut, his new kitchen job, is still there—his first training shift is at 6 p.m. Until then, he needs to be composer. He is looking for a piano.

Across the Piazza lawn, the hill of trees is gone. And so are the holes, all refilled. The only evidence of last night's fire: a ring of dead grass around the flagpole, the filled holes covered with straw and grass seed. *Bonus evidence*: him hearing "Joy to the World" in his head all damn day. After his lesson with Dr. Long, which had ended on a bad note (something about midget sex), Torbjorn went to the Music Library. He tried to compose there, at a research station with this fancy computer and electronic piano, but its music notation software (Finale 2007) was complex and he was distracted—in his head: Christmas carols and the mold of a blue dress. So he opened a word-processing document (Word 2007) and composed the following:

[141] That is, a condensation of Knut's sixth, seventh, and eighth chapters, a stack of un-paginated paper which originally stood some 3⅛" tall, but is now shorter, more "action-packed," and brings us to nightfall in this 24-hour narrative, which, I assume, will end with midnight's "thing with a shotgun" (BE 1.1) in his ninth and final chapter.

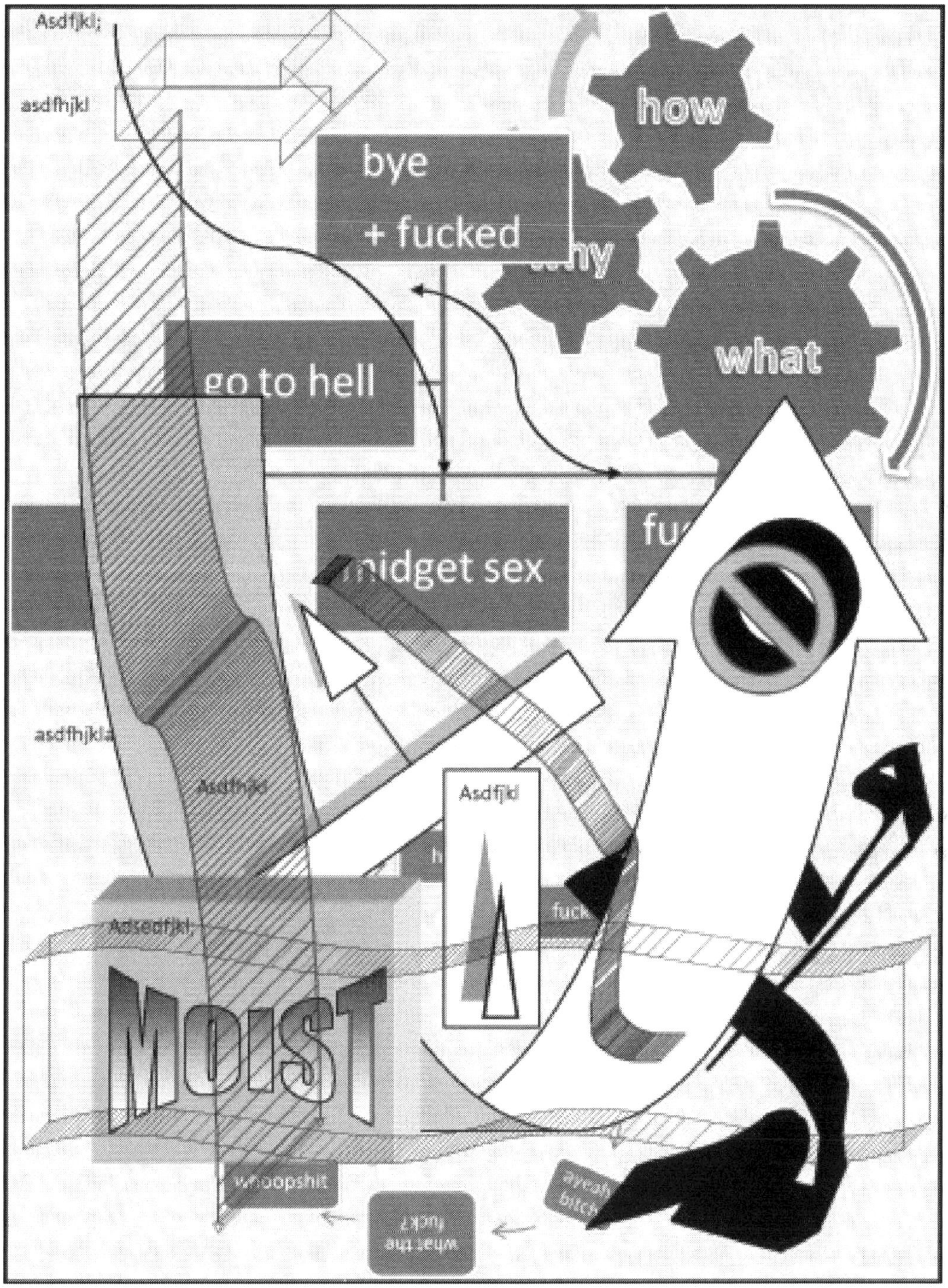

Figure 6.1. Torbjorn embraces Word 2007. (DOCX, 6½”×9”×0”.)

Before he knew it, he was kicked out of the library: Apparently, in the summer, the Napoleon Institute of Music closes early, has got to lock its doors at 4:30.

So now, looking for a piano, he grips the Piazza flagpole with his right hand. It is cool, the metal of the pole. God bless America, he thinks, we got a flagpole up our ass. And that's not cool. He lets go. His palm is black: ash from the fire. He wipes his four-fingered hand on his black jeans, but the black does not come off. Burning leaves a trace.

He kicks the pole like a martial artist.

So there. No, Torbjorn doesn't know shit about martial arts, but it had to be the foot, not the "piano hands." And no, the flagpole didn't snap and *timber* to the ground and, no, his foot's not injured—his jungle boots have steel toes—but, yes, kicking the pole felt good.

"Yeah, kid, you show that flagpole who's boss." It's Janitor Guy from last night: Older than the average Slobodic protestor, he looks a bit like Richard Nixon, and now, this Janitor Nixon is sitting on the bicycle rack by the Annex front entrance, smoking a cigarette, and smiling at him. What is it, Torbjorn thinks, with Napoleon and smiling? Where he's from, you'd need plastic surgery to smile this much. Torbjorn doesn't need plastic surgery, nor a flag-side chat with Nixon. He needs to talk to a piano. Also, there's no smoking on campus.

"Hey," Torbjorn says and joins Nixon, yet smoking with a smile by the Annex front door. Napoleon: a safe place to smoke with a smile. "So," Torbjorn says, "I see you didn't get fired."

"We'll see," Nixon says. "Flag didn't burn. That would've done it, probably. Folks around here can get touchy on flags. That and Jesus. Yeah, Jesus 'round here's like a goddamn American hero, goddamn Rambo walking tall and carrying a big-ass M20A1/A1B1 Super Bazooka.[142] But we'll see. Probation and a few hours of community service, I'm guessing. We janitors are known for second chances."

"Maybe I should be a janitor," Torbjorn says.

Nixon drags: "Fuck you, kid," he says, blowing smoke in Torbjorn's face, "what would you know about it?" Torbjorn coughs, Nixon chuckles. Unlike Santa, his *ho-ho* is presidential, bitchy: "Yeah, I see how you're thinking. You're all, *Hey, guys, look at me*," he says, adopting

[142] This, I think, would be difficult—even for Jesus—such models being five feet in length.

a baby voice, *"I'm a janitor and I clean toilets, so I must be all crazy into Toiletgate."*[143]

"Uh, no, man," Torbjorn says, "I wasn't thinking that at—"

"Well, I ain't," Nixon interrupts, dropping baby voice. "I may have mopped a floor or two, but I don't give a damn about no chess masters cheating on a toilet seat. Nor that Towelgate or whatever you call it—what's Mexican for towel?"[144]

"Spanish?" Torbjorn suggests.

More smoke blown in face: Torbjorn coughs, Nixon chuckles.

Torbjorn tries again: "Yeah, sorry, man, but I wasn't like thinking that at all. Actually, I was just wondering if you knew where I could find a piano?"

"Why? You a penis-t?" Chuckle. "You tried the Music Annex?" he says, pointing to the door beside them.

Torbjorn tries the door: It's locked.

"Yep, that's right," he adds, "Annex is locked to the public at 4:30." Janitor Nixon fondles a big ring of keys attached to his belt. "Suppose you be needing a key?"

"Well," Torbjorn says, "I *am* a music student."

"Really? Then how come you don't got a key?" Nixon's keys jingle at his hip.

"I'm new," Torbjorn says.

"Uh huh. Too bad you don't got a key. There's a *nice* piano on the opera stage. Best one in the Institute. Brand new, nice and shiny. But I wouldn't, if I were you…" He pauses to blow more smoke in face—*cough*—then continues, "Sounds like the asbestos is getting to you."

Cough: "What's that? Asbestosgate?"

"It ain't no conspiracy, kid. This building right here, the Annex, with the opera stage and all. Full of asbestos, asbestos everywhere. You know how the walls got that pitted organic look to them? Coral walls, we call them. Well, walls is all solid asbestos, they tell me, asbestos to the bone. So, yeah, I'm pretty much the only guy crazy enough to work this building." He

---

[143] Naturally, we have a Nixon-looking janitor who, unnaturally, alludes to "-gate" scandals: Toiletgate refers to a chess match in Elista Kalmykia (2006), in which Bulgarian Veslin Topalov accused Russian Vladimir Kramink, reigning World Champion, of cheating with an online analysis program during frequent visits to the "loo." (See Leonard Barden, "Kramnik's carry on over his own convenience," September 30, 2006, *The Guardian*.)

[144] Toallagate? An older scandal (2001) due to the cost of towels ($400 USD each) in the Mexican President's bathroom. (See El 'toallagate' como modelo de lucha anticorrupción, RIDHUALC, 25 Jun 2001.)

flicks his cigarette toward the flagpole. It lands in the straw—sparks—but doesn't start a fire.

Torbjorn asks: "So, you said there's a piano on stage?"

Nixon ignores him: "Which is probably why I haven't been fired, yet. That asbestos, man, is *bad* shit. Bad for the lungs."

But, Torbjorn thinks, smoking's fine?

Nixon can read minds: "Unlike cigarettes, kid, you can't buy asbestos at the pharmacy." Nixon lights another cigarette, then leans back his head and blows smoke at heaven's face, instead of Torbjorn's, and blows harder, like he's trying to get a reading on a breathalyzer. "Of course, maybe you haven't heard about the ghosts."

"No, actually," Torbjorn says, eyeing Nixon's keys. "So what's that—Ghostgate?"

"Hey, School Shooter, how about you knock it off with the -gate crap, why don't you? This is a real. It's all due to the asbestos that they're haunting the place."

"Really?"

"Yep, buncha fat ladies singing. On the opera stage, you know. Some nutcase started a rumor it was Joan of Arc, but that's bullshit. Just opera singers. Yep, them old divas way back when. Late at night, you'll hear them singing on the stage. And they're angry, too. Asbestos has pissed them off *real* good, they say. So that's another reason I haven't been fired yet."

"Isn't the Annex new?" Torbjorn asks. "Building looks new. How could it be haunted?"

"Shit, kid, opera's been around for ages. Just because some diva wasn't murdered on this here particular stage, that doesn't mean she can't be pissed about the asbestos."

"Right. But…so you said there's a piano?"

"Yep, on the opera stage, but you won't be able to use that one."

"Why? Students not allowed?"

"No, ghosts, kid. Weren't you listening? Evenings is when they drop by."

"Yeah, I'll take my chances," Torbjorn says. "So, you got a key?"

Nixon smiles. "Your neck, not mine." With cigarette smoking between his lips, Nixon thumbs through his big chain of keys. He finds the right one and steps over to the door. "Just know," he says, unlocking it, "if I hear you screaming for help, I ain't gonna save your ass. Also…this door will lock behind you." He swings the door open.

Torbjorn catches the swinging door before it closes and locks again. "Thanks," he says.

But then, standing there, holding door open, he suddenly recalls how Nixon knows Slob. And Torbjorn has questions: "Hey, Nixon, I was—"

"Shit, kid, how you get off calling me Nixon?"

"Sorry…man, but you know that chick that called the cops last night. Turns out, she's my music-theory professor. But, yeah, anyway, I wanted to ask you—is she Slob's daughter?"

"Now, listen here, kid. That ain't no -gate to go sticking your nose in." He flicks his cigarette at the flagpole, then lights another. "I say, stay out of it. Boss is a good man—genius, actually—used to teach fancy math at Gengulphus before it went to hell and—"

"Really?" Torbjorn asks.

"Yeah, he's like Philanthropy Central in this shithole. And that's philanthropy minus Jesus and a bazooka, so when I—"

"What's he done that's so philanthrop—"

"Hey, School Shooter, let's focus—you wanna hear about this girl shit or not?"

"Yeah, sorry." Torbjorn leans back against his open door.

"Uh huh, so what I'm saying is, old Slob, he's got a philanthropic flagpole up Napoleon's ass, helping the homeless and shit—free of charge—but when it comes to that girl, well, he don't have much of a sense of humor about that kind of thing. Let's just say, he takes it seriously."

"No kidding…so, is she his daughter or what?"

"Kid"—smoke in Torbjorn's face—"why don't you go piss off them divas?" Janitor Nixon flicks his cigarette straight down, at his feet. Sparks erupt. "Smoke break's over," he says, "and I'm on the clock. Smoke breaks is frowned upon, on the clock. And I got shit to do: doors to lock, floors to mop. You know, janitor shit." And just like that, Nixon turns and departs across the lawn, towards the flagpole, and lights a cigarette as he goes.

"Fine," Torbjorn calls after him, "I'll see you later, I guess—at Community Service, or whatever." But Nixon's gone.

Torbjorn enters the Annex—yeah, the front door *does* lock behind him—and crosses the lobby to the nearest double-door entrance to the concert hall, the opera stage. Gripping a handle in each hand, he opens both doors, dramatically, like a goddamn hero, arms flung to his sides, then stands there, in the doorway, holding them open: It's dark inside. No lights, except for a shaft of lobby light, the ray emanating from him at the open doors. He doesn't see any light switches, but the hall is massive: a main floor, plus three balcony levels above, and the walls, rough and pitted—yeah, like coral—but scarlet. His double-door entrance opens into a side aisle that borders the main-floor seats, starting from the back row and ending in a staircase that rises to the stage. The stage is empty, except for one grand piano in the center. No ghosts. Perfect, he thinks: Here, with hall empty and Annex all locked up, he can finally be alone. He enters, jogging down the aisle towards the stage: The doors shut behind him, and all lights go out…

Interpolation 6.2. Concerning a Book Excerpt which probably belongs here somewhere…but condensing Knut's three chapters is a pain in the ass, so let's just splice it here into the middle of Excerpt 6.1.[145]

4:45 P.M.: Claire unlocks the Annex front door. Apparently, Dr. Long needs to change his clothes. So Claire has "volunteered" to get to the rehearsal of Long's *Dissociative Fugue* fifteen minutes early and unlock the doors for the string quartet performers.

Her second meeting with Dr. Long to discuss his Ant Book was not particularly edifying: After his confession that he has no clue what his quartet sounds like, their tête-à-tête focused primarily on ears:

LONG: I agree: My quartet, it suck big time! But the knowing of not how it sounds—good!

CLAIRE: Why is that, Long?

LONG: Ears same as the brains!

CLAIRE: (*No response…self-reminder about Long's residency in concentration camp.*)

LONG: Brains go into bad places, so we get the ears are the brain.

CLAIRE: (*More concentration camp.*)

LONG: Or is it maybe that we have no ears and it is only the brains?

CLAIRE: So you're saying it is sufficient to examine your composition with the—with the brain, without knowing how it sounds with the ears?

LONG: Never mind! I think it wrong how I say it. Ears not brains! They is—how you say?—

[145] For students of plot, the first and last sentences of Interpolation 6.2 contribute to the present action. The rest of this excerpt explores the influence of superstring theory on Long's creative process; i.e., his string quartet is an ant.

just alike them. Ears alike the brains in your follow them to bad places—jingles tune!

CLAIRE: I'm sorry, Long. I don't under—

LONG: Beethoven better when deaf!

CLAIRE: (*Concentration camp.*)

LONG: Perhaps it better I cut off my ear!

CLAIRE: I—I don't think I—

LONG: Van Gogh retard! Should be poke the eyes out. Not his ear.

LONG: (*Etc.*)

LONG: Nothing beats midget sex! (*End meeting.*)

But before this closing digression on ears, Claire had gathered that, although Long has no idea what his quartet sounds like, he is in control: *Dissociative Fugue: Seven Planets for String Quartet*, it's the first piece he's written with a reason for every note, rhythm, and slur, with a purposive distinction between every piano, pianissimo, and pianississimo. As Craftsman and Creator, he can say why 7/8+5/16 here, why quartertone-up there, why harmonics here or there, why doubly-dotted eighth-rest everywhere. Design: There's no doubt involved. None. And Claire's doubting him is immaterial, is her opinion, her point of view. Who cares what it sounds like? It is perfection. Sound follows form. (There is no function.) How it sounds, that's up to you.

Nor does Long need point of view. He has something better: zoom of view (ZOV). POV is dead. But ZOV, this is new. *Example*: For Claire, blood is scary, but zoom-in enough and blood cells through a microscope are fine. For Long, bread is good to eat, but zoom-in too much and it's a whole new world of wormy protists and microbes. But that's OK because, when you get right down to it, down to the subatomic level, everything in the universe (even protists) is pretty much just empty space. This is interesting, because you can't walk through walls, but also because, if all the matter in the universe, if all these subatomic particles would just sit still, side-by-side, get along, and not create a bomb, then the entire universe could fit in…in something smaller. It's logic. And this makes him happy, because we're mostly empty and don't collapse, because the universe is nearly nothing and all that nothing holds together. *Logic*. Moreover, he has a statistic. Namely, if you extracted the empty space from a 70-kilogram small-ish male or large-ish female, he or she'd occupy approximately 0.00000001 teaspoons—isn't that amazing! And Long weighs less than 70 kilograms, so, essentially, he could collapse into nothing, but he doesn't, he is alive, can think, can write *Dissociative Fugue* and has a reason for all of its musical elements, all of its musical matter, all that matters, and this gives him ground to fall back on—he matters, exists, but also amounts to nothing—without ZOV, the world is chaotic and confusing: He'd be a nihilist, if it weren't for Ant Book.

And ants are all he needs. All this argot about violent quantum foam, superstrings, and curled-up dimensions is a bit silly, much like Kepler's harmony of the spheres—but Mr. Greene's picture of an ant on page 186 of *The Eleg-Ant Universe*, that was smart. The guy with the garden hose in the "ant picture," though, he was rather dumb: You see, this guy owns a canyon with his house on one side and his garden on the other. Now, as fate would have it, the only water source is in the house. So, to water his garden, he needs a really long garden hose. The picture illustrates this well, his hose extending like a tightrope across the top of the canyon, and not lying in it... which is unlikely, which suggests this guy, hose in hand, leapt across the canyon to his garden... or not, perhaps somebody *not* in the picture, but *at* the house, has pulled the hose tight so you could see it better in the picture, which, granted, is just a diagram...yeah, if we're going to be all *technical*, the guy's almost as tall as his house, so, actually, the picture's not too realistic, but that's not why it's smart. See, there's a zoom-in window shooting off his hose, and in this window, the garden hose is magnified so that it's twice as tall as the house, and on this zoomed-in hose, there is an ant. That's smart.

So *Dissociative Fugue* is all about ants' ZOV, except that the ant is also the hose, and the canyon, and the house, and the guy, and the garden, and the whole universe, because, when you zoom-in on the ant, there's another ant, always is—no matter what the ZOV, there's always an ant. So, Miss Tenured, the reason you choose doubly-dotted eighths or 7/8+5/16 is because it's an ant. And that's smart. Quantum foam has something to do with it too, probably, but ants make more sense. And 7/8+5/16 being ant is good enough for Dr. Long and, thus, for whomever, but especially Claire. Indeed, his string quartet is an ant.

4:45 P.M.: Having unlocked the door, Claire enters the Annex and crosses the lobby to—

She stops. Suddenly, through the concert hall doors, she hears it: the tritone, B and F...

Onstage, he is looking for a piano: nothing but black. But that's how Torbjorn likes it, how, door shut and Annex locked, the blackness hides him and the piano, how he can't see the boundaries, how the hall is gone—stage, keyboard, hands: gone—and he is alone. Comfort is a closed door.

Crawling onstage, he finally finds the grand piano. He stands and, with all doors securely shut and locked, undresses. All the way. All the way, shaking—no gin today, just caffeine and ephedra—shaking, he attacks the frayed double-knotted laces of his black jungle boots; shaking, he unbuckles his belt (jeans fall on their own); shaking, he peels off socks, Hanes, and T-shirt; shaking, he tosses all into the dark. There, he thinks. Black and cool. Done with shaking.

Almost ready. He paws about blindly for the piano bench. He finds it and sits: Gripping the outer shoulders of the piano, he slides his knees beneath its smooth ebony chest, then hands slip down the shoulders to touch the outermost keys, and there, from the keyboard's outer edges, nine fingers, careful not to depress any of its 88 keys, glide across, inward, fingertips grazing the surface of the keys, until hands kiss at middle-C. The notes are there. *Exhale*: That mantle of blackness inhales all things. He improvises best, naked in the dark. Blind is his point of view.

How he always starts: Damper pedal floored beneath right foot, torso leaning left, his four-fingered right arm—ignored—hanging limp at his side, he suspends his left fist high above his head, over the keyboard's contra octave no eyes can see, but fist knows is there.

Gravity snatches his fist. And left index knuckle *bombs* double-pedal B. Then up a tritone to pedal F. And the pitted asbestos walls make B and F scream, and, underfoot, floored pedal keeps them screaming. His soul gets greedy, so left hand finds more notes: a chromatic turn—biting, *staccatissimo* on E—then down to B-flat, hammered. The tritone E to B-flat, hammered. And Torbjorn listens: It's kinda like that "Being Fucked" theme, he thinks, from last night, sitting in his tree.[146] Yeah, his hands get back to B and F: A barrage of knuckles fall, flagrant fouls—*tuh-tit, tuh-tika tah, tika-tit-tit tah—sempre marcato, con forza e fuoco*. But then *subito piano*: some more B-and-F shit, *ma cantabile*—you know, something like this:

[146] Yes, "kinda"...but transposed to B and F, etc. See Figure 1.3 in §1.

Figure 6.2. Improvisation on "Being Fucked" theme. (*BF*, meas. 1-9.)
(*the notes of which Torbjorn be ignorant*)

Of course, Torbjorn doesn't know what the fuck he's doing. You say, "Transposed-B-and-blah-tuh-tika-tritone-blah-blah-blah," and he says, "Screw that: Know a note, monitor modulations, resource reharmonizations, think about *real* composers' crap, that's when the music stops," because metacognition, meta-aware, all that "meta-blah" is the music-killer. Because Torbjorn doesn't play piano; his hands do. Hands have no eyes. That's why the dark is best.

Question: Is Torbjorn God?[147]

If Torbjorn, a wannabe composer who abstains from beer and women, is God, then, as far as composing music is concerned, God's fucked. *Why God's Fucked*: Torbjorn can improvise in the dark, but not write in the light. When He sits at a piano with the lights turned on, with blank sheet music and a pen, and stares at the empty staff's five parallel lines, looking for notes, God gets writer's block: It's the notes' fault, not His. It's thinking in notes, their (non) existence on a (blank) score, that blocks, that stands between Him and the music. But when He shuts off the lights and improvises (naked) at a piano in pitch black, there is music—in Him, in His hands—in the dark, His hands have ideas. Unfortunately, there is no written record of this: When He turns the lights back on, the music's gone and He can't remember the notes He's just improvised, notes belonging to hands—body—and not to mind.

So what we're saying is God's got problems. *Solution*: God must not exist, must escape

---

[147] Good question…

HOW TO PROVE YOU'RE GOD: ***A Naïve Metaphysical Proof.***

Proof Assumptions: To prove you're God, assume the following two premises, a pair of seemingly contradictory claims posed a pair of centuries apart by (I) René Descartes and (II) Friedrich Nietzsche, both hold:

I. God exists.
II. God is dead.

Proof Outline: (Need to Show: You're God.) Define the spectrum of existence as follows:

1. Like Descartes, assume your existence is "'intermediate' between God and nothingness, between the supreme entity and nonentity,"* and may be denoted:

   1*a*. nonexistence ≤ YOU ≤ perfect existence

   For God, the perfect benevolent supreme being, write:

   1*b*. perfect existence = GOD

2. Assume that Nietzsche's claim (II) "God is dead" implies that God does not exist.

Now, given 1*a* and 1*b*, along with naïve notions of set inequality and reflexivity, it follows that

3. nonexistence ≤ YOU ≤ perfect existence = GOD (from 1*a* and 1*b*)
4. GOD = nonexistence (from 2)
5. GOD = nonexistence ≤ YOU ≤ perfect existence = GOD (from 3 and 4)
6. GOD = GOD (reflexive property)
7. Therefore, by set inequality, we may conclude that

   7*a*. YOU = GOD. (from 5 and 6)

   7*b*. Neither GOD nor YOU exist. (from 5 and 6)

   7*c*. Nonexistence = perfect existence. (from 5 and 6) Q.E.D.

* See Descartes' argument in his "Meditation IV: On Truth and Falsity" from *Meditations on First Philosophy: In which the existence of God and the real distinction of mind and body, are demonstrated.*

self-awareness. Cognition is Satan. God doesn't know the notes, His goddamn hands do—the things got a mind of their own—so when Godhead steps in and asks "What's the next note?", God remembers He exists and we got a problem: The Lord is afraid—yes, God fears—and God-fearing's not a pretty thing: God fucks up. For example, suppose God's on stage, giving a concert, performing Chopin or God knows what, and God's hands are doing fine, doing who knows what (God sure doesn't), but then, suddenly, mid-performance, in butts Godhead and shit goes to hell. Godheads don't know the notes, and, all the sudden, we got God-fearing in the mix. And hands stop doing whatever. God freezes up. Then off goes God, running off the stage and wasting people's money, people who paid a goddamn fortune to hear God play piano. Embarrassing. Quite the spectacle. But here, in the Annex, with doors shut and lights off, God can just be, because there are no notes, no keys, no Godheads fucking up, there is only the dark, and there, in a bunch of black, the music sings, hands just fall into keys, and sound rises:[148]

Figure 6.3. Example of hands falling, sound rising. (*BF*, meas. 13-14.)

[148] It appears that God is misinterpreting Descartes' treatment of the mind-body problem as follows:

1. I think, therefore I exist.
2. I have a body, therefore I am.

Here, as a bicameral organism, as both improviser and composer, His half-Selfs function on mutually exclusive operating systems, at war with each other: To generate music, you must destroy the mind, must dismantle your existence, must become the body and be, an ontological state which necessitates that, when He finds a piano, He let there not be light—light is bad—and He embrace doubt, cuddle skepticism, and parade all that "perplexed" Descartes in "Meditation I: Concerning Those Things That Can Be Called into Doubt" (e.g., that He have not hands, that underwater sticks be bent, that God's head be a pumpkin, that dreaming is believing, that these illusory perceptions be true, clear, and distinct, that evil deceiver be perfect and benevolent), for here, in God's eyes, it be right to fear the light, to vanish into veracious dream, to reverse representationalism, as well as Creation, to return to a time when "the earth was without form, and void; and darkness *was* upon the deep."

That's how it's gotta be. And sitting here, improvising, deep down Torbjorn knows that he, like God, can't write music—and never will—because there are no notes, just him and the black and cool. Hands just fall into the keyboard, wrapping around shapes that bring fingers to their keys, bring bodies together—like gravity, that general relativity jive where gravity slips time around the universe, a theoretical blanket, and makes sure stars can spin and planets dance around their suns. Hands revolve around chords and gravity pulls them into orbits of melodies, and you don't think about some grand compositional method: In the dark, flesh and bone just float about the calibrated sheet of a keyboard, and the music sings, and the planets go around the sun—

The lights flip on. Stage lights, not hall lights. They are bright as hell: He shuts his eyes.

A woman screams. Her scream: onstage, behind his back. Near a light switch, no doubt.

How embarrassing. Torbjorn feels self-conscious. *Plan of attack*: Don't be weird. Just behave as if everything is normal. He opens his eyes, but does not turn around to face—

The screamer shrieks: "What are you doing?!"

It's worse. Even with back to her, Torbjorn recognizes the voice: Professor Two Can. *Just stick to the plan*: Pretend you're not embarrassed, nothing's weird, and You're God.

Torbjorn is completely naked, sitting on a piano bench, with ass facing Two Can. His clothes—the jeans, T-shirt, boots, and briefs He tossed into the dark—are now scattered across the stage floor. Nothing He can do about it. No, instead of getting all embarrassed and running around the stage like a crazy person, frantically gathering up His underwear, He will take this opportunity to introduce Himself, formally. He still doesn't know His teacher's name. And this is the first time she's ever spoken to Him, directly.[149]

The second time: "I said, just *what* do you think you are doing? This is the Annex."

Just be natural, He thinks: Introduce Yourself and find out her name. Scooting the piano bench back a few inches, He stands up straight and tall, then turns around to face Two Can—there she is, some ten yards away, at stage's edge—and answers her question: "Hi," He says, "I was playing piano."

"But you're naked!" As if she just noticed, her hands pop up to block God's bod from

---

[149] Apparently, their conversation in the faculty parking lot this morning doesn't count; e.g., her speaking directly to Torbjorn when she shouted "And you, you stay away from me!" and drove off to Starbucks. (See Excerpt 3.2.)

view. This doesn't seem to work. She turns around and, back to Him, just stands there, by the short staircase rising to the stage, her blue dress wrinkled and lovely.

Torbjorn needs to *relax*, to think about something besides ripping off her blue dress. He will not, however, abandon "the plan" and put on clothes. Instead, He will take this opportunity to make Himself more comfortable: With the grand piano's lid lowered and shut, He leans back against the keyboard, places both palms on the lid behind Him, and, with one push, hops up on top of the piano. Finding that comfy slouched pose, legs dangling over the edge, He sits there, facing her shrouded behind and proceeds with the introductions: "Yeah, suppose you're right. I certainly *appear* to be naked. But, whatever, my name's Torbjorn…but I guess you already—"

"Appear?" she asks.

"Yeah, no worries. It's like—it's an optical illusion. So what's your name, Professor?"

Back still turned to Him, Two Can puts both hands on her hips (or rather, hands slap her hips and stay there) and, titling her head back to look at the ceiling (or rather, the blinding stage lights obscuring the ceiling), she sighs. Her sigh is also a growl: a harsh exhale and, beneath it, in the bass, a grumbled growl. But she does not speak (words).

Sexy, He thinks, I can tell she's flirting with Me. And really *responds* to that illusion bit. "So yeah," He says, "optical illusion. Frankly, it's become something of a problem."

No growl this time. Nor does she turn around. She folds her arms across her chest.

If God had the nerve, Torbjorn thinks, He'd go over there, to the stairs, and smooth the wrinkles out of that dress. (God-hands, you know, they got a mind of their own.) "So sure, I may look naked," He says, "but, seriously, how are we ever gonna prove it?"

Now, her hands grasp each side of her head. She is pulling her hair—He wants to be those hands—but she still has nothing to say.

Torbjorn will not creep up behind her and also pull her hair—that would be weird. He needs to think of something else to say: This optical illusion shit's getting old. He recalls the Münchhausen trilemma, how this Baron guy pulled himself out of a swamp by his own hair.[150] But she's probably not in the mood for Münchhausen, right now. Nor a proof of how He's God. No, something less weird, more normal, like the weather…or local gossip: "So," He says, "I

[150] For full narrative of how Baron Münchhausen pulled himself out of a swamp by his own hair, see H. Albert, *Traktat über kritische Vernunft* (Tübingen: J.C.B. Mohr, 1991), 15.

heard this hall's supposed to be haunted or something. You know, asbestos and shi—stuff."

She stamps her foot on the stage floor. It is loud in that hall, like a crack of thunder against those asbestos walls, but her heel does not break.

Torbjorn's not sure what this means. It probably doesn't mean: Come here, Torby, and rip off my dress. So He tries a new topic: "So, Professor, interesting class today...although the whole *tritone* thing did get a bit messy, but I'm sure nobody—"

"Shut up!" she shouts. She doesn't stamp, doesn't pull her hair. She flips around and looks: Professor Two Can isn't shy. She is marching straight for Him.

Torbjorn is half-worried, half-excited. Her behavior is not normal. What did He say?

She halts in front of the piano bench, her face just feet from His abdomen. He forgot about those scary Medusa eyes. She points to His underwear on the stage floor. "I'm asexual," she says. "But I don't care: Put some clothes on, or I'm calling the cops *again*."

Yeah, He also forgot about the whole asexual thing. He is losing His grip, but gives normalcy one last shot: "So what's it like...you know, being asexual?"

"Shut up! Clothes and get out. It's our hall. Rehearsal. We have a reservation. Rehearsal, in less than ten minutes." She stamps that foot, again, and points: "Clothes!"

"Yes, Miss Professor, sorry." He slides off the piano and almost bumps into her, but she does not move, not a muscle. This annoys Him, for some reason. He raises His voice: "Fine, I suppose putting clothes on would *rectify* the situation, even though it's an optical—"

"Shut up! Yes, the situation must be rectum-fied—recti—fixed this instant."

"Yes, Miss Asexual, I'll rectum-fy the situation right away." Back to her, He picks up His underwear. Then steps into His Fruit of the Loom briefs and yanks them up. "So I delivered your *note*," He says, looking for some pants. "Yeah, that's right, I *helped*, even drove him home. So, like, what the hell? I mean, this Slob, is he really your...is your name Bisera or—"

"Whoa, hello! And what do we have here?" says a male voice, high-pitched. "Hope I'm not *overdressed*."

Briefs on, Torbjorn spins around to see some guy in a tuxedo mounting the staircase and carrying a violin case—or viola, rather (too big for violin)—but, yeah, that tux says everything about him: tall (over six-foot) and thin, dark-haired, with extra hairspray and aura of wannabe movie-star, but old-school, more of a Cary Grant kinda thing...except his high, breathy voice sounds more like Brittany Spears or Madonna trying to do a sinister Peter Lorre impression. Torbjorn needs to put on some pants. There they are: His jeans are under the Steinway.

"Really, Claire," says Madonna Lorre, "I'm…impressed. Where'd you find him?"

"Your name's Claire?" Torbjorn asks, pants in hand.

Having reached Professor Claire, Madonna Lorre sets his viola case on the piano bench and revises his question: "Hmm, I guess I meant to say: Where'd you *just* find him?"

Torbjorn remembers: Put on pants.

Two-Can Claire does the sigh-and-growl thing, then says, "I didn't. He was just here."

"Really?"

With one leg in His jeans, Torbjorn pauses to look up. Madonna Lorre winks at Him.

"Hey, what's going on?" Two blonde girls approach them across the stage. Though not twins—you know, not biological—they are nearly identical: Aside from matching violin cases, the blondes also wear matching pajamas, plain pink, except for the words St. Gengulphus on the T-shirts, written in gold letters across their large breasts—four large nearly identical breasts.

Torbjorn steps into the other leg of His jeans, then pulls them up and buttons.

"Jeez, Claire," says the Left Blonde, "or is he yours, James?"

Torbjorn zips up. It doesn't seem normal that they don't talk to Him, like He's not even there, like He doesn't exist.

"No, no," says James Madonna Lorre, "Claire *just* found him here."

"Really?" says the other, the Right Blonde. They both set their violin cases down beside their feet, their matching puffy pink slippers.

Torbjorn has managed to put on His T-shirt, but one of His boots is missing.

Arms crossed, Professor Claire lowers her voice, abandoning sigh-and-growl: "Look, Jenny…or Jessie"—*"No, no, I'm Jenny"*—"Sorry, but Jenny, honestly, I don't even really know the guy. He's just one of my students."

"Naughty, naughty Claire. A student!" says Madonna/James. "Getting brave."

"Has anybody seen my other boot? It's not under the piano," Torbjorn says, looking everywhere. Except for the Steinway and a bunch of people ignoring Him, the stage is empty.

"It's on the stairs," Claire answers, pointing to the staircase to the stage, where she first stood with her back to Him. "Nearly tripped over it," she adds.

Torbjorn catches another wink from Madonna/James.

Professor Claire notes the wink, as well: "He lost it, *James*, because…well, the lights were off and it was in the way and—oh, never mind."

Torbjorn minds. Perhaps it's just the missing boot, but, for some reason, her ignoring Him, so persistently, has finally pissed off God: "Thanks for your *help*, Professor—and not Bisera, I guess. So I don't know if this Slob's your dad or what. But I *helped*, like you fuckin' asked. And he's been ill. Why he's been out of touch. So maybe he's lying, stalking you or—"

But Torbjorn stops: Professor Claire is pale. And perhaps it's just her silent suck-hole face, so sickly in the bright stage lights, but, for some reason, he feels less godlike: "Sorry, guys," he says. Then, embarrassed, adds, "Yeah, I guess I was just—you know—leaving."

"Don't worry about it," says Madonna/James. "You don't ever got to apologize to me."

Torbjorn tries to smile back at M/J, but can't. Done with smiles. He walks around them, across the stage to the stairs to get his boot. The blondes are whispering behind his back.

Torbjorn stops at the top of the short staircase: His missing boot is not on the stairs, not anywhere. Two Can is a liar. He looks back at Professor Claire, Blondes, and Madonna. Except for Prof. Claire's back, they are all staring at him, and Madonna is giggling. His boot is not onstage. He walks down the steps, then down the side aisle, down to the double-doors through which he first entered. He pauses with one hand on the door. He takes one last look back. His boot is nowhere in sight. Prof. Claire is arranging chairs and music stands. Fuck it, he decides.

Suddenly, the door opens, and a large woman, Valkyrie-sized and lugging a cello case behind her, bashes into him and steps on his bare toes. Torbjorn hops up and down on his booted foot. Valkyries have big feet.

"Oh, sorry," she says, "where's your other shoe?"

"Lost it," he says, limping out of her way.

"Ah, that sucks." Cello Valkyrie maneuvers into the hall quickly, bashing her cello case into the door on her way through. "Sorry," she adds, "but there was like this weird guy outside and he was like just standing there, smoking. I always got guy issues."

Torbjorn can imagine.

"Yeah, it's like *drama*, wherever I go. Sorry, again. Hope you find your shoe." The Valkyrie hauls her cello-on-wheels down the aisle toward the stage. "Sorry, everyone," she shouts, "sorry I'm late, but I couldn't find my way, and there was like this guy, and I—"

Torbjorn isn't listening. He's gone, heading for the nearest exit. It's after 5 p.m. Less than an hour until his first training shift at Gator's. But it's right across the street. So he's still got time. Time to look for another piano.

Exiting the *unlocked* Annex front door, he finds, not Nixon standing outside, smoking, leaning against the flagpole, but his other teacher: "Care Bear!" But Dr. Long has changed: In addition to his giant mirrored sunglasses, he is now wearing a sequined bullfighter's costume.

Torbjorn decides Dr. Long does not exist, and speed-walks through the grass towards Third Street, hugging the Annex wall to avoid the flagpole's toreador, who seems to have recovered his other "disguise," his mock Chinese-French accent: "Hey, Care Bear, what happen your shoe? Hey, Shoeless Bear, where you go? OK, I see it is Care Bear got the *issues*..."

Yeah, thinks Torbjorn, turning right around the corner of the Annex, towards the back lot. He knows about this Dumpster, where you can hide.

Book Excerpt 6.3. (Keyboard #2.) *Concerning what Knut does know shit about—flipping burgers,*[151] *a fictionalization of his kitchen job at the hospital where he cooked Mother's food.*

Torbjorn's got issues. He is troubled by this, so he decides to get to work early and face the facts. *Fact*: Tonight is Torbjorn's first night on the job, his new kitchen job at Gator's Hut. *Issue*: He's never stepped foot in a kitchen before, even though his application form boasted ten years of cooking experience at four restaurants in New York City. *Fact*: Torbjorn's never been to New York and fucks up Ramen in the microwave. Also, he's missing a boot.

Standing directly across Third Street from Gator's front door, Torbjorn is ten minutes early for his 6 p.m. training shift. *Issue*: This doesn't mean he'll be on time. It is now clear that being early to the outside of a building is different from being early to the inside. *Fact*: Gator's Hut, it's a restaurant-bar with shit going on—jazz nights, standup, a foreign-film series, karaoke, free anarchist newsletters by the toilets, brain sandwiches—but *fact*: It's also a real

[151] A discipline about which I, however, know nothing—hence, this excerpt's lack of footnotes. (Frankly, I'm getting a bit sick of the footnote thing.)

shithole, and *fact*: It's a real convenient shithole, right across Third from the Dumpster behind the Annex. So he didn't expect any issues with crossing the street and getting through the front door in under ten minutes, didn't expect to find this "line," this mass of bodies, coming out the front door, stretching up and down the sidewalk, and trespassing on the lawns of two adjacent frat houses, as well as in the Village Pantry parking lot on the corner of College and Third. Now, beholding this clusterfucking line, he assesses his issues and decides to quit this job: He hides from crowds, rather than in them. But then, *fact*: He's only wearing one shoe. He needs money to buy a shoe. So he decides to keep his job and cross the street. And, for the first time, as he tries to "cut" in line, walking back and forth in the gutter of Third, attempting to mount the sidewalk packed full of intoxicated college students, who look to be underage and scantily dressed, it occurs to him what working in a shithole kitchen could really mean—*fact*: Shithole kitchen means free food.

How to Get a Kitchen Job at Gator's Hut: In general, lie. In particular, your proficiency with two types of lies (written and oral) shall be examined in the following order:

(1) *Written*: The application form should take five minutes max. But job experience is key, so don't fear the research: Hit the net and find the websites of four ethnic restaurants in NYC. Scroll to the bottom of the webpages and copy the contact info (correct street address numbers are OK, but change a digit or two in the telephone numbers). Make sure the foreign-sounding names of your made-up managers are compatible with respective cuisine ethnicities (by bearing in mind mobsters in *The Godfather* trilogy): You will need two Italian surnames (pick names like Tattagli or Clemenza, but avoid Corleone), one German (pick Hagen, reportedly German-Irish), and one Tibetan (you don't know any Tibetan mobsters, so you're stuck with Batista, the Cuban dictator in *Godfather II*). If possible, cite a dishonest buddy as a reference (one who can pretend he was your former manager over the phone). Never admit to felonies.

(2) *Oral*: The Q&A of the personal interview will be much easier. Once the owner of Gator's has explained that his discharge from the Navy was honorable, he'll ask two questions:

Q1. "Only nine fingers, huh—can you hold a gun?" he'll ask.

This Question #1 is disorienting, but it is also rhetorical, for he'll immediately reply:

A1. "Well, sure you can, and like I always say: If you can shoot a gun, you can flip a burger."

However, Question #2 is more difficult:

Q2. "Lotta smoking round here. You got a problem with that? You know, with smoking?" Given higher level of difficulty, he'll wait several seconds before responding for you:

A2. "Well, sure you don't. If you're not pro-legal-weed and all, then you don't work here." He'll conclude the interview by explaining that "You do work here."

Torbjorn is now two minutes early to work. He is even inside the building, getting yelled at as he pushes and shoves through the wall-to-wall bodies to the front of the "line," wherever that might be. *Issue*: He can't see shit, nor does he know what the fuck he's supposed to do, nor does he know where to find the kitchen. *Fact*: There was no orientation after the interview—"Yeah, no time for that," the owner said, "not with cook getting arrested and me getting overworked: Why the hell else would we be hiring?" So Torbjorn just keeps pushing through the crowd, peering for future peers. But it's as hard to see in Gator's as it is to breathe.

What Torbjorn Will Learn if He Survives the Night and Keeps this Job: Not seeing and breathing is good for business. When Indiana introduced the indoor smoking ban, the owner decided Gator's was more of a bar with food, than a restaurant with a bar, and he opted for the 24-hour 18-and-over policy that allowed indoor smoking. Business skyrocketed. Ever since the ban, with nowhere else to go, all smokers go to Gator's. Day or night, there's a wait. And no reservations, no hostesses. Just a bouncer, with a multitask job description: (1) Check IDs and the clock simultaneously, because (1*a*) from 11 a.m. to 7 p.m. Gator's is 18-and-over, (1*b*) from 7 p.m. to midnight it's 21-and-over, and (1*c*) from midnight to 2 a.m. there is no bouncer, and (2) Be a human-wall/babysitter, who (2*a*) prohibits the entry of underage students with bad fakes and (2*b*) administers the "One-in, One-out" policy to maintain the legal seating capacity, a policy that (2*b*i) rips families and fraternity brothers apart, (2*b*ii) forces strangers to sit together, and (2*b*iii) permits waitresses to walk down the aisles. However, on nights like tonight, Wednesday night, Karaoke Night, none of the above applies. As the owner will explain, respecting the maximum seating capacity and minimum drinking age, such legal policies are bad for business. So, tonight, there are no "aisles" (a.k.a. "unobstructed pathways"), just wall-to-wall half-naked bodies, squeezing and squirming between the Hut's front, back, and back-back barrooms.

Torbjorn is now several minutes late to work. But he has shoved his way to the front of the "line" and located what appears to be a bouncer. The bouncer appears to be a mountain, a defensive lineman with off-season breasts and a lone well-greased curl of hair fixed front-and-center to his forehead like a Christopher Reeves Superman. And this mountain sits on a barstool near the front of the front barroom and scrutinizes the IDs of a wall-like front of nearly-naked "line-women," all sporting baby-face pouts and looking underage, drunk, and posed in that unsportsmanlike on-your-mark-get-ready-set-go stance, all ready to charge (offsides or not) into the crowd, as soon as the bouncer's not looking. *Issue*: The mountain hasn't noticed Torbjorn.

When Curly Top Mountain notices Torbjorn, he screams: "Hello, darling! Got your two forms of ID?" His scream is high and nasal, like a beginning oboist who can't hit the high notes.

"No," shouts Torbjorn, "I'm the—"

"What's that, doll?"

He shouts into Curly Top's ear: "I'm the new guy. My first night."

"Praise Jesus!" Curly Top hops off the barstool. "Finally," he shouts, "I can quit."

"What?"

Mountain winks. "Don't worry, darling. I'll be around. Hut's Long Islands are to die for. But, anyway, you know what to do: Just don't let the Neanderthals in if the fakes are too obvious. Actually, don't let anybody in at all." The mountain pats Torbjorn's cheek. "Nice meeting you—toodles!"

"No, wait," Torbjorn shouts. He grabs the guy's shoulder.

Mountain transforms: He catapults Torbjorn's hand away with a martial-artist-like move. "Hey, no touchie," says Curly. "What the hell's your problem?"

The lone curl is too close to Torbjorn's nose. "Nothing," Torbjorn says. "It's just I'm supposed to get trained in the kitchen, tonight."

"No way, sugar, I'm the one's supposed to be quitting. It's my turn."

"But the owner guy, he said kitchen."

"What?"

Torbjorn shouts louder: "Owner Guy said kitchen."

"Fuck him. He promised I could quit."

"Look, man, I'm sorry, but how about I go to the kitchen and ask. That cool with you?"

"Whatever." Mountain plops back down on the stool. "And fuck you, too."

"Yeah, OK, but where's the kitchen?"

No answer. Curly Top Mountain turns his back on Torbjorn. "Fine," Torbjorn says and faces the smoky depths of Gator's, the wall-to-wall bodies. Torbjorn bores into an orgy of skin, backless-shirted underage chicks with variously sized love-handles and frat boys with silk shirts uniformly unbuttoned down to the navel, orgy participants drinking straight from pitchers, pitchers bumping and fountain-ing onto the already wet tile floor, orgy experience punctuated with shrieks from cigarette burns, burns treated with healthy splashes of beer.

Torbjorn is now ten-plus minutes late to work. The sock of his bootless foot is soaked. Finally, he finds somebody who doesn't belong: an employee, a waitress, tall but beefy, her bare bulging calves like snakes digesting cantaloupes. She carries four pitchers in each fist and, like Moses, parts the Student Sea with magic words: "Sit down, or get the fuck out of my way."

But it's not until she stands towering over Torbjorn, her head emerging from the smoke and entering into the dim lamplight, that he notices her face: Jesus, she has a Quasimodo face. Or Polyphemus, rather, given her size and eye patch.

Torbjorn is brave: "Ma'am?" he shouts.

"Sit down."

"I'm new. Supposed to do kitchen training, tonight."

"Great, kid." She raises the eight pitchers above her head, then out and over Torbjorn's. She is a wave about to crash over him. "Just great," she shouts, "now, out of the way."

"Sorry." Torbjorn tries to push and shove his way out of her path. He slams *onto* a standing pile of students, which he would have knocked over, if they weren't so tightly packed. Leaning there, he shouts, "But, ma'am, where's the kitchen?"

She lumbers through the rift in the wide Student Sea. "Where do ya' suppose?"

"Please, ma'am. The bouncer wouldn't tell me, either."

"Yeah, well fuck him." She bulldozes past him. But then, without turning around, yells to Torbjorn behind her: "Just keep going straight. Open-air kitchen. At the back of the front barroom. Hit the back-back barroom, and you gone too far. Just follow the glossy grease road."

Torbjorn is now twentyish minutes late to work. But it turns out that following a winding trail of grease along the floor was sensible advice: The glossy grease road has finally led him to the entrance to the open-air kitchen, the kind of swinging doors you see in Wild West saloons.

Beside these, through a window and across a countertop, the owner, bent over a register, slams his fist onto the counter and shouts at Torbjorn: “You’re late!”

“Yeah, sorry, sir,” Torbjorn says, “but it was so crowded I—”

But Torbjorn’s apology is interrupted: “Two big boys, one wiener!” the owner screams, as loud as possible, in Torbjorn’s face.

From inside the kitchen, a voice responds: “Two big boys, one wiener.”

This *Call and Response* continues, as some unseen cook in the kitchen repeats the screamed food-orders that the owner, reading from a stack of tickets, *keys* into the old-fashioned register, the typewriter type that goes ping, while Torbjorn, ignored, studies a flier taped to the register advertising a “Peanut Butter and Jam Festival” in 1987:

Call (*Owner Guy*)	Response (*Unseen Cook*)
“14 little boys”	“14 little boys”
“4 Peters, 2 beehives, 3 veggies”	“4 Peters, 3 beehives, 2 veggies”
“No, that’s 2 beehives, 3 veggies”	“Got it”
“2 Japs, 1 bones, 1 pussycat, 4 bowls of reefer”	“We’re out of pussycats”
“Gotchya, pussycats been 69-ed—”	

Suddenly, Owner Guy pounds the counter and shouts at Torbjorn: “Kid, what the hell you doing? You’re late. I’m not paying you to just stand around.”

Torbjorn tears himself away from the PB&J Festival flier. “Sorry, sir. So crowded I couldn’t find the kitchen. Name’s Torbjorn.”

“Sure it is. From now on, you’re T-Bone. Now, find an apron, T-Bone, and get on your grill line. And remember, no smoking on the line.”

“Right. Don’t smoke, sir.”

“Sure you don’t. But I don’t care whether you’re pro-legal-weed or whatnot. Fact is, you’re late, and you got a flat-grill waiting for you.”

“Yes, sir.” Torbjorn enters, pushing through the swinging doors, but his booted foot slips on the greasy floor, slips back and out from under him. He doesn’t reach the kitchen floor.

Owner Guy catches the back of Torbjorn’s belt and holds him up by it, letting Torbjorn hang midair. The *Call and Response* resumes: “Ten little boys, two tenders, one pussy—no, never mind, scratch the pussy.” Owner Guy drops Torbjorn and then, with both hands cupped around his mouth, screams louder into the restaurant: "Hey, ladies, pussycat's been 69-ed."

Tobjorn gets up off his stomach, onto his hands and—

"Too slow!" Owner Guy grabs Torbjorn's upper arm and jerks him to his feet. "T-Bone, aprons are by—Christ, T-Bone, what happened to your shoe? It's SHIRT AND SHOES REQUIRED."

"Yeah, sorry, sir, I was…" But then Torbjorn decides not to tell Owner Guy how he lost his boot playing piano naked in the—

"Chrissake, T-Bone, what you standing there thinking for?—aprons are by Dish. Just head to the back, past the walk-in, down to your north end—kitchen's a square, west-side grill—now go on and git." And with that "git," *Call and Response* resumes: "Oh Christ, here we go: two big boys, three gollums, four cups of reefer, four santiagos, one hairy slut…"

Kitchen Territory and Torbjorn's Journey West to the Grill: With saloon doors at his back and Owner Guy screaming "hairy slut" on his left, Torbjorn baby-steps straight ahead—northbound, he assumes—down what appears to be a dry-stock aisle: On his left, the dry-stock shelves display canned goods, gallon tubs of ketchup, mayonnaise, and salad dressings, but also a Winnie-the-Pooh stuffed animal. On his right, halfway down the aisle, he finds the entrance to the so-called "walk-in," a closet-sized cooler. Its metal door is scratched and scarred, like a zinc engraving, with depictions of cannabis leaves and human reproductive organs. At the end of this aisle, in an alcove on his right, he discovers standing water, aprons, and large sinks overflowing with tubs of dishes. This must be "Dish." From a nail on the wall, he selects a damp apron. His hand is now covered with ketchup. On the upside, excluding "Dish," the kitchen does appear to be a "square" of aisles, with food-prep "lines" on the north/south sides of the square and dry-stock shelves on the eastern side. In the center, though, a series of vents completely fills the square's interior and rises to the ceiling like walls, blocking visibility to any other side. Torbjorn is looking for a grill. So, dressed in apron, he heads west, baby-stepping down the northern aisle towards a cloud of smoke. On each side of him, two lines of hot-tubs extend to aisle's smoky end: The tubs on the left hold vegetables and mystery meat marinades; on the right, cracked dried-up soups. One contains an unopened eight-pack of hotdogs, half-submerged in what might be grits or possibly Campbell's Cream of Mushroom. At the far end of the soupy-substance line, there is a big basket of saltine crackers, with label "Wolf Biscuits." Finally, reaching aisle's end, Torbjorn turns left around the northwestern corner, into the heat and the smoke. Journey complete: Welcome to the "west-side grill." And to the cowboy. Shit, thinks Torbjorn.

Torbjorn says, "Shit."

"What the wolf are you doing here?" The cowboy's kitchen uniform is special: no apron, no hairnet. In *fact*, Wolfer looks no different than he did this morning—cowboy hat, boots, giant turquoise belt buckle—except he's tucked his foot-long beard down the front of his snap-down flannel shirt, and smeared black char-grease-whatever on his face like mascara.

Owner Guy hollers from the register: "Cup of reefer, one big boy, two egg, one wiener, two rubies, and—and mother-F'ing-Christ—seven cowboys. Hear that, partner? We got seven cowboys."

Wolfer stares down Torbjorn, but responds to Owner Guy: "Yeah, cowboys, every day of the week. But, Captain, what the wolf's this kid doing here? Kid's a school-shooter, missing a thumb…*and* a shoe."

Captain Owner Guy pops around the southwestern corner. "What you saying? That there's T-Bone. Kid's training, tonight."

"On a Wednesday?" With the back of his hamburger-flipper, Wolfer slaps a burger on the char grill and a burst of yellow flames leaps up through its black corroded slits.

Captain Owner sighs: "Yeah, I know, I know."

"On Karaoke night?" Another slap and flames. "The wolf's missing a shoe. Where's Skittles, Captain? Where's my wolf-man Skittles?"

"Tony ain't coming. Took thirty days. Was either that or two years of community service."

Slap and flames: "No Skittles?"

"Sorry, partner. T-Bone's got experience, though. City boy. Helluva résumé. Should learn nice and quick. You got the cowboys up?"

Slap and flames: "Where's his shoe?"

"Yeah, I know. We discussed it. But what about them cowboys?"

Slap and flames: "What?"

"Seven cowboys."

No slap, no flames.

Without taking his eyes off the Captain, Wolfer slowly places his hamburger-flipper on the cutting board countertop and opens a refrigerator, sandwiched between his char grill and a trio of deep fryers. From the fridge, Wolfer extracts a slab of meat in each hand—large slabs, two-pounds-plus—and plops each one on the countertop, like he's using a flyswatter. He then gets a second pair of "cowboys" from fridge, always staring down the Captain, and plops them just the same. Then back to fridge, three more, then plop goes one, plop goes two—but not the third. Wolfer holds this third giant slab of raw red meat in his fist. There it hangs, like a Dali clock. Finally, he looks away from the Captain, looks to the west. Torbjorn follows the path of this gaze, from the mound of six raw cowboys on the countertop, then rising slightly up to the dressing tubs (full of lettuce, tomato, onion, pickle, mayonnaise, etc.), then up to a large window stretching the whole length of the western line, the expo-line window with finished orders for servers to pick up, and then, finally, through the window, to the wall of guests just outside. Suddenly, Wolfer mutters, "It's show time." And Captain mutters, "Oh Christ, not dodge-beef."

"Mother-wolf!" shouts Wolfer, as he launches the cowboy through the window—"Ah!" screams some cute little sorority blonde just outside, as the cowboy slams into her bare back, her spine butterfly-ing a faint but well-defined imprint of beef blood.

And then, with another *Mother-wolf,* Wolfer's second cowboy flies—*Score!*—"Ah, help, help," screams the blonde.

A third flying cowboy nails some guy with spiked hair in the back of the head: "Jesus, what the—hey, man, just what the hell you"—

Fourth flying cowboy: "Ah, fuck," shouts Spiked Hair, "what're you"—*fifth cowboy*—"you crazy"—*sixth cowboy*—"Jesus"—*seventh*—"Help!"—*out of cowboys.*

"Cup of reefer," says Owner Guy, loudly, but not angrily, more like he's in a trance. He rereads the ticket: "reefer, one big boy, two egg, one wiener, two rubies, seven cowboys."

"Aye, aye, Captain." That "captain" is a snap of the fingers, a gun at a racetrack.

Accordingly, the owner snaps out of it: "And now, partner, I'm gonna grab those cowboys you just wasted. If we can't salvage them," he says, his shouts receding, as he exits kitchen territory, "if they're no good, they're coming off your paycheck—menu price."

"Aye, aye, Captain." Cowboy Wolfer's back in action, back to his grill: With his flipper, he catapults the blackened burgers and breasts into a trashcan and replaces them, and then

The Speed Chess: Wolfer knows the moves, maneuvers fast, rotating (strategically, it seems) choice items from central to peripheral regions on his char grill—"gotta respect the hotspots," he mutters—and then *The Frisbee*: Spinning 180, he throws down a line of eight baskets on the dressings countertop across from the grill, throws them down with a flick of the wrist, like baskets are Frisbees, then buns—wheat, sesame, or white—land in eight baskets where, hand-over-hand, top buns flip up, like sports fans doing the wave, and then *The Percussion*: two rows of condiment tubs (twelve in each row) are like a set of 24 drumheads…or not, Torbjorn thinks. Actually, it's more like Rach's g-minor Prelude for piano—you know, the one that starts: *boom titty-tit, buh-boom tit, boom tit, boom titty-tit, bugger-boom tit, boom tit, boom…*

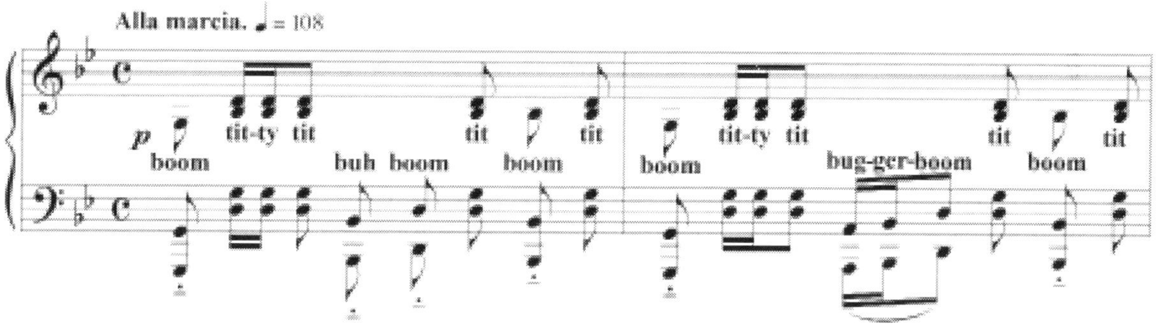

Figure 6.4. Boom Titty-Tit. (Rachmaninoff's Prelude VI, Op. 23, No. 5.)

But not the Boom Titty part, more like the next page, where the keyboard is a grid of condiment tubs and a row of eight burger baskets, and Wolfer's dressing of the burgers' bottom buns is:

Figure 6.5. KEYBOARD #2: Dressing burger buns. (Second theme of Prelude VI.)

So yeah, a lot like Rach. But now we're back to Frisbees, to burgers zooming across the aisle, from grill to baskets, where patties land on their dressed buns, then top buns drop, and just like—no, don't forget the fries—and just like that, eight sandwich baskets pop up in the window and—

"Hey, what the wolf you doing? Hey, School Shooter!"

Torbjorn jumps. "Sorry. What do you want me to do?"

"You're flat-grill. How many times I gotta tell you?" Wolfer slams a fistful of tickets onto the grill-rail counter to his left, which Torbjorn's been sitting on.

The flat-grill, Torbjorn deduces as he turns around to face the grill line, though more potholed than flat, is what this large smoking metal surface must be, this 3×5-foot hotplate.

From the register: "2—4—10—16—17 little boys," shouts the Captain, "four Peters, one beehive, one Santiago, two bowls of reefer, and 2—6—8—9—11 big boys. And listen up, partner, four of your cowboys were salvageable—clean 'em up later—but the other three, too trampled. So, heads up, that's a 3-times-22-equals-66-buck bite out of your next paycheck."

"Aye, aye, Captain." Wolfer opens the fridge and loads his char grill with un-launched cowboys. "But just throwing up seven fresh cowboys, just now. Better let them new wolfs pile up. Gonna need a smoke, too, in a—but hey, what the wolf you doing, kid?"

"We're calling him T-Bone," shouts the Captain, still around the corner by the register.

"Whatever the Wolf-Bone, kid, what you doing?"

Intimidated by the deck of tickets, the potholed flat-grill, and not speaking "Kitchen," Torbjorn's done the only thing he could think of: Dump the bucket of water sitting by the soup station into the dried-up, whitish soup…potato, perhaps? "Sorry, *partner*," Torbjorn says, "but the soups are all dried up."

Wolfer throws his hamburger flipper onto the char-grill: The flipper bounces up and somersaults in the air, spinning fast like a ceiling fan on the highest setting, until its handle falls back into the palm of his hand, like it's a supermagnet. Wolfer hadn't looked at it. Hand just knew where that handle was gonna be. Or vice versa. "First off," he says, "don't you ever go calling me partner. Not ever. You're no partner of mine."

"Then what do you want me to call you?"

"Nothing. Don't call me nothing. No other wolfs in here. And now, secondly, you just poured the rag-wolf in the reefer."

"This—uh—potato soup's the reefer."

"Course it is."

"OK, well, the reefer needed water."

"That wasn't water. That was rag-wolf."

"OK, so, what's rag-wolf?"

"Sterilizes rags. It's got soap and sanitizer-wolf in it."

Torbjorn now notices the poison sticker on the bucket he just poured into the reefer, that green sticker with the tongue sticking out. "Sorry par—sorry, but there weren't any rags in it."

"'Course there weren't. We're running low."

"What's going on back here?" says the Captain. His head pops around the corner.

Silence.

Captain comes all the way around the corner and crosses his arms. "What?"

"Well, Cap'n, this T-Bone just dumped the last of the rag-wolf in the reefer."

"Oh Christ, no he didn't."

"Yep. Outta reefer."

"Jesus, first no pussy and, now, no reefer. Damnit, T-Bone, what the hell you thinking?"

Torbjorn tries: "Sorry, Captain, but—"

"Listen here. Don't you ever call me Captain, T-Bone. You call me sir."

"Sorry, sir, but the potato—or the reefer, I mean, it was all dried up. Needed water."

"Water comes out of a faucet," Captain says. He throws both hands above his head and cries out to heaven, shaking his fists: "Faucet, T-Bone. Not no rag bucket…" Finally, his fists drop to aim two index fingers at Torbjorn, like they're pistols: "From now on, T-Bone, you stick to flat-grill. And you, you keep an eye on him. You hearing me, partner? Like a hawk."

"Aye, aye, Captain."

Captain Owner Guy disappears around the corner, and then yells into the restaurant: "Listen up, ladies. Pussy and Reefer been 69-ed."

"Alrighty, T-Bone," Wolfer begins, flipping a cowboy with his tongs, "so you got flat-grill and all your soup sort of wolfs so let's…" But he trails off, the cowboy in his tongs now pointed at Torbjorn's face, and *in* it, like Wolfer's a reporter with a microphone. "Ah, wolf me." Tossing his microphone on the grill, he picks up their two stacks of tickets, Torbjorn's in his left, his own in his right. One at a time, he smells each stack and goes "hmm," like he's sampling fancy perfume. Once each stack passes the sniffing test, he fans through them like card hands.

"Right, no more reefer," Wolfer says, "so we'll give them wolfs. You got 2—6—7 bowls and 3 cups, and I got—yeah, I got 12 cups and a bowl. So that's 8 bowls and 15 cups, but we only do bowls for wolfs, so that's 23 bowls of wolf. Got it, T-Bone?"

"What are wolfs?"

"Santiagos."

"What's a Santiago?"

"Wolf, T-Bone," he says, slamming fist onto the condiments counter, "Santiago's chili."

"OK, sorry, sorry, but how was I supposed to know?"

"Well, Santiago's capital of Chile, isn't it?"

"Oh yeah, I guess—"

"No time to wolf around. Bowls are the brown wolfs on the top shelf."

Torbjorn locates the brown wolfs: Standing on his tiptoes to reach the top shelf above the soup station, he struggles to grasp a stack of four bowls. *Issue*: Torbjorn has nine fingers. *Fact*: The bowls are ceramic and spherical. And stacked, they don't fit into each other like normal soup bowls, these brown ball-like bowls having mouths with smaller diameters than their bulging middles. (Also, Torbjorn is shaky: no gin today.) But eventually, with both hands, he manages to grip the bottom bowl of the nearest four-stack and lift: The bowls rattle and shake, and slowly he lowers the stack to...*Success*: four bowls on the counter. (Only nineteen more to go.)

"Hurry it up there, T-Bone," Wolfer says. Torbjorn half-turns to see him serving something like hummus onto an oval plate, presumptive hummus dripping like pancake batter from the spatula. "We got rubies and wieners waiting for you."

"Right." Torbjorn picks up the pace. He grips two more teetering stacks of four, one in each hand, the right-hand stack's bottom bowl clamped between his pinky and index finger, and he lifts, and he lowers, and—

bowls are falling—

—and he tries to catch them with his arms and soften their fall with his feet, the booted and the "socked," but they just slip and slide off him like ice cubes (or ice spheres, rather)—

and they all shatter at his feet.

"For Chriss-fuckin-sake." Captain's back. "Now what?"

Torbjorn doesn't see a broom, so he squats down and picks up the shards with his fingers.

"Oh, you know, just Wolf-Bone trying to bowl-up a Santiago."

"Jesus, T-Bone, can't you do anything? What you think, partner? What you think the kid can handle?"

"Well, the wolf can't handle a bowl, that's for sure."

"You're right there. And damnit, boys, the sitters been complaining like crazy, starting to ask to see me. So what's taking you so long? Chrissake, what's the holdup?"

"Told you we needed old Wolfman Skittles, didn't I?"

"Sure we do, but there's cooks and there's crooks, isn't there? Anyways, T-Bone, can you do rubies?"

Torbjorn stands, his fists full of ceramics shards. "Not sure—what are they?"

"Reubens, kid, reubens. You know what's on them?"

"Well, I can learn. I learn fast."

"Sure you do. You done deep-fryers, at least?"

Torbjorn shakes his head, spots a trashcan in the corner between the condiment and soup lines, and tosses the shards.

"Not too tough," Wolfer says, "you know what a Peter is, T-Bone?"

Torbjorn sighs and bends over to pick up more broken bowl.

"Christ, it's codfish, kid."

"Yeah, I know, the wolf ain't too quick. Even though he has got the lost-boy look."

"Sure he does, but tell me, city boy. What the blazes you cook with up there, in NYC?"

"Well, stuck to ovens and stoves. You know, pastas and pizzas and stuff."

"Yeah? I sure didn't see any Pizza Huts on your application."

"Yeah, well, they weren't the specialty dishes."

"Sure they weren't, but this here's Gator's Hut, not Pizza Hut. And tell you what, T-Bone, you're bouncer tomorrow night, that's for sure. Bucky's just disappeared out of nowhere."

Captain's hand plunges into a tub of anchovies. He eats a fistful, like it's popcorn.

"Figures with a wolf like that."

"Well, anyways, we need dishes done, and that's a *fact*. T-Bone, you're on dish. You have washed a dish before, haven't you?"

Torbjorn recalls the mucky water in the plugged-up sinks by the ketchup-splattered aprons. But, he thinks, maybe they've got some kind of long-ass rubber glove, with cuff extending past your elbow to your armpit. "Yeah, sure," he says, "did years of that when—"

"Sure you did." Captain takes Torbjorn's place at the flat-grill. "Now go on and *git*."

Torbjorn does, T-Bone gits.

Back at Dish, he steps into the standing water, sock first.

PROBLEMS

6.1. (a) I'm sick of homework problems. And sick of Book, sick of you, sick of sick, sick to death, and of it, death, so what's the point who gives a shit what am i doing why

(b) I don't want to talk about it.

(c) Fuck this…

Prolegomenon to §7 (The End of Book.) *The guilt surrounding the death of my mother (part 2 of 3).*[152]

Dear Dead Knut,

I've just read the end of *Book*.

Now, I am sick of homework problems. (And don't want to talk about it.) But the end of *Book*—how dare you?! Fictionalized or not, I won't stand for it. Fiction, I'm above it. I do math, I do simple. I do truth.

Granted, I'm getting used to the fact that you wrote my mother as a neurotic old man named Slob, a mathematician (like me) with a brain tumor (like Mom) whose daughter (me) is Torbjorn's professor (as I was yours, until I was fired [like Slob] for screwing you in my office because I didn't have tenure [unlike Claire])—all this, granted, I have accepted, I have become acclimatized to the absurdity of it all, and even embraced it, much like Aristotle: "Poetry, therefore, is more philosophical and more significant than history, for poetry is more concerned with the universal, and history more with the

[152] For part 1 of 3, see footnotes 92-140.

individual."[153] So yes, I say, down with history, glory be to absurdity: I am a mathematician, universals are my thing. But so is the truth. And what happens next (in *Book*'s end, in absurdity) and happened next (in reality), your impending exposé of happenings (in §7) is not absurd enough—how dare you write about it?!

I suppose I'm in denial, suppose it's my duty to get over it, to chronicle the truth, to swallow my vanity and let words warp the world around me. But warping doesn't make it any easier. *Word warp*: It's like reliving the past with a stethoscope; we didn't hear our hearts beating, but now we go back and listen to every damn pump, magnified—the potency of 𝕏, amplified—denial is easier. Denial, my addiction. (Yours was bourbon.) It's time to face the *facts*:

I guess I was jealous. And still am. Even though you're dead—both of you—even though you're both dead. The river took you and forgot to take the jealousy. I am ashamed. No, Knut, I guess it wasn't really all your fault, but you made me do it. You made me be jealous of an old woman with a brain tumor.

Jealous of a mother with a tumor. Did you know? Did you, Knut, notice…anything?

Well, I remember *well* the moment when, for the first time, I noticed jealousy's existence. I remember me, standing outside my own front door after dark, after giving a long day of "midterms" to a bunch of *high-school* students, remember how I stand there, and I can't open the door because I am jealous.

And standing there, I tell myself to *be positive*: I'm young (sort of), I have hair and no varicose veins, and I can see things more than three feet away (when I'm wearing contacts), and my skin fits, doesn't bloodhound sag from my bones, save the pouches beneath my sleep-deprived eyes—if only we could deprive eyes of other things, like what they see—and I don't live on a gurney with built-in bedpan and remote control for some black-and-white TV that only gets a soap channel, 24-hour televised mass from the Vatican, and "mature" pay-per-view. Nor do I have a brain tumor.

But all I can do is stand, stuck and jealous, and think how I don't have time to be jealous. *Be positive?* No, I have worse things to worry about:

1. I've lost my job (because of you) and now substitute-teach six "periods" at a Catholic high school (because an old nun broke her hip): $6 \times 21 = 126$ seven-page midterms to grade.
2. I'm about to lose my house (soon to be the bank's, unless I can find $14,652.72): eight days until foreclosure.

[153] From the following passage in Aristotle's *Ars Poetica*, ed. R. Kassel (Oxford: Clarendon Press, 1966), §1451β: (εἴη γὰρ ἂν τὰ Ἡροδότου εἰς μέτρα τεθῆναι καὶ οὐδὲν ἧττον ἂν εἴη ἱστορία τις μετὰ μέτρου ἢ ἄνευ μέτρων): ἀλλὰ τούτῳ διαφέρει, τῷ τὸν μὲν τὰ γενόμενα [5] λέγειν, τὸν δὲ οἷα ἂν γένοιτο. διὸ καὶ φιλοσοφώτερον καὶ σπουδαιότερον ποίησις ἱστορίας ἐστίν: ἡ μὲν γὰρ ποίησις μᾶλλον τὰ καθόλου, ἡ δ᾽ ἱστορία τὰ καθ᾽ ἕκαστον λέγει. (For the in-text translation above, however, see Aristotle, *Poetics*, ix, trans. Leon Golden [UF Press, 1982].)

So, I think, positively no reason to be jealous. And it's your fault, Knut—yours, writer's, liar's, thief's—not mine. What's mine is guilt. You're the cause. Guilt, like correlation, need not imply causation.[154]

But guilt helps: I open the—it's locked—I unlock the door, then open it, then enter, then shut, then lock. Inside, I'm back to stand and stuck. I drop my suitcase.

As the suitcase, full of student papers and Catholic textbooks, falls to my feet, I decide to be nice to you: Suitcase, almanac of my life—A? or B? or C? or D? or F? is it right? is it wrong?—as my life, as the suitcase, full of rights and wrongs, falls, I decide on nice. Nice, even though my suitcase doesn't really hit the floor, but falls on a pile of your shit, crunched beer cans, and Pizza Hut delivery boxes, reminders of the past week's astounding dinners, of my astonishment that so much grease could be contained, at room temperature, in a solid cohesive food product, grease that sounds so good now, those drops of hot yellow grease on a slice of pepperoni sounding now like drops of fine cognac, grease for which we'd maxed-out our—no, *my*—fourth and final credit card. And I am hungry. But there is no food. Credit cards aren't edible, and you've already scavenged the bottoms of the boxes for stale bits of cheese and leftover crusts I don't eat. But the cash for Keystone, where did you scavenge for that?

Nice, even though, dearest Dead Writer, you shouldn't be sitting at dead Dad's oak Art Deco desk, a beer can—without coaster—on the desktop, beer can's condensation dripping inches away from the laptop, my Apple laptop, the last thing we—no, I—own that Mussolini's would remotely consider (Mussolini's Pawn Shop, a museum for poor people's shit, to which I often go, because it feels like home, a museum to which I'd sell myself, if I could, to be with all my things), but no, you need my laptop, into which you now transcribe her *Requiem* from a cacographic score you treat like a sacred manuscript, reverently, unlike my house, everything I own, and me. Nice, even though, Knut, you shouldn't be here, should be at work, at the hospital, milking my mother for all she's worth, even though I am jealous—me, I decide on nice.

Your face stays fixed to the monitor. "Happy Friday the Thirteenth," says the back of your head.

"Thanks," I say. I do not mention that you're full crap—today is Wednesday, not Friday—nor that the bushy back of your head needs a haircut: mullet not far off. Tonight, I am nice. So I feign a holiday cheer (I prefer thwarting): "And a merry Friday the Thirteenth to you, too."

You ignore my carol-like performance of cheer, your attention fixed to *your* handwritten score of her *Requiem*, a string quartet my mother dictates to you (dictates because, apparently, she's lost the use of her right hand...even though the evidence is against her; for, Dead Writer, I spy on you, have espied her right hand's ability to light cigarettes without any problem, nor any regard for the NO SMOKING policies of hospitals), her dictation of a "Death Mass" you now enter into Finale 2009 (the

[154] Cum hoc ergo propter hoc.

$600 musical notation software, because of which, though eBay cut the price in half, we had to cancel cable), for she is the dictator, but who am I? Her requiem, your novel, you compose them on my laptop, but only save them to your flash drive (just one gig, so pawnshop wouldn't take it), this novel which, Dead Knut, you never let me see, even though you *use* me, your prostituted research tool—no, I don't give a damn about the Death Mass—the novel, though, I deserve that. But I've been trained: Standing here, just inside the front door of my house—jealous—I won't sneak a glimpse of your "work," for which, it seems, my mother functions as confidante, artistic director, life coach—whatever she is, not a mother—and thus trained, standing here, standing her, I know that my options are limited, restricted to four cardinal directions (forward, backward, left, right), that all filaments extending from me lead to dynamite, that, standing here, even though all I need is a place to grade papers, I'm stuck, all four options bound to terminate symmetrically in adversity, until, option launched, the symmetry breaks and I plunge into a vacuum state, into some potential minima, because, whatever choice I make, it's the worst one, because, standing here, stuck, I know that all roads lead to spontaneously broken fields, much like the Mexican Hat Potential:[155]

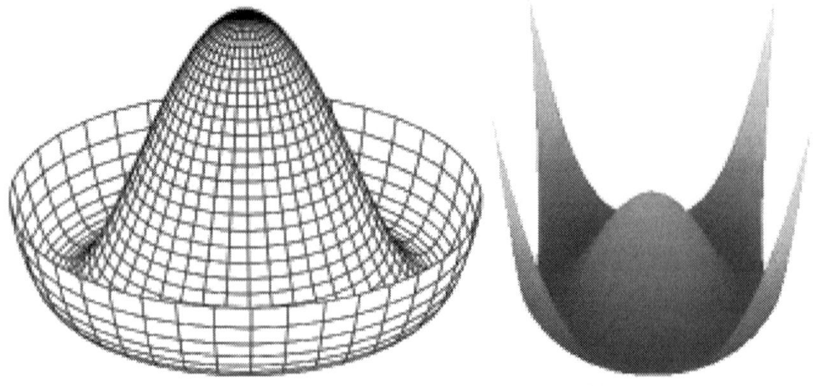

6.6*a*) hat-like **6.6*b*) less hat-like**

Figure 6.6. Spontaneous symmetry breaking. (Mexican Hat Potential.)

For I know that, if I choose the *Right Cardinal Direction*, if I approach you in the dining room, if I walk around the dining room's bookcase/table[156] to the far wall, to Dad's desk, and if I there stand behind you

[155] No, Dead Knut, this graph of the potential term, $V(\varphi) = -10|\varphi|^2 + |\varphi|^4$ in the Lagrangian $L = \partial\mu\varphi\partial\mu\varphi - V(\varphi)$, may not have much to do with my being so intimidated by you I can't move. But it is the simplest example I know in scalar field theory of spontaneous symmetry breaking, with the potential energy term, $V(\varphi)$, having multiple minima (or vacuum states) given by $\varphi = \sqrt{5}e^{i\theta}$ for θ in $[0, 2\pi]$.

[156] A Thanksgiving leftover: See Part 1 of "The guilt surrounding the death of my mother."

and peer over your shoulder within a 6-foot radius, your orbit of tolerance, your plume of permissibility, at a range where my eyes and contacts can see the world how others do, I know you'll then shut off the monitor, until I retreat, like an idiot, like the screen-going-black is a barrage of heat-seeking missiles, know that my mere entry into the—my—dining room will cause "unnecessary" tension. So I have three options left: (1) the *Left Cardinal Direction*: the living room to grade at the "library table," i.e., your altar-like stack of boxes of books I'm not allowed to touch, or (2) the *Forward Cardinal Direction*: the short hallway to the bedroom to grade on the bed we rarely share, not since you started working graveyard shift at the hospital, the bed where I can't grade, where student papers become sleeping pills without danger of addiction, or finally, (3) the *Backward Cardinal Direction*: the door out, where I'll spend more time standing, stuck.

But tonight, I am nice, so I can sit in a chair. I pick up my suitcase and dare to occupy the dining room's kitchen-end chair, one of the bookcase/table's two, the wicker chair, facing your back, at a radial distance with monitor as origin of at least eight feet, far beyond the requisite six-foot perimeter from you, across the "table," at the Dad's-desk end.

I sit. However, on my end of the bookcase/table (your side, empty and bare, except for a couple beer cans and a bowl of empty peanut shells), there are eclectic stacks of library books. *Sample Stack*:

Gertrude Stein's *Geography and Plays*
Albert Einstein's *Die Grundlage der allgemeinen Relativitätstheorie*
Homer's *Odyssey*
Anatoly Karpov's *The Semi-Closed Games in Action*
Catullus' *The Poems of Catullus* (in Latin)
Serge Lang's *Algebra*
Ludwig van Beethoven's *Symphony Number Five in C Minor, Opus 67*

I need space to grade. Objective evaluation needs space. Still seated, I push the stacks toward the middle of the bookcase/table.

You spin around on your—my—office chair, as if my sliding of the stacks were an alarm, had been startling, like a gunshot, like lightning striking.

"Thought I'd grade in here, tonight." The tone of my voice, absurdly singsong—like a kindergarten teacher—makes me sick.

Your eyebrows, those thin, dark, high-arching eyebrows, they seem suspicious of my newfangled kindergarten handicap. But you still spin *slowly* back to face my laptop—slowly, like a planet rotating on its axis, and I want to revolve with that rotation, revolve at the pace that fixes your face, so it stays in sight, that fuses my revolution to a fixed point on your face. And it wouldn't matter that the surface of face moves faster than I do, because that's what happens when you revolve from a distance, because crawling down the revolving radius from me to you, my instantaneous velocity increases. Yes, I need a revolution.

Instead, over the stacks of books, I get to see the back of your head, which still needs a haircut, and the trapezius region of your skeleton, which needs muscle—though frightfully loud is your hammered clicking of the mouse and heavy-handed pounding of the keyboard of my fragile laptop.[157] And I want to say: Go ahead, put as many dents in my keyboard as you can. In the end, your jackhammering achieves nothing.

But I am nice, so I let you destroy my laptop, and remove the manila envelope of second-period pre-Algebra midterms and a red pen from my suitcase. Beginning with the top exam in the stack, I discover that this Catholic high-school student has chosen to scribe her "solutions" in neon-orange ink:

Question 1: Divide the expression $\frac{3i}{2+i}$. Write the final answer in standard form.

Answer 1: $\frac{3i}{2+i} = \frac{3i}{2} + \frac{3i}{i} = 3 + 1.5i$

Midterms: My questions are fixed, but student answers vary: I want a world where questions have single answers, and I don't care if they're right or wrong—as long as there's only one.[158] Be nice: I write a question mark in the right margin and a 0/5 in the left, my red primary-colored ink clashing hideously with the neon secondary-colored orange. I can't take it. I focus on the back of your head. Nice. Nice…

"Do you need any help?" I ask.

"No," says the back of your head.

"It's so nice of you to help Mom with her *Requiem*."

You spin around again. Eyebrows, stitched with suspicion, picking up a pleasant signal coincident with the word "Mom:" Your antenna's not used to picking up waves of pleasantry. My pleasantness has poor reception.

I smile. "Especially with your working *double*-shifts in the kitchen." And I don't say: Why aren't you at work? Nor: You better have a damn good reason to be skipping your second hospital shift.

Now, your eyebrows seem to be frightened. I smile, and your antenna picks up a horror film: From my lips to your eyebrows, the waves become corrupted, the reception is wrong. You attach a lisp to my lips. But once again, you revolve slowly back to the screen. And it's the back of your borderline-mullet head that says, "Yeah, well, I got to get the rest of this entered before tomorrow. Surgery coming up. And she wants to show the 'Dies Irae' to her astrologer."

"Ridiculous." I (unfortunately, perhaps) giggle. So I regroup: "Poor old *thing*," I say, exerting

[157] Cf. Dr. Peng S. Long's typing skills in Excerpt 5.1.

[158] And no matter how much you abhor imaginary numbers, this division problem has a single answer: $\frac{3}{5} + \frac{6}{5}i$

the self-control to not say *bitch*. "Poor Mom, I mean, as if that'd help."

Silence. You mute the volume. Neither keys nor mouse clicking. Now, we are a silent film. I surmise, however, that the silence could yet be attributed to my giggle. Yes, Knut, my sense of humor is, has always been, perhaps...different from yours. But I am not yours to be evaluated. I am not wax to carve, not clay to mold—I have already been fired. You have no right to mute me.

Finally, the back of your head has something to say: "She's sick. I think she's allowed an eccentricity or two." Back to pounded keys and stabbed mouse. I'm not sure how much more abuse they—I—can take. It doesn't always have to be a decomposition reaction.

I return to grading, where evaluations are simple. I give no partial credit. But the neon-orange ink is too much. Even if I weren't grading with red ink, the neon-orange is outrageous, abominable, a deliberate affront, especially after my clear mandate (also written across the top of the midterm) that all exams be completed in pencil. Too much. This Catholic ninth-grader is just asking for an F. But I am nice, so I toss the pre-Algebra stack back into the suitcase. Calculus, I decide...

The top midterm exam of my fifth-period Calc class has not been defiled with neon-orange, but pencil—yes, good—but the student's handwriting is small, smaller than I'd thought possible for any mechanical pencil or surgical instrument, the pencil marks like a product of nanotechnology, like reading an invisible odorless gas, like reading the protein markers on a cell's surface with the naked eye:

Question 1: Find an equation of the tangent line to each of the following curves at the indicated point.

a. $y = \tan x$ at $x = \pi/4$

b. $x\sin(xy - y) = \dfrac{x-y}{y}$ at (1,1)

Answer 1: [This is the exception. It's blank...I think.]

Question 2: Let $z = \tan\dfrac{x}{2}$. Prove that $\dfrac{dx}{dz} = \dfrac{2}{1+z^2}$.

Answer 2: [This one also *looks* blank...]

Question 3: Differentiate each of the following functions:

a. $y = \cot(4-3x)$. b. $f(x) = \sin^3 \cos\dfrac{x}{3}$.

Answer 3: a. $\dfrac{dy}{dx} = -4\sec^2(3x-4)(3) = -12\sec^2(3x-4)$

b. $f'(x) = \dfrac{1}{3}\sin^2(\sin\dfrac{x}{3})\dfrac{1}{3}\cos^2(\cos\dfrac{x}{3})\dfrac{-1}{3}(-\sin\dfrac{x}{3}) = \dfrac{1}{27}\sin^3\dfrac{x}{3}\sin^2(\sin\dfrac{x}{3})\cos^2\left(\dfrac{\cos x}{3}\right)$

I write a "?!" in the margin of Question 3,[159] then three 0/5's, one by each of Problems 1 through 3. My eyes (and contacts) deserve a break, eyeballs forced to focus so hard they've turned to cubes. I allow

[159] Similarly, the derivatives of the expressions in Question 3 have unique standard forms:

myself to look up at the urgently-needing-a-trim back of your head and bony trapezius, just above your ridiculous collection of books which—yes, Knut, you might as well accept it—you'll never read, or, at most, will open, point to a page, and ask me to explain it (that is, by asking, "What do *you* think this means?"). You've signed a lease on my brain, but I'm still the one making the payments. But nice. Tonight's Nice Night...

"So I see you've been doing a lot of reading. Doing a little research? Starting a new section of your novel?"

Back of head: "No."

"So, just reading for pleasure?"

"No."

"For inspiration?"

"No."

"For intellectual enhancement?"

"No."

"For taking up table space to piss me off and ignore me?"

The 180-degree rotation is fast. And eyebrows have no reason to be suspicious—this is what they're used to—but your face, your face is blank, blank like I'm staring at blinds, at a curtain, like the play's performance has started, but some idiot forgot to raise the curtain. And yes, I slipped up, but you, Dead Writer, were not being nice, and this face (or lack thereof) is new, and its implications, that you've learned self-control, a trait you didn't exhibit before—before that crazy old bitch barged into your—our—my—life. And moreover, you now say what you're thinking, unnecessarily bring up things that don't need to be brought up, which is not nice: "They're for your mother. If you must know, she gave me a list of things she never had a chance to learn and always wanted to. But would like to before she dies."

"That's ridiculous. How's she supposed to learn grad-level abstract algebra in a day?"

"Who cares?"

"But it won't mean anything."

"Again, so what?"

"It'll just look like nonsense. Probably just make her more depressed."

Answer 3a: $\frac{dy}{dx} = -\csc^2(4-3x)(-3) = 3\csc^2(4-3x)$

Answer 3b: $f'(x) = 3\sin^2(\cos\frac{x}{3})\cos(\cos\frac{x}{3})(-\sin\frac{x}{3})\frac{1}{3} = -\sin\frac{x}{3}\sin^2(\cos\frac{x}{3})\cos(\cos\frac{x}{3})$

You revolve back to back of head, and then, only then, in the context of my being unnecessarily reminded that you need a haircut, that you might even be growing a mullet on purpose, just to irritate me, same as how you bite off bottle caps with your teeth and chew un-ground coffee beans, how you want to see me explode, be your rhapsody, your chaos and catastrophe, how these are your theories of love, how you oxidize my reduction just because you want a chemical reaction, how you're full of shit, how the world can be chaotic, catastrophic, but I cannot, how I am in control—have to be—because the world is not, and it's in this context of my being unnecessarily reminded that you're full of shit that you say, "You know, dear, you really need to lighten up."

Your telling me to lighten up is heavy. Not nice. Definitely not. And as we know, *dear* Dead Knut, I never lose my temper—am not allowed to—much less my self-control, but that little attack of yours, that overtly belligerent statement, was quite unnecessary. So I make an exception: I stand up and accidentally knock over my wicker chair. I am embarrassed. So I cross the forbidden boundary, invade radial-ly less-than-six-foot-with-monitor-as-origin territory—monitor goes black—and then camouflage my accidental awkwardness by purposefully throwing, one at a time, your twenty-plus library books across the room, into the kitchen (instead of at your head), until finally, no books left, I stand right beside you and have no idea what to do next. So I get to the point, and we have a conversation that goes something like this:

"Well, *dear*," I say, "I'm so sorry, but we're broke."

You stand up, but your face stays blank, insinuates that you're in control and I'm not. Your blank face is a slap in the face. "I know," you say.

"Good. But we need money."

"I know."

"And need it, right now, or we lose the—my house."

"I know."

"What? How?"

"I saw the notice."

"Oh. That's nice. But frankly, *dear*, what's under discussion here is that maybe—just maybe—it's time to ask her for the money."

"But she's up for surgery. Now's not the right time."

"Fine. What about the hospital?"

"Already gave me an advance."

"Oh. I know that. But did you—?"

"Look, it's not like they'll just hand us fifteen-grand."

"Well, we can use all the help we can get. And, homeless or not, we need to eat. And it's not fifteen, it's less.[160] So just get what you can."

"I can't."

"What do you mean, *can't*?"

"I got fired."

"What?" And now, Knut, it's at this point that I have the ability to be neither nice nor not nice. I just have the ability to take two steps, pick up the wicker chair, stand it up on its legs, then sit on it and say, "What?"

You sit in the office chair and scoot next to me. You are too close. I do not look at you, but I can feel you too close to me. Feel the heat and potent odor of your bony un-bathed body. I dissolve. You are my solvent. And I am solute. But we do not form a solution. And what you say is what you think. "Look, you're the one who told me to spend more time with her."

"I know."

"And told me to speed it up."

"I know."

"To get her ripe for the big one."

"I know."

"Well, I guess the manager just got tired of me not doing a damn thing, OK? So it's not my fault."

"I know." I turn to look at you. Our heads nearly collide. No mapmaker could draft the topology of your look. It is the same blank face as before, but blank is not right. I can't filter your look. The osmotic pressure between us is irrelevant. I capture no filtrate, no sediment, nothing settles. I can't isolate your parts, can't label them, can't split you up into a line spectrum, can't label the frequencies of your look. I am no prism. No spectrometer. And blank is not right. There is control, but control is not right. And neither is confidence, nor resolution, nor decision, nor stability, nor calm, nor nothing. It is none of these things. None. But perhaps it is all of them at once. Perhaps it is all of them (and more of them, far more that haven't occurred to me), all of them, but an awareness, your awareness, your consciousness, of none of them. Unconsciously, you just are them all. You just are—you, not the writer; word, not its spelling; alphabet, not the letters; the color of minor/major, not the scale's notes; ellipse, not $(x - h)^2/a^2 + (y - k)^2/b^2 = 1$, with semimajor axis a and semiminor axis b, and center (h, k);[161] the waltz's dance, not its rhythm; death, not the tumor; the requiem, not the voices; chance, not probability; conclusion, not the premise; know, not prove, not right, not conclude, not see, not discover, not think,

[160] $14,652.72.

[161] Of course, we could also express the ellipse parametrically by: $x = h + a\cos(t)$ and $y = k + b\sin(t)$ with parameter t on the interval $-\pi < t < \pi$.

just know—I do not know you. Dear Dead Knut, I do not know you. You see through me, and I wonder: Was there anything to see?

And you say: "I'll get the money. She'll give it to me. Don't worry. She'd do anything for me."

"I know."

SECTION SEVEN

SECTION 7
THE END OF BOOK

If you endured the above Prolegomenon to §7, the end of *Book* might make more sense. Or not. Regardless, it is longish, so the "murder" of my mother has been left as a homework exercise.

Book Excerpt 7.1. ("The Incident" According to Claire [Part 1 of 3].) *Concerning what Claire's mom must have been thinking, twenty-seven days and eleven years ago...*

I hope he'll be OK, if he eats me.

Book Excerpt 7.2. (C_4 = {to, be, or, not}.) *Concerning Slob's ringing a doorbell.*

Without his broken glasses, everything is fuzzy.

Even so, although all this My-Tube-Face/Google-Blog-Book/Space-Tunes.com nonsense is evil and although, after all his circuitous "surfing," the link between the Universal Tube & Rollform Equipment Corporation and her videotaping a dinner party continues to elude him,[162] Slob hasn't spoken to his daughter in a decade, not since "the incident" eleven years ago—this morning's trial run beside a Dumpster doesn't count—so he rings her doorbell.

Should he have rung her doorbell: Yes or no? Yes or no: Life would be simple, if fuzzy logic[163] applied to doors, if doors didn't make life so two-dimensional—so two-sided, so yes/

[162] Knut may be suggesting that Mamma Slob prematurely terminated his "surf" with a perusal of a webpage at, say, uTube.com. However, I suspect that such a surf on May 2, 2007, may be anachronistic: Although the Universal Tube & Rollform Equipment Corporation, an American supplier of tube mills, pipe mills, and roll-forming machines, did receive some publicity when, in August 2006, the company's website received 68 million "hits," causing its computer servers to crash relentlessly, and, subsequently, on October 30, 2006, took legal action against YouTube over the website confusion, it remains that the company has since moved their website to utubeonline.com.

[163] I.e., a multi-valued logic anchored in fuzzy sets to engage reasoning that is approximate, rather than "crisp," and permit a variable's degree of truth to range from 0 to 1, just as fuzzy sets assign a degree of membership to its elements. For the birth of fuzzy set theory, see L. Zadeh, "Fuzzy sets," *Information and Control* 8 (1965): 338-53.

no, true/false, to-be/not-to-be, before/after—if "the incident" weren't the door-like axis of symmetry between all these perfidious pitchfork-bifurcating dualities, if all (two) roads didn't lead to calamitous pre- and post-incident incidents which may or may not concern sugar beets and hence, ineluctably, politics.[164] Yes or no: Should he run away?

Be positive: Slob, you're old—senior citizens don't *run* away—the sunset's pretty, rarely do you see sugar beets at dinner parties, and Bisera needs you. Her letter said so. The letter (i.e., scribble on the back of a Wal-Mart receipt delivered via Crazy Youth) made this need quite clear (i.e., clear from what Slob remembers of a single reading, given that the pigments/dyes of the letter's ink were soluble in the urine of his Siamese cat, Ramanujan): *Need you, Daddy*, she'd written (or had she written "Slob"?); *please come to dinner tonight*; *you add scientific touch*; *filming a dinner party of artsy* (was "artsy" the word?) *friends to post on Tube-Space* (or was it "Tube-Face"?); *need to get past it* (unnecessary reference to "the incident"); *miss you so much* (i.e., "just come"); *love, Bisera* (i.e., if she had written her name, she'd have written "Claire," which, as post-incident name change, would have been another inappropriate reference to "it").

There is laughter behind the door—*Stay positive*: Her home, despite the noisy nightclub (Gator's Something?) on the ground floor, appears to be a splendid example of Second Empire architecture, and here, basking in the eclectic splendor of Napoleon's historic district at the top of the back-alley stairs rising to her second-floor flat, neither father nor daughter would dream of mentioning "the incident," nor post-incident repercussions (e.g., her use of laptop as a weapon).

Footfalls, heavy, behind the door—*Think positive*: He could drop dead at any moment. And this could be his last chance to apologize for everything, to tell her his tumor is—[165]

The deadbolt clicks—*Think more positive*: Even if it's his second-to-last chance, supposing he were to run away, just think of all that sweat—literally—all for nothing: How sweating, he scrubbed his white shirt with bleach, and then, having hung his wet shirt to air-dry above the stove's burners turned on high, he sweat some more as he blacked-out the bleach stains in his black slacks with a Magic Marker; how sweating, he scoured his stacks of math

[164] This relation between sugar beets and politics will be explored later, after "dinner," in Excerpt 7.6.

[165] For students of plot, this break is significant.

books for something “artsy”—for a single “artsy” thought—something with which he could impress her “artsy” friends, could make Bisera proud, but the only “artsy” texts he could find were Kant’s *Critique of Pure Reason* (how can reason be pure?), Usha Jain’s *Intermediate Hindi Reader* (which he can’t read), and Julian Jayne’s *The Origin of Consciousness in the Breakdown of the Bicameral Mind* (which he opened to a promising chapter titled “Of Poetry and Music,” but promptly shut when he reached the third paragraph that begins “I shall state my thesis plain. The first poets were gods.”), and hence, duly frustrated and sweating, he stepped outside his trailer for a breath of fresh afternoon air (and a whiff of the sewage treatment plant a mile upstream) and encountered Wolfer, who adjourned his search for the missing shotgun to show Slob a pod-phone device, which Wolfer’d nabbed from the LOST & FOUND bin at work, and with which, sitting on Slob’s cinderblock frontsteps, they “surfed” far and wide the treacherous pages of the World Wide Web, until finally, hours later, their quest for the ever-elusive My-Book-Tube-Face going nowhere, Slob reentered his oven-warmed trailer, collapsed in his rocking chair, and there, sweating, stared at his “wallpaper,” a collage of doodles, mementos, and documents of diverse nature (which, given Ramanujan’s thing for paper, Slob has taped to the walls), things that, though highly distracting (and far from “artsy”), always cheer him up:

a.

$$
\begin{array}{ccccccccccccccccc}
 & & & & & & 1 & + & 2 & = & 3 & & & & & & \\
 & & & & 4 & + & 5 & + & 6 & = & 7 & + & 8 & & & & \\
 & & 9 & + & 10 & + & 11 & + & 12 & = & 13 & + & 14 & + & 15 & & \\
16 & + & 17 & + & 18 & + & 19 & + & 20 & = & 21 & + & 22 & + & 23 & + & 24 \\
. & . & . & . & . & . & . & . & . & = & . & . & . & . & . & . & .
\end{array}
$$

b. A drawing depicting the “spaghettification” of Dean Mendenhall (the guy who fired Slob), whose being sucked into a black hole—its sequence of increasingly stretched Mendenhalls (white) against the black hole (black)—exploits chiaroscuro effectively.

c. 8589934592 × 116415321826934814453125 = 1000000000000000000000000000000000.

d. The juxtaposition of a poster of Pascal’s triangle (11¼” × 11¼”) beneath a hard-to-find photo of a young Irene Papas (7” × 11¼”), her photo taped precisely beneath the poster so edge lengths conform to the golden ratio.

e. “There are three signs of senility. The first is that a man forgets his theorems. The second sign is that he forgets to zip up. The third is that he forgets to zip down.” —Paul Erdos.

f. The "Notice of Summary Suspension" of his driver's license disclosing a BAC of 0.214.

g. The relics of abandoned research projects: a collection of overdue library notices for Stephen Baskerville's *Taken into Custody: The War Against Fathers, Marriage, and the Family* (2007), as well as the loose-leaf pages—pages 24 to 27 that Slob ripped out of *The Family Law Section*, Vol. XX, No. 1, Fall/Winter 2003—of J. Michael Bone's article "Parental Alienation Syndrome: Examining the Validity amid Controversy."[166]

and thus, staring for hours at his wall, that's how it came, the eureka moment, his single "artsy" thought: While contemplating the only literary quote he could think of, he doodled as follows:

to	**be**	**or**	**not**	**to**	**be**	**or**	**not**	**to**	**be**	**or**	**not**	**to**	**be**	**or**	**not**	**...**
be	or	not	to	be	or	not	to	be	or	not	to	be	or	not	to	...
or	not	to	be	or	not	to	be	or	not	to	be	or	not	to	be	...
not	to	be	or	not	to	be	or	not	to	be	or	not	to	be	or	...
to	be	or	not	to	be	or	not	to	be	or	not	to	be	or	not	...
be	or	not	to	be	or	not	to	be	or	not	to	be	or	not	to	...
or	not	to	be	or	not	to	be	or	not	to	be	or	not	to	be	...
not	to	be	or	not	to	be	or	not	to	be	or	not	to	be	or	...
to	be	or	not	to	be	or	not	to	be	or	not	to	be	or	not	...
be	or	not	to	be	or	not	to	be	or	not	to	be	or	not	to	...
or	not	to	be	or	not	to	be	or	not	to	be	or	not	to	be	...
not	to	be	or	not	to	be	or	not	to	be	or	not	to	be	or	...
to	be	or	not	to	be	or	not	to	be	or	not	to	be	or	not	...
be	or	not	to	be	or	not	to	be	or	not	to	be	or	not	to	...
or	not	to	be	or	not	to	be	or	not	to	be	or	not	to	be	...
not	to	be	or	not	to	be	or	not	to	be	or	not	to	be	or	...
to	be	or	not	to	be	or	not	to	be	or	not	to	be	or	not	...
be	or	not	to	be	or	not	to	be	or	not	to	be	or	not	to	...
or	not	to	be	or	not	to	be	or	not	to	be	or	not	to	be	...
not	to	be	or	not	to	be	or	not	to	be	or	not	to	be	or	...
to	be	or	not	to	be	or	not	to	be	or	not	to	be	or	not	...

[166] It should be noted that parental alienation syndrome is considered a legitimate syndrome by neither the critics of the fathers' rights movement nor the American Psychological Association.

be	or	not	to	be	or	not	to	be	or	not	to	be	or	not	to	…
or	not	to	be	or	not	to	be	or	not	to	be	or	not	to	be	…
not	to	be	or	not	to	be	or	not	to	be	or	not	to	be	or	…
to	be	or	not	to	be	or	not	to	be	or	not	to	be	or	not	…
be	or	not	to	be	or	not	to	be	or	not	to	be	or	not	to	…
or	not	to	be	or	not	to	be	or	not	to	be	or	not	to	be	…
not	to	be	or	not	to	be	or	not	to	be	or	not	to	be	or	…
to	be	or	not	to	be	or	not	to	be	or	not	to	be	or	not	…
be	or	not	to	be	or	not	to	be	or	not	to	be	or	not	to	…
or	not	to	be	or	not	to	be	or	not	to	be	or	not	to	be	…
not	to	be	or	not	to	be	or	not	to	be	or	not	to	be	or	…
to	be	or	not	to	be	or	not	to	be	or	not	to	be	or	not	…
be	or	not	to	be	or	not	to	be	or	not	to	be	or	not	to	…
or	not	to	be	or	not	to	be	or	not	to	be	or	not	to	be	…
not	to	be	or	not	to	be	or	not	to	be	or	not	to	be	or	…
to	be	or	not	to	be	or	not	to	be	or	not	to	be	or	not	…
be	or	not	to	be	or	not	to	be	or	not	to	be	or	not	to	…
or	not	to	be	or	not	to	be	or	not	to	be	or	not	to	be	…
not	to	be	or	not	to	be	or	not	to	be	or	not	to	be	or	…
to	be	or	not	to	be	or	not	to	be	or	not	to	be	or	not	…
be	or	not	to	be	or	not	to	be	or	not	to	be	or	not	to	…
or	not	to	be	or	not	to	be	or	not	to	be	or	not	to	be	…
not	to	be	or	not	to	be	or	not	to	be	or	not	to	be	or	…
to	be	or	not	to	be	or	not	to	be	or	not	to	be	or	not	…
be	or	not	to	be	or	not	to	be	or	not	to	be	or	not	to	…
or	not	to	be	or	not	to	be	or	not	to	be	or	not	to	be	…
not	to	be	or	not	to	be	or	not	to	be	or	not	to	be	or	…
to	be	or	not	to	be	or	not	to	be	or	not	to	be	or	not	…
be	or	not	to	be	or	not	to	be	or	not	to	be	or	not	to	…
or	not	to	be	or	not	to	be	or	not	to	be	or	not	to	be	…
not	to	be	or	not	to	be	or	not	to	be	or	not	to	be	or	…
to	be	or	not	to	be	or	not	to	be	or	not	to	be	or	not	…
be	or	not	to	be	or	not	to	be	or	not	to	be	or	not	to	…

or	not	to	be	or	not	to	be	or	not	to	be	or	not	to	be	…
not	to	be	or	not	to	be	or	not	to	be	or	not	to	be	or	…
to	be	or	not	to	be	or	not	to	be	or	not	to	be	or	not	…
be	or	not	to	be	or	not	to	be	or	not	to	be	or	not	to	…
or	not	to	be	or	not	to	be	or	not	to	be	or	not	to	be	…
not	to	be	or	not	to	be	or	not	to	be	or	not	to	be	or	…
to	be	or	not	to	be	or	not	to	be	or	not	to	be	or	not	…
be	or	not	to	be	or	not	to	be	or	not	to	be	or	not	to	…
or	not	to	be	or	not	to	be	or	not	to	be	or	not	to	be	…
not	to	be	or	not	to	be	or	not	to	be	or	not	to	be	or	…
to	be	or	not	to	be	or	not	to	be	or	not	to	be	or	not	…
be	or	not	to	be	or	not	to	be	or	not	to	be	or	not	to	…
or	not	to	be	or	not	to	be	or	not	to	be	or	not	to	be	…
not	to	be	or	not	to	be	or	not	to	be	or	not	to	be	or	…
to	be	or	not	to	be	or	not	to	be	or	not	to	be	or	not	…
be	or	not	to	be	or	not	to	be	or	not	to	be	or	not	to	…
or	not	to	be	or	not	to	be	or	not	to	be	or	not	to	be	…
not	to	be	or	not	to	be	or	not	to	be	or	not	to	be	or	…
to	be	or	not	to	be	or	not	to	be	or	not	to	be	or	not	…
be	or	not	to	be	or	not	to	be	or	not	to	be	or	not	to	…
or	not	to	be	or	not	to	be	or	not	to	be	or	not	to	be	…
not	to	be	or	not	to	be	or	not	to	be	or	not	to	be	or	…
to	be	or	not	to	be	or	not	to	be	or	not	to	be	or	not	…
be	or	not	to	be	or	not	to	be	or	not	to	be	or	not	to	…
or	not	to	be	or	not	to	be	or	not	to	be	or	not	to	be	…
not	to	be	or	not	to	be	or	not	to	be	or	not	to	be	or	…
to	be	or	not	to	be	or	not	to	be	or	not	to	be	or	not	…
be	or	not	to	be	or	not	to	be	or	not	to	be	or	not	to	…
or	not	to	be	or	not	to	be	or	not	to	be	or	not	to	be	…
not	to	be	or	not	to	be	or	not	to	be	or	not	to	be	or	…
to	be	or	not	to	be	or	not	to	be	or	not	to	be	or	not	…
be	or	not	to	be	or	not	to	be	or	not	to	be	or	not	to	…
or	not	to	be	or	not	to	be	or	not	to	be	or	not	to	be	…

not	to	be	or	not	to	be	or	not	to	be	or	not	to	be	or	…
to	be	or	not	to	be	or	not	to	be	or	not	to	be	or	not	…
be	or	not	to	be	or	not	to	be	or	not	to	be	or	not	to	…
or	not	to	be	or	not	to	be	or	not	to	be	or	not	to	be	…
not	to	be	or	not	to	be	or	not	to	be	or	not	to	be	or	…
to	be	or	not	to	be	or	not	to	be	or	not	to	be	or	not	…
…	…	…	…	…	…	…	…	…	…	…	…	…	…	…	…	

a doodling which triggered the discovery that the set $G = \{to, be, or, not\}$, with binary operation $\bullet : G \times G \rightarrow G$, forms a group $(G, \bullet)$ isomorphic to the cyclic group generated by the element *be*, $C_4 = < be >$, with identity element *to*, and produces the group table

Table 7.1. {to, be, or, not}

•	**be**	**or**	**not**	**to**
be	*or*	*not*	*to*	*be*
or	*not*	*to*	*be*	*or*
not	*to*	*be*	*or*	*not*
to	*be*	*or*	*not*	*to*

a discovery which is perhaps why, sweating, he's half-an-hour late to Bisera's Tube-Face dinner and why, only now, for the first time, he notices the quarter-sized hole in the crotch of his slacks.

The door handle rotates 45° counterclockwise—*Bisera, who is she?* He can't remember much: Bisera (alt., Claire), she'd been sweet, obsessive, assiduous, silent, had never bugged him while he was busy working (or drinking), had always joined and endured (unlike the wife) his chalkboard parties, and, though too skinny, had never been a fan of sugar beets. He hopes she got past all that. Hopes she rebelled against her parents who weren't there. Hopes she's learned to hate her father, because if she has, she will be OK and, if she is, he will be ready to die.

Comfort is a closed door. It opens.

Book Excerpt 7.3. ("The Incident" According to Claire [Part 2 of 3].) *Concerning what Claire's mom must have thought next, twenty-seven days and eleven years ago...*

I rubbed myself all over with a dead rabbit. He seems to appreciate this—he *is* strangling me to death—but what if he eats me, too? I should have washed my clothes first. True, it was a rabbit, so no chance of Salmonella, but what about me, what if I have parasites? Who will take care of him? Who will notice the signs: mouthrot, respiratory infection, stargazing? What if he chokes on me? I will try to keep still, keep calm, but what if I lose control during the digestion process? What if his digestive juices get into my brain, make me lose my mind, and I try to claw my way out of his stomach like an alligator? No, he knows to kill me first, but I'm definitely not a healthy choice. I am going to make him so fat.

Book Excerpt 7.4. (Slob's "Last Chalkboard Supper" According to Claire.) *Concerning Knut's fictionalization of my childhood home as Claire's memory of the hours leading up to "the incident," her recollection prompted by her father's ringing the doorbell.*

The doorbell rings—her father, Slob, who has *apparently* been "ill" for twenty-seven days and eleven years, is now at the door—and suddenly, Claire's wine glass of chilled Evian spring water[167] is a bottle of Tangerine Gatorade, her name is Bisera, and she is seventeen.

And instead of a windowless white dining room furnished with one white china cabinet, one camera tripod, eleven white chairs at a round-ish table, and one dead plant in a white porcelain vase, we have her childhood's dining-slash-living-slash-music-slash-laundry-slash-Dad's-bedroom-slash-kitchen-slash-library furnished with books, bookshelves covering every inch of wall and more books stacked-slash-piled everywhere—every surface, covered with books—except for the rim of the sink around which Mom's African fertility sculptures huddle, the pile of unfolded laundry on top of the dryer, and the most recently traveled paths between stove, fridge, table, and door (and, obviously, the large hole in the floor by the washing machine from which, of late, though primarily at night, a possum has been known to emerge).

Granted, it may not have been that bad. But one thing is certain: Touching books can be disastrous. For although the piles of books may suggest a chaotic distribution, Mom assures them (Dad and Claire) that every text has its place, according to the call number classification

[167] Knut was fond of noting that, backwards, Evian is naïve.

system of the Library of Congress. And they don't argue with her, because, from memory (even though books haven't been labeled with call numbers, nor have piles with corresponding ranges), she can identify the (sub)division letters and number sets of each and every volume and, thus, according to the twenty-one major divisions of the Library of Congress' classification system,[168] has renamed their four rooms and bathroom as follows:

a. Claire's room = the LMUV-room: *Education* (L), *Music* (M), *Military Science* (U), and *Naval Science* (V).
b. Mom's room = the ADEFNP-room: *General Works* (A), *History* (D, E, & F), *Fine Arts* (N), and *Language and Literature* (P).
c. Dad's Office (i.e., Barney's room) = the QRST-room (i.e., "Cursed-room"): *Science* (Q), *Medicine* (R), *Agriculture* (S), and *Technology* (T).
d. The bathroom = the GZ-room (an unsuccessful pun, given that the topic *Masturbation* [HQ 447] is in the dining-kitchen-etc.-room): *Geography, Anthropology, Recreation* (G) and *Library Science and Information Resources* (Z), with G containing, notably, the topic *Nudism, Sunbathing* (GV 450), a subdivision of *Physical Education and Training* (GV 201-555), a subdivision of *Recreation, Leisure* (GV 1-1860).
e. The dining-kitchen-etc.-room = the BCHJK-room: *Philosophy, Psychology, Religion* (B), *Auxiliary Sciences of History* (C), *Social Sciences* (H), *Political Science* (J), and *Law* (K).

And although, over the years, adolescent Claire gains a working knowledge of her house's organization as Library of Congress, Dad's retention of divisions by letter (much less number) is quite poor, limited to neologisms that *he* finds humorous and/or necessary for survival:

1. The topic *The Bible* is denoted BS.
2. *Indexes (General)*, denoted by AI, reflects Mom's "Artificial Intelligence."
3. *Slavic*, denoted PG, suggests "Parental Guidance."
4. And perhaps more seriously, when Mom says, "We're out of chemical technology," she means, "Out of toilet paper," given that *Chemical Technology* is denoted TP.

So, naturally, touching books results in mass hysteria.

And finally, instead of a father ringing a doorbell (her father, who, according to the

---

[168] I.e., given the five unused letters I, O, W, X, Y.

nudist slobber Torbjorn, has been "out of touch" for twenty-seven days and eleven years because he's been "ill"[169]) and a troop of asexuals getting intoxicated before tonight's YouTube film shoot (the script for which is now being revised extensively, at the very last minute, to address her poor father's lengthy "illness"), we have a seventeen-year-old Claire, a missing mother—still refusing to come to dinner, still sulking in Dad's "study" with Barney—and three plastered math professors (Dad included), nibbling silently on peanuts, and spilling their beer and bourbon more and more frequently, as they—transfixed—squint at Dad's mobile chalkboard, which now also belongs in this all-purpose room, ever since Mom designated Dad's study the construction site for Barney's new cage (Barney being Mom's 22-year-old, 22-foot-long, 235-pound Burmese Python, and "Prometheus A. Barney" being, of course, Dad's clever anagram of "Are A Burmese Python"). For instead of Claire's imminent "YouTube dinner party," we have the penultimate stage of Dad's "chalkboard party"—of *the* chalkboard party, on the night of "the incident," twenty-seven days and eleven years ago[170]—the penultimate stage when, finally, father and math colleagues notice that Bisera (alt., Claire) exists and, alas, attempt to include her in the dinner-table conversation (dinner being bourbon, beer, peanuts, and Tangerine Gatorade).

<u>CHALKBOARD PARTY</u>: A TECHNICAL DEFINITION

1. *Prerequisite for Chalkboard Party*: No Mom. Absence of matriarch arising from a pre-dinner fight between Mom and Dad of such cataclysmic magnitude that Mom refuses to cook dinner, shuts herself in Barney's room, and there waits for Dad to knock on the door and apologize (which, ever since Claire learned to talk "effectively," never happens, because, once Dad and Company pass out, Claire will knock on the door to "fix things").
2. *Chalkboard Party Stage One*: Dad's math colleagues arrive—arrive promptly (having received the call/signal: "Wife out of picture")—and Dad gives them all a beer.
3. *Stage Two*: They drink beer (Dad drinks bourbon) and attempt small talk: "How's work?" "Oh, you know, work's fine." "And the wife and kids?" "Fine, fine." … "But, boy, these peanuts are good." "Yep, darn good peanuts." "Nothing like a peanut." "Nope."

[169] Actually, what Torbjorn said was: "I don't know if this Slob's your dad or what. But I *helped*, like you fuckin' asked. And he's been ill. Why he's been out of touch. So maybe he's lying, stalking you or—" (Book Excerpt 6.1).

[170] So it's Friday, April 5, 1996?

… "Helluva drought." "Yep, farmers hurting this year." "Yep, probably even peanut farmers."

4. *Stage Three*: Silence. Dad serves more beer and bourbon and replenishes the peanut bowl.
5. *Stage Four*: Silence. Then somebody says, "You guys see that Putnam Problem #3, the graph theory one?" "Nope, sure didn't. Wish I had." "Well, actually, I got it right here."
6. *Stage Five*: The party really picks up: Dad and colleagues solve math problems on the chalkboard, their ebullient efforts interrupted if and only if (a) beer and peanuts run out or (b) standing up becomes problematic.
7. *Stage Six*: Standing up is impossible. And, no matter how tenaciously they stare at the chalkboard from the dining table, their discussion soberly (albeit inebriated-ly) drifts to woman problems and related topics. The following, often revisited examples made a profound impression on teenage Claire:
    a. Incest taboo and Claude Lévi-Strauss' "Alliance Theory."[171]
    b. The Fathers' rights movement.
    c. Solon's discriminatory laws against slaves on the issue of pederasty.
    d. The etymology of the word "Cuckold" (from "Cocu," the Old French for Cuckoo bird) and the translation of its Chinese equivalent (戴綠帽) as "wearing a green hat."
    e. Chinese ghost marriages.
    f. The lower divorce rates of mail-order brides in the U.S.
    g. Sexual dimorphism and the relative sizes of testes in the evolution of monogamy.[172]

[171] See Claude Lévi-Strauss' *Les structures élémentaires de la parenté* (1949).

[172] In short, the testes of species with promiscuous mating systems tend to be larger. This trend applies particularly well to the family of primates: Chimpanzees, who enjoy a promiscuous mating system, have significantly larger testes than gorillas, who practice a monogamous mating system, while humans are "the monkey in the middle;" i.e., espousing a socially monogamous mating system, accompanied by moderate amounts of sexual non-monogamy, humans have moderately sized testes. For students new to testes, I recommend beginning with the following texts:

- Birkhead, T.R., *Promiscuity: An Evolutionary History of Sperm Competition* (Harvard University Press, 2000).
- Dixson, A., & Anderson, M., "Sexual selection and the comparative anatomy of reproduction in monkeys, apes, and human beings," *Annual Review of Sex Research* 12 (2001): 121-44.
- Harcourt, A.H., Harvey, P.H., Larson, S.G., & Short, R.V., "Testis weight, body weight and breeding system in primates," *Nature* 293 (1981): 55-57.
- Simmons, L.W., Firman, R.E.C., Rhodes, G., & Peters, M., "Human sperm competition: testis size, sperm

8. *Stage Seven*: Dad pours himself more bourbon and smiles at Claire. The penultimate stage: Claire exists. She knows what's coming. Should she leave: Yes or no?

Dad belches. He reaches for a peanut, but stops. "Dirk? Cornelius?"—Dirk and Cornelius, Dad's math (and only) cronies: one's fat and short, and the other's skinny and shorter, but Claire can never remember which is which—"Boys, what would you say to a little music?"

Though staring at the chalkboard, they both respond in the affirmative with something like, "My dear Watson, what an excellent notion." All it takes is one beer and they're all Sherlock Holmes, and everyone else is Watson, and Dad has a handle of bourbon (1.75 L).

Claire: no response.

"Fates are against you, Watson," says Fat Holmes.

"My dear Watson," says Thin Holmes, "could it be due to a sugar beet?"

"Difficult to say, Watson. Ask Slob, his father was a sugar beet farmer, after all."

This is true about Slobodon's being the son of a sugar beet farmer and is, in fact, the only fact that Claire (or perhaps anyone) knows about her father's past.[173]

"Shush there, Watsons," says Daddy Holmes. Then addresses Claire, the daughter: "Please, Bizzy—just one well-tempered fugue?"

"No," she says. But *no* never works, and it is due to a conversation of the following nature between Fat, Thin, and Daddy Holmes (their stab at "artsy" subject matter the daughter might appreciate) that Claire, eventually, changes her mind: "Probably not well-tempered, my dear Watson." "Watson, it's elementary logic I was referring to Bach's *Well-Tempered Clavier*." "Naturally, Watson, Bach's dead, and this is the modern era of 12-tone-equal-temperament, when even sugar beets are genetically altered." "Truly, Watson, and a tragic one: All of Western music, out-of-tune." "Indeed, Watson, but we wouldn't be wanting a wolf interval."[174] "No, Watson, we wouldn't, nor would any sugar beet farmer." "Wouldn't want Z_{12}-scales generated by more than one element, would we, Watson?" "Ah, Watson, 'these are deeper waters than I

---

production and rates of extrapair copulations," *Animal Behavior* 68 (2004): 297-302.

[173] Nevertheless, the link between sugar beets and politics shall be revealed later, after dinner, in Excerpt 7.6.

[174] I think it's safe to assume that Wolfer is not one of Slob's math cronies: "Wolf interval" is the term for the most out-of-tune interval on the circle of fifths in any tuning system, the interval "sacrificed" for the benefit of all others.

had thought.'" "Fear not, Watson. 'I am a brain. The rest of me is a mere appendix.'" "Must be difficult, my dear Watson, for a brain to drag around such a large appendix."

Claire sits on the piano bench of the black Baldwin upright. She opens Bach's *Well-Tempered Clavier: Book One* to "Fugue 1, C-Major," and, resting her left hand in the middle of the keyboard, ring finger on middle-C, she waits for the Watsons to be quiet: "My dear Watson, 'I am familiar with forty-two different impressions left by tires.'" "Shush, she's gonna play." "What's she playing?" "Sugar beets me." "Looks like we're starting at middle-C…That's 261.626 Hertz." "Shush, Watson, she's ready…"

The Watsons finally shut up. Claire plays Bach's "Fugue 1, C-Major":

9. *Stage Eight*: The Performance (cf. YouTube parties, 27 days and 11 years later):

<u>WHY MOM DIDN'T COME TO DINNER</u>: A BACH FUGUE IN C-MAJOR[175]

from *The Well-Tempered Mom-&-Dad-Never-Say-What-They're-Thinking Klavier: Book I*

by Claire, the daughter

S: Mom Says: "76°F. I leave for six hours and 76°F. Damn it, Slob, it's 78°F, night; 86°F, day;
A:
T:
B:

S: 90°F, basking—can't I trust you with anything?"
A: Mom thinks: *Look at him. Drinking*

A: *already. Not listening. Thinking some math function. Balancing equations between us.*
T: Dad

----

[175] It appears that Claire's performance of Bach's "Fugue 1, C-Major" is Mom and Dad's pre-dinner fight: In Bach's four-part fugue, Knut seems to have first restricted Mom to the soprano and alto voices, and Dad to tenor and bass. Then, by including only fugal subjects (initially in the tonic) and answers (in the dominant) and omitting the rest, subjects/answers expressing a tonic-like function here coincide with spoken dialogue, and those having dominant-like function with tacit thoughts. For further examination of my writer's "method," see Problem 7.2 at Book's end.

T: THINKS: *I'm hungry. She'll overcook my steak; always does when she's angry. She cooks*

T: *shit at whatever temperature it is in Hell.*

B: DAD SAYS: "I'm sorry, honey. Dirk called, and then, it

S: MOM SAYS: "Of course not, go take a

T: DAD THINKS: *How am I gonna*

B: was one thing after another. Poor Barney. Is he OK?"

S: look: He's depressed. You know the cold makes him depressed. And glossy eyes: He's sick."

A: MOM

T: *tell her Dirk's coming to dinner? She'll be angry. Turns everything into a disaster.*

A: THINKS: *Theorems. He's not listening, thinking the math of black holes and astrology—it's*

A: *passive-aggressive. Him thinking math is passive-aggressive.* MOM THINKS: *Pathetic.*

B: DAD SAYS: "Oh, I forgot. Dirk

A: *Passive-aggressive. Inviting dorks just to piss me off. And now, getting drunk to piss me off.*

T: DAD THINKS: *Of course, we could always eat Barney. Been getting fat ever since he*

B: and Cornelius are coming to dinner, but if Barney's sick, we can cancel. Poor Barney."

A: MOM SAYS: "What are you doing?

T: *switched to rabbits. Delicacy in southeast Asia, they say.* DAD THINKS: *Should*

A: Stop. That book belongs in 'The Soul' stack, BL 290. Not BT-98-to-180, that's 'God.' Stop,

T: *probably cut off Barney's head first. Can't eat you without a head. Need an axe. Old Barney*

B: DAD THINKS: *There she goes. Move a book, no dinner. Better*

S: MOM THINKS: *He can't do it. He*
A: you stupid, drunk, unemployed piece of—no, I said stop."
T: *won't hold still. I'm hungry.*
B: *drink more. Although, it's true that last lecture hadn't gone too well.*[176]

S: *knows not to. No, not BL "Religion"—no, no, "Psychology" is BF.* MOM SAYS: "No, no,

----

S: no—stop. That's CC 700-to-705: 'Stone Heaps, Cairns, etc. of Unknown Purpose.' They're
A: MOM THINKS: *No, H is "Social Sciences." He's doing it on purpose, messing up HQ 1-2039*
T: DAD SAYS: "Whoops—sorry, dear—but just look what we got
B: DAD THINKS: *She would organize*

S: organized. You know how much time—no, stop."
A: *"The Family, Marriage, Woman"—passive-aggressive.*
T: in this stack, a family-planning sort of pile. Shit on the family."
B: *them this way: masturbation, family violence, men all in the same pile—passive-aggressive.*

A: MOM THINKS: *No, "Divorce" is HQ 811-to-960.7—why's he doing this?*
T: DAD SAYS: "And look at these. I never knew we had so many books on eunuchs and

----

A: *"Emasculation, Eunuchs, etc.," that's HQ 449, not "Family Violence," HQ 809-to-809.3.*
T: emasculation—oh, sorry, dear—and here we go: This pile's got a lot of divorce in it."

S: MOM THINKS: *I can't. "Destitute, Neglected, and Abandoned Children."*
B: DAD THINKS: *Passive-aggressive. And on top of that, no dinner, for sure...and darnit, frankly,*

S: *It's passive-aggressive. I'm a good mother, and that's HQ 873-to-887.*
T: DAD THINKS: *As if*
B: *eating Barney's going a bit far—but oh, look: Can't forget child abuse.*

----

[176] For final lecture, see Evisceration 4.4, Slob's pre-incident "Reason Y: Barney."

T: *she's any better. So I lost the job. I think I'm entitled to a drink or two. Maybe it's OK to*

S: **[BRIDGE]**
A: **[BRIDGE]** MOM THINKS: *I*
T: *feel a little sorry for myself, for once.* **[BRIDGE]** DAD SAYS: "Honey, are you gonna
B: **[BRIDGE]**

A: *can't. All he does is try to hurt me, me and Barney. Barney needs me, though. Depressed*
T: make dinner or not? You look upset. It's Barney, isn't it? Yeah, I'll fix dinner; you go take
----

A: *probably. Sick probably. Vet probably. Better check on Barney.*
T: care of Barney. Hell, my father was a sugar beet farmer."

THE END

Claire turns the page: Bach's "Prelude 2, C-minor." The party, however, seems to be over...

Time to check on Mom: Claire stands and leaves, tiptoeing around Fat and Skinny Holmes, both of their heads on the table, then over Daddy Holmes, who's lying on the floor, and finally down the short hallway to Dad's (alt., Barney's) study, to Mom—to *fix* things.

She knocks on the QRST-room door. It does not open.

"The incident" begins.

Book Excerpt 7.5. ("The Incident" According to Claire [Part 3 of 3].) *Concerning what Claire's mom must have thought, twenty-seven days and eleven years ago, as Claire pounded on the QRST-room door...*

A dead rabbit is not enough. He wants me to be afraid. I am not. And this, he thinks, is no fun: You are not prey unless you are afraid. I am ruining dinner. He would like it if I screamed. But I feel no flight or fight—*knock at the door*—I do not fear death. But Barney, he needs that, fear—*"Mom?"*—Yes, I am not doing it right. He needs me to fear, to fly, to struggle, to tense one muscle at a time—*knock, knock*—*bang*—Yes, there, that's better: He is tightening, constricting, crushing—*bang: "Mom?"*—Oh God, so tight: This, yes, this is what he needs from me, my role. The role I play in my death. To die, I must be afraid—*bang*—without fear, death will have no—*bang*—God, please, I can't breathe. I am ready—*bang: The door opens.*

Book Excerpt 7.6. (Claire's "YouTube Dinner" According to Slob.) *Concerning Knut's juxtaposition of cryptanalysis, medieval medicine, and elementary linear algebra.*

The door is open.

Blocking Slob's entrance and having an ellipsoid head, a young man—huge, chesty, barefoot—stands in the doorway, silently, and chews a *large* mouthful of something. Even without his glasses, Slob can tell there's something fuzzy about this giant barefoot masticator, who is not his daughter, and whose black tuxedo, along with his dark brown Hitler mustache, accentuates the otherwise blond hair and pasty skin of his large skull, which, with its narrow face, goitrous double-chin, and long blond hair pulled up into a bun, held fixed with chopsticks, and rising like a mound from skull's "north pole," is not merely ovoid, but sublimely elliptic.[177]

Ellipsoid Head finally swallows, then welcomes Slob in an oily high-pitched voice: "You must be Dad, so your name is"—he thrusts a nametag in Slob's face—"Mr. Hilbert Hawking Heisenberg."

Slob takes the nametag, laminated and larger than a four-by-six note card, the name

[177] We should probably attribute Mamma Slob's invocation of the "elliptic" to his missing broken glasses, since otherwise his proposal—mathematically, beginning with a head (in 3-space) whose height (along the z-axis) is probably greater than its width and depth (in the xy-plane), but whose face is "narrow" so the distance from ear to ear (along the x-axis) is likely less than that from back of head to nose (y-axis), and, finally, whose double-chin and chopstick-fixed bun ultimately define an ellipsoid $x^2/a^2 + y^2/b^2 + z^2/c^2 = 1$ with $0 < a < b < c$—is preposterous.

typed in some kind of Old English font. He now notices Ellipsoid's nametag: MR. HOMER HERSTEIN.

"Yeah, we all got different tags for the big show," says elliptic Mr. Homer Herstein, "but we couldn't decide with you being all Einstein and quantum and whatnot, so we gave you a little of each, but—what am I saying?—why don't you come on in and meet the others?"

Slob doesn't move. Ellipsoid seems worried, sad even—yes, his eyes appear to be watering—"It's OK," he says, placing a wide pudgy palm on Slob's shoulder. "We're all real sorry, you know, about your *illness*," he adds, with a watery-eyed wink.

"Illness?" Slob asks. The pudgy palm slides down, to squeeze Slob's bony bicep.

"Yes, yes, we know all about it." Ellipsoid sniffles. "But don't worry, Hilbert, we got the *cure*." A second wink sends tears down his cheek. Slob's bicep is released: Ellipsoid wipes his face, rubbing hard, to remove the tears. He also removes half of his moustache, one side now hanging vertically, perpendicular to his thin crimson lips.

Slob doesn't wish to discuss fake Hitler moustaches. "What cure?" he asks.

"Oh, sorry." Ellipsoid fixes his moustache, then perks up: "Yeah, sorry, but I just ate this whole jar of jalapenos like all at once, and my eyes got all watery."

"Oh," Slob says. "But what do you mean *cure*? I thought it was just dinner?"

"Yep, first we cure you, then it's dinner—didn't you get the text?—but seriously, Bert, come on in," he says, taking back Slob's nametag, "I'm supposed to be in the kitchen." Mr. Herstein pins the nametag on Slob's well-bleached shirt, the tag completely covering the breast pocket, then slaps Slob's shoulder and, slap turned clamp, pulls him inside. The door slams shut behind them. "Haven't started filming, yet. Still working on preparations for *dinner*"—wink—"but the rest of the cast's already taken their seats at the *round table*"—wink—"follow me."

Slob follows Hitler/Homer down a narrow hallway, a bare white wall on their left, while on their right a first then a second doorway open into nearly identical parlors, identically bright and white, the furniture in each camouflaged in white; and Slob, perturbed by (many things, but mostly) false moustaches, continues following Ellipsoid's heavy barefoot flops on the hardwood floor, until they pass through a doorway at the end of the hall, which opens into the *SET*: a windowless white-walled dining room, a large square-shaped room with another doorway, directly opposite the hallway's, opening to a kitchen (most likely), but dining room furnished only with one dead plant on the left wall, a white china cabinet on the right, and a large "round table," at which a daughter and eight other cast members (three with Hitler mustaches) sit in a circle around a toreador, who stands in the center of the room with a video camera on a tripod.

"Everyone, meet Professor Hilbert Hawking Heisenberg—you know, Einstein and shit."

The cast greets Slob with an assortment of nonverbal grunts and gestures signifying "hello," except for (1) a shout of "Dad!" from a short middle-aged Asian man wearing large sunglasses and a sequined bullfighter's costume, and (2) Bisera's (alt. Claire's) nothing.

Ellipsoid continues, "Professor, meet the Napoleon Asexual Society. First off, we got…"

Despite nametags all around, Mr. Herstein proceeds to introduce the predominately asexual cast, and despite his failure to explicate the foreign symbols on the table's twelve place cards (e.g., facing Slob, on the opposite arc of the round table, we have ♑, ♒, ⚮,♈, ♉, ♊), not to mention the gallon-sized bag of what appears to be ketchup by the ⚮ place card of the empty seat beside Bisera, Mr. Herstein's *Homeric* introductions persist…so Slob surveys the *SET*: dead plant on left, cabinet on right, and, in the middle, a toreador surrounded by "round table," which is neither round nor a table, but rather, a collection of six small tables, varying both in the height of their legs and the surface area of their rectangular tabletops, each covered with a white tablecloth, and tables arranged in a circle or ring, around which sits the mostly asexual *CAST*: Suppose the round table is a clock face, so that the positions of its eleven chairs and "the bar" may be assigned a numeral 1 through 12; then we have the following numeric listing of cast member positions, descriptions, and place-card symbols:

1/♈ MLLE GERTRUDE HERSTEIN: fictional daughter of Homer and Alberta; Slob's daughter, Bisera/Claire; dark hair; blue dress, ratio of bare skin to dress is greater than one; President and founder of NAS (Napoleon Asexual Society).

2/♉ N/A: "the bar," the smallest of circle's six tables, at which no one sits, but on which rests an 18-case of Busch Light and three six-packs: Guinness, Purple Haze, Evian.

3/♊ MRS. ALBERTA HERSTEIN: fictional wife of Homer; professor of philosophy; zaftig; no Hitler moustache, but otherwise looks like husband; also wearing tuxedo; V.P. of NAS.

4/♋ N/A: elliptic Mr. Homer Herstein's seat.

5/♌ MR. KARPOV KING: Hitler mustache; preschool administrator; wears leather; shy.

6/♍ Ms. Paula Gram: elderly; born in Indiana, but wearing tweeds and speaking with British accent; collector of Civil War surgical instruments; amateur astrologist; NAS Treasurer.[178]

7/♎ Mr. Ulysses J. Jameson: Hitler mustache; wedding planner; sombrero, but strong Minnesotan accent (frequent *Oh yahs*); born in Duluth, *not* Minneapolis.

8/♏ Ms. Cataline Caesar: employee of morgue for over 25 years; hair hiding eyes and face, to yield inverted paraboloid head;[179] Secretary of NAS.

9/♐ Ms. Alberta Camel: horse face; jogging outfit; college student, wants to major in like psychology or premed or something, if she like doesn't become a lawyer; new to NAS.

10/♑ Mr. Serge Lang: Hitler mustache; cop, not Walrus; not embarrassed by lisp.

11/♒ Mr. Ludwig Hornet: tuxedo, but no Hitler moustache; professor of viola; hairspray; not a member of NAS, and never will be, not ever; fictional fiancée of Gertrude.

12/♓ N/A: Slob's seat; gallon of ketchup.

N/A Mr(s). Peng S. Long: toreador/cameraman at circle center; composer; handwritten "s" added to end of nametag's "Mr.;" spiked hair; giant sunglasses; hiccups.

Introductions complete: awkward silence. Solitary hiccup from toreador.

But no joyful reunion of father and daughter: Slob, standing behind Mr. Jameson's chair (7/♎ o'clock), stares across the room at Bisera (1/♈ o'clock), and for the first time in—well, no, there'd been this morning's brief exchange, cut short by laptop—for the second time in eleven years, his daughter, Bisera, returns his gaze. But Slob doesn't understand her face which, though lacking moustache, makes no effort to welcome him to her Tube-Face dinner party. Nor invite him to his assigned seat beside hers at their table for three, to the empty seat (12/♓) between Mr. Hornet (at 11/♒) and herself (at 1/♈). Instead, the room is silent. And white. Bleached.

Finally, beside Slob, Homer whispers: "As you all know, Mr. Heisenberg is a sick man."

Chuckles erupt from the cast—party atmosphere, restored—so Slob doesn't contradict Ellipsoid, who continues: "That's right, an eleven-year illness like his is no laughing—"

"Dad!" Suddenly, across the room, Bisera stands up, bumping the table—her wine glass of water *rocks*, but Mr. Hornet, his arm lunging across their table's gallon-bag of ketchup,

[178] An apt "characterization" of my dead mother's astrologer.

[179] $z = -(x^2/a^2 + y^2/b^2)$ with $0 < a = b$.

catches and steadies it. "I mean, Homer Dad," she says (as Gertrude), addressing her fictional father (Ellipsoid), "is dinner about ready?"

"Yeah," Homer says, "not really. But almost. Was just adding the finishing touches"—wink—"five more minutes." Walking around the circle of tables, Ellipsoid leaves Slob at the hallway entrance and exits through the opposite doorway. His head is less elliptic from the rear.

"I better help her," Bisera tells the cast. Then bumps her table—"him, I mean. Better help Homer with the *food*." She winks, convulsively, then follows Homer into the kitchen.

"I'm sorry, Professor Heisenberg," says Mrs. Alberta Herstein (3/♊), "but don't worry: Miss Herstein, she's just nervous about the…about your illness. We all are. But perhaps you'd like a beer?" she asks, indicating the bar, the small table (2/♉) beside her seat.

Slob declines: "No," he says. "Thanks, but I don't drink—"

"French water!" shouts the toreador. Mr(s). Peng S. Long abandons his post at center tripod. From a six-pack at the bar, he removes a bottle of water, then holds it above his head and shouts: "Evian, I am French water!" He remains there, by the bar, posed like the Statue of Liberty: arm up, fully extended, with Evian as torch. It seems Slob must go fetch this beverage.

"Yes, perhaps you've met Dr. Long?" Mrs. Alberta Herstein says, wearily, as Slob walks counterclockwise around the circle, behind her table, to the bar, to obtain his water from the toreador. "Professor Long is a composer, you know…his string quartet is an—"

"Bug juice!" The Toreador of Liberty's arm lowers and, from circle's interior, hands the Evian to Slob, now standing across the bar in circle's exterior. "Yes, it true," Long says, "your daughter with the tenure, we is thinking hard to make Kepler into an ant. But it turn out, my string quartet is bug juice, so I drink many of the beer now." Long taps his Busch Light bottle into Slob's unopened Evian, then chugs. "Ah," he finally sighs, "bug juice, I explain it…"

But, as Long proceeds to explicate the "quantum foam" of his bug juice quartet, Slob is distracted by "the bar" between them. Its array of beverages is extraordinary: On this small table (2/♉), there rests, firstly, an 18-case of Busch Light (B) whose cardboard insert partitions the case into a 3×6 matrix of 18 slots, where c_{xy} denotes the slot in the xth row and yth column of

$$B = \begin{pmatrix} c_{11} & c_{12} & c_{13} & c_{14} & c_{15} & c_{16} \\ c_{21} & c_{22} & c_{23} & c_{24} & c_{25} & c_{26} \\ c_{31} & c_{32} & c_{33} & c_{34} & c_{35} & c_{36} \end{pmatrix},$$

and, secondly, three six-packs—a Guinness Extra Stout (G), an Abita Purple Haze (A), and a Evian Natural Spring Water (E)—having representations

$$G = \begin{pmatrix} c_{41} & c_{42} \\ c_{51} & c_{52} \\ c_{61} & c_{62} \end{pmatrix}, A = \begin{pmatrix} c_{43} & c_{44} \\ c_{53} & c_{54} \\ c_{63} & c_{63} \end{pmatrix}, \text{ and } E = \begin{pmatrix} c_{45} & c_{46} \\ c_{55} & c_{56} \\ c_{65} & c_{66} \end{pmatrix};$$

and these three 3×2 six-packs have been placed below the 3×6 case B of Busch Light

$$\begin{pmatrix} & \text{18-CASE} & \\ & \text{(B)} & \\ \text{6-PACK} & \text{6-PACK} & \text{6-PACK} \\ \text{(G)} & \text{(A)} & \text{(E)} \end{pmatrix} = \begin{pmatrix} c_{11} & c_{12} & c_{13} & c_{14} & c_{15} & c_{16} \\ c_{21} & c_{22} & c_{23} & c_{24} & c_{25} & c_{26} \\ c_{31} & c_{32} & c_{33} & c_{34} & c_{35} & c_{36} \\ c_{41} & c_{42} & c_{43} & c_{44} & c_{45} & c_{46} \\ c_{51} & c_{52} & c_{53} & c_{54} & c_{55} & c_{56} \\ c_{61} & c_{62} & c_{63} & c_{64} & c_{65} & c_{66} \end{pmatrix}$$

so that six-packs and eighteen-case together form, en masse, the 6×6 square matrix (B-GAE) with c_{xy} entries taking values 0 (if bottle be empty/missing) or 1 (if bottle be full):

$$B\text{-}GAE = \begin{pmatrix} c_{11} & c_{12} & c_{13} & c_{14} & c_{15} & c_{16} \\ c_{21} & c_{22} & c_{23} & c_{24} & c_{25} & c_{26} \\ c_{31} & c_{32} & c_{33} & c_{34} & c_{35} & c_{36} \\ c_{41} & c_{42} & c_{43} & c_{44} & c_{45} & c_{46} \\ c_{51} & c_{52} & c_{53} & c_{54} & c_{55} & c_{56} \\ c_{61} & c_{62} & c_{63} & c_{64} & c_{65} & c_{66} \end{pmatrix} = \begin{pmatrix} 0 & 0 & 1 & 1 & 0 & 1 \\ 1 & 0 & 1 & 0 & 0 & 0 \\ 1 & 0 & 1 & 0 & 1 & 1 \\ 0 & 0 & 0 & 1 & 0 & 0 \\ 0 & 0 & 1 & 1 & 0 & 0 \\ 0 & 1 & 0 & 1 & 1 & 0 \end{pmatrix}.$$

But that's not what's so extraordinary. What is extraordinary: B-GAE appears to be invertible, to have linearly independent rows, so that—

Belch.[180]

Mr(s). Peng S. Long has finished his beer: Into case B, he returns his empty Busch Light bottle to an open spot in the cardboard insert, the fourth slot in the third row—Slob denotes this

[180] Unfortunately, Dr. Long's belch has interrupted Mamma Slob's thought process. But B-GAE is invertible, i.e., there does exist a 6×6 square matrix $[B\text{-}GAE]^{-1}$ such that $[B\text{-}GAE]^{-1}\,[B\text{-}GAE] = [B\text{-}GAE]\,[B\text{-}GAE]^{-1} = I$:

empty bottle 0_{34}—and, having returned 0_{34} to the case, Long then removes 1_{35}:

$$B = \begin{pmatrix} c_{11} & c_{12} & c_{13} & c_{14} & c_{15} & c_{16} \\ c_{21} & c_{22} & c_{23} & c_{24} & c_{25} & c_{26} \\ c_{31} & c_{32} & c_{33} & \mathbf{0_{34}} & \mathbf{1_{35}} & c_{36} \end{pmatrix}.$$

This is bad: If Long consumes 1_{35}, *B-GAE* will no longer be invertible—[181]

"No!" Slob shouts.

Silence. *Party interrupted*: Once again, all eyes on Slob.

But it's too late. Having twisted off the cap, Dr. Long takes a long swig of 1_{35}. Then wipes his wet chin and asks: "No? What you mean *no*?"

More silence. The room full of stares is embarrassing, but Slob is not in the mood to explain basic Linear Algebra to the artsy cast…

Mrs. Alberta Herstein has a solution: "Professor Heisenberg, perhaps you'd like to make

---

$$[B\text{-}GAE][B\text{-}GAE]^{-1} = \begin{pmatrix} 0 & 0 & 1 & 1 & 0 & 1 \\ 1 & 0 & 1 & 0 & 0 & 0 \\ 1 & 0 & 1 & 0 & 1 & 1 \\ 0 & 0 & 0 & 1 & 0 & 0 \\ 0 & 0 & 1 & 1 & 0 & 0 \\ 0 & 1 & 0 & 1 & 1 & 0 \end{pmatrix} \begin{pmatrix} 0 & 1 & 0 & 1 & -1 & 0 \\ 1 & 1 & -1 & -1 & -1 & 1 \\ 0 & 0 & 0 & -1 & 1 & 0 \\ 0 & 0 & 0 & 1 & 0 & 0 \\ -1 & -1 & 1 & 0 & 1 & 0 \\ 1 & 0 & 0 & 0 & -1 & 0 \end{pmatrix} = \begin{pmatrix} 1 & 0 & 0 & 0 & 0 & 0 \\ 0 & 1 & 0 & 0 & 0 & 0 \\ 0 & 0 & 1 & 0 & 0 & 0 \\ 0 & 0 & 0 & 1 & 0 & 0 \\ 0 & 0 & 0 & 0 & 1 & 0 \\ 0 & 0 & 0 & 0 & 0 & 1 \end{pmatrix} = I.$$

That said, $B\text{-}GAE^{-1}$'s entries are problematic. In particular, what would the negative number "-1" have to do with beer? Could there, for example, be an inverse-world, an under-world, where, on the underside of Claire's dining-room floor, there is another case of beer hanging upside down, an identical inverse-case reflected through the floor, in which a -1_{xy} is a full upside-down bottle corresponding to a right-side-up 1_{xy} above the floor, and would this under-world, this inverse-world, extend to Mamma Slob himself, to the existence of an inverse-self, to an upside-down inverse-Slob hanging from the underside of his feet and matching his every movement, reflected through the floor?

[181] I.e., if Long drinks beer 1_{35} (where drinking is a map D_{35}: $1_{35} \rightarrow 0_{35}$ with all other c_{xy} fixed for $(x, y) \neq (3, 5)$), then the resultant matrix with empty bottle 0_{35}, call it $B\text{-}GAE_{35}$, would not be invertible. Equivalently, the rows of $B\text{-}GAE_{35}$ would be linearly dependent: That is, let r_x be the xth row of the transposed matrix $[B\text{-}GAE_{35}]^{T}$, denoted by $[\, r_1\, r_2\, r_3\, r_4\, r_5\, r_6\,]^{T}$. Then the third row r_3, containing 0_{35}, is a linear combination of rows r_1, r_2, and r_5, with $r_3 = r_1 + r_2 - r_5$:

$$\begin{array}{rlrl} & r_1 & & (0\ 0\ 1\ 1\ 0\ 1) \\ + & r_2 & + & (1\ 0\ 1\ 0\ 0\ 0) \\ - & r_5 & - & (0\ 0\ 1\ 1\ 0\ 0) \\ \hline & r_3 & = & (1\ 0\ 1\ 0\ 0\ 1) \end{array}$$

yourself comfortable"—she points to Slob's assigned seat (12/♓)—"there, beside Mr. Hornet."

Slob has a better solution: He transfers bottle 1_{36} to slot c_{35}, then addresses Long across the bar: "When you're done with that," Slob explains, pointing to the now empty slot c_{36}, "put your empty bottle here."[182]

"Yes, dear, he will," Alberta says, yet pointing, "but perhaps you'd like to have a—"

"Pow!"—the toreador slaps the adjacent table at Slob's seat, denoted by ♓ and bag of ketchup, the tables of Slob and Alberta flanking the bar along circle's circumference.

"Yes, ma'am," Slob says, "I'd love to have a—"

But before Slob can reach his seat, Mr(s). Peng S. has straddled the center of Slob's table for three: one foot in the seat of Slob's chair, the other dangling in circle's interior, the gallon-bag of ketchup between his thighs. "I drink with men," Long says. He points at Slob's crotch.

Slob had forgotten about the quarter-sized hole in his slacks. His sit is a collapse. He has collapsed in Bisera's seat (1/♈), next to the bar.

Long swings his dangling leg over the table (and Slob's head) from interior to exterior, then hops to his feet and, pointing at his own crotch, mimics Slob's collapse in Slob's seat (12/♓), between Slob in Bisera's (1/♈) and Hornet (11/♒). "We men!" Long shouts, slapping Slob's back on his left, then Mr. Ludwig Hornet's on his right: "Hornet is men, too, but he play viola. The rest, though," he says, now pointing to everyone else in the circle, "they is all the ladies wearing the moustache. Yes, I explain it—"

"Professor Heisenberg," interrupts Ms. Camel (9/♐), the young one in the jogging outfit, circa 120° counterclockwise from Slob: "Professor, we're like so grateful you came."

"My pleasure," Slob says.

---

182 *Mamma Slob's solution*: Switch c_{35} and c_{36}? This would solve the "problem," provided Long listens and puts his empty 0_{35} into 1_{36}'s old slot, which is now 1_{35}…i.e., *before* Long drinks his beer, we're switching 1_{35} and 1_{36}, but *after* he drinks it, we're switching 0_{35} and 1_{36}, so the old 1_{36} becomes the new 1_{35}, and the old 1_{35} becomes the new 0_{36}. Anyway, after the switch, the resultant matrix $B\text{-}GAE_{\text{switch}}$ would be invertible, having inverse $B\text{-}GAE_{\text{switch}}^{-1}$:

$$B\text{-}GAE_{\text{Switch}} = \begin{pmatrix} 0 & 0 & 1 & 1 & 0 & 1 \\ 1 & 0 & 1 & 0 & 0 & 0 \\ 1 & 0 & 1 & 0 & 1 & 0 \\ 0 & 0 & 0 & 1 & 0 & 0 \\ 0 & 0 & 1 & 1 & 0 & 0 \\ 0 & 1 & 0 & 1 & 1 & 0 \end{pmatrix}, B\text{-}GAE_{\text{Switch}}^{-1} = \begin{pmatrix} 0 & 1 & 0 & 0 & 0 & 0 \\ 0 & 1 & -1 & -1 & 0 & 1 \\ 0 & 0 & 0 & -1 & 1 & 0 \\ 0 & 0 & 0 & 1 & 0 & 0 \\ 0 & -1 & 1 & 0 & 0 & 0 \\ 1 & 0 & 0 & 0 & -1 & 0 \end{pmatrix}.$$

"Especially with a fever like yours," she adds. "Thank God it's not Sunday morning."[183]

Slob does not have a fever. And it's Wednesday night, not morning. He better clear this up: "Isn't it Wednesday?" he asks.

"Well, in reality—yeah," she says, then turns to her neighbor, Mr. Serge Lang (10/♑): "But what day is it *supposed* to be, again?"

"Early Friday morning, Ms. Camel," he says, adjusting his Hitler mustache.

"Which," she says, "is like so much better than Sunday, isn't it, Ms. Gram?"

"Naturally, dear, with a wicked fever like his," says Ms. Gram (6/♍), in a "British" accent.

Slob has a tumor, not a fever: "I'm fine," he says. "Nothing wrong with me."

Ms. Gram disagrees: "*Actually*, Professor Heisenberg, you've had a nasty fever for twenty-seven days and eleven years, ever since eleven years ago three Fridays before last. So you're lucky we're having dinner tonight, on Friday morning, when we can cure you."

"Which we like couldn't in reality," Ms. Camel says, "with its being Wednesday night."

"Yes," says Gram.

"But," says Camel, "he's not going to die because, tonight, it's Friday morning?"

"Yes, first six hours of the day, when blood has dominion."

"So it's blood-letting?"

"Phlebotomy, dear. But only for six hours. After dark, it's a question of phlegm…"

But Slob is distracted from Camel and Gram's phlegmatic discourse by an intruder: A Hitler-mustached Mr. Karpov King has left his seat (5/♌) and approached the bar. And this Mr. King, the shy one who wears leather, removes bottle 1_{35} from the case of Busch Light to yield

$$B\text{-}GAE_{\text{KingSwitch}} = \begin{pmatrix} 0 & 0 & 1 & 1 & 0 & 1 \\ 1 & 0 & 1 & 0 & 0 & 0 \\ 1 & 0 & 1 & 0 & 0 & 0 \\ 0 & 0 & 0 & 1 & 0 & 0 \\ 0 & 0 & 1 & 1 & 0 & 0 \\ 0 & 1 & 0 & 1 & 1 & 0 \end{pmatrix},$$

[183] For students of medieval medicine, astrology, and natural magic, the remainder of Excerpt 7.6 may make sense. I, however, shall be focusing on the invertibility of B-GAE matrices.

which is clearly not invertible, possessing the linear dependence $r_2 = r_3$—

“No!” Slob shouts.

“What?” King shrieks. Up-close, even without glasses, Slob can now see that Mr. King’s moustache does little to disguise his female body, dressed in tight leather from the neck down.

“Never mind,” Slob says, switching 1_{31} to 0_{35}, to yield invertible $B\text{-}GAE_{\text{SwitchKingSwitch}}$.[184]

But Mr. King has not left, (s)he is stroking Slob’s earlobe: “Was supposed to get two,” (s)he says. “Mr. Jameson was needing a Busch, same as me.”

“Right, I’ll get it.” Slob removes her finger from his ear, then bottle 1_{23} from the case, which is fine,[185] but which requires instructions: “Just put your bottles here and here,” he says,

[184] So that *later*, when King’s drunk 1_{35} becomes the old 0_{35}, it will not be 0_{35}, but the new 0_{31}, to yield the matrix

$$B\text{-}GAE_{\text{SwitchKingSwitch}} = \begin{pmatrix} 0 & 0 & 1 & 1 & 0 & 1 \\ 1 & 0 & 1 & 0 & 0 & 0 \\ 0 & 0 & 1 & 0 & 1 & 0 \\ 0 & 0 & 0 & 1 & 0 & 0 \\ 0 & 0 & 1 & 1 & 0 & 0 \\ 0 & 1 & 0 & 1 & 1 & 0 \end{pmatrix}, \text{ with inverse } B\text{-}GAE_{\text{SwitchKingSwitch}}^{-1} = \begin{pmatrix} 0 & 1 & 0 & 1 & -1 & 0 \\ 0 & 1 & -1 & 0 & 0 & 1 \\ 0 & 0 & 0 & -1 & 1 & 0 \\ 0 & 0 & 0 & 1 & 0 & 0 \\ 0 & 0 & 1 & 1 & -1 & 0 \\ 1 & 0 & 0 & 0 & -1 & 0 \end{pmatrix}.$$

[185] Yes, sort of fine, given that the matrix

$$B\text{-}GAE_{\text{JamesonSwitchKingSwitch}} = \begin{pmatrix} 0 & 0 & 1 & 1 & 0 & 1 \\ 1 & 0 & 0 & 0 & 0 & 0 \\ 0 & 0 & 1 & 0 & 1 & 0 \\ 0 & 0 & 0 & 1 & 0 & 0 \\ 0 & 0 & 1 & 1 & 0 & 0 \\ 0 & 1 & 0 & 1 & 1 & 0 \end{pmatrix} \text{ has inverse } B\text{-}GAE_{\text{JamesonSwitchKingSwitch}}^{-1} = \begin{pmatrix} 0 & 1 & 0 & 0 & 0 & 0 \\ 0 & 0 & 1 & -2 & 1 & 1 \\ 0 & 0 & 0 & -1 & 1 & 0 \\ 0 & 0 & 0 & 1 & 0 & 0 \\ 0 & 0 & 1 & 1 & -1 & 0 \\ 1 & 0 & 0 & 0 & -1 & 0 \end{pmatrix}.$$

But a “-2_{xy}” is potentially problematic, an unexplored facet of Mamma Slob’s inverse-world. For now, assume that the -2_{24} in $B\text{-}GAE_{\text{JamesonSwitchKingSwitch}}^{-1}$ is an upside-down bottle containing twice as much beer as it should.

pointing to empty slots 0_{31} and 0_{23}, "when you're—"

"*Professor*?" Across the bar, Mrs. Alberta Herstein has said something to Slob—loudly: "Professor Heisenberg, would you *please* stop playing with the beer case?"

"But *B-GAE*!" Slob protests.

Alberta is unsympathetic: "What do you mean, *Be gay*?" she asks. "We're asexual."

Slob is confused, Slob is irked—King has escaped to his/her seat with a pair of Büsche—Slob needs glasses: "Darnit," he says, "why are you ladies wearing moustaches?"

Silence. Sympathetic giggle from Long, who seems to have reached the *nonverbal* stage.

Crash. Metal. Behind Slob, in the kitchen. As if several metal pots had fallen on a tile floor, then wobbled and rolled until they banged into hollow metal—a stove, perhaps.

Bisera shouts from the kitchen: "Don't worry. Everything's fine."

"OK, dear," Mrs. Alberta Herstein answers, then removes Busch Light 1_{16} from the case.

Slob transfers 1_{14} to 0_{16}.[186]

Mrs. Herstein frowns at Slob, but addresses the cast: "I suppose Mr. Heisenberg can't be held accountable for his phlegmatic complexion." She sighs. "He was born that way."

Mr. Lang (10/♑) nods: "Cold and moist," he says.

"Oh yabetcha," says Mr. Jameson (7/♎), opening his new Busch, "excess of cold moist phlegm, on top of a fever like his—it's the brain that suffers most in such cases."

"His poor brain," says leather-clad King (5/♌), opening hers. "And a scientist, too. But I agree with Alberta. The professor can't be blamed for his brain."

"True enough," Alberta says. "Perhaps we've been excluding Professor Heisenberg and

---

[186] Given the disastrous linear dependency ($r_1 = r_5$) in Alberta's callously vilified $B\text{-}GAE_{\text{AlbertaJamesonSwitchKingSwitch}}$, thank God Mamma Slob had the scruples to switch 1_{14} and 0_{16}, to yield $B\text{-}GAE_{\text{SwitchAlbertaJamesonSwitchKingSwitch}} =$

$$\begin{pmatrix} 0 & 0 & 1 & 0 & 0 & 1 \\ 1 & 0 & 0 & 0 & 0 & 0 \\ 0 & 0 & 1 & 0 & 1 & 0 \\ 0 & 0 & 0 & 1 & 0 & 0 \\ 0 & 0 & 1 & 1 & 0 & 0 \\ 0 & 1 & 0 & 1 & 1 & 0 \end{pmatrix} \text{ with inverse } B\text{-}GAE_{\text{SwitchAlbertaJamesonSwitchKingSwitch}}^{-1} = \begin{pmatrix} 0 & 1 & 0 & 0 & 0 & 0 \\ 0 & 0 & 1 & -2 & 1 & 1 \\ 0 & 0 & 0 & -1 & 1 & 0 \\ 0 & 0 & 0 & 1 & 0 & 0 \\ 0 & 0 & 1 & 1 & -1 & 0 \\ 1 & 0 & 0 & 1 & -1 & 0 \end{pmatrix}.$$

his brain." She then turns to Slob: "But don't worry, Professor. With you coming and being science-oriented, we all did a little research, and frankly, we're all puzzled by this fascinating little quantum field matter." She stands at her seat and removes a small notebook, a Moleskine, from the inner breast pocket of her tux. She clears her throat. "Professor Hilbert Hawking Heisenberg, what is your view of quantum consciousness?"

"What's that?" Slob says.

Belch. The toreador, it seems, has finished his beer. Yet nonverbal, he scoots his chair back, not to stand up, but to get on the floor, onto his hands and knees, and under the table.

Ignoring Slob's question and Long's crawling under the table to circle's interior, Mrs. Alberta Herstein reads directly from her Moleskine notebook: "All the varying epistemological assumptions and discrepancies in neurophysiological levels aside, could quantum randomness—mathematically, of course, in the discourse of quantum mechanics—could its fundamental features of complementarity and entanglement function to assuage the conflict between conscious free will and physical determinism?"[187]

Silence. And, even though Long is crawling in circle's interior toward the bar—at least, peeking above the opposite edge of Slob's tabletop, the gold-tipped cones of Dr. Long's spiked hair seem to be bouncing in bar's direction—everyone is staring at Slob. "Sorry, what's that?"

"I said," Alberta continues, "could quantum consciousness..."

Slob doesn't care: Nonverbal but standing, Dr. Long, bent over the bar, grimaces at Slob, but wavers: Long's hand, hovering over the bottles, roams above them in circles, as if to tease Slob—suddenly, Long's hand darts for the six-packs and seizes 1_{53}, an Abita Purple Haze.

Slob answers: Noting linear dependence $r_4 = r_5$, he deftly moves 1_{65} to 0_{55}, to obtain

$$B\text{-}GAE_{\text{SwitchLongSwitchAlbertaJamesonSwitchKingSwitch}} = \begin{pmatrix} 0 & 0 & 1 & 0 & 0 & 1 \\ 1 & 0 & 0 & 0 & 0 & 0 \\ 0 & 0 & 1 & 0 & 1 & 0 \\ 0 & 0 & 0 & 1 & 0 & 0 \\ 0 & 0 & 0 & 1 & 1 & 0 \\ 0 & 1 & 0 & 1 & 0 & 0 \end{pmatrix},$$

[187] There are so many problems with this statement that I don't know where to begin. (So I won't.)

and then shouts at his short pointy-haired opponent, victoriously, with a "Ha!"[188]

Alberta is shouting something, but the toreador in sunglasses is not intimidated: Long answers with a "Ha!" of his own and tosses the unopened Purple Haze 1_{53} over his shoulder—tossing hand snapping back to hover-position above the bar where, like a vulture, it slowly circles over the bottles, as tossed bottle soars over the tripod behind him, and Alberta keeps—

Dr. Long snatches bottle 1_{54}. And, before Slob can respond, Long tosses this second Purple Haze over his shoulder with another "Ha!"

But Slob doesn't care since $B\text{-}GAE_{\text{LongSwitchLongSwitchAlbertaJamesonSwitchKingSwitch}}$ is invertible.[189]

Unlike Alberta: "Professor Heisenberg!" she shouts. "Yes or no?"

Slob is not a fan of yes-or-no questions: "What?" he shouts back.

"I said, yes or no? Is science just another realm of discourse limited to its own socio-epistemic concerns? Yes or no: Is science socially-constructed?"

Slob shouts: "My dick is socially-constructed."

Silence. That's not what Slob meant to say, but B-GAE's been—

A plate, covered by a metal inverted paraboloid, slams onto the table in front of Slob.

"Dinner's ready," says Mlle. Gertrude Herstein (i.e, Bisera [i.e., Claire]). "And keep your food covered until we're filming. No peeking." She returns to the kitchen.

---

188 À propos, $B\text{-}GAE_{\text{SwitchLongSwitchAlbertaJamesonSwitchKingSwitch}}{}^{-1} = \begin{pmatrix} 0 & 1 & 0 & 0 & 0 & 0 \\ 0 & 0 & 0 & -1 & 0 & 1 \\ 0 & 0 & 1 & 1 & -1 & 0 \\ 0 & 0 & 0 & 1 & 0 & 0 \\ 0 & 0 & 0 & -1 & 1 & 0 \\ 1 & 0 & 0 & 1 & -1 & 0 \end{pmatrix}$ dodges -2_{xy} conundrums.

189 $\begin{pmatrix} 0 & 0 & 1 & 0 & 0 & 1 \\ 1 & 0 & 0 & 0 & 0 & 0 \\ 0 & 0 & 1 & 0 & 1 & 0 \\ 0 & 0 & 0 & 1 & 0 & 0 \\ 0 & 0 & 0 & 0 & 1 & 0 \\ 0 & 1 & 0 & 1 & 0 & 0 \end{pmatrix}$'s inverse $B\text{-}GAE_{\text{LongSwitchLongSwitchAlbertaJamesonSwitchKingSwitch}}{}^{-1} = \begin{pmatrix} 0 & 1 & 0 & 0 & 0 & 0 \\ 0 & 0 & 0 & -1 & 0 & 1 \\ 0 & 0 & 1 & 0 & -1 & 0 \\ 0 & 0 & 0 & 1 & 0 & 0 \\ 0 & 0 & 0 & 0 & 1 & 0 \\ 1 & 0 & -1 & 0 & 1 & 0 \end{pmatrix}$

Mr. Homer Herstein and Bisera reenter and re-exit the dining room to set the circle of tables with ten more covered plates, one for each guest, except for the toreador who, returning to the tripod at circle's center, peers into the camera lens.

Finally, table(s) set with eleven identical covered dishes, Bisera stands at the bar, beside seated Slob, ignores him, and asks the cast: "Anybody need another beer, for dinner?"

Three Büsche are called for...

Slob restrains himself, as Bisera removes 1_{13}, 1_{21}, and 1_{33} from the case, so that $r_3 = r_5$ and $r_2 = \textit{all 0s}$.[190] But then, having delivered the Büsche and butchered *B-GAE*, she returns to the bar and performs a miracle: Of her own volition, she makes the following switches:

$$1_{16} \rightarrow 0_{11},\ 1_{62} \rightarrow 0_{22},\ 1_{35} \rightarrow 0_{33}, \text{ and } 1_{64} \rightarrow 0_{66},$$

to yield $B\text{-}GAE_{\text{Bisera'sSwitchForDinnerLongSwitchLongSwitchAlbertaJamesonSwitchKingSwitch}}$, a matrix which not only has an inverse, but is itself its own inverse, a self-inverse—i.e., the identity matrix:

$$B\text{-}GAE_{\text{Bisera'sSwitchFor DinnerLongSwitchLongSwitchAlbertaJamesonSwitchKingSwitch}} = I = \begin{pmatrix} 1 & 0 & 0 & 0 & 0 & 0 \\ 0 & 1 & 0 & 0 & 0 & 0 \\ 0 & 0 & 1 & 0 & 0 & 0 \\ 0 & 0 & 0 & 1 & 0 & 0 \\ 0 & 0 & 0 & 0 & 1 & 0 \\ 0 & 0 & 0 & 0 & 0 & 1 \end{pmatrix}.$$

Slob is filled with love: He looks up at his daughter, yet standing beside him, and she, Bisera, is looking back at him, and, sitting there, under the gaze of her dark eyes, for the first time in eleven years, or twenty even—for the first time in his life, Slob feels no shame. Regret: yes. Sorrow, pain, disembowelment: yes. But no shame. His own daughter, Bisera, just look what she did to the beer case: This is love. And now, looking up, lost in her eyes, finally—tumor or no tumor—Daddy knows he can tell her anything: In her eyes, here and now, he is forgiven.

---

190 I.e., $B\text{-}GAE_{\text{For DinnerLongSwitchLongSwitchAlbertaJamesonSwitchKingSwitch}} = \begin{pmatrix} 0 & 0 & 0 & 0 & 0 & 1 \\ 0 & 0 & 0 & 0 & 0 & 0 \\ 0 & 0 & 0 & 0 & 1 & 0 \\ 0 & 0 & 0 & 1 & 0 & 0 \\ 0 & 0 & 0 & 0 & 1 & 0 \\ 0 & 1 & 0 & 1 & 0 & 0 \end{pmatrix}.$

And thus, finally, eyes fixed to his, she speaks: “You’re in my seat,” she says.

“Oh.” Slob switches himself, from seat 1/♈ to 12/♓: “Sorry,” he says, “but I just—”

“Who’s got the script?” she asks.

“Right here, dear,” says Ms. Gram (6/♍), who then sends a document, passed hand-to-hand, around the circle. “Made a few last-minute changes,” she says, “like we discussed.”

“Thanks.” Bisera takes the thick stapled document (ca. twenty pages) from Alberta, then sits beside her father and, silent, bows her head. They all do, around the circle, all heads bow.

Except for Mr. Homer Herstein, who silently approaches Slob with a roll of duct tape. Standing by seated Slob, Homer bites off a yard-long strip of tape, then points at the gallon-bag of ketchup: “Don’t worry,” he whispers, “you won’t have to do much—actually, just don’t do anything at all—but I’m still going to need that arm.” Onto Slob’s left forearm resting on the tabletop, Homer plops the bag of ketchup. “OK, now just hold her steady there,” he says, suspending Slob’s arm midair, and, with Slob’s aid, Homer, wrapping five times around, tapes the gallon of ketchup to the forearm. “And don’t you dare take her off.” He takes his seat.

Dr. Long, attentive at tripod, sips his beer and aims the camera lens at Slob and daughter.

Into the lens, Slob whispers: “I have a brain tumor.”

“That’s not funny,” Bisera whispers back. She stands, script in hand.

No, Slob thinks, it isn’t (funny). *Yes or no*: Should he tell the daughter his tumor is—?

“Press record!” shouts Mr. Homer Herstein.

<u>CLAIRE’S TUBE-FACE DINNER</u>: THE FILM VERSION

BLACK SCREEN.

(O.S.) [1/♈] MLLE. GERTRUDE HERSTEIN (CLAIRE)

It is a time long ago, when calendars were different, but taxes were not.

(BEAT)

Two lovers must marry, for fiscal reasons to do with taxes—their love is pure and asexual—but the biological father of the bride has been fatally ill for twenty-seven days and eleven years. There can be no rehearsal dinner until a cure is found.

(BEAT)
And everyone is hungry.

CAMERA is turned on (via power button) to reveal actors and set.

INT. DINING ROOM—NIGHT

As before, our eleven characters sit at a "round table" with a covered plate in front of each. Much like the twelve numerals on a clock face, characters correspond to a sign of the zodiac.

CAMERA follows Mrs. Alberta Herstein (3/♊), who now has a stethoscope around her neck, as she approaches Slob with a 7" cleaver in one hand and a 10" Sabatier chef knife in the other.

(O.S.) [1/♈] MLLE. GERTRUDE HERSTEIN (CLAIRE)
Early Friday morning, just twenty-seven days and eleven years after malady's beginning, a physician is called.
(indicating Mrs. Alberta Herstein)
And all the dinner guests look to the wise physician, who knows well the stars, and hope for a quick cure, because everyone is hungry.

CAMERA zooms out from the 7" cleaver and pans past Slob to frame Claire, reading script.

[1/♈] MLLE. GERTRUDE HERSTEIN (CLAIRE)
Fortunately, there is a good chance of recovery. For planet Luna, ruler of phlegm, now resides in watery Cancer, where she is powerful in producing cold and moist humors.

(O.S.) [N/A] ALL OTHER DINNER GUESTS
(in chorus)
Cold and moist.

[1/♈] MLLE. GERTRUDE HERSTEIN (CLAIRE)
And on this Friday morning, Mars, in the seventh house, is weakened and falling from Libra, while most beneficent Jupiter dwells in Gemini where, in strong oppositional aspect with Saturn in Sagittarius, He neutralizes the malignancy of this grave infortune…
(BEAT)

And thus on Friday, Saturn is rendered helpless…
(BEAT)
And Mars is weakened…
(DOUBLE BEAT)
And Luna, not strongly aspected to any wicked planet and rejoicing in her…
(TRIPLE BEAT, as she flips through the pages of her script)
And everyone is hungry…
(now reading the last page of her lengthy script)
And thus, on Friday, under this happy configuration of stars, during the first six hours of the day, when blood is in ascendency, our wise physician must bleed the feverish patient.

With her shiny 10" Sabatier chef knife, rather than tarnished cleaver, wise Alberta punctures the gallon bag of ketchup taped to Slob's arm. She then squishes the bag with the flat of her cleaver: It squirts like a geyser, such as Old Faithful. Slob's bleached shirt is splattered with ketchup.

(CONT'D) [1/♈] MLLE. GERTRUDE HERSTEIN (CLAIRE)
…and all the while, everyone is hungry.
(BEAT)
But on this Friday, the patient's eleven-year fever should subside during the last six hours of the natural day, when phlegm is in ascendency, if…or *not*…but possibly if—oh hell.
(tossing script on floor)
So, sometime on Friday, recovery is assured if the feverish father is phlegmatic. And all are hopeful, for everyone is hungry.
(to Mrs. Alberta Herstein)
O wise physician—how hungry we are—please, tell us: According to his nativity, is the patient's complexion phlegmatic?

[3/♊] MRS. ALBERTA HERSTEIN
Behold, dear malnourished dinner guests, Mr. Hilbert Hawking Heisenberg is…
(consulting her Moleskine notebook)
Ladies and gentlemen, we got phlegm on our hands!

[N/A] ALL OTHER DINNER GUESTS
(in chorus)

Praise be to phlegm!

Alberta returns to her seat. Slob opens his Evian and washes the ketchup off his face.

[1/♈] MLLE. GERTRUDE HERSTEIN (CLAIRE)
(to Mr. Homer Herstein, fictional father)
Daddy, I'm starving. Can we eat now?

[4/♋] MR. HOMER HERSTEIN
Excellent idea, dear. Our food must be getting cold.

All dinner guests bow their heads in prayer.

[N/A] ALL DINNER GUESTS (not SLOBODON)
(chanting "The Lord's Prayer" in Old English, in unison)
Fæder ūre þū þe eart on heofonum, Sī þīn nama ġehālgod. Tōbecume þīn rīċe, ġewurþe ðīn willa, on eorðan swā swā on heofonum. Ūrne ġedæġhwāmlīcan hlāf syle ūs tō dæġ, and forgyf ūs ūre gyltas, swā swā wē forgyfað ūrum glytendum. And ne ġelǣd þū ūs on costnunge, ac ālȳs ūs of yfele. Sōþlīċe.

[4/♋] MR. HOMER HERSTEIN
(loudly)
Dear guests, bawn appetite.

[N/A] ALL DINNER GUESTS (not SLOBODON)
(in unison)
Mercy.

The characters, numbered according to our cosmological clock, lift the metal covers off their plates and throw them over their shoulders: The metal paraboloids clang, wobble, and roll about the floor. However, instead of "food," each person has a different book on their plate:
1/♈ Mlle. Gertrude Herstein (Claire): Gertrude Stein, *Geography and Plays.*
2/♉ The bar: N/A.
3/♊ Alberta Herstein: Albert Einstein, *Die Grundlage der allgemeinen Relativitätstheorie.*
4/♋ Mr. Homer Herstein: Homer, *Odyssey.*
5/♌ Mr. Karpov King: Anatoly Karpov, *The Semi-Closed Games in Action.*
6/♍ Ms. Paula Gram: Linus Pauling, *General Chemistry.*

7/♎ Mr. Ulysses J. Jameson: James Joyce, *Ulysses.*
8/♏ Ms. Cataline Caesar: Catullus, *The Poems of Catullus.*
9/♐ Ms. Alberta Camel: Albert Camus, *L'Étranger.*
10/♑ Mr. Serge Lang: Serge Lang, *Algebra.*
11/♒ Mr. Ludwig Hornet: Ludwig van Beethoven, *Symphony No. 5 in C Minor, Op. 67.*
12/♓ Mr. Hilbert Hawking Heisenberg (Slob): N/A.

[4/♋] MR. HOMER HERSTEIN
Let's eat.[191]

All the characters (except Slob) open their books and start speed-reading, turning a page once every three seconds, in unison. After a minute or two, conversations begin in pairs around the table, except for silent Slob who stares at his plate, the "food" upon which is always off camera: When Slob's in frame, we can only see he's looking down at his plate.

CAMERA (shooting, as always, from the center of the table) pans right from Slob to frame: Mr. Homer Herstein and his wife Alberta. Other conversations murmur (O.S.) in the background.

[4/♋] MR. HOMER HERSTEIN
How's the Einstein, dear? Too spicy? My stomach can't usually handle relativity.

[3/♊] MRS. ALBERTA HERSTEIN
No, no. Iron stomach, you know. It's quite nice.
(reading from her Einstein text)
If a system of coordinates K is chosen so that, in relation to it, physical laws hold—*but dear me. That's a bit bland.*
(turning some pages, then reading again)
Ah, here we go: A-sub-μ-ν equals the differential of A-sub-μ with respect to x-sub-ν minus the tensor—*ah, you can smell the infusion of red pepper in the words.*

[4/♋] MR. HOMER HERSTEIN
Truly. But dear Alberta, would you like to taste some Homer? It's really quite tender:
(reading from Homer's *Odyssey*)
But come now, cut out the tongues of the victims and mix the wine bowls…

---

[191] For the "consumption" of books in the hours before my mother's "murder," see homework Problem 7.3*b*.

CAMERA pans left to frame: Gertrude Herstein and Mr. Ludwig Hornet. (Slob in middle.)

[1/♈] MLLE. GERTRUDE HERSTEIN (CLAIRE)
(reading from Stein's "Sacred Emily")
Rose is a rose is a rose—*hmm, so succulent*—is a rose is a rose is a rose is a rose is a rose is a—*how's the Beethoven?*

[11/♒] MR. LUDWIG HORNET
(singing Beethoven's Fifth, with commentary)
Sublime, my dear. Here, have a taste: Clarinet in B with all strings, fortissimo: tee-tee-tee-taaah, tee-tee-tee-taaah—*ouch! Too hot, think I burned my tongue*: now piano, Violin Two: tee-tee-tee—plus Cello and Bassoon—taaah. Viola: tee-tee-tee-taaah...

[1/♈] MLLE. GERTRUDE HERSTEIN (CLAIRE)
...rose is a rose is a rose is a rose—

[11/♒] MR. LUDWIG HORNET
Violin One: tee-tee-tee-taaah...

CAMERA, panning right, rotates ca. 225° to Ms. Cataline Caesar and Ulysses J. Jameson.

[8/♏] MS. CATALINE CAESAR
(reading Catullus)
Solis putatis esse—*ah, the aroma of rosemary always perks me up*—mentulus vobis solis licere quidquid est puellarum confutuere et putere ceteros hircos—*and thyme: It's as if I could taste the goats myself.*[192]

[7/♎] MR. ULYSSES J. JAMESON
(reading Joyce's *Ulysses*)
Oh, you and your goat-sex. Joyce tastes better than goats any day: touched his trousers outside I was dying to find out was he circumcised he was shaking like a jelly—what kind of jelly, I wonder? Green currant maybe? Is there such a thing as a green currant?

CAMERA pans right to Ms. Alberta Camel and Mr. Serge Lang.

[192] SUBTITLES (skipping over italics): Do you think that you alone have cocks, that you alone may screw all the girls, and that the rest of us stink like goats?

[10/♑] MR. SERGE LANG

(reading Lang's *Algebra*)

Assume that φ-of-F-to-the-i is defined for all i, φ-of-F-to-the-i equals zero for almost all i—*tad sweet, isn't it?*

[9/♐] MS. ALBERTA CAMEL

(reading Camus' *L'Étranger*)

At least there's no icing: Aujourd'hui, mama est morte. Ou peut-être hier, je ne sais pas—ugh, I can feel the calories congealing on my gut.[193]

CAMERA pans left (ca. 120°) to Mr. Karpov King and Ms. Paula Gram.

[5/♌] MR. KARPOV KING

(reading Karpov's The Semi-Closed Games in Action)

Hm, hm, hmm—pawn to f3, knight to a5. Twelve: bishop takes f7 check, rook takes f7.

[6/♍] MS. PAULA GRAM

(reading Pauling's *General Chemistry*)

Since a kilogram of Uranium—*Uranium's heavy, like cream. I prefer skim products, you know, lighter ones like Hydrogen or Helium*—contains 4-point-2-6 gram-atoms, the complete fission of 1 kilogram of this element…

CAMERA pans left *faster* to Mr. Homer Herstein and Mrs. Alberta Herstein.

[4/♋] MR. HOMER HERSTEIN

(reading Homer, *faster* and *louder*)

Good friends, Nobody is killing me by force or treachery…

[3/♊] MRS. ALBERTA HERSTEIN

(reading Einstein, *faster* and *louder*)

…tensor μ-ν-comma-ρ times A-sub-ρ; i.e. the extension of the four-vector…

CAMERA pans right (ca. 120°) *faster* to Ms. Cataline Caesar and Mr. Ulysses J. Jameson.

---

[193] SUBTITLES (not italics): Mother died today. Or, maybe, yesterday; I can't be sure.

[8/♏] MS. CATALINE CAESAR
(reading Catullus, *faster* and *louder*)
Siquoi iure bono sacer alarum obstitit hircus…[194]

[7/♎] MR. ULYSSES J. JAMESON
(reading Joyce, *faster* and *louder*)
Ghoul! Chewer of corpses!

CAMERA pans right *as fast as possible* to Ms. Alberta Camel and Mr. Serge Lang.

[9/⛎] MS. ALBERTA CAMEL
(reading Camus, *as fast as possible* and *shouting*)
…j'ai effleuré ses seins…[195]

[10/♑] MR. SERGE LANG
(reading Lang, *as fast as possible* and *shouting*)
…χ-sub-φ-of-F is defined…

CAMERA pans left (ca. 285°) *as fast as possible* to Gertrude Herstein and Ludwig Hornet.

[11/♒] MR. LUDWIG HORNET
(singing Beethoven, *as fast as possible* and *shouting*)
…tee-tee-tee-tee-TEEYAH-tip-tip…

[1/♈] MLLE. GERTRUDE HERSTEIN (CLAIRE)
(reading Stein, *as fast as possible* and *shouting*)
…is a rose is a…

[11/♒] MR. LUDWIG HORNET
(singing Beethoven, *as fast as possible* and *shouting*)
…TEEYAH-tip-tip…

(O.S.) [4/♋] MR. HOMER HERSTEIN
(shouting)

---

[194] SUBTITLES: if ever a good fellow was justly affected with the vile stench of armpits…

[195] SUBTITLES: I brushed my hands over her breasts…

Silence!

Everyone falls silent—CAMERA pans right *as fast as possible* to Mr. Herstein, then pulls back into a wide shot, to include Slob's table: Mr. Homer Herstein stands and points his finger at Slob.

[4/♋] MR. HOMER HERSTEIN
(accusatory, but no longer shouting)
Mr. Hilbert Hawking Heisenberg is not eating his food.

[1/♈] MLLE. GERTRUDE HERSTEIN (CLAIRE)
Daddy, perhaps it's because Hilbert's dick is socially-constructed.

(O.S.) [8/♏] MS. CATALINE CAESAR
Excuse me, dear, but, if I may, Catullus, in his ninety-fourth poem, has something to say on the subject: Mentula moechatur moechatur mentula.[196]

(mostly O.S) [N/A] ALL DINNER GUESTS (not SLOBODON)
Mentula moechatur moechatur mentula.[197]

[3/♊] MRS. ALBERTA HERSTEIN
(suddenly, enthusiastically)
You know, Mr. Hilbert Hawking Heisenberg has a point. One could certainly raise the question: Would, for example, men in today's society get an erection from, say, Tolstoy's description of Anna Karenina's lovely plump arm or one of Reuben's nudes? No, I'd argue the probability of erection in the modern male would be far greater with anemic—

[4/♋] MR. HOMER HERSTEIN
(irately)
All right, all right, Alberta, you're not helping. Mr(s). Peng S. Long, please stop filming.

THE END (of Claire's Tube-Face Dinner: *The Film Version*)

CUT to:

[196] SUBTITLES: The cock fornicates. What a fornicating cock!

[197] SUBTITLES: The cock fornicates. What a fornicating cock!

There is a sugar beet on Slob's plate. He regards it: It is fuzzy, he is queasy.

Bisera speaks to her nauseous father: "Well, Slob? Aren't you going to say *anything*?"

Slob's shirt is covered with ketchup. And now, a sugar beet. What is Slob supposed to say? Why's he here? Why'd he come? Why? Darnit, he came for dinner. And to say things. He came to apologize, to eat a hot meal, to tell her about the tumor, to say "Hi" and "Bye" and something artsy in between. He did not come to discuss sugar beets. As Bisera *well* knows, Slob's father was a sugar beet farmer. What she doesn't know is when you're a little boy and your father is a sugar beet farmer during the Greek Civil War and a truck full of "gorillas" (i.e., a confusing term for the members of the Democratic Army of Greece [i.e., the military branch of the Communist Party of Greece], a term which adult Slob, finally, in his mid-thirties, learned to spell "guerillas") visits your mountain village, and when these soldiers, like gorillas, eat all your father's sugar beets and then, once they're done with Mommy, leave, driving their military truck back down your mountain's gravel roads, driving like the crazy youths they are, with no regard for speed limits, nor the ten-foot rope dragging behind, one end tied to truck's back bumper and the other end to Daddy's ankles, and your father dragged behind, skinned alive, screams, unlike Mommy, they're done with Mommy, but not with you, the little boy, you they rescue, you they take,[198] you are evacuated by these Democrats to be raised under Communist regimes until, years later, you escape to the good old USA where, one day, you learn algebraic number theory and how to spell guerilla—in other words, what the daughter doesn't know is the species Beta vulgaris (a.k.a. sugar beet) implicates politics and thus induces nausea, and there's no point in explaining why and he never has, not to anyone, and never will.

"Well—*Dad*?" says the daughter.

Slob picks up the sugar beet and looks at it, rather than the daughter sitting beside him. Even without his broken glasses, he can tell it is unpeeled, but washed. And raw. Definitely not cooked. And sitting there, regarding the fuzzy beet in his fist, he senses the slow ebbing of his nausea: dwindling, draining, dead. Until finally, with nausea gone, he is tired. Just tired. Tired and covered with ketchup. "Bisera," he says, staring at his beet, "I'm sorry. But I blacked out. You know I did. Never meant to kill Barney. Not my fault your mother was—the way she was."

[198] Along with 30,000 other children in the epic paidomazoma…one of whom was my mother.

The daughter snorts.

Slob drops his beet on his plate: "And sorry," he says, "but I got a brain tumor, whether you like it or not." Shaky, he unpins the giant ketchup-spattered nametag from his shirt's breast pocket. "But I still got questions," he says, flinging the tag at plate's beet. Then, from his breast pocket, he removes the decrepit 3×5 note card and slams it, message-side up, on the table in front of her: 10001100101110001110101110101100011101101111000101111000 0110001110100011. "And darnit, think I deserve to know what it means before I croak. Wouldn't you agree?"

The daughter stands, suddenly, bumping their table—her wine glass of water *rocks* beside the card—"What do you mean, tumor?" she says, as her glass tips and—

Slob swats her glass into circle's interior: The wine glass falls and its water spills onto the floor below, where glass shatters and water splatters, but above, on the tabletop, the aged card is safe and dry: the ink of its handwritten message, unblemished.

Yet seated, Slob takes the card from the table and shows his daughter the message, her goodbye note, hand-delivered to him in a prison visitation cubicle some eleven years ago.[199] He holds it up, its string of 0s and 1s, in his standing daughter's face: "What's it mean?" he shouts.

The daughter seems upset: "I told—I thought…" She falters, trembling, standing there in a skimpy blue dress daughters don't wear. "It's ABCs," she says. Then yells: "ABCs and 123s."

The daughter seems to be leaving: She has left her father's side, quickly, stumbling in her high heels toward the white china cabinet behind Alberta and the bar. There, kneeling down at cabinet's base, she opens its bottom door and extracts a black boot—just one—then stands up tall, boot in hand, and shouts at Slob once more: "Fibonacci!" she screams, then charges out of the dining room, out the hallway door opposite the kitchen, and Slob and cast listen to the hurried steps of her high heels clipping down the hall's hardwood floor toward her flat's back-alley entrance, until finally, with a loud snap of a deadbolt, followed by the bang and wobble of a door crashing into the spring mechanism of a doorstopper, the daughter screams "Fibonacci!" and the front (back-alley) door slams shut—she is gone.

Silence. Slob and cast: immobile, mute. Their host has left them. The party seems to be—

Hiccup. The toreador seems to have a question: "Anyone interest in the karaoke?"

---

[199] As dramatized, several hundred pages ago, in *Book*'s fourth chapter. For excerpt, review Evisceration 4.5.

The toreador's proposition seems to be a good one, but Slob is not interested in the cast's recollection that it's Wednesday night (rather than Friday morning) and hence Karaoke Night at the Alligator-something club on the ground-floor of Bisera's Second Empire building—no, Slob has recovered his daughter's twenty-page script from the floor and removed a Sanford King Size Permanent Marker from his pants, and, ignoring the cast's decision to leave their departed host's flat (and all attempts to persuade Slob to do so: "Professor Heisenberg," they said, "I think we really should be going—Claire's gone," to which Slob replied, "FUC? No. How could it be FUC? Too simple. FUC—no," by which he'd meant the acronym FUC for Fibonacci Universal Code, but which the cast misinterpreted as "fuck"), instead, in black marker, Slob scribbles the following on the blank 8½" × 11" backsides of his daughter's lengthy script:

Let X = 10001100101110001110101110101100011101101111000101110000110001110100011 and $F(k)$ be the sequence of Fibonacci numbers—1, 2, 3, 5, 8, 13, 21…—defined s.t. $F(0) = 1$, $F(1) = 2$, $F(k) = F(k-1) + F(k-2)$, for all $k \in \mathbb{N}$, $k > 2$. Now, for FUC: Construct a vector $A(n)$ of Fibonacci numbers s.t. the ith element of $A(n)$, $A(n)_i = F(i)$, $i = 0, 1 \ldots d$, with $F(d)$ the largest Fibonacci number $\leq n$. Choose a second vector $B(n)$ of binary digits of dimension d s.t. the dot product $A(n)^{\mathrm{T}} \cdot B(n) = n$ and $B(n)_d = 1$. Then the codeword $FB(n)$ is a vector of dimension $d + 1$, where $FB(n)_k = B(n)_k$ for all $1 \leq k \leq d$ and $FB(n)_{d+1} = 1$. Now, since any $B(n)$ must be chosen without successive 1s and $FB(n)_{d+1} = 1$, all codewords end in 11

10001100101110001110101110101100011101101111000101110000110001110100011

1000**11**0010**11**1000**11**1010**11**1010**11**000**11**10**11**0**1111**00010**11**10000**11**000**11**101000**11**

1000**11** 0010**11** 1000**11** 1010**11** 1010**11** 000**11** 10**11** 0**11** **11** 00010**11** 10000**11** 000**11** 101000**11**

which implies the daughter's message X is the following sequence of vectors in $B(k)$:

10001 00101 10001 10101 10101 0001 101 01 1 000101 100001 0001 1010001

Then, computing the dot products $A(n)^{\mathrm{T}} \cdot B(n) = n$ with $B(n)_d = 1$, we have

$$(1\ 0\ 0\ 0\ 1) \cdot (1\ 2\ 3\ 5\ 8) = 1{\cdot}1 + 0{\cdot}2 + 0{\cdot}3 + 0{\cdot}5 + 1{\cdot}8 = 1 + 8 = 9$$
$$(0\ 0\ 1\ 0\ 1) \cdot (1\ 2\ 3\ 5\ 8) = 0{\cdot}1 + 0{\cdot}2 + 1{\cdot}3 + 0{\cdot}5 + 1{\cdot}8 = 3 + 8 = 11$$
$$(1\ 0\ 0\ 0\ 1) \cdot (1\ 2\ 3\ 5\ 8) = 1{\cdot}1 + 0{\cdot}2 + 0{\cdot}3 + 0{\cdot}5 + 1{\cdot}8 = 1 + 8 = 9$$
$$(1\ 0\ 1\ 0\ 1) \cdot (1\ 2\ 3\ 5\ 8) = 1{\cdot}1 + 0{\cdot}2 + 1{\cdot}3 + 0{\cdot}5 + 1{\cdot}8 = 1 + 3 + 8 = 12$$
$$(1\ 0\ 1\ 0\ 1) \cdot (1\ 2\ 3\ 5\ 8) = 1{\cdot}1 + 0{\cdot}2 + 0{\cdot}3 + 0{\cdot}5 + 1{\cdot}8 = 1 + 3 + 8 = 12$$
$$(0\ 0\ 0\ 1) \cdot (1\ 2\ 3\ 5) = 0{\cdot}1 + 0{\cdot}2 + 0{\cdot}3 + 1{\cdot}5 = 5$$
$$(1\ 0\ 1) \cdot (1\ 2\ 3) = 1{\cdot}1 + 0{\cdot}2 + 1{\cdot}3 = 1 + 3 = 4$$
$$(0\ 1) \cdot (1\ 2) = 0{\cdot}1 + 1{\cdot}2 = 2$$
$$(1) \cdot (1) = 1{\cdot}1 = 1$$
$$(0\ 0\ 0\ 1\ 0\ 1) \cdot (1\ 2\ 3\ 5\ 8\ 13) = 0{\cdot}1 + 0{\cdot}2 + 0{\cdot}3 + 1{\cdot}5 + 0{\cdot}8 + 1{\cdot}13 = 5 + 13 = 18$$
$$(1\ 0\ 0\ 0\ 0\ 1) \cdot (1\ 2\ 3\ 5\ 8\ 13) = 1{\cdot}1 + 0{\cdot}2 + 0{\cdot}3 + 0{\cdot}5 + 0{\cdot}8 + 1{\cdot}13 = 1 + 13 = 14$$
$$(0\ 0\ 0\ 1) \cdot (1\ 2\ 3\ 5) = 0{\cdot}1 + 0{\cdot}2 + 0{\cdot}3 + 1{\cdot}5 = 5$$

$$(1\ 0\ 1\ 0\ 0\ 0\ 1) \cdot (1\ 2\ 3\ 5\ 8\ 13\ 21) = 1{\cdot}1 + 0{\cdot}2 + 1{\cdot}3 + 0{\cdot}5 + 0{\cdot}8 + 0{\cdot}13 + 1{\cdot}21 = 1 + 3 + 21 = 25$$

which implies $X = (9\ 11\ 9\ 12\ 12\ 5\ 4\ 2\ 1\ 18\ 14\ 5\ 25)$. So, given the daughter's screaming

"It's ABCs," she shouted, "ABCs and 123s!",

we might then ask the question:

Was the screaming daughter implying that A = 1, B = 2, C = 3 ... Z = 26?

If so, then $X = (\text{I K I L L E D B A R N E Y})$, and the decrypted message X is "I killed Barney."

Slob stops scribbling: *Bisera? Bisera killed Barney?* Suddenly, Slob is ashamed:

Yes or no: Should he tell the daughter that his tumor is benign?[200]

Yes or no.

Book Excerpt 7.7. (Coda to "The Incident" According to Claire.) *Concerning Knut's fictionalization of me as the murderer.*

Claire does not drink. Not ever. So when she orders a jumbo virgin Southern Snow Peach Daiquiri from a large Gator's waitress, Claire means virgin. And when she orders her second and third jumbo virgin daiquiris, she still means virgin. But Claire does not drink. So when daiquiris taste funny, that means Gator's Hut must not make their daiquiris with freshly-squeezed organic peaches, but rather, from juice concentrate containing organophosphate pesticide residues.[201] But tonight is the twenty-seven-day-and-eleven-year anniversary of Barney's murder and, now, her father has a brain tumor, so she decides that maybe, just this once, she will have a drink, and when she orders her fourth daiquiri "non-virgin" from the scary waitress with an eye patch, who laughs and asks, "So you mean virgin or *virgin*-virgin?", then laughs a second time when Claire, who's feeling out of sorts because her father's probably cracked the card by now and discovered that his daughter is not only a liar but also killed Barney, shouts more urgently, "Non-virgin! Non-virgin!", but does not laugh a third time when

[200] As disclosed, almost a 1000 pages ago, in *Book*'s second chapter, "The Twins: Sex," which we skipped… We'll come back to this tumor thing later: The "murder" of my mother has been left as a homework exercise.

[201] Actually, organic foods contain pesticides, too, though typically "one-third as many residues as conventionally grown foods," according to Brian Baker et al., "Pesticide residues in conventional, IPM-grown and organic foods: Insights from three U.S. data sets," *Food Additives and Contaminants* 19.5 (2002): 427-46.

Claire, later, after drinking two-thirds of this fourth daiquiri, sends it back and asks for another because "It's virgin," she says, "and don't think I clan-not tell the differ—iffer—", but can't even say the word "difference" because she's so upset about Barney's death and Daddy's brain, and when the bartender himself brings the fifth daiquiri, assures her it's not virgin, and says, "Trust me, honey, that Jumbo's got a triple shot of rum in it, same as your last four," and Claire asks, "Are your daiquiris made from concrete? I mean, from consent—from consternate—or from organic peaches?", and when the bartender says something else that doesn't matter, Claire doesn't care that they're trying to destroy her liver and just asks, "Why was it bug juice!", but the bartender's gone, but that's OK because it's late, nearly midnight, and Gator's is packed, and she's sitting at a booth with three, maybe four, possibly five guys, all at least a decade younger than her, but they're sweet for buying her daiquiris and teaching her that the Colts are a football team, not basketball, that the Pacers are basketball, and she tells them how you can't write a seven-note scale without a tritone and how they'd all be filthy rich if they started farming fireflies and harvesting them for luciferase, and they all agree and they're nice and friendly and eager to learn more about luciferase, but frankly, Claire just wants to go upstairs and go to sleep and never taste a peach again, but that's impossible, because Slob might still be there, in her apartment, and she can't confront him, not now, because she keeps thinking how, just hours ago, her father stared at his sugar beet and didn't look at her, how that *not looking* was the same—how, twenty-seven days and eleven years ago, her mother had not looked at her, had only watched Barney's twitching, the twitching which, despite Claire's having speared him through the eye with a nineteenth-century African artifact and sawn off his cantaloupe-sized head with a ten-inch Sabatier chef knife, wouldn't stop; how her mother had not looked at her when Claire called the police, had only watched her husband breathe as he slept under the kitchen-etc.-room table; how her mother had not looked at her when Claire told the police that it was not she but her father, the drunk lying under the table, who had killed Barney; how her mother hadn't looked when she left and never came back—so, yes, the same as Mom and, no, Claire can't go to bed yet, because Dad might be there, plus her student, the nudist composer and pianist, appears to be the Gator's dishwasher, and she really ought to give him back his boot before she heads to bed.

Book Excerpt 7.8. (The End of Book.) *Concerning Knut's "thing with a shotgun."*

Torbjorn does not smoke. Not ever. He is looking for a plunger.

He's been trying to "do dish," after a strenuous karaoke-rush that resulted in Cowboy Wolfer's deep-frying, among other things, an iPhone. But as midnight and Torbjorn's fortieth hour without sleep slowly approached, as sleep-deprivation began to obscure the boundary between the territory of dream (bubbling dishwater, curtains of indoor rainfall, etc.) and "Dish Territory," as his clothes became more and more wet, especially the sock of his bootless foot, as the dishes he scrubbed in the plugged-up sink adopted personalities and he talked to them about his day, about a blue dress and how he lost his boot, and they reminded him how the dishwater in this plugged-up sink is disgusting, and he apologized for the whole sink situation and told them about nice places, clean ones, and they asked, "Oh yeah? Like where?", and he said, "Like dorm rooms," and he tried to tell them what his dorm room looks like, but he couldn't remember, could only recall a mattress without sheets, so he should probably buy sheets when he buys a shoe, but it's likely he'll have to buy a pair of shoes because they don't usually sell those individually, and as these talking-dish and indoor-rain hallucinations (despite a second dinner of Yellow Swarm) *accelerando*'d, Torbjorn finally faced reality: He's got to find a fucking plunger.

So now, standing in the middle of the dry-stock aisle, facing the "Walk-In" door, Torbjorn is looking for a plunger. But Torbjorn does not smoke. Not ever. And he's long lost patience with Wolfer, who, having finally snapped under the pressure of the karaoke-rush, dumped an iPhone, along with other choice items from Gator's Lost & Found bin (notably, an assortment of cell phones and Bic lighters, two wallets, a Nikon Coolpix digital camera, a Harry Potter action figure, and a 13-inch Dell laptop computer), into the deep-fryers, and who is now, Torbjorn knows, behind this Walk-In door, inside this closet-sized cooler, where the cowboy now pursues less stressful experiments in 3D geometry—simples ones, involving various volume-wolfs—that is, on top of himself, how many waitresses can he fit in the 5×5×8-foot Walk-In (in addition to its vats of chili, boxes of fries and beef patties, tubs of marinating breasts, and the Lost & Found bin), while maintaining a constant temperature of 41°F and smoking marijuana. The experiment is, no doubt, going well. Torbjorn's search for a plunger, however, is not. The Captain Owner Guy had said, "Chrissake, T-Bone, check your nail." Eventually, Torbjorn gathered that the plunger's handle has a loop, a rusty ring of steel wire that slices your hand and gives you tetanus, so it can hang from a nail above the sink. But the plunger was not on its nail, so the Captain doesn't know where it is. Nor do the dishes. But Wolfer might.

Anyway, Torbjorn does not smoke. Not ever. So when he opens the Walk-In door and, peering into the dark smoke-filled cooler, beholds a globular mass of smoky bodies that reminds him of Ligeti's *Atmospheres* or JJ's plum-pudding model,[202] Torbjorn has a coughing fit. On the upside, however, as the pungent scent of pot diffuses throughout the open-air kitchen and his coughing fit subsides, the first object to materialize out of this foggy pudding is in fact the plunger, aimed, as weapon, at Torbjorn's face.

"Either come in or shut the door," shouts the plunger—its voice, also much like pudding. Torbjorn attributes this voice to a lone cherry burning red between the lips of a bearded cowboy.

Torbjorn has no desire to join their jam-packed pudding. Nor the energy to get Wolfer to heel and surrender the poised plunger. "Wolfer," Torbjorn scolds, "I need the plunger."

No answer. A waitress giggles. Other waitresses join the giggling.

Torbjorn applies pressure: "*Man*, Wolfer, the Captain is like all pissed and said you better come out right away and break down the grill-line so I can do dish, because I need the plunger."

Pressure backfires: "What you talking about there, T-Bone?" It's the Captain Owner's voice, coming from *inside* the Walk-In, from the nucleus of the pudding.

"Well, I need the plunger, anyway." Torbjorn grabs the plunger by the handle, just behind the rubber cup aimed at his head. But the plunger comes alive: It rips free from his grip, then bops him on the top of his head. This *bop* has consequences:

First the cherry comes alive: Sparks erupt, like fireworks—"Stop! You wolfed the joint."

Then the Walk-In comes alive: It erupts, like a volcano—"Where's the wolf? I dropped it!"—first it spews a small waitress, who tumbles into Torbjorn's arms and clutches, clawing him with her sharp fingernails—"I said, where's the wolf?"—then a second spewed waitress

[202] I see no relation between the following: (1) a cooler full of potheads, (2) an orchestral work by György Ligeti, (3) the atomic model of British physicist Joseph John Thomson, who received the 1906 Nobel Prize for his discovery of electrons, which, like raisins, he embedded in the uniform, positively charged sphere of his pudding-like atom.

grabs Torbjorn, as he attempts to dislodge the sharp claws of the first—"The wolf, where is it?"—but the second grabs tighter, as Walk-In spews a far larger third waitress, who tumbles into the first—"There it is. There's the—wolf, no, you're gonna step on her!"—and finally, the spewed Captain Owner slams into the large third, as Torbjorn, falling backwards from the impact, catches his balance on the dry-stock shelves behind him, but then the second waitress slugs the Captain for having grabbed her boob—one helluva slug—and, like dominoes, the Captain and two waitresses, the first and large third, all collapse into Torbjorn and the dry-stock shelves, which, in turn, as eight hands grasp for them, all give way, and tubs of mayonnaise, bags of buns, Winnie-the-Pooh, and large cans of beans, tomatoes, and whatever fall on a pile of four bodies, Torbjorn at bottom, then scatter, tubs and cans rolling wherever across the slick greasy floor.

"Ah wolf, Captain, just look what you did." Standing in the Walk-In doorway, Wolfer regards the papery remains of what must have been the dropped joint.

With plunger yet in hand, Captain Owner gets to his knees, and the apologetic second waitress lends her boss a hand (rather than a boob) to help him stand. "Chrissake, Partner," he says to Wolfer, "was that really necessary?"

"Wolf was gonna step on it."

Cowboy's explanation seems satisfactory: "Sure she was," says the Captain.

The third waitress helps the far smaller first to her feet. But the assembly line ends there: Nobody, not even the first waitress with long red-painted fingernails, helps Torbjorn.

"Chrissake, T-Bone," Captain says, bopping Torbjorn on the head with the plunger, "was that really necessary?"

"Sorry, sir," says Torbjorn, standing on his own, "but sinks are plugged-up."

Though spared a third head-bopping, Torbjorn's explanation is less than satisfactory: "Course they are, T-Bone," Captain says, "that's no excuse. Sinks is sinks—but hey, Partner."

"Yes, Captain," Wolfer says, rolling another joint.

"Not out in the open."

"Yes, Captain." Wolfer takes one step back, into the Walk-In, and out of the open.

"Good, but should probably save her for later," Captain says, indicating Wolfer's joint. "It's dish-time and, apparently, past T-Bone's bedtime—and hey, ladies."

"Yes, Captain?" three waitresses ask, nearly in unison.

"You, too, you three," he says, "don't you got tables?"

"Yes, Captain. We do." The three waitresses disperse, with parting frowns at Torbjorn's bootless foot, and Wolfer, sliding joint into his breast pocket, takes a step forward, into the open.

"Right, now you and T-Bone clean up this mess," Captain says, as he points, with plunger, to the fallen shelves, cans, tubs, buns—points everywhere—his plunger wandering *distractedly*, as if he's weaving a cleaning spell over the entire kitchen, or tracking fireflies.

Wolfer waits for Captain to finish pointing, then replies: "Aye, aye, Cap'n. It's a wolf."

"Sure it is." Captain kicks a can of peeled tomatoes across the floor, and it rolls under the swinging doors by the register. He follows it out of the kitchen. Taking the plunger with him.

Torbjorn starts the cleanup process: He picks up a shelf, a long wooden plank.

Wolfer comes alive—"Wolf!"—he knocks the shelf out of Torbjorn's hands with a karate chop across the wrists: "Time for that, later," he says. "We got wolfs to talk about." Grabbing a wrist, he yanks Torbjorn into the Walk-In. The door shuts: Cold and dark—the walls lined with tubs, boxes stacked on the wet floor—the ceiling's fluorescent lamp, glowing dimly, flickers.[203]

"What the hell, man?" Torbjorn says.

"Enough of your wolfin'." The cowboy sits on a case of fries and fires up a joint. He takes a deep drag, like a vacuum cleaner, then holds it in: Leaning forward, forearms on his knees, his beard hangs giant between his thighs. Roaches litter the floor between his feet.

Torbjorn sits beside him on a case of "Big Boy" patties. Cold and tired, he waits. The *whirr* of the cooler's refrigeration is loud. His clothes, soaked. His bootless foot, numb. Also, in the far corner, below a shelf of soup tubs, in the LOST & FOUND bin, there is a shotgun.

Finally, Wolfer exhales: cloud of smoke. "So," he asks, "what happened to your boot?"

The room, full of smoke. "Lost it," says Torbjorn.

"Yeah..." Another drag, another cloud. "I lost a dog recently."

Torbjorn laughs. "Yeah?" he asks.

"Yeah," says the cowboy, not laughing, "her name was Wolf."

---

[203] Obviously. Fluorescent lamps don't work well below 50°F. The moron who installed a fluorescent lamp in this cooler should invest in a plastic lamp sleeve. High-output lamps (HO) are also available, operating down to 10°F.

"Yeah?"

"Yeah, a little Weiner dog, she was. Miss her little wolf-face. Ever since she passed away…I don't know. I started saying 'wolf' all the time. All I ever say is wolf this and wolf that, but she don't wolf back."

The cowboy takes another long drag, sucking hard, like a black-hole woman, then holds: This time, the wait is longer, an infinity, and Torbjorn thinks how infinity looks like ∞. How he hasn't slept in days and Captain's got the plunger. How the Walk-In is cold and full of smoke. How its smoke spirals slowly, but convulsively, in the flickering fluorescent light: a slow dance, in strobe light. How there's a shotgun in the LOST & FOUND bin and Wolfer's still holding.

Torbjorn stands. "Dude, I gotta go. Sorry about the dog, seriously. But I haven't slept in like forty hours and I got dishes. Plus, dry-stock's on the floor. And Captain's got the plunger."

"No!" The cowboy chokes—coughs of smoke—then seizes a wrist. "Told you, we got wolfs to talk about." He jerks Torbjorn back down, onto his Big-Boy seat. "Got a message," he says, but then pauses, releasing Torbjorn's wrist, to relight his joint. "Right, so, message is: Boss wants you to lay off the girl."

"What?"

"You know, the wolf. The one that called the cops."

"Who—Claire? You mean the one your *boss* is stalking?"

"No, wolf's name is Busy-something-bee. Something B-wolf. Starts with B."

"Her name's Claire," Torbjorn says. "I should know. She's my music-theory professor."

Wolfer taps his joint, ash falls between them. "Your neck, not mine," he says. "You're the school-shooter. I'm just the messenger-wolf. And Boss says, lay off the wolf."

"Whatever, man, I ain't the stalker."

"Messenger-wolf, is all. But I'd be careful. She's out there, right now."

"Yeah, I saw."

"Well, the wolf never comes here. Not her. Which is…*fishy*."

"What?" Torbjorn asks.

"*Fishy…*" The cowboy seems distracted: He is rolling a second joint, the first smoking in his lips. "Girl's here, and never is. *Fishy*. Wolfs'll be suspicious. They're always watching."

"Who's watching?"

The Walk-In door swings open: the light blinding like a flashlight, the silhouette large like a Walrus. But it's just Captain Owner Guy: "T-Bone!" he shouts, pointing his plunger.

Torbjorn stands up quickly. He slips on the wet floor, but catches his balance on the shelf beside him, where—shit—his fist flattens a cheesecake. "Sorry, sir. I slipped."

"Sure you did." But the Captain, still aiming the plunger, does not seem angry: "Just a cheesecake," he says, almost sadly, his tone as docile as his bloodshot eyes, stoned. "Excuses," he says, lowering the plunger, "that's all it ever is. But right now, T-Bone, you got a visitor."

"What?"

"Some girl asking for you—so Wolfer!"

"Yes, Captain."

"Wolfer, you're cleanup. Dry-stock shelves is on the floor. That won't do—T-Bone!"

"Yes, sir."

"You go talk to your girl. See if she wants a job, while you're at it."

Torbjorn steps around the Captain and out of the Walk-In. By the register, above the swinging saloon-style doors, is Professor Claire's head. It is smiling at him.

"But, sir," Torbjorn says, "I got dishes to—"

"Darnit, T-Bone, you go take care of that girl—and Wolfer!"

"Yes, Captain."

Suddenly, Captain is chipper: "Christ, you got another one going there, Partner?"

"Aye, Cap'n." Wolfer offers him a pair of joints: one long, one short. "Got two going."

"Good." Captain hands Torbjorn the plunger: "T-Bone, why don't you take care of that girl?" he says, and then, selecting the longer of Wolfer's two joints, steps inside the Walk-In and shuts the—"Christ!"—he opens the door. "T-Bone!" he shouts. "What the blazes—Chissake—is this yours?" Through the Walk-In doorway, the Captain is holding out the shotgun.

"No, sir," Torbjorn says.

"Sure it isn't, but—"

"Belongs to Boss-wolf," says the cowboy behind him. "Was missing, but not anymore. *Antique*," he adds.

"Sure it is. And a beauty—pre-'64, or I'm a city boy—but why's it in LOST & FOUND? Not allowed. We got policies." Captain shakes the gun at Torbjorn: "Take it! Quick! Quick!"

Torbjorn takes the shotgun shaking in his face: "OK, sir, but what do you want me to—"

"Don't care," Captain says. "No guns in the Walk-In." The door slams shut.

"Shit," Torbjorn says, plunger in one hand, shotgun in the other.

"Nice Winchester," says a voice.

"Shit," he says, turning back to his music-theory professor: Claire wears the saloon doors well—her smiling head above, bare legs below—but her hair is messy, and her words, slurred: "Got something for you, *Torby*," she says. "Come on out." Her head and legs depart to the left.

Torbjorn should not follow. He had a mother figure once, and Mother Figure'd called him "Torby." This is bad. He's out of Yellow Swarm—midnight, the cusp of his fortieth hour, has now struck—and Professor Claire is not her best: She's *lost* the suck-hole face, but *found* a drunken smiley face. Plus, she's got some serious stalker issues, corroborated by Wolfer's warning: Lay off the girl, people are watching, something's fishy. Also, Torbjorn is holding a shotgun. A Winchester, according to his music teacher. As well as a plunger.

Torbjorn follows. Laying plunger and shotgun on the counter by the register, he pushes through the swinging saloon doors and exits the kitchen. Gator's is still packed, but to his left, perhaps ten feet away, Professor Claire, still wearing that blue dress, is leaning against the edge of a booth table. Under this table, Dr. Long, still dressed in a sequined bullfighter's costume, appears to be unconscious. But at this booth sit six guys, and, unlike the rest of the screaming scantily-clad college kids squeezing into booths to escape the wrath of angry waitresses, these guys are silent, sitting with their feet up, knees to chest, to accommodate the comatose composer under their table, and staring at Claire, hypnotized by this asexual professor's—

A large boot is flying toward him: Torbjorn holds up his arms and ducks—

Too late: The boot hits him in the head, anyway. *His* boot. His missing jungle boot.

Claire is swaying gently and looking in his direction. "Brought your boot," she says.

"I can see that," Torbjorn says. He bends over to cram his foot into his black jungle boot, but it slides in easy: his soaked sock, slick and greasy. He kneels down to lace, then tie.

"I'm drunk," Claire says.

Torbjorn doesn't say that he can see that. He's not sure what to say to his drunk-ass professor. None of that black hole she had at noon. She's sucked it all in, might be ready to explode. He finishes tying his lace, slowly. Then stands and asks: "Where'd you find it?"

"What?" she asks.

"My boot."

"Oh, it was in my china cabinet. Come over, so we can talk."

She doesn't seem to be holding any other potential projectiles, so Torbjorn does. He stops in front of her, just out of reach. She scoots back and sits full on the booth table, so that her bare legs dangle off the edge, and also so she knocks over a pitcher of beer that spills onto a hypnotized guy's lap. "Ah!" she shouts. "What are you doing?" She hops off the table, holding her ass. She twists and turns, chasing her tail. Her tail is wet. Torbjorn grabs a fistful of napkins from a basket at an adjacent booth. He holds them out to her.

"Hey, professor," he says, offering napkins.

She smiles, almost sweetly. "Oh, thanks. I'm all wet." She scrubs vigorously—this is too much, it seems, for the booth of six staring guys—but Claire's scrub effort is short-lived, as napkins drop, fly, and scatter to the floor, next to Dr. Long. Out of napkins, Claire seems satisfied: She stamps one high-heeled foot and crosses her arms, same as she did this afternoon, on stage, in the Annex—except this time she slips: Torbjorn catches her before she hits the floor.

"Don't touch!" she shouts, slapping her way out of his arms. She stands OK on her own now, but still sways gently. "Floor's all wet," she says.

"I can see that." Torbjorn also sees that an audience (male) has gathered, forming a semicircular wall behind him, while Claire's six guys, evacuating their wet booth (Long left under table), join the wall behind her, completing the circle behind her beer-stained ass.

But Claire seems oblivious of their new audience, of their being surrounded by a wall of large males: She stamps her heels successively and says: "I don't care if it's bug juice."

"What?" Torbjorn asks.

"Bug"—stamp—"juice"—stamp.

"OK."

From audience: laughter, whistles, and a "You go girl!"

Claire ignores her male audience: "Why do you hate me?" she asks Torbjorn.

"What?"

"There's no reason," she explains, "just because his quartet's bug juice, for you to hate me." She then turns and shouts behind her: "Dr. Long!" she calls.

No answer from Dr. Long.

Unlike audience: "Yeah, man, why do you hate her?" says an elbow in Torbjorn's back. Followed by an "Ah baby, *I* don't hate you."

Torbjorn gets the message: "I don't hate you," he says.

"Yes, you do."

"OK, I hate you."

No response from audience.

"Ah Torby," she says, "your piano composition, this afternoon, that was no bug juice."

Audience back into it: They seem to like the bug juice comments.

"What composition?" Torbjorn asks.

"On stage, silly. You were playing it naked."

Audience: whistles.

Torbjorn attempts to justify his creative process: "Yeah, I was just—"

"What do you want with me?" she asks.

"I don't—"

"Fine!" she shouts.

Audience: *Oh yeah*'s, whistles, *Hoot-hoot*'s, and one "Bug juice!"

"Fine what?" Torbjorn asks.

"Fine, you can take me home. I don't care anymore."

"What?"

"Take me home, now." She falls, she hugs him, her face hidden in his neck—*Ah*'s from audience—then in his ear: "Please," she whispers, "I'm afraid. I can't go alone. He's there. I know he is. I need you to take me home. He rapes me, in my dreams. Please, take me. Now."

Torbjorn is tired, T-Bone's got dishes to do: "OK," he says, "but first I gotta—"

"You're wet," she says.

"Yes," he says.

"And you stink."

"Yes."

"Just don't tell anybody you're my student." She wraps her arms around his neck and looks up into his eyes. It's romantic, but not really.

Audience agrees: "Kiss her, dude."

She smiles and whispers: "I brought your boot."

Chant from audience: "Kiss! Kiss! Kiss! Kiss!"

"No!" Claire shouts. She pushes Torbjorn away, pushes hard, and he slips and falls on the wet floor, falls flat on his back.

"No!" she shouts, stepping back. "No, stay away! I mean it. I said, go away."

But Claire is not addressing Torbjorn: She is looking at Slobodon, who is standing over, but not looking at, Torbjorn. And Slob, staring back at her, appears more haggard and disheveled than usual, especially here, against the backdrop of their audience, against this wall of frat boys modeling for Abercrombie & Fitch, and especially now that, in addition to his too-short trousers and earth-stained sport coat, Slob's white shirt appears to be covered in blood.

The audience, however, doesn't seem to notice this pipeline between bloodstained Slob and beer-stained Claire—not with a maiden in distress: "Help!" Claire shouts, and they all rush to the rescue, some two-dozen bodybuilding frat-boys pushing and shoving to gain a place by her side, to form a squirming protective wall around her—"What did he do?" they ask. "What? Are you hurt?"—and Claire is crying and shaking: "Please help. Get him out of here. He's always there. Wherever I go. Following me. Please, I'm not crazy. Not dreaming. It's always the same—rape!"[204] And while the nearest members of the protective squirming wall, including the six booth guys, comfort Claire, the angel dressed in blue with a wet ass, the angel who spilled beer on their laps, while these inner members shield her from danger, the outer dozen-or-so members, having observed that she's not hurt, well-protected, and safe, this outer dozen attends to her malevolent stalker, and possibly a rapist, Torbjorn.

Some guy lifts Torbjorn from the ground and, from behind, locks Torbjorn's arms behind his back, as the others, ignoring Slob, form a squirming imprisoning wall around the stalker and interrogate him: "What's your problem, man?" they ask Torbjorn, but instantly conclude: "Think it's time to leave, buddy, and I mean, like, right now." And Torbjorn—arm-locked, unable to point, and surrounded by a wall of Abercrombie automatons who seem to be

[204] Cf. Satan in Excerpt 3.1.

majoring in weightlifting and ignoring bloodstained Slob—Torbjorn explains their mistake: "It's not me, it's him," he shouts, nodding to elderly Slob, to an old bald guy in an earth-stained sport coat who stands with his back to them.

Torbjorn's explanation seems less than satisfactory: "Bullshit," they say. And Slob, silent, takes this opportunity to leave, to wedge his way away from Torbjorn's Imprisoning Squirm Wall and toward Claire's Protecting Squirm Wall.

Torbjorn shouts: "Quick, he's getting away," and, from behind Protecting Squirm Wall, Claire shouts back, hysterically: "Get him out. Help. Rape."

Imprisoning Squirm Wall takes steps: "All right, buddy," says the arm-locker, "you're coming with us." And they—well, he, the arm-locker, aided by on-looking Imprisoning Wall—proceed to drag Torbjorn, with difficulty, down a packed aisle (the booths now chiefly occupied by women, their males eager to enlist in the Squirm Wall effort) toward the front entrance.

Minor progress is made, as Torbjorn struggles to glimpse Slob in the widening breach between the two Squirm Walls, in the rift by the kitchen's swinging doors, and though Protecting Squirm Wall appears to yet thwart Slob, Torbjorn hears the shouts: Claire's "Out, get him out!" and Slob's "Bisera—Bisera, please!" and Claire's "That's not my name! I'm not crazy. Help."

And as her shouts of "Help!" and "Rape!" continue, a door opens in Protecting Squirm Wall, an opening of bodies, who turn around to face aged Slob. Torbjorn can't see Claire, only Slob stepping closer to this opening, to a hidden screaming Claire. Then, suddenly, Wolfer and Captain emerge from the kitchen, through the swinging doors and into the breach between the Walls: "Wolf, Boss, what's going on here?" And Claire screams louder.

Torbjorn back-kicks, his heel stomping the shin of his large arm-locker, and breaks free. He charges into the wall of tipsy frat boys, who slip and fall and knock each other over like bowling pins on the slick floor, and Torbjorn keeps skating, tunneling through the crowd like a ball through pins, and somewhere, Claire is screaming "That's not my name. I mean it. Get back or I'll"—but all Torbjorn sees, as he bursts into the breach, is Slobodon, and, finally, with no pins left between them, Torbjorn hurtles, accelerating, sliding fast in his boot-skates across the greasy floor, until they collide and Torbjorn grabs hold and Slob shouts "Tumor!" and they tumble, together, face to face, the old man in his arms, the old face shouting "It's benign!" and the young "What?" and, as one, they both shout "What?" when suddenly, out of nowhere, for just a split second, a pair of black holes (they look like this: ∞) swings into view, just before ∞ fires into their face, and all lights go out.

PROBLEMS

7.1. My mother's tumor was not benign.[205]

7.2. Nor was the *germination* of Claire's performance of Bach's Fugue 1 in C-major (see Excerpt 7.4). The following document, recovered from Knut's box, appears to be his analysis of the fugue in question:

[205] Nor did I shoot her in the face.

Figure 7.1. Knut's analytical process.

7.3. *The Guilt Surrounding the Death of My Mother (Part 3 of 3).*[206]

(a) *On germs and marriage.*[207]

Dear Dead Knut,

Recall: In the "Prolegomenon to §7" I chronicled the night I tried to be nice, and although I threw your library books on the floor, you promised to procure my mother's money. You had a plan. Your plan was a "catastrophic," and the following sequence of catastrophes in equations of less than five variables begins the next day, at noon—in nineteen hours, my mother will be dead:

Catastrophe That's All Your Fault Number One: *Fold Catastrophe*, $F_1(x, u) = x^3 + ux$:[208] Firstly, my dearest Dead Knut, you didn't launch the catastrophe sequence well by interrupting my fifth-period Calculus lecture on Fixed Point Theorems, which hadn't been going well in the first place, given that (1) I hadn't graded their exams because, instead, the night before, I'd decided to be nice and (2) I was right in the middle of proving

> *Rolle's Theorem*: Let f be continuous on $[a, b]$ and differentiable on (a, b), and suppose that $f(a) = f(b)$. Then there is some c with $a < c < b$ such that $f'(c) = 0$.

which wasn't going well because my proof of Rolle's, which I'd copied on the board from my notes, had nothing to do with Rolle's Theorem (a blunder which none of the Catholic high-school students had noticed [and, although I was stuck and knew something wasn't right, neither had I]), but rather, what I'd written was the proof of the subsequent theorem in my notes

> *Mean Value Theorem*: Let f be continuous on $[a, b]$ and differentiable on (a, b). Then there is some c with $a < c < b$ such that $f(b) = f(a) + (b - a)f'(c)$.

the proof of which *uses* Rolle's, which, in turn, provoked

Catastrophe That's All Your Fault Number Two: *Cusp Catastrophe*, $F_2(x, u, v) = x^4 + ux^2 + vx$: When Ms. Elsa Something, the principal's administrative assistant, by opening the door as quietly and discreetly as possible, entered the classroom, that's when I, thus stumped by the proof of this elementary theorem, shouted, "Damn it, Elsa, didn't your mother ever teach you how to knock?", and then, gaining my composure, said, "I'm sorry, but I've totally screwed up this—oh—oh, I'm so sorry, but—", at which point I stopped mid-sentence, brain and mouth suddenly forming a right angle, because, firstly, the students in the front row were paying attention for once, perking up (as if, as my father used to say, mid-colonoscopy) at the idea that I, their substitute teacher, had "screwed up" something, and, secondly,

---

[206] Students of my guilt may wish to review footnotes 92-140 (for part 1) and the Prolegomenon to §7 (part 2).

[207] **Irrelevant Definition 7.9. (Germs.)** The GERMS of catastrophe geometries are degenerate critical points of the potential function, and have nothing to do with the above narrative.

[208] My listing of catastrophe geometries is mathematically irrelevant, as well: They are headings, nothing more.

because I'd suddenly recalled a soul-killing conversation I'd had with Ms. Elsa Something over lunch break last week when she, drinking a Heineken, had confessed, confidentially (albeit excitedly, as if it were hot gossip), that she was, among other things, an orphan, and therefore, Dead Knut, it was coldly that she announced (to the class): "I have an urgent *anonymous* message for you," which she then read (to the entire class) from a large *neon-orange* post-it note: 'Problem solved, but come hospital immediately—emergency.'"

"Is that it?" I asked.

Ms. Elsa Something slammed the door as she left.

<u>Catastrophe That's All Your Fault Number Three</u>: *Swallowtail Catastrophe*, $F_3(x, u, v, w) = x^5 + ux^3 + vx^2 + wx$: For the first time in my life, I let my students go ten minutes early—which was inappropriate because this is high school (not college)—but I didn't give a shit, grabbed my "briefcase" (alt. suitcase), and ran out of the room, which brings us to

<u>Catastrophe That's All Your Fault Number Four</u>: *Butterfly Catastrophe*, $F_4(x, t, u, v, w) = x^6 + ux^4 + vx^3 + wx^2 + tx$: I'd forgotten to erase my egregious error on the chalkboard.

<u>Catastrophe That's (Probably Not) All Your Fault Number Five</u>: *Hyperbolic Umbilic Catastrophe*, $F_5(x, y, u, v, w) = x^3 + y^3 + uxy + vx + wy$: Traffic.

<u>Catastrophe That's (Definitely) All Your Fault Number Six</u>: *Elliptic Umbilic Catastrophe*, $F_6(x, y, u, v, w) = x^3/3 - xy^2 + u(x^2 + y^2) + vx + wy$: Four Simultaneous Traffic Violation Tickets: (1) speeding, (2) no proof of insurance, (3) damaged windshield wiper, and (4) driving on the wrong side of the road.

<u>Catastrophe To End All Catastrophes</u>: *Parabolic Umbilic Catastrophe*, $F_7(x, y, t, u, v, w) = x^2y + y^4 + ux^2 + vy^2 + wx + ty$: I doubt that you, Dead Knut, given the catastrophic nature of the festivities, remember what it was like, how I, running through the hospital's maze of halls (which I knew well) to the long-term patient wing, charging down the crowded halls "like a ball through pins," bumping into shrieking nurses (and one old guy in a wheelchair), until finally, out of breath, gasping, sides burning, I reach my mother's room, but stop: Paralyzed, unable to walk through the open door, I just stand there, looking in—stuck—because you'd married my mother, and I missed the wedding. (In eighteen hours, my mother will be dead.)

(b) *On eating books.*

A sunrise is a striptease between day and night…

Why?

Dead Writer, Why?

Why, the dawn you die, did you say this?

Yes, the sun was beginning to rise, far away. Through your window, the driver's-side window, we could see a sliver of the sun, clenched between the horizon's crooked line of black backlit treetops and the outer edge of black cloud, one cloud, one black ceiling that, except for that slice of sunrise, covered the rest of the sky, that stretched over us from east to west and battered the roof of your Jeep with hail and darkness, and I was afraid. I was. But through your window, far away, at the feet of the eastern horizon, at storm cloud's end, a thread of yellow-red purpled the black cloud's outer rim, and I hoped. I did.[209]

But you—Why?—with the river rising and the hail and Jeep rocking in the wind, why did you hand me the sealed envelope and say, "A sunrise is a striptease between day and night"—Why?

And why, you ask, am I asking this? Well, Dead Knut, there was another window. Before she died, there was another—another one of yours—and there was no storm, but the sun rose the same, wedged between the earth and a purple-edged cloud. It was the window beside your wedding bed, the sunrise that ended your wedding night, and you didn't know I was there, on the other side of the door. You didn't know I was listening just outside my mother's hospital room, the door cracked open just slightly, listening to you read to your new bride, read those stupid books, read chess moves and Homer, and stumble through math equations and Latin, and tonguing Beethoven's Fifth, and you didn't know I cried. Ridiculous. But I did. And it was ridiculous: The night of the wedding, the night before her brain surgery, your reading things neither of you could understand, couldn't even pronounce, things she'd always wanted to learn but never had, and the prognosis wasn't good, and because of the surgery, she couldn't eat, so you fed her books. Ridiculous. And hidden outside, uninvited, I listened, listened all night to your rasping voice, and I cried and wasn't sad. I wasn't and I did. But near dawn, I got brave: I peeked through the slit in the door and saw the back of your nearly-mullet head and the same slice of sunrise through the window. And I saw her bald head's face shine in the yellow light.

This is the dawn she dies.

What I did was wrong.

Atone.

Forgive me.

(c) My mother's tumor was not benign. My mother's tumor was not benign. My mother's tumor was not benign. My mother's tumor was not benign. My mother's tumor was not benign. My mother's tumor was not benign. My mother's tumor was not benign. My mother's tumor was not benign. My mother's tumor was not benign. My mother's tumor was not benign. My mother's tumor was not benign. My mother's tumor was not benign. My mother's tumor was not benign. My mother's tumor was not benign. My mother's tumor was not benign. My mother's tumor was not benign. My mother's tumor was not benign. My mother's tumor was not benign. My mother's tumor was not benign. My mother's tumor

[209] In retrospect, I was an idiot. Storms travel from west to east. My window was black.

was not benign. My mother’s tumor was not benign. My mother’s tumor was not benign. My mother’s
tumor was not benign. My mother’s tumor was not benign. My mother’s tumor was not benign. My
mother’s tumor was not benign. My mother’s tumor was not benign. My mother’s tumor was not benign.
My mother’s tumor was not benign. My mother’s tumor was not benign. My mother’s tumor was not
benign. My mother’s tumor was not benign. My mother’s tumor was not benign. My mother’s tumor
was not benign. My mother’s tumor was not benign. My mother’s tumor was not benign. My mother’s
tumor was not benign. My mother’s tumor was not benign. My mother’s tumor was not benign. My
mother’s tumor was not benign. My mother’s tumor was not benign. My mother’s tumor was not benign.
My mother’s tumor was not benign. My mother’s tumor was not benign. My mother’s tumor was not
benign. My mother’s tumor was not benign. My mother’s tumor was not benign. My mother’s tumor
was not benign. My mother’s tumor was not benign. My mother’s tumor was not benign. My mother’s
tumor was not benign. My mother’s tumor was not benign. My mother’s tumor was not benign. My
mother’s tumor was not benign. My mother’s tumor was not benign. My mother’s tumor was not benign.
My mother’s tumor was not benign. My mother’s tumor was not benign. My mother’s tumor was not
benign. My mother’s tumor was not benign. My mother’s tumor was not benign. My mother’s tumor
was not benign. My mother’s tumor was not benign. My mother’s tumor was not benign. My mother’s
tumor was not benign. My mother’s tumor was not benign. My mother’s tumor was not benign. My
mother’s tumor was not benign. My mother’s tumor was not benign. My mother’s tumor was not benign.
My mother’s tumor was not benign. My mother’s tumor was not benign. My mother’s tumor was not
benign. My mother’s tumor was not benign. My mother’s tumor was not benign. My mother’s tumor
was not benign. My mother’s tumor was not benign. My mother’s tumor was not benign. My mother’s
tumor was not benign. My mother’s tumor was not benign. My mother’s tumor was not benign. My
mother’s tumor was not benign. My mother’s tumor was not benign. My mother’s tumor was not benign.
My mother’s tumor was not benign. My mother’s tumor was not benign. My mother’s tumor was not
benign. My mother’s tumor was not benign. My mother’s tumor was not benign. My mother’s tumor
was not benign. My mother’s tumor was not benign. My mother’s tumor was not benign. My mother’s
tumor was not benign. My mother’s tumor was not benign. My mother’s tumor was not benign. My
mother’s tumor was not benign. My mother’s tumor was not benign. My mother’s tumor was not benign.
My mother’s tumor was not benign. My mother’s tumor was not benign. My mother’s tumor was not
benign. My mother’s tumor was not benign. My mother’s tumor was not benign. My mother’s tumor
was not benign. My mother’s tumor was not benign. My mother’s tumor was not benign. My mother’s
tumor was not benign. My mother’s tumor was not benign. My mother’s tumor was not benign. My
mother’s tumor was not benign. My mother’s tumor was not benign. My mother’s tumor was not benign.
My mother’s tumor was not benign. My mother’s tumor was not benign. My mother’s tumor was not

benign. My mother's tumor was not benign. My mother's

(d) *On exploding head.*

The dawn she dies, I enter the room. In bed, her bald head still shines in the yellow light.

Silence. Except for the snoring. You are asleep, Dead Knut—done with reading, on to snoring—you and your mullet head, you sit, asleep, snoring, in a chair in the far corner of the hospital room. Except for Beethoven's Fifth lying open in your lap, you are naked.[210]

For the first time in twenty-seven days and eleven years, I stand beside my mother. She is different, lying there in her hospital bed: Unlike Knut, she is wearing clothes, a purple nightgown that *complements* her bald, yellow head. Unlike Knut, she is awake—

She speaks: "Are you the nurse?"

"No," I say.

In the chair, naked Knut snorts, but does not wake. He snores in snorts.

"You," she says. "Is it you?"

I do not answer. Cannot. Her bald head faces me—the tumor behind her eyes is large—she is blind in one eye. Her other eye is gone, the tumor's shoved the other from her head.

(e) *On last words.*

My mother has no eye patch. I stare at the growth where her eye used to be. According to Knut, she hadn't gone to a doctor until it popped from its socket.

Her last words: "The tumor," she says, "is not benign. Please help. I can't do this on my own."

(f) *On help.*

Her pillow. With difficulty, she removes the pillow from behind her head. She holds it out, up, near me, near my voice.

I take the pillow. Knut's asleep, snort-snoring soundly.

Last-last words: "It shouldn't be you, but your father's gone.[211] Your father wouldn't let them keep me this way. I'm sorry. Sorry it's you. But I need your help."

(g) *Help.*

Knut got it wrong:[212] There is no snake, no strangulation, no coiling constriction. Just a pillow.

There is no daughter to save the day, no decapitation, no twitching decapitated snake. Just her arms and legs, twitching. Just her head beneath the pillow. The tumor, bulging from the socket of her missing eye, hidden beneath the pillow.

Pressing, I feel the tumor bulging back beneath the pillow.

(h) *Post-mortem.*

---

[210] Ergo, a sunrise is a striptease between day and night?

[211] And has been, for twenty-seven days and eleven years. But that's another story.

[212] I.e., the thing with Claire's Mom and a dead rabbit in Excerpts 7.X, where X is odd: $X = 2k - 1$ for $k = 1, 2, 3, 4$.

After death, no twitching.

After death, the sun had risen full. And so had Knut. (Beethoven's Fifth, no longer on his lap.)

I had not seen him stand, not seen him wake, not heard his snoring stop. So I explained: "It's better," I said. "What she wanted. The tumor was not benign. She asked me to help."

"Bullshit," he said.

Bullshit: The last thing you said to me before you left, before you sat on your box in the street, before I called the cops and they took you, before you disappeared and I couldn't find you, before the rain, the weeks of rain, before I sat in my mother's house—same as now—until the laptop beeped itself dead, until, one night, you showed up and left a box, the night the river took you—before all this, the last thing you said to me, as you stood, naked in a hospital room beside my dead mother's wedding bed, was: "Bullshit."

(i) *The Knudson hypothesis.*[213]

Bullshit is right. That's not what happened. The truth is: Knut's hypothesis is correct—I am full of shit—I've fictionalized my mother's death, condensed the time. And I got a gallon of gasoline.

The truth is: We did hospice, and my mother's death was slow and dull and morphine-induced. Blind, delirious, Mom didn't recognize me as I gave her the morphine and, drop by drop, she drifted into death.

The truth is: I imagined suffocating her with a pillow, but never did. Instead, I got to watch Knut be depressed as I slowly "killed" my mother, as I sat by her side, night after night, dripping morphine under her tongue, as she smoked imaginary cigarettes I wouldn't give her and spoke in Greek I couldn't understand.[214] Instead, I got to watch my new "stepfather" try to drink himself to death, because he married my mother for her money, because her money should have been mine. Poor Knut, bottle after bottle, his drunk, glossy, blue-gray eyes, blaming me, hating me—tell me, Knut, is that love? Is it? Is it guilt, sadness, is it shame? And for what? What am I doing, sitting here, writing this—why?

Damn it, Knut, the truth is: I am a river, my annotation of your *Book* has been my levee, but now I'm done. And yes, I suppose we could do more: Chapters have been skipped. And paintings, ignored. Not to mention your string quartet, my mother's *Requiem*. But I don't care: The levee cannot hold—I am flood, I am collapse, I am ready to explode.

---

[213] I.e., Mr. Knut Knudson's proposal that I be full of shit—not to be confused with the hypothesis that cancer results from the slow accumulation of DNA mutations, first formulated by Alfred G. Knudson in 1971. For *this* so-called "Knudson hypothesis," see A.G. Knudson, "Mutation and Cancer: Statistical Study of Retinoblastoma," *Proceedings of the National Academy of Sciences of the United States of America* 68.4 (1971): 820-23.

[214] Her father was a sugar beet farmer.

Also, I got a gallon of gasoline.

And frankly, Knut, if you were alive, I'd know exactly what to do: "Shut up!" I'd say. "That's right, Knut, you don't get to talk. I mean, who the hell do you think you are to do this to me, to write this shitty *Book*?" "I'm sorry," you'd interrupt. So I'd be forced to shout: "Damn it, Knut, shut up, for once, and listen. You don't have the right to play games with people in order to make yourself feel better for a moment, or in order to create some dramatic situation so you feel important, or whatever the fuck it is you think you're doing. I'm a real person, not some fucking character for you to manipulate. I have actual feelings and dreams and hurts and you have no goddamn right to hurt me this way for no reason other than you were fucking bored. You are not the center of the universe, no matter what you do to convince yourself otherwise. So. Fuck off. Just fuck off and wallow around in your paradoxical self-loathing egotism and Jack Daniels. Go treat other people like shit so you can constantly have something awful to keep your attention. I don't fucking care. I've been beaten up and cheated on and made broken-hearted enough by better men than you are, and I don't have the time to waste on your bullshit anymore. It's revolting. And I'm done. Go play somewhere else now."

And if this were a movie, there'd be this tense moment of silence and then we'd have angry sex on my dead mother's desk.

But this is not a movie, and Knut is dead, and I am alone and lost, sitting at her desk, squatting in her empty house, because everything is gone—job, home, lover, money, mother—all I got is Mr. Knudson's giant box of crap.[215] And now, this Book I've annotated, this *Book of Knut*. And a gallon of gasoline.

The truth is: I can't explode. Cannot. And never will—*Why?*—because I am boring, and far from artsy, unlike Mom, unlike Knut. Because every proof of love is a string of ideals.[216] Because the truth is: I am no Knut, no wannabe writer. Words are not my medium—I am a mathematician—what I can do is this: I can dump Knut's box of crap on my dead mother's desk and drench it all in gasoline. And, as I stand here, clutching *Book of Knut*, this manuscript of *Book* I've worked so hard to annotate and Knut will never see, and watch my mother's house burn to the ground, I can toss this *Book of Knut* into the fire and be free.

(j) THE END?

[215] For itemization of crap, see footnote 42 to Fluid 3 in Problem 3.5*a*.

[216] **Irrelevant Definition 7.10. (Ideals.)** An IDEAL is a subring I of a ring R s.t. $\forall\ a,b \in R$: $aI \subseteq I$ and $Ib \subseteq I$.

ANSWERS TO SELECTED HOMEWORK PROBLEMS

1.1. Fiction.

Fiction, life—in the end, what's the difference?

I was born and raised in southern Indiana, on the Ohio River. At the age of two, according to my mother (she's not dead), I ate Hegel's *Phänomenologie des Geistes*. I spit most of it on the floor.

After that, I remember practicing the piano until the age of eighteen, until 1999, when I went to music school, where I studied composition (even though I had ten fingers) with a composer named Phuc Q. (rather than Peng S.), but soon abandoned music for a more rewarding kitchen job, where I studied burger-flipping with a cook who said "wolf" occasionally (rather than compulsively). He collected swords.

The first decade of the new millennium is a blur. According to the records of four academic institutions and the IRS, a pattern emerged—with studies in music, math, chemistry, etc., episodically forsaken for bartending gigs and graveyard shifts at gas stations—but frankly, I don't remember much…

I remember a bar manager who owned a twenty-foot Burmese Python named Buster—Buster was in his car when he got the DUI.

I remember, one Fourth of July, from dusk to dawn, I painted a gas station red—on my black jungle boot, even now, there is still a speck of red paint on its steel toe.

I remember spending one summer in a château on the Seine, outside of Paris, where I finally accepted I couldn't compose music worth a damn. I didn't touch a piano for ten years.

Back in Indiana, I remember being homeless for a year, sleeping behind a Dumpster, and learning not to freeze to death. Wherever I went, I carried a giant cardboard box, full of scores and books and paper.

I remember women. A decade of women, with beds, AC, and alcohol. I'd write them to apologize if only I knew their names.

By decade's end, I remember ending up in Florida, where now I've lived three years, but never seen the ocean. It's here I came to study fiction with a writer I call the Colonel: One summer, some raccoons ate his chickens, so he set traps and ate the coons. Me, I store books in the fridge, my bathroom mirror looks like this:

Figure A.1. Halvor's bathroom mirror.

But what I'll remember best about Florida is the rehab: the mothers, deprived of crack, screaming for their kids. Most were poor, some wealthy, and one maintained to be the wife of a French Emperor, Napoléon Bonaparte. And I remember, on the day I graduated from rehab, this woman ("Miss Bonaparte") stood behind me and wrapped her arms around my neck, as I sat at a piano in the common room and played Chopin's Ballade in g-minor. I hadn't touched a piano in ten years, so it sucked. But the feeling of her arms around my neck, her hands down my chest, her breasts in my back, the feeling of her lips as she wept, it is this memory of her touch and her tears that's kept me sober, that's resulted in my answering this homework problem, in writing this Book, in searching for its end—an end—now, as I sit in a bus heading north on CA-1 from Antigua to Chichicastenango, and sitting here, writing this, I think: So what? Why? What do I know? What can I do? What have I learned? And why? Through the bus window, I see a little girl, standing on the side of the road, naked, tracing graffiti on a rock wall with her finger: I know nothing. This nude roadside child, her bare bony ribs—she knows more than me. The bus has passed her by—and me, sitting here, stuck on this Guatemalan "chicken bus," what can I do?—in the end, all I can do is this: I can tell you Knut's alive. I can tell you he survived the crash, the river, the barge crushing bridge, and Jeep, falling, buried under river in a ditch. I can tell you that our mathematician, annotator, and prolific author of homework problems is not an arsonist, is still sitting at her dead mother's desk, yet squatting in her mother's empty house, when suddenly, behind her, she hears a loud knock on the door. I can tell you she opens the front door and has an emotion, call it $\mathbb{Y}$, and, door open, she faces Knut, standing there, his clothes still soaked from the flood, and she doesn't know what to say, given $\mathbb{Y}$.

"Why?" she asks.

"Yeah," says Knut, "Jeep's in a ditch. Think she's done for."

7.3. (j) THE END.

To my mother, the writer, who got cancer after
I wrote Knut's Book, but who died before it was
published, and never read a word I wrote.

Halvor Aakhus
April 2012

ABOUT THE AUTHOR

Halvor Aakhus was born and raised in southern Indiana, on the Ohio River. There, he practiced the piano until 1999, when he went to the Jacobs School to study composition but soon abandoned music for various kitchen jobs and graveyard shifts at gas stations. The first decade of the new millennium is a blur. Despite himself, Aakhus earned a B.A. in Mathematics (2006) and an MFA in Creative Writing from the University of Florida (2011). *Book of Knut: A Novel by Knut Knudson* won the 2011 Henfield Prize for Fiction from University of Florida, and has been turned into a math textbook containing musical scores and oil paintings, as well as homework problems. Aakhus lives in Pennsylvania, where he teaches at the University of Pittsburgh.

12630866R00144

Made in the USA
Charleston, SC
17 May 2012